RUNNING WILD

AN LCR ELITE NOVEL

BY CHRISTY REECE

Running Wild

 An LCR Elite Novel

Published by Christy Reece

Cover Art by Patricia Schmitt/Pickyme

Copyright 2016 by Christy Reece

ISBN: 978-0-9967666-3-0

To obtain permission to excerpt portions of the text, please contact the author at Christy@christyreece.com.

PROLOGUE

Cali, Colombia

Ernesto Diaz chewed nervously at his lip as he checked his watch once again. He cursed beneath his breath. The two men he'd hired to help him with this job were late. He'd had no choice but to go with local talent, which usually wasn't an issue. There were more than enough available men to do this kind of work. The problem wasn't the lack of assistance, the nature of the job, or even the money. The problem with this job was the target.

Ernesto was fifty years old. Forty of those years he'd been running various cons and scams. Made a good living. For the past five years, he'd turned to information gathering. Being a short, squat man with average looks had its advantages. Few people noticed him or saw him as a threat. Being a snitch and informant was a much more lucrative endeavor.

It was because of his past association with the target that he'd been chosen for this job. Ernesto wasn't above taking the occasional kidnapping assignment. When finances were low, there wasn't much he wouldn't try his hand at. So when he had been offered this opportunity, he had eagerly accepted. The money was excellent, and the setup was minimal. All in all, it should've been an easy way to make a nice profit. The issue, once again, narrowed down to one specific problem—the target.

He had known Aidan Thorne for several years. The man had paid him handsomely for various bits of intel Ernesto had collected. Ernesto didn't know the reason Thorne needed the information he asked for…didn't want to know. Sometimes, the more you knew, the better your chances of getting dead. Ernesto made sure he knew just enough to make a living and not enough to cause his death.

If he'd had a conscience, he might feel guilty for betraying a man who'd always been kind of decent to him. But Thorne understood the way of the world they both inhabited. In a battle between money and loyalty, money always won.

Ernesto peeked around the corner. This time of day there were few people on the streets. And in this neighborhood, the ones who were on the streets were the people you wanted to avoid.

Maybe once this job was over, he'd go somewhere else. Get out of town, at least for a little while. Did Thorne have people who might come looking for him? If that was the case, then Ernesto knew he wouldn't want to be around.

He didn't know what the people who hired him wanted with Aidan Thorne. He didn't want to know. Whatever it was, he doubted Thorne would survive the outcome.

A shiver that had nothing to do with the temperature zipped up Ernesto's spine. If Thorne somehow got away, he'd come looking for Ernesto. The thought made his gut twist. He'd seen dead men with more warmth in their eyes than Aidan Thorne. Without a doubt Ernesto would not survive any kind of skirmish with the man. That was the reason he'd hired two men to help him. Thorne would be a ruthless, formidable enemy.

If the men he'd hired didn't arrive soon, he would have to do this on his own.

Ernesto unconsciously shook his head. No way would he take on Aidan Thorne by himself. Only one man would survive such a confrontation.

Ernesto knew to his soul it wouldn't be him.

CHAPTER ONE

The bar was both sleazy and filthy. Smoke swirled through the big room like an industrialized bug fogger belching out its last toxic dregs. From the sticky fake-wood floor that hadn't seen soap and water in decades to the light fixtures with grimy coats of dirt and dead bugs, the ambience of Claudio's Cantina bellowed, *Enter at your own risk.*

Aidan figured it'd take at least a half-dozen showers before the stink left him.

Slouched in the corner, his back to the wall, he gave the appearance of being half wasted and all the way bored. He was neither. His informant was fifteen minutes late. Punctuality had never been a priority for Ernesto Diaz. Aidan had no illusions about the man. Though less corrupt than most in his business, if Diaz got a better offer, he'd sell out without a thought. Which was why Aidan was going to give the vermin only five more minutes to show. The back of his neck was getting that twitchy feeling, which usually meant trouble was brewing. Ignoring that twitch had once gotten him shot. He hadn't ignored it since.

He shifted in his chair, noting and appreciating the lack of pain. Three months ago, he'd been laid up with a broken leg. Weeks of doing almost nothing but waiting for it to heal had made him antsy and out of sorts. The minute he'd returned to full LCR duty, he'd jumped into the action as if all of hell's demons were on his ass. Too much time to think and remember. Too much time to regret. Nothing like staying on the edge of danger to help focus a man's thoughts.

In fact, he'd been so focused, that when he'd gotten the call from Diaz, he'd almost delayed the meet. After all this time with no viable intel, what was the point of rushing just to find out there was nothing new? After that thought, the inevitable guilt had followed. How dare he not follow up? Had he not made a promise? Had he not sworn that he would follow every lead, no matter how minuscule or far-fetched, until he found the murdering bastard?

So, despite the fact that Diaz was about as reliable as a politician and most likely had nothing new to tell him, Aidan had taken the bait.

His family thought he was certifiable. Not that they'd come right out and say it. His mother and father, ever supportive, just gave him that sympathetic, helpless look that basically said, *We're here for you, but we're completely lost on why you're not living up to your potential.*

His sister was a little more blunt. Last time he'd talked to her, they'd had a shouting match. She thought he was wasting his life and didn't mind saying so. He thought she was a nosy, opinionated buttinski who needed to stay out of his business. A day later, he had sent her flowers to apologize. She had sent him a bottle of his favorite wine. Both of them knew that all was forgiven.

To his family, it probably did look as though he was wasting his life. Or at least not living up to his potential. They had a vague idea of what his job with LCR entailed, but he did his best to shield them from the more hair-raising details. Rescuing kidnapped victims from the most dangerous places in the world was a far cry from the safe, secure world he'd left behind.

But that world stopped being safe and secure a decade ago. His family could stay in denial as long as they wanted. Aidan knew the truth. The monster was still out there. Watching. Waiting. Looking for his next chance to strike. Too many had paid the price for Aidan's carelessness. He would never let his guard down ever again.

Without moving a muscle, every inch of Aidan's body went on high alert. His eyes searched the reason for his unease. Detected nothing. Still, the hair on the back of his neck was screaming a warning. What the hell was going down?

"Let me go, you big gorilla! I don't want to go in here."

What the hell?

A woman was shoved into the middle of the room. All eyes were on her, and almost every damn one of them had the salacious look of a predator about to pounce. This was not going to be pretty.

The room was too smoky to tell much about her, but that wouldn't matter to a bunch of drunk, horny, soulless men. Fresh meat had arrived in their vicinity, requiring no effort to obtain. The woman was in a shitload of trouble.

With a casualness in direct contrast to the circumstances, Aidan stood and eased himself over to the bar. Calling attention to his movements wouldn't be good for either him or the woman. He was her best chance to get out of here unscathed. If he was taken down, she was toast.

There were three men at the bar. An additional eight were at various tables. Four men had been playing pool. Two had been throwing darts. Of course, all activity had ceased. No one was doing anything now but staring at the woman and salivating.

Already trying to figure out which man he could pit against the other, Aidan leaned against the barstool and pretended to eye the woman just like everyone else. Acting as if he wasn't interested would call attention to himself, but in truth, he didn't bother to look at her. All other eyes were on their single target. Aidan's attention was on the safest way to get this woman out the door.

The music on the ancient jukebox ended. Since no one had bothered to pay for another song, silence filled the room.

"Look," the woman stated in a firm, no-nonsense way, "I'm just looking for my friend. If you've not seen her, that's fine. But I'm not going to stand here anymore. I'm leaving."

Aidan's involuntary gasp took in a giant gulp of smoky air, and he almost choked on the fumes. Probably would have if he wasn't in shock. His eyes finally settled on the woman, and even though his mind screamed a denial, he couldn't avoid the truth. Holy, holy hell. That was no girl, no mere woman. And definitely no stranger. That was the one, the only, Anna Bradford.

What the hell was she doing here? Most important, how was he going to get her out alive?

Anna stood in the middle of the smoke-filled room and concentrated on acting tough and in control. She told herself she'd been in worse predicaments. A dozen bee stings in Arizona, a snakebite in Peru, and a severely broken heart in the ninth grade. Not to mention being kidnapped and tortured a few years back. She could darn well figure her way out of this situation. Admittedly, while all the men surrounding her looked as though they would murder their sainted granny for a dollar, she had learned to look beyond dirt and grime to the person beneath the surface. Out of all of these not terribly reputable-looking people, there had to be at least one with enough decency to help her get out of here.

So far, coming to Cali had been an abysmal failure. Counseling traumatized children was a challenge on the best of days. It was especially difficult when the parents of those children were less well-behaved than a one-year-old with diaper rash. But when the psychologist scheduled for the clinic had canceled because of a family emergency and Carrie had called her at the last minute, Anna had gotten swept up in the notion that if she didn't help, no one would. Now not only had she not helped a single child, Carrie was missing.

And to make matters a thousand times worse, Anna was now going to die a horrible death.

At that thought, her spine went stiff with indignation. She was most certainly not going to die today. She would simply explain what was going on to these men. Surely they had tender feelings for their mothers or sisters. She would just appeal to their human side.

Giving them the smile she often used to put a frightened child at ease, she stated firmly, clearly, "Gentlemen, I find myself in need of assistance. A friend of mine has gone missing. She's about five-feet-five, with blond hair and light green eyes. Her name is Carrie. Has anyone seen her?"

No one answered. Not even a headshake. She tried again. "I know if your mother or sister were missing, you'd want someone to help her. Wouldn't you?"

What came next burned her ears. These men were definitely not fond of their mothers or sisters.

She made a three-sixty-degree turn, looking for a friendly face. It wasn't to be found. Deciding a quick and graceful retreat was her best recourse, Anna started to back away. She took slow measured steps and began to feel optimistic. No one was coming after her. Maybe they were going to just let her—

She slammed into what felt like a brick wall. Heart thundering, her breathing almost to the point of hyperventilating, Anna turned around. Her eyes were on the level of a large, well-formed chest. The man stood before her like an immovable boulder. Tall, broad-shouldered, and so muscular that the sleeves of his olive green T-shirt were molded around his well-developed biceps.

Anna swallowed hard and finally found the courage to raise her gaze to his face. Beautiful, golden brown eyes, sensual, unsmiling mouth, sexy facial scruff. A wave of dizziness swept over her, and if he hadn't grabbed her shoulders, she would have keeled over at his feet.

Of all the gin joints, in all the towns, in all the world, why did she have to walk into his?

Casablanca was a million miles away. She was no Ingrid Bergman, and the man in front of her was definitely not Humphrey Bogart. Rick never would have glared at Ilsa like that.

"Having trouble staying out of trouble, Anna?"

"Hello, Aidan. It's nice to see you again. How are you?"

Despite the tense situation, Aidan had trouble keeping a straight face. "Only Anna Bradford could have two dozen salivating drunks surrounding her and act as if she's attending a Sunday social."

She lifted her chin. Such a lovely, stubborn slant. "Politeness never goes out of style."

"You think we could save the social niceties until after we get you out of here?"

Without moving her head, her gaze swept nervously around the room, the only indication that she was aware of the trouble she was in. Clearing her throat, she said, "I was just leaving."

"Very wise," Aidan said dryly.

Though he kept his eyes on Anna, Aidan was hyper-aware of everything that was going on around them. The three men at the bar were discussing their plan of attack. A half dozen other men were looking for their own chance to strike. The rest of them were hanging back. No doubt waiting to see what their friends could accomplish without them.

So for now, it was nine against two. Not the worst odds he'd ever faced. If he could get out of here without bloodshed, all the better. Protecting Anna was his priority.

She swallowed loudly. "Any suggestions?"

"Yes. Get ready to be offended."

Wide-eyed, she looked up at him. "What?"

He took advantage of her open mouth, swooped down, and slammed his mouth over hers. His tongue swept inside, and in an instant, Aidan knew the men surrounding them were the least of his troubles.

He'd dreamed about tasting her, and dammit, now he'd gone and done it. She was more delicious than anything he'd ever tasted in his life. He could stand here all day, drowning in her sweetness, savoring her flavor.

Oh hell no.

Before she could struggle or kick him in the groin, Aidan pulled away from her. Giving her no time to scream or slap his face, he scooped her up with one arm and threw her over his shoulder. With the other, he pulled his Glock from the holster on his thigh and glared around the room. And just in case they didn't get it, he shouted, "Mine! Anybody got a problem with that?"

Not waiting around for an answer, Aidan turned and stalked out of the bar.

CHAPTER TWO

Stunned into silence, Anna couldn't decide whether she should be thanking him for the rescue or slugging him for his audacity. Since he had most likely saved her life, Anna decided gratitude would be the most appropriate response. But first he was going to have to put her down.

"Aidan, you can let me down now."

His only response was a slight grunt.

Bouncing against his hard shoulder, Anna lifted her head and noticed they were at least a block from the bar.

"Okay, Thorne. This has gone on long enough. Put me down."

"I'll put you down when I feel like you're safe."

"And when do you think I'll be safe? When I'm back in the States?"

"Maybe. Or at least on the plane."

"I'm getting nauseated. If you don't want me to puke all over your very fine ass, you'd better put me down right now."

Her world tilted again as Aidan at last put her on her feet. He did it with such ease and casualness, she wanted to haul off and hit him just for that alone.

She blew out a disgruntled breath, then tossed her long hair out of her face so he could get the full benefit of her glare. "You know, that caveman attitude is one of your most unattractive qualities."

"Yeah, but as you noted, I have a very fine ass. So I at least have that going for me."

"I was attempting to take you off guard. Placate you with false confidence. It's not really all that fine."

"Now I'm wounded."

As abrupt as the flip of a light switch, the teasing glint in his eyes disappeared, and Anna swallowed hard at the change in his demeanor. Only Aidan Thorne could go from charming rogue to hard-as-nails LCR operative in the blink of an eye. And, as usual, she found both frustratingly irresistible. She had never been attracted to the bad-boy type until she'd met Aidan Thorne.

"You want to tell me what the hell you were doing in that sleazy bar in the most dangerous part of the most dangerous city in the country?"

"You're here."

That got a raised brow. "You came to see me?"

"No. I'm just pointing out that you're in a dangerous part of the city, too."

"And I have reason to be."

"Well, so do I."

He took a step forward and stared down at her with the ice-cold eyes of a pissed-off man. "Don't push your luck, Bradford. I'm about five seconds from hauling you back over my shoulder and carrying you to the airport. Talk."

"Okay. Okay. I need your help anyway. I'm here with a coworker. We're doing some counseling at the medical clinic a few blocks up the street. She didn't show up this morning for a session. I couldn't get her on her cellphone, so I started looking for her."

"And you thought she might be in Claudio's?"

"No. I walked farther than I intended. I stopped to get my bearings, and that was when that odious man pushed me inside the bar. Since I found myself in there, I thought I'd ask if they'd seen her."

"And almost got yourself raped and killed, too."

"Thankfully, that didn't happen. But my friend is still missing."

"When's the last time you saw her?"

"Last night, around midnight. We had some snacks in my room, and then she left. Her room is three doors down from mine."

"Which hotel are you staying in?"

"The Hotel Cali."

"Did you contact the police?"

"Not yet." She grimaced. "I've heard they're not always cooperative."

"No? Really? I'm shocked."

"Sarcasm isn't helpful."

"You're right." He glanced back toward the bar and then looked at his watch.

"Look"—she backed up a step—"if you're meeting someone, don't worry. I'll be fine. I'll just go—"

"Shut up, Bradford." He said the words almost absentmindedly. "We'll find your friend."

Anna wanted to smack herself upside the head as it abruptly occurred to her that Aidan was here on an LCR mission. The shock of seeing him, along with her worry for Carrie, had obscured everything else. Had she inadvertently messed up a rescue?

"Aidan, did I—"

"Come on." He grabbed her wrist and started pulling her farther away from the bar. And farther away from her hotel.

"Did I mess up a mission? If you're here on LCR business, don't let me stop you. I don't want—"

"I'm not on LCR time right now."

"So I didn't screw up a rescue attempt?"

"No."

The answer was abrupt and blunt, telling Anna that if she persisted, she risked alienating him. Since she needed his help, she decided to table her questions until later. But she couldn't help but wonder why Aidan Thorne, an LCR Elite operative, would be here in Cali, Colombia. Had he come here on his own time? If so, for what reason?

Her mind whirling with questions, she kept up with Aidan as he strode down the street as if he owned it. Where did that kind of confidence come from? And why, oh, why did she find it and him so fascinating? A man who had made it clear that being around her was the last thing he wanted. She still didn't know why he didn't like her. She assumed she just pissed him off on general principle.

When she stumbled over a stone on the sidewalk, Aidan glared at her as if she'd done it on purpose. Then she noticed something else. He was no longer limping. Only a few months ago he had fractured his leg.

"How's your leg?"

"Fine."

Realizing getting anything more out of him was futile, Anna gazed about at their surroundings. She wasn't familiar with this part of the city. It was older but seemed less run-down than the area where she and Carrie were working.

"Where are we going?"

"A friend of mine has a business a couple of blocks away. We'll talk there." His hand still wrapped around her wrist, he kept his eyes on the path in front of them. But she knew he was on alert and aware of everything around them.

She stayed silent. Having Aidan Thorne's help in finding Carrie was a blessing. She had no idea who to go to or where to look.

She told herself that her friend could get herself out of any kind of situation. From the moment she'd met Carrie Easterly, she been impressed with the woman's calm, determined attitude. In her mid-forties, Carrie was a widow and one of the most dedicated people Anna had ever met. She was compassionate without being emotional or condescending. Her no-nonsense demeanor inspired confidence. Carrie was also the most reliable person in the world. If she said she would be somewhere, then it would take something major to make her break that promise.

And that was Anna's biggest fear. That something major had happened to her kindhearted friend.

They stopped in front of a small grocery store. Instead of going inside, Aidan turned to look down at her. The scowl was in full force, but she also saw a tinge of worry.

"What's wrong?"

"There are a few rules you need to observe. Don't look anyone in the eye. Do not speak to anyone. If anyone speaks to you, look at me before you answer. If I nod, you answer. If not, don't say a word."

"I can't even talk to you?"

"When we're alone, yes. If we're with other people, follow those rules."

"I thought you said this guy was a friend."

"Friend is a relative term in this part of the world." With that, he opened the door and pulled her inside.

The instant Aidan walked inside with Anna, he wanted to haul her back out. That twitchy feeling at the back of his neck was going haywire. Since it had started at the bar, right before Anna walked in, he had attributed the feeling to her. Now he wasn't so sure. Damn, he didn't like this at all.

A tall, thin man with a thick mustache and wire-rimmed glasses called to him from behind the counter. "Thorne, my friend. Welcome."

"I need a place, Munoz."

"Of course. Up the stairs, two doors down."

Still dragging Anna by the wrist, Aidan went up the stairway. The dim lighting gave off a sinister atmosphere, but out of all the places in the city, this was the one he'd always felt the safest. Until today. Something wasn't right. But he needed to talk to Anna, and getting her off the street, out of sight, was a priority.

They stopped at the designated door. Aidan pulled his gun and pressed a finger to his mouth to tell her to keep quiet. So far she'd been amazingly cooperative.

Easing open the door, gun at the ready, Aidan peered inside. The room held a single bed, table and two chairs, and a hot plate. Luxurious accommodations for this part of the city.

With a jerk of his head, he told Anna to go inside. Then, with one last look around the dim hallway, he followed her, closing the door behind him.

She was safe for now, but the next step would be the hardest. He had to get her out of Cali without anyone else seeing them together.

Chapter Three

"So tell me again why you're here, Anna."

"I've already told you. I'm here to do counseling for the family and children's center. I came with Carrie Easterly. I work with her occasionally in the States. She said she was coming here and invited me. We thought we could do some good."

Aidan pulled out a chair for her. Anna wondered if he knew his absentminded actions revealed the man behind the gruff mask of indifference. Aidan Thorne had been raised to be a gentleman. For whatever reason, he fought hard against that upbringing, especially when she was around.

"Do you have a photo of her?"

"I..." She frowned and then jumped from the chair, excited. "Yes. On my phone." Pulling the phone from her back pocket, she clicked through several photos till she came to the one she had taken last month at her birthday party.

She handed the phone to Aidan. "Carrie's the older woman in the middle with the short blond hair and glasses."

"What do you know about her?"

"What do you mean?"

"Personal life? Married? Kids? Boyfriends? Girlfriends? Does she have friends here? Who else came with you? Does she have a reputation for disappearing?"

Anna scrambled to come up with answers to the conglomeration of questions. "She's widowed. Has two children, two boys, both in college in the States. She has a few gentleman friends, but none that are serious. She lives in Atlanta, Georgia. As far as I know, she has no friends here. She would have told me if she did.

"We came to Cali alone, but we have a young man, named Miguel, who is helping us. The center assigned him to us. He was the first person I went to when I couldn't find her. He said he hasn't seen her since last night when we both went upstairs for bed.

"She's in trouble, Aidan, I know she is. Carrie would no more disappear on purpose than I would eat snails."

A little twitch at the corner of his mouth made her think he almost smiled. Despite her worry for Carrie, she wished he would smile. Aidan had a great smile. Only problem was, he never gave her one. Apparently, he saved them for people he liked.

Brushing aside her moment of self-pity, she asked, "So what should we do? Call the police? Or maybe Noah?"

"You contact McCall, he'll just tell me to investigate."

"Then can we do that?" She stood again. "Now?"

"You got transportation?"

"No. Miguel runs errands for us, but we haven't had the need to go anywhere."

He glanced down at his watch, stood, and walked over to the window. "Five more minutes and we'll leave."

"What are you looking for?"

"Lots of things. Right now, I'm looking for our ride."

"You have a car?"

"Of sorts."

"How would anyone know to bring one to you here?"

"I arranged for it earlier."

"Aidan, if you're not here for LCR, why are you here?"

It didn't surprise her that he didn't answer. To almost everyone else, Aidan Thorne kept up a charming façade. For some reason, he had never done that with Anna. She didn't know why, and part of her resented it. What she wouldn't give for just one of those beautiful, sexy smiles he gifted to other women. For her, he was either surly, sarcastic, or downright rude. So why in the world did she find him so unbelievably fascinating?

She'd always felt a certain amount of dismayed pity for women who seemed to fall for the guys who were the meanest to them, attributing it to low self-esteem. She could not say that was the reason for her fascination for Aidan. She had a healthy sense of her own worth and didn't take crap from anyone. But with Aidan, it was different. Not that she let him get away with being rude. She had called him out on his bad behavior more than once. But she also had never walked away from him.

Her training as a psychologist notwithstanding, something about Aidan Thorne spoke to her. There was a connection beyond the superficial one he tried to enforce. Call her crazy, a very relative term in her book, but this man, beyond any other man she'd ever known, made her yearn.

"He's here. Let's go."

Accepting that this was the best she was going to get from him, Anna followed him out the door. She knew his full concentration needed to be on their surroundings, so she did her best to help him look out for any danger. It would be helpful to know exactly what he was looking for and why, but she could at least alert him if she saw anything suspicious.

Instead of going out the front, the way they'd arrived, Aidan led her through the store and into a storage room. They crossed to the other door. Before opening it, he stopped and looked down at her. For an instant, an infinitesimal one, she saw a touch of tender warmth in his eyes. Then, as if it had never happened, the cool arrogance was back. "Stay here for a second."

He opened the door and walked out. With anyone else, she might have had a thousand questions. But with Aidan, she had total trust in his abilities, his knowledge about what to do.

Trusting him with anything else, though, like her heart? Nope, never going to happen.

Aidan paid the man who'd made the delivery and waited until he'd disappeared around a corner to examine the bike. Offending the man who had provided his transportation would not be taken well. Right now, Aidan figured he had more than enough troubles without adding the hurt feelings of a renowned thief to his list.

Assuring himself that the bike was in good enough shape to get them where they needed to go, he took one last glance around and then opened the door for Anna.

He handed her a helmet. "Make sure your hair is secure under it and keep your shield on until we get to your hotel."

He had to give her credit. She didn't ask why or even look the least offended. He was well aware that all the extra caution might not be necessary, but he refused to take the chance. Anna was too important to take her safety for granted.

He straddled the bike. The instant she settled in behind him, put her hands on his waist, he was off. Concentrating on keeping them alive kept him from having to think about her soft, fragrant body pressed up against his, the slender hands touching him, or the firm thighs pressed against his. No, he wasn't thinking about that. At. All.

They drove through the center of town, zigzagging around yellow taxis, other bikers, and the multitude of pedestrians. The open-air market with its millions of diverse scents, heated to a zenith by the soaring temperatures, was an oppressive weight.

He could've chosen a less congested road to travel, but the more people around them, the better to blend in and get lost in the crowd. He had no reason to believe that Simon was in Cali, but that didn't mean he didn't have people watching. Paranoia and caution had been Aidan's mainstay for years. He wasn't going to change now, especially when Anna's life could be on the line.

He stopped in front of the small hotel. Anna got off the bike. The instant her hands went to her helmet to pull it off, Aidan grabbed her wrist. "Wait till we get inside."

She nodded, not saying a word. An unwanted and inconvenient feeling tugged at his heart. She really was a trouper.

He swung his leg over and stood, noting that the curtains twitched on the third floor. Someone had noticed them. Still holding Anna's wrist, he steered her toward the entrance. The minute they were in the lobby, he began to breathe easier.

Turning to her, he unbuckled her chinstrap and pulled the helmet off her head. She shook her hair out in an ultra-feminine way that was a natural part of Anna Bradford. From the top of her thick, lustrous brown hair to the bottom of her long, slender feet, she was pure femininity.

"Where do we go from here?"

"Let go talk to Miguel."

"He's usually in the kitchen around this time, eating lunch."

As they started toward the back, Aidan made note of their surroundings. It wasn't an expensive hotel, but it had a homey feel to it.

"Has Carrie been to Cali before?"

"A few times. She has some acquaintances here but no one close. Another counselor was supposed to come with her instead of me, but had to cancel at the last minute. So Carrie asked me to come."

"Have you been on other trips with her?"

"Uh-huh. Two last year. One earlier this year. I promise you, Aidan, she's a responsible person. She wouldn't just leave. I'm really afraid something has happened to her."

He didn't say it, but he was thinking the same thing. And when people went missing in this part of the world, the outcome was rarely a good one.

Aidan pushed open the kitchen door, stuck his head inside. A couple of men stood in front of a stove. One woman was at a giant sink. He spotted a young man in his late teens sitting on a barstool, eating. They all turned and looked at Aidan, their eyes wary. The kid eating his lunch stopped in mid-chew and swallowed hard.

Aidan pulled Anna into the kitchen with him. The instant the kid spotted her, he sprang from his chair and took off, exiting out a back door.

"Aw, hell." Aidan took off at run, throwing over his shoulder, "Stay here."

Not sure who she was more worried for, Aidan or Miguel, Anna followed them. Yes, she'd been told to stay put, but Miguel didn't know Aidan. He might think he meant him harm. And the reason behind Miguel running was more than a little suspicious. Did he know something about Carrie's disappearance after all?

She went through the door and found herself in a small storage room. Hearing no noises, she went farther and spotted another door. She peeked out and then gasped. Aidan had Miguel up against a brick wall. The kid's feet were dangling, not touching the ground, and Aidan's hands were wrapped around Miguel's neck.

"Where is she, kid?"

Miguel's dark eyes were wide with fear.

Surprised at Aidan's behavior, Anna said firmly as she walked to them, "Let him go, Aidan."

"Not till he talks."

"He can't talk if he can't breathe."

"He can breathe." He paused, then added, "For now."

Shaking Miguel a little, Aidan growled, "Answer the question, kid, and I'll let you go."

Apparently seeing her as his only hope, Miguel gasped out, "Señorita Anna, help me."

"She's not the one you need to be talking to, Miguel. Tell me where Carrie is, and I'll let you go. It's as simple as that."

Miguel shook his head. "I don't know anything."

"Then why'd you run?"

"Because I know who you are. You are the Thorne. You have a reputation of being ruthless and deadly."

Aidan's laughter, incongruent considering the situation, sounded genuine. "Good try, kid. Trying to boost my ego like that. But you didn't run when you saw me. You ran when you spotted Anna, which tells me you're more worried about her than me."

Aidan shook him again. "You know where her friend is, and you're going to tell me. I got no place to go right now, and holding you here all damn day long is no big deal."

Big tears rolled down Miguel's cheeks, and he started sobbing.

Furious, Anna reached out to pull Aidan away from Miguel. Before she could touch him, Aidan had dropped him. "The tears were a good move. Doesn't mean you're free, though. You know something. Spill it."

Miguel looked up at Anna, his eyes filled with sorrow and tears. "I'm sorry, señorita."

She squatted down and took Miguel's hand. "What are you sorry for? Do you know where Carrie is?"

"I cannot say."

"Won't say," Aidan snarled.

"Aidan, enough. He's obviously terrified of someone."

"He's going to be more than terrified if he doesn't talk." Aidan grabbed Miguel's arm and pulled him to stand. "Spill it, kid."

Instead of answering, he sent Anna a pleading look. "They said they would not hurt her."

"Who said?"

"I can't say."

"How much did they pay you, kid?"

"No, it wasn't the money." He shook his head rapidly. "They said—"

"What did you do, Miguel?" Anna asked.

"I just told them where to find Dr. Carrie. They said they wouldn't hurt her."

"What did they want with her?"

"Someone is hurt. They want Dr. Carrie to make him better."

"Oh no, Miguel." Anna sent a worried look to Aidan. "Carrie isn't a medical doctor. She's a psychologist."

Aidan gave her a grim nod and then turned his attention back to Miguel. "What's the name of the person they wanted her to treat?"

Miguel shrugged his thin shoulders, refusing to meet Aidan's eyes as he said, "I do not know."

Aidan wasn't having it. "Try again."

Evidently thinking she would have pity on him, Miguel sent a dark-eyed, pleading look to Anna.

Anna wasn't in the mood to be gentle anymore. Carrie could be in serious trouble.

"Miguel, either you tell us where Carrie is, or I'm going to leave you with Señor Thorne and walk away."

"But…but…" Realizing he couldn't get out of it, he said, "It's the Garcia family. One of their people is sick. They can't risk going to the hospital."

"And they thought a psychologist was their best bet?"

The harshness in Aidan's tone confirmed Anna's fears. Carrie was in deep trouble.

CHAPTER FOUR

Bogota, Colombia

"Thorne arrived in Cali yesterday."

"Excellent." Something that might have been a smile at one time twitched at Simon Cook's mouth. "He took the bait. When can we expect him to arrive here?"

"There was a small glitch."

"And that would be?"

"Today's planned meeting didn't happen. Diaz didn't get a chance to grab him."

His blood pressure shot up, but he gave no indication of his ire as he said in a mild tone, "And why not?"

"There was a disturbance at the bar where they were to meet. A woman came in, and Thorne helped her out. Diaz saw them leave together."

"This girl. Who is she?"

"Name's Anna Bradford. A do-gooder doing counseling at a free family clinic. She's an American."

He rubbed his chin as he considered this new development. "Interesting. So Thorne was being his typical knight-in-shining-armor self, or is there more to it?"

"Possibly."

"Explain."

"Thorne is still with the girl. We're studying the situation. There is a possibility that he knows her. He seemed familiar with her. Diaz asked some discreet questions at the bar. Word is, Thorne kissed her."

His heart jumped. "Is that right?"

"Yes, sir. Some believed he did it just to keep anyone else from bothering her."

"You disagree?"

Patrick shrugged his beefy shoulders. "Seems out of character for the man. Thorne's not known for his impulsiveness."

"Indeed, he's not. You'll find out more about this young woman, won't you, Patrick? In the most discreet manner, of course."

"Of course, sir. What do you want me to do with Diaz?"

He waved his hand as if swatting away a fly. "His services are no longer needed. If Thorne happens upon him, I don't trust Diaz to keep his mouth shut. He's a liability we can't afford. As usual, discretion is of utmost importance. I would be quite put out if Thorne finds out about Diaz's demise."

"Yes, sir. Consider it done and to your specification."

"Thank you, Patrick."

Without even having to tell him, Patrick knew to leave. It was one of the man's best qualities. Anticipating the needs of his employer had earned him a permanent position long ago.

He sat back in his chair. Hearing a slight squeak, he made a mental note to have one of his servants take care of the matter.

Everything, including furniture, should perform perfectly. If not, they would be replaced. Just like people.

A grim smile played around his mouth. Even though Aidan Thorne was still alive and breathing, he couldn't help but be glad the plan had been foiled. It would have been so simple, too simple. For ten long agonizing years, he had been waiting for an opportunity. On two occasions he had exacted a small amount of revenge, but never full victory. Those small incidences had been nothing in comparison to what Thorne was owed. But circumstances had changed, and he had been ready to accept that his ultimate act of revenge could never be as spectacular as he hoped.

He had thought to hold Thorne here, performing various tests and experiments, and then allow events to unfold as they would. It was so rare to have such a healthy specimen for his research. He had fantasized about the last days of Aidan Thorne's life and had told himself that would have to be enough.

But now? Had fate intervened, giving him a second chance? Energy and excitement surged through him. After all this time, did Aidan Thorne have a new woman in his life? Someone he cared for? Someone he would miss when she was gone?

His imagination took flight again. This time, a real smile stretched across his mouth.

The possibilities were endless.

Cali, Colombia

"What should we do?"

Aidan looked into Anna's trusting eyes. What he wanted to do was haul her over his shoulder and get her on a plane out of here. Pronto. The Garcias were one of the oldest families in

Colombia. A half century ago, the family had been affluent and well respected, earning most of their money from agriculture and emerald mining. Then one family member had discovered that smuggling drugs was a much more lucrative moneymaker. Other family members were either coerced or persuaded to agree. Since then their wealth had increased, but their respectability had taken a hit. They were widely feared, though, and that was the kicker.

Aidan glanced down at Miguel. If he wasn't still holding the kid's arm, Aidan knew he would've disappeared in a second. Miguel knew more than he was telling them. Part of it was fear of retribution. Aidan believed that. He also knew there was something else that kept the kid from talking. Money.

"I don't care how much they paid you, kid. You can't spend it if you're in prison, and I'll personally walk you to the cell and watch them lock you up tight if you don't spill it here and now. Where did they take Carrie?"

Aidan gave him the look he used to interrogate hardened, soulless men and women who'd sell their firstborn for whatever stupid-assed cause they believed in. The cold-as-death stare usually got a response. Directed at a teenager who was probably about to lose control of his bladder and bowels, it had an immediate effect.

"It's about an hour away from here. In a large place. I've never been there, but a cousin of a friend said it is hidden within the hills"

"When did they take her?"

"Last night when she was going to her room."

"Would they have hurt her, Aidan?" Anna asked.

"They didn't," Miguel said.

Anna turned her eyes on the kid. "You were there?"

The look in Anna's eyes made Miguel back up. If the situation weren't so serious, Aidan would have laughed. She might appear as pretty and fluffy as cotton candy, but the look she'd given the kid might've worried even the most badass criminal.

"I...I wanted to make sure she was all right. She—"

"Fine," Aidan said. "Our priority is to find her."

He pulled out his cellphone, searing Miguel with a look. "You got family here?"

"No. My mama...she is gone. She is all that I had." He glanced over at Anna, tears filling his eyes again. "Lo siento, Señorita Anna. I should not have done this, I know." Straightening his shoulders and lifting his chin, he made the most pitiful declaration Aidan had ever heard. "I will take my punishment like a man."

The kid probably hadn't seen his twentieth birthday yet. Yeah, he'd screwed up, but Aidan wasn't about to throw him to the wolves. Money was a powerful motivator, especially for someone who didn't have much opportunity. Problem was, the Garcias wouldn't leave Miguel alive if they knew he'd ratted on them.

Aidan shifted his focus to Anna. "Stay here with him. Don't let him out of your sight."

"Where are you going?"

"I've got a couple of calls to make."

Moving his gaze back to Miguel, Aidan gave the kid his best *I mean business* glare. "Stay here with Anna. She may not look like it, but she can and will beat your ass to a bloody pulp. I've seen her take down men twice your size. Got me, amigo?"

Sending Anna a wary glance, Miguel nodded. "Si."

Turning away from them, Aidan put the phone to his ear and made his first call.

Anna didn't bother to pretend she wasn't eavesdropping. Was Aidan contacting LCR? Could a rescue team arrive in time to save Carrie? What would happen when the Garcias realized she was a doctor of psychology and not a medical doctor?

"Hola, amigo. Como estas?"

Whoever Aidan's first call was to, it was someone fluent in Spanish. Anna managed to understand his first words, but then he spoke in a dialect she didn't recognize and at a speed she had no hope of following.

"He is asking someone to help me."

Miguel seemed to have no trouble following the conversation, but then Aidan moved farther away from them, and neither of them could hear.

Giving up, she turned back to Miguel. "Why didn't you come to me, Miguel? I would have been glad to help you."

"No one could help against Garcia's men."

"Aidan will. And so will I."

Before she could continue a reassurance she in no way felt certain of, Aidan returned.

"Okay, here's the plan. A man will be here soon to pick you up, Miguel. He'll take you to get a passport and then will fly with you out of Cali."

She said, "You can't get a passport that fast," at the same time that Miguel asked, "Where am I going?"

Aidan sent her a raised-brow look that she understood totally. It wouldn't be a legitimate passport, but it would do the job. He then turned to Miguel. "Unless you have other options, you're going to the US."

Anna knew one of the people he'd called and why. The one man they both trusted to take care of Miguel and see that he had a chance. Noah McCall, the leader of Last Chance Rescue, would make sure Miguel got opportunities he'd never get on his own.

"It's where I've always dreamed of going. But where—"

"You'll be taken to a man who can help you. But it's up to you what you do with your opportunity. This isn't a handout, it's a help up. Understand?"

"Si. Gracias, Señor Thorne."

"You can call me Aidan, kid."

"Señor Aidan. Gracias."

"What about Carrie?" Anna asked. "What are we going to do?"

His face hardening, he turned back to her. "I'd like to send you with Miguel."

She sent him the same kind of raised-brow look Aidan had given her a few moments ago. She was going nowhere.

"Yeah. That's what I thought."

He gave her an up-and-down look that was in no way sexual or inappropriate. Her libido didn't care. Where Aidan Thorne was concerned, the most innocent of looks from him could cause a mild earthquake in her body. The man was potent without even trying.

"You got some hiking boots?"

"Yes."

"Thick socks? Sunscreen? A hat?"

"Yes. Yes." She grimaced, then said, "And yes."

"You don't like your hat?"

"My mom snuck it into my suitcase before I left. It was my grandfather's."

He didn't smile, but a glint of amusement flickered in his eyes. "It'll be perfect, then."

He glanced at his watch. "Come on. Our ride will be arriving soon."

Anna and Miguel followed Aidan back into the hotel. The curious eyes of the small kitchen staff bored holes into their backs as they made their way through the room they'd dashed through moments ago.

Aidan stopped in the tiny lobby. "Where's your room, Anna?"

"Third floor. Room 301."

"Let's go."

"Me, too?" Miguel asked.

"Yeah. Neither of you are leaving my sight."

Anna sent Aidan a frustrated look that he ignored. Being in the dark and having orders thrown at her without explanation was irritating. She held her tongue. Not only had she interrupted whatever plans he'd had, he was helping her rescue Carrie and had arranged a new life for Miguel.

They trudged up the three flights of stairs together, Aidan in the lead, his gun once more in his hand. No matter the situation, she had noticed that Aidan was always first through a door. His overprotective gene had been well honed.

Aidan stopped at her door and held out his hand. Anna fished in the pocket of her jeans for her key card and gave it to him. Giving one sweeping glance down the hallway, he shoved the card into the slot, eased open the door, and peered inside.

Seconds later, he pushed the door the rest of the way open. "Looks clear."

They walked into the room, and Anna grimaced at the mess she'd left behind. She hadn't been expecting company. Her clothes looked as though they'd exploded from her suitcase. The thong panties she'd thought were too uncomfortable were hanging from a bedpost where she'd flung them in her rush to get dressed. Her bed was unmade, and her birth control pills were lying on the nightstand.

The look on Aidan's face was a mixture of bemusement and humor. A burning blush started at the tips of her toes and zoomed like wildfire throughout her body.

"Excuse me." She sped through the room, scooping up clothes and her thong on the way to her suitcase.

Aidan got to her suitcase before she did and was already pulling clothes from it, throwing items left and right.

"What are you doing? It looked bad enough before."

"No time to be modest, Bradford." He pulled out a pair of khaki pants, a light blue tank top, a long-sleeved button-down cotton shirt, and a pair of thick socks. "Put these on, along with your hiking boots." He nodded toward her backpack hanging from a chair. "Call me when you're dressed, and we'll pack the rest together."

Before she could answer, he grabbed Miguel by the shoulder and pushed him out the door.

Aidan closed the door behind him and then leaned up against the doorjamb, his eyes on alert for any kind of threat.

"Señorita Anna. She is your woman?"

"No. Barely know the girl."

He gave a casual glance toward the kid, checking to make sure Miguel bought that. No way in hell was he going to answer the question truthfully. Besides, Anna *wasn't* Aidan's woman. Just because he wanted her like a starving man wanted a meal, or a thirsty man craved water, didn't make her his woman. Didn't matter what he wanted. He'd never endanger Anna that way.

"You seemed…how you say…familiar with her."

"I know her name. Nothing more." Aidan made the words as offhand as possible, wanting to shut down even the slightest suspicion. Even though Miguel was headed to Noah McCall, one of the few people Aidan did trust, it didn't mean the kid needed to know anything about his personal business. It was safer for everyone.

The door opened abruptly. Aidan had to give her credit. Anna's independent spirit was most likely howling protests at his bossiness, but she gave no indication of her ire. She was dressed in the clothes he'd set out for her, and in her hand was the ugliest hat he'd ever seen. It was the color of brown mustard, with a wide green brim and decorated with some kind of insect design.

"Put the hat on."

Though temper glinted in her eyes, she plopped the hat over her silky dark hair. Only Anna could make something so damn ugly look kind of cute.

He removed the hat from her head and almost smiled at the relief on her face. "Bunch your hair up." Frowning her confusion, she did as he asked. Aidan plopped the hat back on to her head. "Perfect. Now, let's get you packed. Smith will be here soon."

Instead of arguing with him, she led the way back into her room. Less than five minutes later, Aidan had filled her backpack with the essentials for their trip, and they were headed out the door. He had been impressed with Anna's clothing choices almost as much as her packing efficiency. For someone who always looked so feminine and effortlessly lovely, her apparel was surprisingly practical and minimalistic.

They reached the first floor just as his cellphone vibrated. A signal that Smith was close. Aidan pushed both Miguel and Anna into a small alcove. He pulled a handful of bills out of his wallet and handed them to the kid.

"This should last you till you get to where you're going." He put his hands on Miguel's shoulders and eyed him, man to man. "Listen, kid, I trust Smith more than any other person in this city, but that's not saying much. If you get an idea that anything is off, you tell him you need to take a leak and then get away from him."

From his other pocket, he took a burner phone, keyed in a couple of numbers, and hit save. He handed the phone to Miguel. "Something like that happens, you hit speed dial for either of these numbers and then hide until someone comes for you. Got it?"

"Si. Gracias."

"Okay. Let's get going."

Walking in front of them, Aidan went through the front door and spotted Smith getting out of a beat up looking Land Rover. Dressed in a long-sleeved black shirt and black jeans, the man should've looked like a wilted weed. Instead, he looked as cool as if he were in air conditioning instead of the ninety-plus degrees and one hundred percent humidity of Cali, Colombia.

Words weren't necessary. The arrangements had been made. He just hoped Smith didn't have another agenda. He'd asked the man for help a couple of times before, and Smith had always come through. Didn't mean Aidan trusted him, though. He just distrusted him less than others.

His expression impassive as always, Smith handed Aidan a key to the Land Rover. Giving the other man a nod, Aidan squeezed Miguel's shoulder and backed away. Should've known Anna had other ideas.

Hugging Miguel hard, she whispered something in his ear, which made him smile and then redden with a deep blush. Releasing the kid, she turned to Smith and gave him what was probably the meanest look Anna Bradford could conjure. In Aidan's opinion, she looked like a spitting kitten.

"You'll take good care of him?"

"Yes." Smith wasn't one to talk much. Another reason Aidan kind of liked him.

"See that you do, or I'll come gunning for you."

Instead of commenting, he glanced over at Aidan with a raised brow.

Aidan shrugged. "She means business. She's meaner than she looks."

In a deep but surprisingly gentle voice, Smith said, "I will take very good care of your friend."

With that, Smith grabbed Miguel by the elbow and led him to Aidan's motorcycle. Without another glance back, they sped off.

Aidan turned to the woman at his side. "Let's go find your friend."

CHAPTER FIVE

Anna followed Aidan to their ride. Mud, at least two inches thick, caked the giant tires. The hood and doors were only slightly cleaner. The Land Rover looked as though it had driven through hell at least twice.

She was about to open the passenger door to get in when Aidan grabbed her arm. "Hold on." He bent down, pulled a small handgun from his ankle holster, and handed it to her. "Hold this at your side. You see anything suspicious, let me know."

With that, he stooped down and looked underneath the vehicle. Determined to be as helpful as possible, Anna did as he'd asked and kept her eyes open for anything odd or suspicious. This part of town was filled with small businesses, and traffic was light. A few people walked down the sidewalk but seemed lost in their own worlds. Still, she kept a wary eye on them. Aidan's paranoia was contagious.

Standing, Aidan opened the front door, hit the hood release, and then went around to the front of the vehicle and lifted the hood for inspection. After careful examination, he gave what sounded like an approving grunt and slammed the hood shut. He took the gun from her hand and said, "Let's go."

Relieved, Anna jumped inside. An instant later, Aidan climbed in beside her and started the engine. He glanced over and gave her the first smile she'd seen from him today. "You hungry?"

She was so startled by the question, she burst out laughing.

"What's so funny?"

"I guess that wasn't what I thought you'd say. Don't we need to get going finding Carrie?"

"We will, don't worry." His eyes shifted to the rearview mirror. "Soon as I'm sure we're alone."

"Who would be following us?"

"You think the Garcia family trusts Miguel to keep his mouth shut?"

"Miguel's in danger?"

"Not anymore."

"Do you think the Garcias know we're coming?"

"Maybe. Probably." He turned onto a street filled with food vendors. "We'll keep 'em guessing for a while."

He sent her another look, this one almost lighthearted. "So, what are you hungry for?"

If ever there was a loaded question. She decided to take the question at face value and answered truthfully, "Anything sounds good. Breakfast was a long time ago, and I missed lunch."

"You like empanadas?"

Her stomach growled an answer before she got the chance.

At the sound, she was treated to another smile. Two in less than five minutes was almost more than her heart could take.

"I'll take that grumble as a yes. There's a hole-in-the-wall restaurant down this street. Best empanadas in the city. Got a takeout window, too. We'll eat on the road as we head on up to see Garcia."

It struck her then. "You don't think Carrie's in danger, do you?"

He steered the Rover onto a dusty gravel road. "No. At least not yet. I put out some feelers to a few of my more reliable contacts. No one knows of any injuries to the family or his people. One of my contacts thought a baby might be on the way for a daughter-in-law."

"If Garcia is so powerful and wealthy, couldn't he afford a full-time physician?"

"My sources say the family had one, but he died." Apparently seeing her alarm, he added, "Stroke. Not murder."

Feeling only slightly less worried, she was about to ask about his plans to rescue Carrie when he pulled up to the window of a small brick building. A harsh-faced man glared at them and barked out, "What do you want?"

She listened as Aidan placed an order large enough to feed a small army. The man nodded and snapped, "Five minutes."

Aidan winked, gave her a quick grin. "Customer service sucks. Food's better."

A buzz sounded. Aidan grabbed his cellphone from the console and swiped the screen to read a text. His expression never changed, but Anna noted a slight tightening of his jaw.

"Something wrong?"

Instead of answering her, he tapped out a reply. Another buzz, then another reply. The rapid rate of replies was both dizzying and worrisome. Had something happened?

In the midst of Aidan's rapid-fire texting, the dour-faced man returned to the takeout window and growled out an amount for their order. Anna grabbed her wallet, determined to pay. It was the very least she could do. Without taking his eyes from his phone, Aidan pulled a wad of bills from this pocket and held them out to the man. It must have been more than enough, because the man's mouth actually moved up into what might've been a smile.

Seconds later, two giant white sacks were shoved through the open window. Aidan grabbed them and handed them over to Anna.

With a nod and a "Gracias" to the man, Aidan pulled away from the building.

Anna dealt with the food. She was a little surprised that instead of pulling over so he could eat, he pressed a key on his cellphone and then held it to his ear.

Anna shamelessly listened to the short and very one-sided conversation.

"Yeah. You're sure?" Aidan said. He listened for several long seconds and then gave two "Okays," one grunt, and an "All right" before ending the call and dropping the phone back onto the console.

Frustrated, Anna said, "Want to tell me what's going on?"

He didn't give her an answer, just an odd, concerned look as he pulled into the parking lot of a small strip mall.

"Let's eat, and then we'll talk."

Aidan was more than a little surprised he got away with that. Instead of demanding to know what was going on, she silently withdrew several paper-wrapped meat pies from the sack. She handed him two and unwrapped another, taking a healthy bite.

He downed one pie in three bites, then started on the second one, eating only slightly slower. After finishing that one off, he twisted in his seat and pulled open a cooler in the backseat. Smith had come through once again. The cooler was filled with ice-cold bottles of water, along with sports drinks and sodas.

He handed a bottle of water to Anna and then took several chugs from his own bottle before he looked at her again. He was impressed that she'd managed to handle two empanadas and was now working on her third. He liked a woman with a healthy appetite.

"Taste good?"

She nodded. Chewing and then swallowing, she said, "Truly excellent."

Aidan grabbed another from the bag between them and ate slowly. His thoughts were anything but slow. Circumstances had changed, and he didn't like it one damn bit. But he'd learned a long time ago that accepting the shit that happened and liking it were two different things.

He took one last swig from his water bottle. "Why have you never accepted Noah's offer to come work for LCR?"

If she was surprised by his question, she didn't let on. "For one thing, I love what I do. For me, there's nothing more rewarding than making a difference in a child's life. Seeing a traumatized child recover and know that I was a part of that is a phenomenal feeling."

He liked the way her brown eyes gleamed and her expressive face glowed when she talked about her job. He liked that she didn't overreact at the bar earlier. She'd been in danger but had kept her wits about her. He liked that when she didn't like something, she spoke up. He liked the way her hair glinted with different colors when the sun hit it at a certain angle. He liked the light spatter of freckles across her nose and that when she smiled, her entire face lit up. He liked that—

He slammed the door on those thoughts. Oh hell no, he would not go there. He had successfully tamped down his attraction to Anna Bradford for over two years. Damned if this event would throw him off course.

"McCall says you've had training. Said that you've been through some practice missions with Riley."

Riley Ingram was one of Anna's best friends. She was also one of the toughest operatives Aidan had ever worked with.

"Yes, Riley and I have done some training on occasion. Whenever we've got some extra time together." Her eyes narrowed. "What's going on?"

Aidan sprawled back in his seat. No point in beating around the bush. McCall believed she could handle this. The LCR leader would never put anyone, especially a civilian and someone he cared about, in harm's way unless he had total confidence in her abilities.

"Circumstances have changed."

"In what way?"

"Your friend was taken to a Garcia family compound. Only, it's not the one we figured. This one is several hours away."

"Do you know how to get there?"

"McCall is sending me coordinates."

"There's more, though. What?"

"This compound belongs to Garcia's youngest son. Julio's not known for his even temper even in the best of times. Does Carrie have a good head on her shoulders?"

"She's the most level-headed person I've ever known."

"Good. She should be safe."

"But not us?"

"He won't be as accommodating as his father would have been. We'll have to use stealth. It could get dangerous. You need to tell me if you don't want to do this. I can handle this alone."

What an odd feeling it was to want to slap a man and kiss him at the same time. Only Aidan Thorne had ever made her think that way. He was telling her she didn't have to put herself in danger. That he was willing to take the risk on his own. Aidan Thorne was a hero in every sense of the word. But he had shown her on more than one occasion that he didn't have a lot of faith in her abilities.

"Yes, you can handle this alone, but you don't have to. I'll be with you every step of the way. And I will be an asset, not a liability."

She spoke with a quiet confidence. Anna knew what she was made of.

"Good enough for me."

Something loosened inside her. She had always believed in her abilities, but having Aidan's support and trust did something to her. She so wanted this man's approval. Pushing that needy feeling aside for now, she asked, "What's the game plan?"

"The compound is on a mountain, situated between Medellín and Arauca. Give or take any interruptions along the way, that's about a six-hour drive to the base of the mountain. McCall's intel says the compound was once easily accessible, but after Julio finished building his home, he had all access roads blocked off."

"How does he get supplies?"

"Other than on foot, helicopter is the only way on or off the mountain. It's been a couple of years since Julio finished his home, so there's no telling what kind of growth has built up. We'll drive up as far as we can, hike the rest of the way. Could be a couple dozen miles or so. Depending on the terrain, it could take a day, day and a half to get to the top."

Hiking was one of her favorite pastimes. She was in good shape and was thankful for it. Hiking in the humid ninety-plus-degree heat would be a challenge.

"Do you expect resistance before we arrive?"

"Colombian authorities aren't crazy about having Americans wandering into unknown territory. If we get stopped, I'll handle things.

"Once we get to the compound, it could get dicey. Juan Garcia turned the bulk of his business over to his two sons. Julio's hotheaded and arrogant. Got a double dose of machismo." He paused a beat, then gave her that bone-melting sexy smile. "But that's a weakness we can exploit."

"How so?"

"You get too cocky, you screw up."

He glanced at one of the bags still full of empanadas. "You finished?"

"Yes."

He took the sack from her and dropped it into the backseat. "So what now?"

"We're going shopping."

CHAPTER SIX

An hour later, armed with more weapons and equipment than they might need, they were headed out of Cali. Aidan was taking no chances. McCall had sent as much information as he'd been able to gather on short notice. No matter how Aidan looked at it, this rescue would be no picnic.

He glanced over at his passenger. So far, she had been the biggest surprise. From this morning's encounter at Claudio's Cantina to learning that her friend had been abducted, she had taken everything in stride. No, Anna Bradford was not one to overreact.

And because of her maturity and calm demeanor, Aidan was taking her on a rescue mission. Even though he really had no choice, he didn't feel as uneasy as he might have with another civilian. McCall, who was nobody's fool, believed she could handle herself. Just because she looked like candy sprinkles on an ice cream sundae didn't mean she was delicate.

What she had survived a few years back, abduction and torture, might've destroyed most people. He knew Anna Bradford was no weakling.

"You ever been to Medellín or Arauca?"

She'd been gazing out the window but turned to him when he started talking. "No. This is my first time in Colombia."

"You've had an interesting introduction. Sorry your work got interrupted."

She turned away to look out the window, but not before he saw the grimace. "I wasn't having much luck anyway."

"Why not?"

"Some of the kids I worked with have been through more trauma than most people will see in a lifetime. Their parents—some, not all—want to push it under the rug, pretend it never happened."

"It can't be the first time you've dealt with parents in denial."

She gave a little strangled laugh. "No. I was raised by parents in denial. I know the symptoms. Doesn't make it any easier to understand or deal with."

"Your parents are divorced. Right?"

"Yes. Not that it's done them a lot of good."

"How so?"

"They can't move on. They were miserable when they were married. Now they're miserable apart. Always wanting to know what's going on with the other. Is she seeing anyone? Does he have a new bimbo?"

She shrugged in that nonchalant way people did when they were trying to pretend something didn't bother them when it bothered them a helluva lot.

"Putting you right in the middle."

"I've been there most of my life. You'd think I'd be used to it by now." She threw him a wry look. "I shouldn't complain. If there's one thing my parents agree on, it's their love for me. There are too many children…people in general, who never know the love of one parent, much less two. I'm lucky, I know."

"Doesn't make it any easier to bear."

Another shrug, she then shifted in her seat to face him. "What about you? Were you one of the lucky ones, too?"

"The luckiest. Great parents. Wonderful sister. I hit the jackpot."

Anna's expression was easy to read. She was wondering where his damage was. Most LCR operatives had something in their past that compelled them to dedicate their lives to rescuing others from a similar fate. He couldn't say his own hellacious experience was a typical one, but in a roundabout way, it had brought him to LCR.

"You're wondering what happened to me."

She didn't even try to hide her curiosity. Instead, she nodded and waited.

For the first time in a long time, he found himself wanting to spill his guts, tell her the whole sorry mess. The pain, the betrayal. The waste of a beautiful life. The destruction of other lives. The gut-wrenching ache of his own.

The temptation was so great, he actually opened his mouth to say the first words and then slammed his trap closed. What the hell? How damn selfish would he be to put any of his shit into Anna's head? The less she knew, the safer she was.

"You can trust me, you know."

She said it so sweetly, no judgment, no artifice. Just the compassionate words of a caring, beautiful soul. It was all he could do not to reach over and hug her. Dammit, why did she have to be so damned sweet?

"I know I can. It's just best for both of us if you don't know."

"You're still in danger?"

He looked away from her, away from temptation. "Let's not go there."

"But… I—"

"Drop it," he snapped.

He didn't see her flinch, but he felt it like a blow.

"Shit, Anna," he rasped out. "I'm sorry. It's just—"

"No. Sorry. Prying is my business, and sometimes I overstep my boundaries."

"You didn't overstep. It's just best not to talk about it. Okay?"

"It's fine. Really." Her best fake smile in place, she glanced out at the sky. "Will the weather be this humid and hot where we're headed?"

Anna knew he didn't buy her false cheerfulness. Her change of subject—the weather, for heaven's sake—was more than a little awkward. The man beside her was quiet for a few seconds, and she wondered if he would give an explanation after all. She hoped he wouldn't. She didn't want one. Not this way. Having him tell her out of guilt was a form of coercion. That wasn't the way she wanted to get to know Aidan Thorne.

"Weather will probably be about the same. Hot and humid." He gave her a teasing, lighthearted glance. "Good thing we've got plenty of sunscreen and bug spray."

Anna drew in a relieved breath. The awkwardness had passed. Even though he hadn't given her any information, what she had learned was almost as important. There was something in his past, a darkness that loomed over him. It hurt her to know that he was still hurting.

Pushing aside feelings that she could not allow to grow, she said, "How are Justin and Riley doing?"

"Good. Seem content."

She almost smiled at the bland description. She knew they were more than just "content." The last time she'd seen them, Riley had a glow of happiness that Anna had never believed was possible for her friend. And Justin had the look of a deeply satisfied man.

"Thank you again for helping me set that up."

He shrugged as if it had been nothing. It had been a whole lot more than nothing. Without hers and Aidan's interference, Riley and Justin might still be hurting today. Anna had believed that just getting them together in the same place was all that was needed. It had taken a little convincing, but she had talked Aidan into helping her arrange a meeting. He had offered his family's place in the Caribbean.

"Riley told me that she and Justin were spending their days off house hunting. I wouldn't be surprised if he pops the question soon."

He gave a slight grunt. Anna wasn't sure if he was agreeing with her or just wasn't listening.

"You don't think they'll get married?"

He glanced over at her, and she saw something flicker in his expression, his eyes. Sadness? An acceptance?

"What's wrong?"

"You're a romantic, aren't you?"

"You say that like it's a bad thing."

"No. We all have to be who we are."

"I agree. So who are you?"

"Who am I?" He shifted his gaze forward again. "Guess I'm still trying to figure that out."

She didn't believe him for a minute. Aidan Thorne knew exactly who he was. She thought that might be the first time he had ever lied to her and wondered if she should call him on it. No, this wasn't the time or place. Getting Carrie safely back home was the only thing they needed to be concentrating on. But when this was over and everyone was safe, she was going to confront Aidan Thorne. Their odd animosity had existed for too long. Aidan was gruff, surly, and occasionally downright hateful to her. To most everyone else, he was polite or friendly, and to some, he was incredibly charming. What was it about her that put him on edge?

Anna told herself she needed to remember that learning the truth wasn't always pleasant. Maybe Aidan just didn't like her. If that was so, no matter how painful, she would accept it and move on. How self-defeating was it to be attracted to a man who couldn't stand her?

Attracted?

She determinedly ignored the laughing sarcasm of the little voice inside her.

CHAPTER SEVEN

Aidan listened to the shallow, even breaths of his sleeping passenger. Anna had gone under a while ago, and he thought it might've been the sweetest thing he'd ever seen. One minute she'd been talking about a documentary about Colombia that she'd watched before her trip, and the next she'd just dropped off. He'd seen her head loll forward and had used his hand to catch her. She hadn't even noticed when he'd pulled to the side of the road and leaned over her to push her seat back. She'd given the sexiest, sweetest little groan, wiggled a little to get more comfortable, and then burrowed into her seat.

He had been avoiding this woman for almost two years now. Having her show up in a bar halfway across the world was both unexpected and inconvenient. He knew strange coincidences happened every damn day, but this was one he could definitely have done without. Being in the same room with Anna Bradford was something he avoided at all costs. Having her close reminded him of what he couldn't have. Being on a rescue mission with her was pure, unadulterated hell. Not only would she be in danger—the very thought twisted his gut—she would be within touching distance, kissing distance.

The buzzer on his cellphone jerked him out of his pity party. He glanced at the screen. Bracing himself for a million questions, he answered, "Hello, Ingram."

Riley Ingram was her usual direct and to-the-point self. "Justin and I are headed to Colombia."

"Thanks for the assistance, but it's doubtful you guys can make it in time. We need to act ASAP."

"Anna isn't trained for an actual rescue, Thorne."

"No, but she *is* trained. McCall believes she can do it."

"I disagree. She's not tough enough."

"You know she'd kick your ass if she heard you say that."

"No, she wouldn't," Riley replied. "She'd just smile and hug me for my concern."

Aidan's chest tightened. "Yeah, you're probably right about that."

"We can be there by tomorrow, midmorning."

"We'll keep in contact. You guys can head up after us."

"But you're not going to wait."

His eyes flickered over to the sleeping woman beside him. He'd give his life to protect her, but it was his job to rescue kidnapped victims. McCall believed Anna would be an asset, not a liability. Ingram was thinking with her heart, not her head. If Anna wasn't her best friend, Riley would probably have a different opinion.

"No. We can't take that chance. The situation is too volatile. I'll send you our location. Come when you can."

"Can I talk to Anna?"

"She's sleeping."

"Okay. I—"

He heard some whispering in the background, then Riley said, "Hold on. Justin wants to talk to you."

"You okay?"

He almost smiled at the concern in his friend's voice. Justin Kelly was one of the few who knew what he felt about Anna.

"I'll make do."

There was a long pause, and Aidan figured Justin was trying to come up with something that wouldn't get Riley's suspicions up. She had no idea that the animosity Aidan often showed Anna was one big lie.

Finally, Kelly released a sigh, saying, "Don't do anything stupid."

"That's the plan. As soon as we arrive, I'll send you our location."

"I looked at the map. You've got a long haul on foot."

"Yeah. Will take us a day. Day and a half tops."

"We'll be in the air in less than an hour."

"Then I'll either see you there or see you on the way down."

"Call if you need air transport."

"Will do."

Aidan ended the call and dropped the phone back on the console. They had about two more hours of drive time. When they arrived, he'd take a few hours to sleep, and then they'd head out at dawn.

If things went as planned, Anna, Carrie, and Aidan would be headed back down the mountain in about thirty-six hours.

Problem was, *if* was a damn big word for this op.

***

A wild, unearthly sound jerked Anna awake. Darkness surrounded her, and for an instant she had no idea where she was or what had happened.

"Relax," a sleepy, masculine voice said beside her. "It's just a screech owl."

Memory returned in a flash. "How long have we been here?"

"Few hours. Go back to sleep. We still have a while before dawn."

How embarrassing. Aidan had driven almost the entire trip with her sleeping beside him like a slug. He had to be exhausted. The least she could have done was offer to share the drive time. Instead, she'd fallen asleep and forgot all about teamwork.

"What's that busy mind of yours getting upset about?"

She froze. She had promised herself she would be an asset to him, and now she couldn't even let him get some rest. How could he tell she was still awake and thinking? And why did his gruff, slightly slurred voice have to sound so sexy? Would she still be as attracted to him if he had a voice like Pee-wee Herman or Elmer Fudd? The answer was yes. His sexy voice wasn't the reason for her feelings, but it sure did nothing to hinder them.

"Anna?"

"Shh. I'm trying to stay quiet and still so you can go back to sleep."

"Then how about relaxing? You're as stiff as a board."

"Sorry." She released a long breath and consciously relaxed her entire body. Seconds later, she was wishing she hadn't relaxed quite so much as an awareness of greater need hit her. She was in dire need of the bathroom. They had stopped at a rest stop about a hundred miles out of Cali, but that had been hours ago. She now regretted that bottle of water she'd consumed before falling asleep.

She could hold it for a while longer. At least until Aidan managed a little more sleep. As a disciplined person with tremendous willpower, she told herself she could control her bodily urges. Controlling her bladder was just going to take some extra concentration.

"What's wrong?"

Of course Mr. Hyperaware would notice.

"I'm really sorry, but I really need to pee."

Instead of sounding aggravated, he said, "Let me grab a flashlight."

The interior light came on, and Anna blinked to adjust her eyes. She glanced over at Aidan. Even though his thick blond hair was mussed and she had obviously woken him, he looked as alert as if he'd had a full night's sleep and a gallon of coffee. She didn't even want to consider her own appearance. It was downright aggravating that he could look so good on so little sleep.

Instead of just handing her the flashlight, he got out on his side and came around for her.

She opened the door, glancing up at him. "Um, I think I can do this by myself."

He gave a short bark of laughter. "Good to know. However, it might be best if you let me find you a snake-free area before you drop your pants."

That wasn't something she could argue with. A snakebite on the butt, poisonous or not, would be extremely unpleasant.

She stepped out of the vehicle and immediately understood what he meant. Wilderness surrounded them in every direction.

The area around their vehicle was flattened, but only a few feet away, dense, dark jungle lurked in ominous darkness. Nope, she wasn't going to complain at all about him coming with her to scare away the snakes and whatever else might be slithering in the undergrowth. Embarrassment was the least of her worries.

She followed him. The flashlight was bright, illuminating a small path. He stopped about ten yards from their vehicle and swung the flashlight left and right.

Anna saw no beady eyes gleaming or slithering bodies and sighed her relief.

"This looks safe enough but best hurry."

She agreed. Wasting no time, she moved to the area he'd motioned toward and was grateful that while he was kind enough to keep the flashlight shining on the area, he politely looked up to the sky as she unzipped her pants. Seconds later, she was standing, zipping up as she ran toward him.

"You're fast." He had the flashlight pointed in front of her, helping her make her way back. All she could see of him was the outline of his body, but she heard the smile in his voice.

"Thanks." She reached him in seconds. "Just one of my many talents."

When they were standing by the Land Rover again, she asked, "What's the plan?"

"It'll be dawn soon. Might as well get ready to go."

"Where exactly are we going?"

"Come back inside. We'll eat breakfast, and I'll show you the map."

Once inside, he turned on the overhead light, reached into the backseat. He held the sack of leftover empanadas in one hand

and a wrapped bar in the other. "We don't have time for much else. You want cold empanadas or a PowerBar?"

Her stomach, normally cast iron and adventurous, rebelled at the thought of the cold, spicy meat pie. "As good as they were yesterday, I don't think I can handle cold ones for breakfast."

She took the bar and the bottle of water he handed her.

Aidan had no such qualms, wolfing down one meat pie in three bites and then starting on another.

While she ate, she took in their surroundings. She had been too focused on her need earlier to pay much attention. "Where are we?"

"About seventeen miles from our destination."

"And it'll take over a day to get there?"

"At least. Maybe a little longer. We've got some challenging terrain ahead of us."

Before she could explain that she was in good shape and there was no need for him to take it slow for her sake, he pulled a map from the console and unfolded it.

"Take a look."

Aidan pointed out their location and their destination. He waited while her eyes followed the map and what they would have to travel.

"I'm assuming you brought a raft to cross the river?"

A wave of gratitude swept over Aidan for the lack of panic in Anna's voice. Crossing a river that wide without a boat did look daunting. "I got a text from McCall. He's located a man who helped build Garcia's house. He says there's a bridge." Because he needed her to know all the dangers, he added, "Since it's not been maintained, I don't know how stable it'll be. If we have to, we can hike around it."

"How much longer would that take?"

"Half a day, maybe more."

She settled back into her seat and looked out the window. Aidan figured she had something on her mind that she wanted to say. Was she thinking she shouldn't have come with him? It was too late for that. No way in hell was he going to leave her down here by herself. And they could wait no longer to get started. He didn't believe Carrie was in any immediate danger, but the younger Garcia wasn't known for his pleasant personality. Who the hell knew what he might do if things didn't go his way?

Trust Anna to come out with the unexpected.

"I couldn't bear it if something happened to you."

Her voice was low and intense. He had turned off the overhead light after she'd examined the map. Now he flipped it back on.

"Hey, look at me."

When she turned to him, he said, "We'll both be fine. And so will Carrie. Got that?"

He saw something in her eyes then. Behind the worry, there was something else. Something he had been avoiding. Something he refused to put a name to and could not allow. No matter how much he wanted it.

As if realizing she was revealing more than she intended, she turned to the window again. "I know you're right. It's just—"

Aidan reached for her, just to turn her face back to him. That was all he had planned. The instant his fingers touched her cheek, he knew he was in trouble. Holy hell, had he ever touched anything so soft, so delicate? So damn beautiful?

She was looking at him now, dark brown eyes full of trust, hope, and that something that, heaven help him, he didn't want to deny.

His hand slid behind her head. He leaned forward and touched his mouth to hers. *Just a caress, just a touch*, temptation whispered. A gesture of comfort. Of reassurance. Nothing more. The instant his mouth touched hers, he was lost.

He caught her breath of surprise, took it in as his own as his mouth claimed hers in the most sensually provocative kiss Anna had ever received. Aidan kissed like a conqueror. Like he was staking a claim. The hand cupping the back of her head and his mouth on hers were the only places he touched, yet she felt him everywhere. Her body reacted as if this was a prelude to lovemaking. Foreplay could not be any more erotic, more earth-shattering. She wanted him in a way she'd never imagined wanting anyone. Her mind went blank as her body controlled every thought, every feeling, softening, readying itself for his complete possession. Nipples peaked and heat settled low in her belly. She wanted him in her, around her, covering her.

Whimpering her need, Anna grabbed his shoulder, her fingers digging into the thick muscle. If he wanted her, right here, right now, she wouldn't stop him. Heat and need consumed, washed every coherent thought away.

The kiss ended as quickly as it started. One moment she was lost in a haze of sensuality she'd only ever dreamed of, and the next she was leaning back in her seat, breathless and confused.

Aidan was sitting straight up in his seat, staring out the windshield, a clenched jaw and the stiffness of his body the only indications that he'd been affected. Whereas Anna felt as if her entire life had changed in an instant. She was attracted to him, but had forced herself to deny her more tender feelings. Aidan had always treated her as if he didn't want to be around her, didn't particularly like her. That kiss had altered everything. Revealed that all the other things between them had been lies.

"Aidan?"

He turned to look at her, and she knew that even though everything had changed for her, nothing had, or would, change for him. He might not be able to deny his attraction for her any longer, but his expression made it more than apparent that he would continue on as if it didn't exist.

Aidan Thorne wanted her. He just didn't want to want her.

"Going to be light soon. We'd better get started." His voice was rough, but the words were said coolly, dispassionately.

Anna got the message. This was not the time to confront him. He had allowed her to come along on this rescue. She was not going to be a liability. Their total focus needed to be on rescuing Carrie and all of them getting out alive. Putting her personal feelings aside was her only choice. But when this was over and everyone was safe? Aidan Thorne better hold on to his hat, because the gloves were coming off!

Chapter Eight

Aidan adjusted the backpack on Anna's shoulders, making sure the weight was evenly distributed. "Too heavy for you?"

She shifted the pack slightly, shook her head. "Feels fine. I can carry more if need be."

Of course she would. If there was one thing he knew about Anna Bradford, it was that she was willing to carry more than her weight. He also knew that if he hadn't been around to help her rescue Carrie, she would be heading off to do it by herself. She was resilient, resourceful, and determined.

He stepped back, away from temptation. "By the time we arrive, this pack will feel as if it's about three times heavier."

She turned to face him, a thousand questions in her eyes. He was glad she didn't ask them. There were too many things he wanted to say right now—things he had no right to say.

Dammit, he shouldn't have kissed her. He avoided this woman as much as possible. Had even been rude to her on occasion, just to make sure she knew to stay away from him. And in the span of less than twenty-four hours, he'd kissed her twice. So much for the self-control he was so damn proud of. He needed to get this done and get back to his life, away from her. That was the only way to deal with this. Get it done and over with.

Aidan went to his own backpack and shrugged it over his shoulders. Though he didn't ask for her help, she came over and snapped it into place for him, just as he had for her.

Once the pack was settled comfortably, he turned to face her. "Two things before we get started. You're trained to defend yourself, and no matter what happens, I want you to promise me that you will be your first priority. I'll take care of myself and Carrie. You take care of you."

She opened her mouth, and Aidan held up his hand to stop her. "No. I need your promise on that before we leave. I'm trained for rescuing and staying alive. I'm good at it. It's my job. Let me do it. Taking care of yourself is your only job. You'll make things easier for me if I don't have to worry about you. Got it?"

"All right."

"Secondly, when I give you an order, I want you to carry it out. I don't want an argument or an 'I think this'll work better' suggestion. Once we rescue Carrie and we're all back safe and sound, you're welcome to rail at me for being an asshole, jerk, or whatever newfangled word is popular today. But on this op, I'm your boss. Do what I say without question. Got it?"

"I've got no problem with that." If she resented his autocratic words, she gave no indication. Her words were exactly what he needed to hear.

Relieved she'd offered no protest, Aidan turned to eye the location where they'd hidden the Land Rover, double-checking that it couldn't be seen. If any of Garcia's people spotted the vehicle, they'd know immediately somebody was headed their way.

Satisfied the Rover was well hidden, he said, "Let's go."

They started off at a fast, steady pace. Fresh, rested, and hydrated, they needed to make good time here. This path, though overgrown, would be one of the easiest. There would be several areas up ahead that would require more work.

This time of morning, massive trees and oversized bushes provided so much shade, Aidan had to use his flashlight on occasion. Frustrating now, but when the sun was at its zenith, the shade would be much appreciated.

Wild birds cawed to their mates, a small grouping of bright blue butterflies appeared above their heads, a skinny tree limb creaked as a brown spider monkey swung from one branch to another. An ordinary, peaceful day in the depths of the Colombian jungle. Aidan hoped to hell it stayed that way.

His cellphone vibrated in his pocket. Aidan grabbed it, grunted at the readout, and answered, "What do you have, McCall?"

"More than we did. You guys started yet?"

"Yes, we just have, though." He glanced at Anna and mouthed, *McCall.*

"What do you have?" Aidan asked again.

"Nothing Anna can't hear."

Aidan lowered the phone and hit speaker. "Okay. Speaker's on."

"First, wanted to let you know that Miguel arrived safely. We'll get him a proper visa and a safe place to stay. For right now he's staying in one of our safe houses."

"Thank you, Noah," Anna said. "He'll have advantages he never believed were possible."

"Seems like a good kid. Just needed a chance. Anyway, on to the other. It's what we figured, only worse. All roads and trails headed up to the compound were destroyed several years back. Julio has a helipad for arrivals and departures. The mountain's going to be well guarded. If you're seen, they'll shoot first, no questions asked."

That's what Aidan had figured but had held out a little hope that Julio was less paranoid than Aidan had heard.

"What else?" Aidan asked.

"No intel on any injuries or illnesses, however, Julio has himself a young wife. Rumor is she's pregnant. There's a possibility he wanted a doctor for her."

"How far along?"

"From what I've been able to get, she's just a few months. There could be some pregnancy complication."

With that information, Aidan's concern grew. If Carrie wasn't able to help, or the mother or baby didn't make it, would Julio take out his grief on the psychologist?

"Anything else?"

"It's a fortress. Well guarded. Our informant thinks he has a dozen men. He wasn't sure."

"Not as many as I thought. You got a phone number?"

"Yes." McCall gave a series of numbers. Aidan committed them to memory.

"Ingram and Riley will arrive in approximately five hours. They were delayed. We had some mechanical problems with the plane. They've got your coordinates and will head up right behind you."

Hopefully, the other two operatives wouldn't be needed, but it was good to have backup just in case.

"Roger that."

"Anna," McCall said, "how are you?"

"I'm fine, Noah. We'll all be fine."

"I know you will. Who knows? Maybe this will persuade you to join our team."

She laughed, as Aidan knew his boss had intended. "Maybe it will."

"Okay, you two, stay safe and call if you need anything."

Aidan slid the phone back into his pocket and started walking again. "We can talk as we go. You have any questions?"

"Why did you get his phone number?"

"Depending on how things go, I might call him and let him know we're coming."

"Okay, I know you told me I shouldn't question you, but—"

Aidan threw her a look over his shoulder. "I meant when we're in the middle of the rescue, don't question my orders. You got questions before we get there, spit them out. You've got every right to ask."

That made things easier. She had been determined to go along with him on anything, but being able to ask him the why of something was a relief.

"Calling him and telling him we're coming seems counterproductive."

"Julio Garcia has many enemies. His guards will be trained to shoot on sight. They won't wait to find out if we're friend or foe."

"If I wasn't with you, would you do things differently?"

He wasn't going to lie to her, but he could lessen the blow. "Yes, but look at it this way. If you weren't with me, I could very well get my head blown off. This way you might just be saving my ass."

Her expression told him she wasn't buying his reasoning for a minute, but instead of arguing, she smiled. "And as we've already discussed, it is a very fine one."

Resisting the urge to grab her for a hard kiss, he nodded. "On behalf of my very fine ass, I thank you."

"So how do you think he'll take it when you call him? Will you tell him who you are?"

"Yes and no. I'll explain that you're a coworker of Dr. Easterly's who hired me to find her."

"And then what?"

"We see how he reacts. Go from there."

"Aidan?"

"Yeah?"

"Have I thanked you for helping me?"

He glanced over his shoulder, not surprised to see that intensely serious expression she wore when something touched her. Anna was as easy to read as a children's book.

"No thanks necessary. It's what I do."

He knew his cool, offhand response probably hurt her tender feelings, but he could do nothing else. For almost a decade, his life had been about avoiding relationships of any kind. Anna Bradford was the first person in years who made him hate that restriction with every fiber of his being. But it could be no other way. It was best she accepted that, just as he had. He'd realized long ago that wanting something you could never have was a torture all its own.

Chapter Nine

Garcia Compound

Julio Garcia paced back and forth across the cool tile of the patio. What was taking the doctor so long to make a diagnosis? Two days ago, when one of his men had complained of headaches and nausea, Julio had shrugged it off as no matter, believing the man had imbibed too freely the night before. Every Friday night, the majority of his men were allowed to enjoy themselves at the small cantina he provided for his people. Most of them were mature enough not to overindulge, but it happened on occasion.

He had assumed that was the case this time, until another man fell sick, and then another. Before he knew it, half of his men were lying in their beds, groaning from pain, or bending over their toilets, vomiting their guts up.

His biggest worry was for Elena. She was finally adjusting to her new life as the wife of a Garcia. Having her become ill was something he wanted to avoid at all costs. Her pregnancy had caused her to be sick already. She didn't need anything else to make her feel worse.

So far, just the men had succumbed to the illness. Julio was feeling nauseated as well, but he told himself the sounds of his men retching and groaning were causing his symptoms. He could not afford to become ill.

"Señor Garcia?"

He whirled around. The woman before him looked both troubled and compassionate. He told himself he should feel guilt for snatching her but could find none. He'd had no choice in the matter.

"What have you decided?"

"You realize that my diagnosis is merely opinion, señor. My training is not in the medical field."

"Yes. Yes." Julio waved off her protests. The men who had abducted the doctor had told him they were misinformed. By the time they allowed her to speak, it had been too late. She was already here.

"But you've had some training. Correct?"

"Yes, but I am in no way trained to treat a serious illness."

"You believe this illness is serious?" That was his worst fear.

"Having no way to test blood or urine samples, all I can do is make an assessment of the symptoms."

"Yes, yes. I understand that."

"Then my initial diagnosis is the possibility of food poisoning."

"Food poisoning?" Relieved breath gushed from his body. "You mean, like tainted or spoiled food?"

"Yes."

"Other than a few who have their meals here in this house, most of the people take their meal in the common building."

"Yes, that's my understanding."

"Then why isn't everyone sick?"

"I don't know. Several of the men indicated they'd visited the cantina."

"But not all of them who were at the cantina are sick. How do you explain that?"

"I can't. I've only been here a few hours. I hope to be able to determine more soon." She held out a piece of paper. "Here's a list of the supplies I need. Also, I've drawn blood from the men who are ill. The vials need to be taken to a lab and analyzed."

"And how do you propose I do this?"

"I don't know. However, until I know exactly what this is, food poisoning or something else, I would recommend quarantining those who are ill."

"You believe it could be contagious?"

"If it's not food poisoning, then yes, it could be something that could spread."

Julio's guts twisted. He refused to fall prey to whatever sickness was bringing down his men. And what about his Elena? What if she became ill? The baby could be hurt.

He could not allow that to happen.

***

Carrie shoved fingers through her short hair. She was running on no sleep. On top of that, she had no real clue what was wrong with these men. Yes, they were presenting symptoms consistent with food poisoning, but unless she was able to get their blood tested, then she couldn't be absolutely certain it wasn't a half-dozen other illnesses. Illnesses that could spread and kill with ease. Illnesses that she had no idea how to treat.

She stood at the entrance to the room designated for the sick. A half-dozen cots had been brought inside and were already occupied. While more beds were being rounded up, the remaining ill lay on blankets on the floor. Buckets had been placed beside all of the sick, and the sound of retching filled the air. The stench would soon become unbearable.

She glanced at the two women who had been selected as her helpers. Evelyn was in her mid-fifties and had a worried look in her soft brown eyes. Constance was a little younger and had the same expression of concern on her face. Both women were looking decidedly green, but Carrie figured it had more to do with revulsion than their bodies succumbing to the illness. It took a strong stomach to be in the medical profession. She'd always considered her constitution to be made of iron, but she had to admit that even her stomach lurched a bit at the scene before them.

Since there was nothing to be done but continue on, she eyed the two women. "Make sure you wear gloves before you tend to any of the men." She held out white masks one of Garcia's men had brought her. Though the masks were intended to keep painters from breathing toxic fumes, they were better than nothing. "Keep one of these over your nose and mouth like I showed you.

"Let's start emptying buckets. Rinse them, spray them with disinfectant, and return them to the beds. Once you're through with that, we'll work up a schedule so we can all get some rest at some point."

Neither of them looked too enthusiastic, but both nodded and set to work.

As Carrie slid her hands into gloves and covered her face with a mask, she thought about what poor Anna must be going through. Was it only yesterday they had planned to have a joint counseling session with one of the families?

Would Anna have gone to the police? Had she called Carrie's children? Hopefully not. Both of them tended to worry about their mom way too much already.

If she could find a phone, she could at least call Anna and let her know she was all right. Asking for one would be pointless. When she had been taken, she had been bound and gagged, arriving here in a helicopter. Then blindfolded, she had been taken to the man responsible for her abduction—Julio Garcia. The man had apologized for the inconvenience but claimed he had a couple of people who were ill and he would be most grateful for her assistance.

It didn't take a rocket scientist to realize she'd been abducted by people who were more than just mere criminals. She had been fearful that telling Garcia she wasn't a medical doctor would get her killed on the spot. However, she figured if she didn't tell him, he'd learn the truth on his own.

Garcia had been furious at the news, but thankfully not at her. He had asked her to do what she could, and she had agreed. She had asked for one favor—to call her friend and let her know she was all right. The request had been denied.

Asking again would do no good and possibly make them keep a closer eye on her. She was going to have to steal a cellphone and call Anna. Not that she expected her young friend to be able to do anything other than alert the authorities, but someone needed to know what had happened to her.

And as she looked around the room at the horrendously sick men, a chilling feeling warned her that someone needed to know about this, too.

***

Anna guzzled her bottle of water. Rivulets of sweat were rolling down her body, and she was losing moisture almost as quickly as she could replace it. She slapped at a mosquito buzzing around her head and then tossed a damp strand of hair out of her eyes. She was glad she wasn't a particularly vain person. If she were, she was sure she'd be mortified by her appearance.

Her eyes moved to where Aidan sat on a rock a few feet away, chugging down his own water. He wore camo pants and an olive green T-shirt, and while both were damp and stuck to his skin, they only emphasized his manliness. His T-shirt clung lovingly to his abs, showed off impressive pecs, causing Anna's thirst to grow even more. His thick, blond hair was dampened to a dark gold that only seemed to highlight the golden brown of his eyes.

"How you holding up?"

Anna jerked. Had he noticed that her eyes had been roaming over him like a starving piranha's?

She answered quickly, in case he had. "I'm fine. I'm used to hiking long trails."

"But not in this heat."

"No, don't have this kind of humidity in Arizona."

"Do you live close to both your parents?"

"Close enough to get there if they need me. Not close enough that they can drop by on a moment's notice."

"You dating anyone?"

If that question had been asked by any other man, she might have believed his interest was personal. An entry-level question leading to asking her out. But this was Aidan Thorne. Even though he'd kissed her, she had no illusions about his interest in her personal life.

"Not really. I do so much traveling, it's hard to maintain a steady relationship."

"I know you counsel traumatized children, but why so much traveling?"

"The Timothy Foundation, my employer, is a nonprofit children's advocacy group. They help kids from all over the world and send psychologists and counselors to wherever they're needed."

"How'd you get interested in counseling children? Seems like I remember your major was criminal justice."

Her heart lightened a little. She had never told him that, so maybe he had some interest in her after all.

"That was my major, but after my experience in Tranquility, a lot of my priorities changed."

Having been kidnapped by a cult, brainwashed, and tortured to give up all her free will, her very identity, had brought a lot of things into focus for Anna. After she was rescued, she had reevaluated every part of her life. Who she was, who she wanted to be. And what impact she wanted to make in the world.

"At first I thought I wanted to work with traumatized adults. Seeing what happened to them in Tranquility, I figured my personal experience could better relate to those kind of traumas."

"Why'd you change your mind?"

"My last year of college, I interned at a homeless shelter and had a couple of experiences that made me realize I had a special affinity with children. It fit, you know? Challenged me in a way I'd never experienced before, but in a good way. So I took a few more classes focused on counseling traumatized children. Took a little extra time to get my degree, but the effort was worth it. When I got my masters, that was my main focus."

"Are you going for your PhD?"

"Yes. So between that and my job, extra things like fun have been put aside."

"You enjoy your job?"

"Yes and no. I love helping the kids and watching them recover, but it's painful to see what they've gone through."

"Yeah."

They were quiet for several moments. She knew they would have to get up soon. They'd agreed to ten-minute breaks every two hours simply because the heat and humidity drained their strength so much. She wanted to ask him questions about his life before LCR. He'd indicated yesterday that his past wasn't up for discussion. Which seemed incredibly unfair since there was almost nothing he didn't know about her.

"You did some counseling with some of the victims of Tranquility, didn't you?"

She wasn't surprised Aidan knew this, too. Being rescued by LCR put her in the unique position of having much of her past known by a lot more people than she was comfortable with. She wouldn't, however, ever resent that. LCR had saved her life and her sanity.

"I didn't really do any counseling then. There were a couple of people, victims themselves, who were kind to me. I wanted to be there for them. Counseling victims who have been tortured and brainwashed requires specialized training. I was there as their friend, to support them."

"Are you still friends with them?"

"Not all of them. Most of them wanted to get away from everything that reminded them of what they'd endured. Kelli Cavanaugh and Missy Meads are the two I've maintained friendships with. We see each other every other month or so."

"How are they doing?"

"Remarkably well. Missy finished her degree in finance. She's vice president of the bank where she used to be a teller and got married last year to a great guy. And Kelli, despite her entire family's objections, decided to follow in her Uncle Seth's path and is a cop in Houston."

"Another LCR happy ending."

"They're not always like that, though, are they?"

"Unfortunately, no, but we do what we can."

She got to her feet. Their conversation had brought back memories she didn't care to dwell on. Those dark days of suffering, torture, starvation, and terror would always be with her, but she had learned that thinking about them too much was counterproductive. Moving on was the only way to survive in this world. She'd learned that the hard way, and it was a lesson she would never forget.

Aidan took one last drink from his bottle and stood. "You ready?"

Before she could answer, a buzzing noise sounded. Aidan's phone.

He grabbed it, held it to his ear. The furrow of his brow gave her an ominous feeling.

"Hold on, McCall," Aidan said. "I'm putting you on speaker."

A second later, Noah said, "Anna, I was just telling Thorne that we have some additional information. Might not be pertinent, but it's best to learn everything you can, whether it's relevant or not.

"As you know, Julio is Juan Garcia's youngest son. He's had a few rifts with his father and recently tried to patch up his relationship by agreeing to marry into the Ruiz family."

Aidan gave a snort of disgust. "The Ruiz family are rivals of Garcia's. Joining two powerful families like that…" He shook his head. "Never seen it work."

"Yeah," Noah said. "Rumor is that Julio found it no hardship, though. Not only did he want to please his papa, but he's entranced by his beautiful new wife, Elena.

"Both families are purportedly happy about the baby. It's being touted as the consummation of a Garcia/Ruiz partnership."

Anna swung her gaze to Aidan. "Then the speculation that he abducted Carrie to treat his wife could be right."

"It's a real possibility," Noah answered. "From all accounts, though, neither Garcia nor Ruiz know about any pregnancy difficulties."

"Sounds like we'll just have to find out for ourselves," Aidan said. "Anything else?"

"Nothing other than what you already know. Both families have violent pasts. Pablo, the patriarch of the Ruiz family, is known to be particularly ruthless. I wouldn't turn my back on any of them, though."

"I agree," Aidan said. "Ingram and Kelly still in the air?"

"Yes. Should be landing soon. Delvecchio and Mallory are tagging along, too. Fox is on another assignment."

Anna was watching Aidan, and when Noah mentioned Sabrina Fox, an expression flashed across his face that she couldn't mistake. Disappointment. A sinking feeling zoomed to the pit of her stomach.

"We'll keep you updated," Aidan said.

"Stay safe, you two."

Aidan slid the phone back into a zippered pocket. "Let's go."

Knowing the dejection would show, she kept her face averted as she repacked her bag. When he picked the bag up and helped her settle it on her back, she thanked him with a polite smile. He gave her a little frown but didn't say anything.

In silence, she followed behind him as they continued up the small incline. How silly to be hurt by his disappointment that his partner couldn't join them. It only made sense that Aidan would want his Elite partner, Sabrina Fox, with him. She was trained for rescues, and she was his friend.

Even though he hadn't said it outright, she knew Aidan believed Anna would be a liability. She had promised herself she wouldn't, but new doubts were corroding her positive attitude. What if she messed things up? What if instead of rescuing Carrie, she—

She couldn't finish the thought. She refused to fail either Carrie or Aidan. Or herself.

Chapter Ten

Aidan looked over his shoulder. "Everything okay?"

Her expression unusually blank, Anna nodded. "Yes. Fine."

She obviously wasn't, but Aidan hadn't figured out how to get her to tell him what was wrong. Ever since that phone call from McCall, she'd been quiet. Too quiet. Anna wasn't a chatterbox, but neither was she one to stay silent for long. The first few hours of their trek, she had commented on everything from the vegetation in the jungle, to the kind of music she liked best, to questions about his favorite books and movies, to conversations about their favorite foods. He'd become accustomed to her steady stream of interesting topics. Truth was, he missed it.

"In about a mile, we'll cross a small stream. On the other side of it, we'll need to find a place to hunker down for about half an hour."

He waited to see if she'd ask why. She didn't. And that bothered him.

Coming to an abrupt stop, he turned to face her.

She stopped, too, and frowned up at him. "What's wrong?"

"That's what I'd like to know. You're a million miles away from where your mind needs to be."

Her eyes flashed with anger. "I am not. I'm keeping up. I've not slowed you down one bit. And I'm keeping an eye out for any dangers, just like you told me to."

"Then why do we need to find a place to hunker down for half an hour?"

"Because the rains will start about that time."

Okay, so she wasn't completely distracted, but there was still something wrong.

"Why are you so quiet all of a sudden?"

Her eyes, which had been locked with his, skittered away. "I ran out of things to talk about. Besides, I'm sure you don't need the distraction."

His head told him the wise thing was to back off and leave it alone. When it came to Anna Bradford, his head was all too often in control, because he had no choice. For once, he chose to ignore the wise thing.

His fingers lifted her chin, startling her and making her look up at him.

"What's wrong, sweetheart?"

Anna's stomach dropped to her feet. Any other man using an endearment was either sweet or insulting, depending upon the man. Aidan Thorne calling her sweetheart was a completely different thing altogether. Her insides were melting.

Without conscious thought, she leaned forward. One step closer, and she would be in his arms.

A warm splat on her forehead and a rumble of thunder were their only warnings. A deluge of water splashed down on them as if someone in heaven had turned a river upside down.

The rains might've shown up early, but as far as Anna was concerned, they showed up just in time. Throwing herself into Aidan's arms was so not a good idea.

Grabbing her arm, he shouted over the roaring deluge, "Let's go!"

She squinted to keep her eyes from being flooded. She had never been caught in a torrential downpour. It was both exhilarating and a little scary. Most of the gravel on the road had been washed away already. Heavy streams of water rushed down, eroding even more of the path and making it almost impossible to keep their footing.

Aidan kept his hand wrapped around her wrist. His hold was so firm, she figured she'd have bruises, but she didn't care. If he let her go, Anna knew she'd slide down the muddy hillside.

Glancing back at her, he shouted, "Looks like there's a rock overhang up ahead."

She nodded, but the rain was so thick, she wasn't sure he could see her, so she yelled, "Okay!"

She took another step, and her feet slid out from under her. Anna yelped and scrambled to regain traction to no avail. Her body pitched forward. An inch away from planting her face in the mud, she was lifted to her feet. Raising her face up to Aidan's, she tried to say thank you, but he gave her no time. Wrapping an arm around her waist, he lifted her off her feet and one-arm carried her up the hill. Even though she knew that carrying her put him in a precarious position, Anna knew not to struggle. One slip of his feet, and they'd both be sliding down the hill.

The rain pounded on them from all sides, and just when she was wearily wondering if Aidan planned to carry her all the way up the mountain, she heard him shout, "Hang on!"

She raised her head to see that they were heading toward a giant rock with a large overhang. Aidan's grip on her slipped, and Anna scrambled on her hands and knees, water and mud sliding beneath her, carrying her away. Just when she thought she was a goner, a large wet hand gripped her upper arm and jerked her forward. Her feet found a small amount of traction. Doing everything she could to help him, Anna almost crawled to get to the rock. They reached it at the same time and collapsed beneath its shelter.

Breathless, they lay side by side for several long moments, panting and recovering as the world around them gushed with water.

Aidan was the first to recover. He propped up on an elbow to look down at her, concern etched on his face.

Anna swallowed a breathless giggle. She might be soaked to the skin and covered in mud, but they were both safe and alive, and that was all that counted right now. "Are we having fun yet?"

Warmth and something like awe flickered in his eyes. "You okay?"

"Just a little damp around the edges. How about you?"

She was sopping wet, as was Aidan, but instead of complaining or being afraid, Anna Bradford was not one bit fazed by almost getting swept away in a torrential rainstorm.

He wanted to answer with an appropriate lighthearted response. It was what he should do. Keep it light and humorous. Don't let her see she was getting to him. Don't let her know what was going on in his head or his heart. But she looked so sweet lying there, soaking wet, beautiful brown eyes sparkling with life, luscious mouth curved with the sheer joy of being alive.

It was that last thought that brought him to his senses. Hell yes, she was alive, and he intended to keep her that way.

Sitting up, he shrugged his backpack off and pulled her up to sit. "Let's get yours off and see if we can dry off a bit."

As if realizing his mood shift, she was silent as she allowed him to take the backpack from her shoulders.

Seeing to his own needs, he kept an eye on her as she retrieved a small towel from her bag. She wiped at her face and, after quickly unbraiding her hair, squeezed the moisture from the damp strands. Then, in an unbelievably short time frame, she rebraided her hair.

Aidan swiped down his own face and hair. "How'd you do that so fast?"

"My best friend and I used to compete to see who could braid our hair the fastest."

"And you always won?"

"Nope. Never. Gina was always faster. But I can braid quicker than the average person, so that's something."

Using the now damp towel, she patted down the rest of her clothing.

"Unless you think something's going to chafe, you might as well keep your wet clothes on. Once the rain stops, they'll dry out." His gaze moved down to their drenched feet. "We do need to change into dry socks, though."

She looked out at the pounding rain as she untied her boots. "How much longer will this last?"

"Probably no more than another ten minutes or so. We'll wait a few minutes after that to let the water recede."

As she tugged off her shoes, then wet socks, she eyed him curiously. "How do you know so much about Colombia? Do you come here often?"

"LCR's had several ops here. We learn as much about an area as we can before we embark on a mission."

The statement was true. Aidan had been on a half-dozen missions in Colombia in the past few years. There was no need to expound on that explanation with more information. Inviting additional questions was the last thing he wanted.

He watched as she dried her feet, noting the white daisies painted on her hot-pink toenails. Everything about Anna Bradford surprised him, enchanted him, or turned him on. This whimsical bit of decoration seemed normal for her.

"Aren't you going to dry your feet?"

Embarrassed to be caught ogling her feet like some sort of perv with a foot fetish, Aidan concentrated on getting his shoes off and drying his own feet. They were silent for several minutes, but he was aware of the curious sideways glances she threw him.

Finally, she spoke. "Can I ask you a question?"

Though he maintained a relaxed expression, his insides tensed as he nodded. He figured if she felt the need to ask if she could ask a question, it was going to be personal or shocking.

"Why do you always act as though you don't like me?"

As usual, she surprised him. Not because the question wasn't difficult to answer, but because she was so damned straightforward.

Denying her words would be useless. Not only was she correct, he had too much respect for her to lie. Anna often consulted with

LCR on certain cases. And on occasion she had been too close to danger. Whenever that had happened, he hadn't hesitated in making his disapproval known.

"It's complicated."

"You can do better than that."

That was true. He could. But telling her the whole truth would be admitting that he cared too damn much. He could, however, give her a truthful answer—just not all of it.

He looked out at the gush of rain as he searched for the right words. "Our jobs—LCR operatives—are dangerous. Having you involved when you're not trained isn't something I'm comfortable with."

He glanced over at her, saw that she was about to reply, and held up a hand. "Let me finish. I know that you've had some training, but you're not LCR-trained. There's a big difference between the two. I can't support you being involved in an op because of that. However, I do regret that you think I don't like you. It's not true."

For an instant, he thought the sun had come out in the middle of the rainstorm. Her smile was just that bright. Then it turned cheeky as she said, "Oh, I know you like me."

Aidan cracked a laugh. "And how do you know that?"

"Because you're one of the good guys."

"I obviously have you fooled."

Instead of giving him another cheeky answer, her eyes went distant and sad, as if she was remembering something difficult.

"Remember the day LCR came into Tranquility and rescued me and all the others?"

"Yes."

"I was sitting in the back of one of the medical vans, shivering from shock and pain. I had three blankets wrapped around me, and I still couldn't get warm."

He had no idea where this was going. Yes, he'd been in on the raid to rescue the victims of Alden Pike's cult, but he had barely even talked to her.

"I was looking out the window, trying to come to terms with what had happened, that we had actually been rescued, and I saw you striding across the road. This little boy, he was probably only about five or six, came at you with a knife."

Aidan remembered that all too well. He'd been focused on the job, looking for threats from everywhere. Seth Cavanaugh had been shot. At the time, Seth hadn't been an LCR operative, but he'd been working with them to help find his niece, Kelli, who had also been abducted by the cult. After seeing Seth's injury, no one had expected him to survive. The shooter had come out of nowhere, and Aidan had borne a huge weight of guilt because he hadn't seen the risk.

After Seth had been transported to the hospital, Aidan had been tasked, along with several other operatives, with rounding up the residents. He had been hyperalert, looking for danger in every corner. A noise behind him had him whirling around with his gun, ready to take out the threat. Instead, he had faced a terrified child with a butcher knife.

"Do you remember what you did?"

"Yeah. The kid was no threat."

Anna watched Aidan's expression, wondering if he would explain what had happened next. When he didn't say anything more, she had no problem describing what she had witnessed.

"You went to your knees, put the gun on the ground, and held out your hands. I couldn't hear what you said to him. Do you remember?"

"No."

The answer wasn't abrupt, so she thought maybe he didn't remember. And even though she hadn't been able to hear his words, witnessing that one moment of kindness had given her the warmth she had been seeking.

"Whatever you said made a remarkable impression on him."

Anna saw the scene as if it had happened yesterday. The little boy had dropped the knife on the ground and had thrown himself into Aidan's arms. They'd stayed like that for several moments, and Aidan had talked to him the whole time. Then Aidan had picked up his gun and the knife, and holding the little boy's hand, he'd led him away.

Other than her rescue, that was the best memory she had of those horrific days.

"He was just a kid."

He didn't get it. Probably because he hadn't seen his actions as anything more than doing his job and being the man he was. Anna had seen a tough, strong man with a compassionate heart. She had seen a hero.

"When I saw how you were with him, I thought you probably had kids of your own."

A cool light entered his eyes, and with regret she recognized that the conversation was over. Whatever was in Aidan's past wasn't something he was willing to share with her. That made her sad, not only because she wanted to know him better, but because whatever had happened to him must have been incredibly painful. After all these years, he was still hurting.

"If your feet are dry enough, you might want to get your socks on. The rain should be ending soon."

Anna pulled socks from her backpack, put them on, and then slipped her feet into her boots. She glanced over at Aidan, surprised to see that he was looking at her, an unusual consternation on his handsome face.

"What?"

"I don't dislike you."

She flashed him a lighthearted grin. "I thought we already established that."

"It's important that you understand that."

Her heart turned over at his concern. Aidan cared about hurting her feelings. She was about to tell him that he really was a nice guy, when he opened his mouth and spoiled the nice moment.

"But you need to understand that there can never be anything between us. Not even friendship."

Her hackles rose. He didn't even want to be her friend? Eyes narrowed with temper, she didn't hold back her thoughts. "If I'm not mistaken, you're the one who's kissed me. Twice! I neither initiated, nor did I enjoy your mauling."

Okay, so the last part was a bald-faced lie, but a girl had her pride, didn't she?

"The first kiss was to save your life. I had to make sure those assholes knew you were under my protection."

"Oh, right. And the second kiss? The one in the Land Rover before we got started? What was it for? Was there a snake or a poisonous spider outside the car window that had its evil eye on me? You wanted to make sure they knew not to mess with me, too? Give it up, Aidan. I know you—"

"Dammit, Bradford. Shut up."

"What?"

Grabbing her by the shoulders, he pulled her to him and growled, "Just. Shut. Up." And then his mouth was on hers.

While her mind was telling her to struggle in his arms and demand he let her go, her body said what he was doing was just fine with her. Deciding she could let her mind chastise her later, she went with what the rest of her wanted. Wrapping her arms around Aidan's waist, she gave herself up to the glorious sensation of being exactly where she wanted to be.

Had he ever tasted anything sweeter? Aidan couldn't get enough of her, would never get enough of her. His conscience was blaring a warning in his head. It told him to let her go. Told him to apologize for being a jerk and try to pretend this craziness had never happened. It was too late for that. Way too late.

He pushed Anna until she was lying on her back, and then he was over her, tasting, devouring. Seemed like he'd been dreaming of this forever. His body screamed with the need to be inside her. His hands ached to touch every silken inch of her. He wanted to spend hours exploring what turned her on, what she liked, what would drive her crazy.

Even while he told himself this was not the best place to do all the things he dreamed of doing to her, his hand delved into her shirt, palming her full, round breast. Then, as if it had a will all its own, his hand left her breast and slid beneath the waistband of her pants, gliding over a silken stomach as it headed to paradise.

Anna's mouth was open as she accepted and dueled with his tongue. Her hands were beneath his shirt, caressing his back, pressing his body harder against hers. He didn't want to stop kissing her, but he wanted to see her, had to see her.

Lifting his head, his breath rasping from his lungs, body heavy with need, Aidan looked down at the beautifully aroused woman beneath him. Brown eyes were open, simmering with fire, luscious mouth wet and swollen from his kiss. Her face was flushed, her entire body arched upward in need, acceptance. Surrender.

The hand that had been lying dormant against her belly slid lower. His finger tangled with tight curls, and Aidan had to grit his teeth to keep from ripping her pants down and taking her here and now. His timing was lousy as usual, so while he couldn't do the one thing his body throbbed, demanded, and wanted more than anything, he could at least give them this.

Aidan slipped his fingers into her crease and groaned at the wet heat he found there. He went farther, found her opening, and slid one finger, then two, inside. At first, he just held them there, allowing her to feel the invasion, allowing himself to savor the heat. She was already throbbing. Already on edge. His eyes locked with hers as his fingers began to move, first slowly, easily, and then when she gasped, spread her legs wider for him, his touch was firmer, harder.

The only sounds were her heavy breaths, his pounding heart, and the torrential rain around them. They were alone in this intimate, sensual moment, surrounded by nature and need. He watched as she reached for satisfaction. Her face was flushed, her eyes glittering with heat. Her entire body arched up from the ground, and she gave a half gasp, half scream.

Aidan felt a moment of intense satisfaction. He hadn't found release himself, but seeing Anna let go and lose herself in a sensual moment was mind-blowingly fulfilling. He refused to ask himself why that was.

He lowered his head, kissing her again as his fingers slowed, allowing her to ride out her peak a little longer. She shuddered one last time, and then her body went limp, quiescent.

Her entire body felt floaty, wondrously dreamy. Aidan's kiss, now slow and languorous, was both sweet and sexy. His mouth was soft, coaxing, gentle, almost as if they'd both achieved satisfaction. Anna's mind, blurred from pleasure, could still recognize the signs of a man who, though on the edge of physical pain, could give her this, easing her down to earth.

She could barely comprehend what had happened. One minute, she'd been snarling at Aidan, and the next, he was kissing her like he couldn't get enough of her.

Finally, he raised his head. A part of her told her she should be embarrassed, but Anna never had been, never would be, a shrinking violet. This man, mysterious, sexy, gorgeous, and heroic, had given her something beautiful. She wasn't about to pretend it hadn't happened, or that she didn't want it to happen again.

She could, however, joke with him. "I'm glad you like me."

His smile was almost sad as he sat back and looked around them. "The rain has stopped."

She had noted the cessation of sound. The birds were singing once again. Within a span of a few moments, the world had gone through a metamorphosis. And so had she.

"You ready to go?"

She sat up and adjusted her clothing. Just like that, the moment was over. They dropped onto the damp ground, slipped on their backpacks, and started walking again.

Anna couldn't decide whether she was disappointed in his behavior or not. She couldn't say she was surprised. Aidan had made it clear that, though he liked her, nothing could happen between them. One orgasm, no matter how spectacular, did not make a relationship. It had been a few minutes out of a lifetime. Extremely glorious minutes, but it was over. Now she needed to decide how to move forward.

She shot a sideways glance at the silent man beside her. There was no doubt how he intended to move forward. His blank expression said it all. If anyone saw them now, no one would guess that only a few moments ago, they'd been so immersed in each other that an earthquake couldn't have pulled them apart. Now, although she knew he was aware of everything around them, he acted as if she weren't there. As if she didn't exist.

She reminded herself once again that this was not the time for a confrontation. Rescuing Carrie had to take precedence over everything else. But if Aidan thought he could give her just that much of himself and no more, he was wrong. Whether he wanted it or not, she was going to be part of his life. Just as he was already part of hers.

It was way too late for them both.

CHAPTER ELEVEN

Other than telling her to watch her step on a large slippery rock, Aidan hadn't said a word in almost an hour. What could he say that wouldn't make the situation worse? What he had done was incomprehensible and contemptible. For the first time in thirty-three years, he had let his body overrule his brain. He'd done the difficult thing and told her nothing could happen between them, and then he'd done a great job of convincing her by making out with her.

Real smart, Thorne. All those years he'd spent in school meant nothing when it came to doing the smart thing with Anna Bradford.

"Aidan, you don't have to look so morose. I don't expect a marriage proposal, you know."

"Good to know, since I don't do marriage."

"You don't believe in marriage?"

"For the right person, yeah."

"So you don't see yourself ever settling down?"

His chest went tight. Yeah, at one time, that was exactly who he'd been. Mr. Stable. Mr. Reliable. Mr. I Have My Shit Together Thorne. Mr. So Much In Love With His Wife He Couldn't See

Straight. He'd had it all. He was the golden boy with the perfect, untouchable life. Nothing bad ever happened to charmed people like him. Until the day it had, and everything had been destroyed.

"Aidan? You didn't answer. You don't plan to ever marry?"

"Never again."

"You've been married?"

"Once. It was enough."

"You're divorced?"

"No."

Surprising the hell out of him, she touched his hand and said, "I'm sorry. How did she die?"

"It was a long time ago. I don't like to talk about it."

"Of course. I understand. If you ever do, though, I'll be glad to listen."

His chest went even tighter, and Aidan had to fight every instinct to haul her back into his arms. Why did she have to be so damned sweet?

The farther up the mountain, the denser the jungle. Aidan was grateful for the distraction of the heavy growth. Using the machete to clear a path for them kept his mind off the physical ache he could do nothing to assuage. If he thought that those intimate moments they'd shared would make things awkward, he was right. Going from an arousal so intense he wanted to howl with need to pretending that nothing had happened was out of his realm of expertise.

He wanted her. He couldn't have her. Damned if he would be happy about it.

Even though they had barely spoken in the last two hours, Aidan knew she was right on his heels. If anything threatened her—some wild animal sprang out of nowhere—he'd only have to take one step back. Protecting her was his highest priority. A snarling whisper in his head reminded him that what he had done back there on that rock was the very opposite of protecting Anna. He had indulged himself. Yes, he had given her pleasure. Big damn deal. He was smart enough to know that what he had done was pure selfishness on his part.

"Can we stop for a moment?"

The breathless woman behind him was a reminder that they hadn't stopped in almost three hours.

"Yeah, let me find a place."

"This will do, won't it?"

He turned to see her sitting on an old, fallen tree. "Just be careful of insects and snakes."

Lifting her legs, she looked around her and, seeing nothing threatening, lowered her feet to the ground.

In silence, Aidan sat down on the other end of the tree.

"I won't bite you, Aidan."

He couldn't help but laugh. Anna Bradford was not the type to sweep something under the rug and pretend it hadn't happened. Taking the easy way out was not who she was. It wasn't Aidan's way either, but damned if he could figure out a way to explain his actions without sounding like an idiot.

He had to address it, though, so he took a breath and tried to explain the unexplainable. "Anna, first of all, I'm—

She held up her hand. "Wait. If you apologize, I will not be responsible for my actions."

"I wasn't going to apologize."

"Oh." She frowned, and he wanted to smile at the temper simmering behind her calm façade. "Continue on, then."

"Thank you," Aidan said dryly. "As I was saying, I'm not the type of guy to send mixed messages, but that's exactly what I've been doing for the last two days. I am attracted to you…guess I've made that obvious."

"Aidan…really. You don't have to do this. I'm old enough to realize a heavy make-out session doesn't have to mean anything. We were two healthy adults enjoying a sensual moment, nothing more."

She was giving him an out. All he had to do was take it, tell her he was glad she understood, and that would be that. And he would be the lowest form of sleaze if he let her believe that.

Taking the hand she had fisted on her lap, he unclenched each finger and pressed his mouth against her palm. "It meant a lot to me, Anna. But I had no right to take things that far. You're a beautiful, passionate, intelligent woman who deserves a man she can count on. I can't be that man."

She looked down at their joined hands, squeezed lightly, and removed hers from his grasp. "Thank you for your honesty."

After taking a long swallow from her bottle of water, she stood. "Guess we'd better get going."

Aidan went to his feet, unaccountably sad. He had known whatever he said to her wouldn't make a difference. Telling her the real reason that they could have no relationship wouldn't change anything. He couldn't have her…could never have her.

As Anna followed Aidan, watching him cut a trail through the thick jungle foliage, she tried to convince herself she was glad he had been so forthright with her. Even though he hadn't given her any reasons, he had been clear that there could be no relationship. She had dated guys before who'd said pretty words that meant nothing. At least with Aidan she was safe from the lies. Unfortunately, that didn't help her bruised heart, because despite his blunt assertions, she couldn't change her feelings for him.

She ground her teeth together in frustration. She was not going to be the type of woman to pine over a man. She had too much pride in herself to give anyone that much power over her.

Shoulders straight, chin lifted in a defiant stance, Anna took in a deep breath. She told herself the tears in her eyes were from allergies, not her hurt feelings.

Four hours later, her bruised heart was the least of her concerns. Every single muscle in her body was screaming with exhaustion. Aidan hadn't mentioned stopping for the night. She knew he wanted to cover as much ground as possible. Her aching body was nothing compared to what Carrie might be going through. What would happen to her friend if she couldn't help Garcia's pregnant wife? Was Julio Garcia the type of man to arbitrarily murder an innocent woman?

"Let's stop here for the night."

Her mind on the horrors of what Carrie might be enduring, Anna shook her head. "We can keep on for a few more hours."

Aidan shrugged off his backpack. "You're exhausted, and I'm getting tired, too. In another half hour, the jungle is going to be so dark, we'll have to use our flashlights. If Garcia has guards patrolling around here, no way they won't see the light. Getting shot isn't going to get us to Carrie any faster."

"I know you're right. I just—" She shrugged, feeling helpless. "I'm so worried for her."

Instead of answering right away, Aidan went around to her back and eased the backpack off her shoulders. Anna almost cried at the relief. When they'd started out this morning, she'd thought the bag was quite light. Now she felt as if a fifty-pound bag had been lifted from her.

Aidan dropped her pack on the ground and turned her around to face him. Hands on her shoulders, he bent his knees to make eye contact with her. "Julio may be a hothead, but he's no idiot. Kidnapping an American citizen is already going to bring a world of hurt down on him. He knows that murdering one would be a million times more stupid."

She let the truth of his words settle into her and felt the tension lessen. "You're right. Thank you."

He squeezed her shoulders lightly and stepped away. "Let's get settled before it gets too dark. I don't want to use the flashlight for long periods of time if we can help it."

The place Aidan had chosen to stop was surprisingly inviting looking. The ground was covered with short, springy grass and only minimal twigs and branches. Anna cleared those off while Aidan cut down giant fronds from a large green plant.

He placed several on the area Anna had cleared and grinned. "Not the Ritz, but not bad for sleeping."

Anna bent to touch one of the leaves and stumbled, almost falling onto them. She caught herself just in time and stepped back. "I'm so tired, I think I could sleep on glass tonight and wouldn't notice it."

"Know what you mean."

He sat down and unzipped his backpack. Anna followed suit. They each drank a bottle of water and ate a protein bar.

"Should've brought some MREs but figured we could exist on these for one night. Now I'm having second thoughts."

Since she was having trouble staying awake to eat all of her bar, Anna had doubts she could have finished a whole meal without falling asleep in her plate. She forced the rest of the bar down and swallowed the rest of her water.

Without a word, Aidan got up and walked away from their campsite. He was about five seconds from doing something he would regret. Anna looked so bedraggled and exhausted, but her mouth was set in that determined slant that he'd come to know so well. He wanted to feel that sweet mouth under his own again. The memory of what had happened only a few hours ago played in his brain. She had tasted so damn good, and her sweet body beneath his had been better than any fantasy. The temptation to kiss her again had been a living thing. Leaving, albeit abruptly, was his only choice.

A few minutes later, he returned to find Anna still sitting in the same place. He handed her the flashlight. "I've cleared out an area for you a few yards that way. Didn't see any animals slinking about, but—"

"I know. Don't dawdle." She gave him a quick smile as she passed him. "One snakebite in a lifetime is one too many for me."

Before he could ask what she meant, she was gone. Less than a minute later, she was back.

Since it was now pitch dark and they were both exhausted, there was nothing more to do other than sleep. While Anna had been gone, Aidan had covered the leaves with a thin blanket.

"We can use our backpacks for pillows." He waved at the makeshift bed. "After you."

She lay down, and Aidan followed suit. They lay quiet for several seconds, not touching. Aidan wasn't even sure if Anna had taken a breath. Figuring she was uncomfortable lying beside him after what happened earlier, he rolled onto his side to face her. Hoping to dispel her uneasiness, he asked casually, "So how'd you get a snakebite?"

She didn't answer. He was about to ask the question again when he realized something amazing. Anna wasn't so still because the situation made her uncomfortable. She was already asleep.

Aidan knew he didn't have the right to hold her, but he couldn't resist touching her fingertips with his own. Then, despite the ache in his groin and the even more painful one in his heart, he fell asleep with a slight smile on his face.

CHAPTER TWELVE

Garcia's Compound

Diego appeared at the door of Julio's office. "Señor, the doctor. She says she needs to talk to you again."

Julio waved a hand in consent. He had spent a miserable night trying to convince himself he wasn't sick. It hadn't worked. His skin was clammy, his gut was a roiling mass of pain. He had thrown up twice and knew it was only a matter of time before he vomited again.

More worried for Elena and his child than for himself, he had insisted she stay on the other side of the house in a guest room. He had talked to her via intercom, and she had been so sympathetic it had made him smile in spite of his condition. Marrying her had been the best decision he'd ever made. Not only had he pleased his papa, which was no easy feat, but he had brought a peace between two powerful families. In addition, he had married the most beautiful woman he'd ever known.

The doctor entered his office. Even though her expression was bland, he could feel her disapproval like a thick cloud. What did he care about her opinion? He had brought her here to care for his men, nothing more.

"One of your men has died. Two others won't survive the day."

Fear clenched his already-aching gut, twisting it into a tight ball of pain. Julio turned away from the doctor. He didn't need her seeing his weakened condition.

"What's wrong with them?"

"I don't know." She sounded both furious and exasperated.

Allowing anger to cover his fear, he whirled back to her. "Then you'd better find out, or you're the next person to die."

"Your threats mean nothing to me, Señor Garcia. If the illness is an airborne virus, we're all dead."

Panicked, Julio grabbed her arm. "No. My wife and the baby inside her. You must save them."

Compassion melted Carrie's anger away. She had watched a man die an agonizing death and had been unable to do anything but mop his brow, hold his hand, and pray his suffering ended soon.

Last night had been one of the longest in her entire life. Trying to keep the men hydrated and their fevers down, while hoping and praying that she didn't get sick, too, had been unbearable.

Not only was she exhausted, she felt as helpless as a newborn left to fend for itself.

She'd come to see this man, to demand he do something. The fear in his eyes stopped her from castigating him. Julio Garcia might be an amoral criminal, but in this he was as mortal as the rest of humanity. He loved his wife and child.

"How far along is your wife?"

"I believe almost four months." He gave a little wave of his hand as he spoke. To Carrie, it was the universal language of some men who found the entire cycle from conception to birth a confusing mystery and wanted to keep it that way.

"I can check her. Make sure she is healthy. I would recommend that she stay as far away from everyone as possible."

"She's had no contact with my people."

He didn't elaborate. She assumed he kept his business dealings away from his family. She wondered about the poor girl, who was probably lonely. Had this been a love match? He seemed to care about her, but was that because of the baby she carried? Too often in her work she had seen men treat their wives as brood mares and nothing more.

Carrie mentally shook her head. Exhaustion was making her brain get off track. Whether Julio and his wife were in love was the least of her problems.

Returning to her main worry, she said, "If this isn't an airborne virus, there's a possibility of poison."

"What kind of poison?"

"I don't know. They all ate at the cantina Friday night. Perhaps that is where it happened."

"Food poisoning would cause these kinds of reactions? Even death?"

"Possibly. But some of the men claimed they didn't eat anything. And while all of them had alcohol, they claimed to have imbibed different kinds."

"So you're saying this could be deliberate?"

"I'm only stating what I've learned," she said calmly. "You'll have to make your own conclusions."

"Can you do nothing for them?"

"Your medical supplies are abysmal. I'm keeping them hydrated, but your supplies need to be replenished." She held out the piece of paper he'd refused to take from her last night.

As he stared down at the long list of items, she continued. Her no-nonsense tone was the one she often used to urge the most stubborn of her clients. "I've drawn several more vials of blood. Until they're analyzed, it's doubtful we can figure out what's wrong. You have ten sick. One has already died. They need to get to a hospital where they can receive proper medical care."

She watched as his face went from stark white to a light green. He grabbed his belly. Comprehension came quick. "You're sick, too."

He whirled away and vomited all over the floor.

She reached out for him. "Let me help you."

Instead of accepting her help, he turned around to glare at her. "It can't be food poisoning. I don't eat with my men. And I don't drink alcohol. You do nothing but guess. You know nothing!"

He turned toward the door and bellowed, "Diego!"

The portly man came running into the room. "Si?"

"Take this woman and lock her in her room. I'll deal with her later."

Her sympathy at an end, she said, "If you don't get those men to a hospital, more will die. You might, too."

"Get her out of here!"

Carrie jerked her arm away from Diego and walked out the door. There was no talking sense into this man. He was either too stupid or too worried about his own neck to get help for his people. If this was an airborne virus, what would happen if his wife became ill? Would he change his mind then?

She stepped down into a sunken living room and glanced outside, through huge sliding glass doors. A giant pool sparkled in the sunshine. A young woman in a minuscule bikini stood on the side of it. She was young and incredibly beautiful. Who was she?

Risking censure from Diego, Carrie gestured with her hand. "Who is that young woman?"

"That is the señor's wife, Elena."

The woman turned, and Carrie got a good look at the woman Julio Garcia seemed to be so enamored of. She was stunningly beautiful. Tall, long-legged, curvy but not voluptuous. The woman walked with an indolence and supreme self-confidence. She drew closer, and Carrie thought she was quite possibly one of the most beautiful women she had ever seen. She stopped at a table and lifted a glass of something cold to her lips, and then she turned. Carrie got a side view of her, noting her tight, flat stomach. Elena might be many things, but there was one thing that she was not. The young wife of Julio Garcia was not pregnant.

Carrie's hand touched the reassuring weight in the pocket of her jeans. While one of the men had been throwing his guts up, Carrie had taken the opportunity to go through his pockets. Whatever was going on here was becoming more troublesome as time went on. Whether Julio wanted help or not, she was going to see that he got it.

***

Anna stopped for a second to adjust her backpack. Her muscles were aching, but not as badly as they had last night. After almost six hours of sleep, she'd woken with a much lighter heart. It hadn't hurt that she'd woken in Aidan's arms. Since she was practically lying on top of him, she knew she was the one who had made the contact. Aidan had been nice enough to let her use him as a mattress.

Other than a gruff "Good morning," Aidan had been characteristically silent. Anna wasn't much of a morning person, so it had been easy enough to go along with his quietness. After everything that had happened in the last thirty-six hours, she had more than enough to keep her occupied.

A melodic noise came from her backpack. She stopped again and, reaching over her shoulder, quickly unzipped a pocket, and retrieved her cellphone. Before she could say hello, a breathless voice said, "Anna, it's Carrie."

"Carrie?" Her eyes, wide with shock, zoomed to Aidan, who had stopped in front of her. "Where are you? What's happening? What—"

Aidan took the phone from her and pressed the speaker button. He heard an older woman's voice, sounding both tired and angry.

"I was abducted, brought to this little village in a helicopter. There're a lot of sick people here. I'm worried it's contagious."

"Carrie, my name is Aidan Thorne. I'm with Anna right now. We're coming up the mountain for you."

"The Aidan Thorne from Last Chance Rescue?"

He caught the embarrassed grimace on Anna's face before she turned away.

"Yes. That Aidan Thorne. Can you tell me how many people are there?"

"It's hard to say. I've spent most of my time in the infirmary since I got here. The man in charge, Julio Garcia, he's sick, too. He's also scared."

"What are the symptoms?"

"Vomiting, diarrhea, fever. One of the men died this morning. Two are close to death. I don't know how long the others will last."

"Any coughing or difficulty breathing?"

"No."

"Headaches or joint pain?"

"No."

"Any rashes or sores?"

"None that I've seen."

"We're maybe three hours away from you. Turning back for a doctor or medical supplies isn't an option, but I can help."

"You have a medical background?"

"Yes."

"But Anna—"

"I'll make sure she's safe."

"Can you get more help? Even with your assistance, these men won't last much longer if we can't figure out the cause of their illness and get them medical care. I've drawn blood, but Garcia refuses to send someone to get it tested."

"I'll see what I can do. If you can, without endangering yourself, find out what kind of security Garcia has set up. Call us back when you can."

"I'll do my best."

"To be on the safe side, drink only bottled water, if it's available. And consume only pre-packaged food."

"Thankfully there seems to be an adequate amount of bottled water. With what's going on, I don't think anyone has the appetite to eat anything."

"Probably for the best."

"Anna?" Carrie said.

"Yes?"

"I'm sorry I got you into this."

"Don't be silly, Carrie. Everything is going to be okay. I promise."

"I'll call back when I know more."

The line went dead.

"What are we going to do?" Anna asked.

What he wanted to do was find a safe place for Anna to hide until he could come back for her. Since that would go over as well as a furnace store in hell, he said, "We're going to triple-time it up the mountain."

With a nod, she started to run. Aidan hit speed dial for McCall and took off after Anna.

Her thoughts whirling like a tornado, Anna kept a good, steady pace as she listened to Aidan's conversation with Noah. Of all the things she thought they would be confronting, an airborne illness that might kill them all was not one of them.

Her normal optimism was taking a serious hit. How on earth were they going to rescue Carrie in addition to helping the men who were sick?

"Yeah," Aidan was saying. "From the sound of it, he's got a dozen or more men guarding the place, but if more than half of them are sick, our chances for infiltrating are better."

She couldn't hear Noah's response but assumed it was about her, because Aidan sent her a sideways glance and said, "I agree."

Whatever that meant. She knew he was worried about her. Heck, she was worried about her, and him, too. And she was worried for Carrie. If the illness was airborne, there was no way Carrie wouldn't become ill. Her throat clogged with emotion. Carrie had been her mentor and friend for years. If anything happened to her...

A hand grabbed hers and squeezed it. She glanced over at Aidan, who was still talking to Noah but his eyes were on her. He knew she was scared, and he was trying to comfort her. She told herself it should bother her that he could read her so well. Even though she had never been one to hide who she was or what she was feeling, a little self-preservation would probably be wise when it came to dealing with this man.

Aidan ended his call to Noah with, "I'll wait to hear back from you."

"So what's the plan?"

"Let's stop for a minute and talk."

When she halted, Aidan noted that even though Anna's breath was slightly elevated, she'd been able to keep a steady pace. Anna being in good shape was a plus for them both.

"McCall has a contact with the CDC. He's going to see if they can determine what the illness might be with the symptoms Carrie described."

"That's a long shot, isn't it? Don't a lot of illnesses have the same symptoms?"

"Yes, but there were some particular aspects in Carrie's description that could narrow the options down."

"You told Carrie you have medical experience."

"Yes." Aidan had never gone out of his way to hide his medical background. It just wasn't something that ever came up. It'd been helpful when he'd been in the military, as well as on LCR ops, but he knew that bringing it out in the open would raise more questions than he wanted to answer.

He figured Anna would be full of them, but instead of asking what his medical experience entailed, she said, "Then you have some ideas on what the illness might be?"

"Diagnostics wasn't my field, but this sounds like poisoning, not a contagious virus. I'm hoping McCall's contact with the CDC can confirm that."

"Could it be food poisoning?"

"It's possible. We don't know what kind of health the man who died was in. He might've had other health factors that contributed to his death."

"Or it could be intentional poisoning."

That was Aidan's biggest worry. If there was an enemy in Garcia's camp, then that raised the stakes. If someone was willing to poison a dozen men, they'd have no problem killing a lone woman who might figure out the problem.

"If it is intentional, then there's going to be more than one element of danger we're going to have to look out for."

"But we're not going to wait on anyone, are we?"

"If it's an airborne virus, I'd say yes. Carrie's already been exposed, and there's not much we could do until help arrived. Hopefully, by the time we arrive at the village, we'll have heard from McCall."

"And if we haven't?"

The next part would be the hardest for her to accept.

"Then we wait."

"But—"

He held up his hand. "Running in blind isn't going to benefit anyone. From the sound of it, Carrie has very few medical supplies. We're not going to be able to help her without more supplies or knowing what we're dealing with."

The obstinate look on her face told him she didn't agree. She didn't, however, argue, and that was a point in her favor.

"When we get there, we'll assess the situation."

He didn't know why he was softening his stance. He had been involved in dozens of rescues and was a seasoned operative. Allowing her to have any input was ridiculous. So why...

She smiled at him as if he'd just given her a million bucks.

Okay, yeah. That was why. *Hell.*

"Okay," he said gruffly, "here's what we've got facing us." Pulling his phone from his pocket, he clicked on the map. "We've got the river in front of us. Just because McCall's contact said there's a bridge, we don't know what kind of condition it's in. If we go this way, we'll be at Garcia's hideout within a couple of hours." He pointed to another trail. "The safer way is this path that bypasses the river."

"How much longer would that take?"

"Half a day at least."

"We've got to get there as soon as possible."

He'd already known what her answer would be. He actually agreed with her, but he didn't have to like it.

"You're right. Problem is, with this being the rainy season, even a small stream will probably be gushing like a geyser. The rain we had earlier didn't help. With a river...who the hell knows?"

"We have to try."

"I agree." He huffed a frustrated breath, not liking where this was going but unable to do anything else. "Let's go."

CHAPTER THIRTEEN

Standing on the edge of the rushing river less than an hour later, Anna was having serious doubts about whether they had made the right decision. One glance at Aidan told her he was having the same thoughts.

"Well, there is a bridge," Anna said in what was supposed to be a cheerful tone, but the quiver in her voice ruined the intent.

"Calling that a bridge is a serious insult to bridge builders everywhere."

She couldn't deny his statement. The bridge was a bunch of slats held up by two thick ropes. Most of the slats were either cracked or rotting. There were several open areas where slats used to be. And while the bridge stretched across to the other side, crossing it was going to take more courage than Anna was sure she possessed. If they didn't make it across, the only alternative was the gushing, wild river beneath them.

She was a strong swimmer, but even if she survived the fall... at worst, the wild current would bash her body against the rocks. At best, it would carry her miles downstream.

A hand grasped hers and gave a squeeze. "I'll be with you every step of the way."

Even though she was terrified, she was grateful he didn't say they needed to head the long way around. Aidan wouldn't do this if he didn't believe they would survive.

"This probably sounds pretty selfish, but I'm glad you're with me."

He squeezed her hand again. "I am, too."

"We're going to make it, aren't we?"

"Hell yeah, we're going to make it." Turning to face her, he took both her hands in his. "We do this together. I'll be in front, but you'll be with me every step. You step where I step. Okay?"

Her mouth suddenly bone-dry, all she could do was nod.

If she thought they would discuss the issue further, she was wrong. Pulling her with him, they took the first step together. The raging river below couldn't drown out the creaking of the wood as Aidan's weight pressed down on the first slat.

Her heart pounding so hard the noise from the rushing water almost disappeared, Anna followed Aidan step by step, one hand gripped in his, the other hanging on to his belt.

Aidan took each step as if he were about to step on a land mine. He had faced death more times than he could count, but he didn't know if he'd ever been more aware of what might happen if he died. Because if he went today, so did Anna. That wasn't something he planned on happening. This woman, with her courageous spirit, zest for life, and screwy sense of humor, was precious to him. He might not ever be able to tell her that, but he could damn well keep her alive so she could go on existing. The world without Anna Bradford would be a much sadder world.

The drop to the water below was maybe a hundred feet. The fall probably wouldn't kill them. It was what would happen after the fall that concerned him. It was his responsibility to make sure that didn't happen.

Even though his focus was on taking each step just right, he was hyperaware of the woman behind him. She clung to his hand and was gripping his belt but wasn't touching him anywhere else. Even so, he could feel the rigidity of her body as if he held her. She was terrified and trying so damn hard not to show it. When she had given him her hand, she had placed her trust in him. He would not let her down.

Sweat trickled from his forehead into his eyes, and Aidan forced himself to ignore the sting. One misstep was all it would take to turn this into disaster.

They made it to the middle of the bridge without mishap. He wasn't ready to let out a relieved breath yet, not until they were both back on solid ground, but—

He heard the crack of the wooden slat a second before Anna screamed his name.

Aidan tightened his hand around hers as he whirled around. Her eyes wide with horror, Anna was dangling in the air. She had let go of his belt, and the only thing keeping her from plunging to the rushing river was his grip on her hand.

"Hang on!" Bracing his feet against the rope, Aidan grabbed hold of her forearm with his other hand. "I'm going to pull you up."

"No!" She glanced down at the water, then back up at him. "You'll fall, too."

"No, don't look down. Look at me, Anna." Either she didn't hear him, or she was too frightened to comprehend. He shouted in a harsh, uncompromising voice, "Anna Bradford, look at me. Now, dammit!"

She raised her head and locked eyes with him.

"Bring your other hand up and take hold of my arm."

Even though it was only seconds, it felt like a millennium before she reached up and grabbed his arm.

"Hang on, baby. Just hang on to me."

With every ounce of strength within him, straining with all his might, Aidan pulled Anna up. He knew he was probably hurting her, possibly crushing her hand and wrist, but if he loosened his grip, she was gone. Inch by slow inch, he brought her up. He knew she would do everything she could to aid him, but for right now, she could do nothing but hold on.

Jaw clenched tight and muscles screaming with strain, Aidan pulled her up and into his arms. Even though he wanted to hold on to her and celebrate the fact that she wasn't in the river, neither of them was out of the woods.

"Let's go." Without waiting for her consent, he grabbed her hand again and continued their journey.

Torn between sobbing and throwing her guts up, Anna did neither as she followed Aidan's every step. When they got to the other side, on firm ground, would be soon enough to have a mini breakdown. She would not put Aidan's life in jeopardy again. He had saved her life and almost lost his own.

The rest of the way passed without incident. The slats held. There were no bobbles, no major swaying of the bridge. Only the slightest of breezes ruffled their hair. Though her heart was still pounding like a terrified rabbit's, Anna was finally ready to accept that they were both going to make it. Only a few more steps…

Craaack!

Anna jerked her head around. Her heart flew up into her throat. Panic zoomed through her as she watched the bridge begin to collapse behind them.

"Aidan!"

She was flying through the air without a word of warning. Her terrified mind comprehended that Aidan had grabbed her by the waist and literally thrown her onto the bank. She landed with a crash and a roll, barely noticing the jagged rocks that cut into her skin. Whipping around, she faced the stuff of nightmares. The bridge was completely gone.

And so was Aidan.

Chapter Fourteen

"Aidan!"

"Down here!"

Aidan looked up to see Anna peering over the edge of the hill. Her pale face held twin expressions of terror and relief.

"Are you all right?"

"Yeah," he yelled back. "How about you?"

"I'd be better if you were up here with me. What can I do to help make that happen?"

Despite the fact that he was clinging to the side of a muddy cliff that was rapidly disintegrating beneath him, he couldn't help but feel a lift to his heart. Anna Bradford was good to have around in a tight spot.

"You see a sturdy tree close by?"

"Just a sec."

Anna disappeared from view, and Aidan took a moment to assess his situation. He was maybe twenty feet below her. The footholds he could see looked precarious at best.

Anna reappeared above him. "Yes, I found one not too far away."

"Great. Take the rope I put in your backpack and tie a knot around the tree. Throw the other end to me. I'll climb up, and we'll be set to go."

He made it sound simpler than it was. If she tied a lousy knot, he was a goner. However, there was no time to give her instructions on tying a proper knot. His feet were sliding out beneath him, and he figured he had maybe a minute or less before he slid down the hill into the river.

Her head had disappeared again, and he couldn't help but call out to her. "Anna?"

"Hang on! Be right there."

Half a minute later, she appeared again. "Okay, I'm going to lower the rope down to you."

When the rope was within a few inches of him, Aidan reached up for it. His foot slipped out from under him, and he started sliding. He grabbed hold of whatever he could find and finally stopped his slide. He looked up and grimaced. Now he was about ten feet farther down than he had been. Fortunately, the rope was a long one. This time, he waited until the end of it was right in front of him before taking hold of it.

"Got it."

"What next? Want me to hold the rope?"

"No! You'll rip your hands to pieces. Step back. I'll be up in no time."

Praying he was right, he braced himself with his feet and quickly looped the rope around his torso, tying it in a figure eight. Wishing he had a climbing harness was pointless. The instant the rope was secured, he started to climb. Even though Anna continued to peer over the edge, he concentrated on moving one foot in front of the other. It was slow going. For every solid place he put his foot, the next one dissolved beneath him. Jaw clenched with determination, Aidan continued until he reached the top and collapsed onto solid ground.

Breathless, his entire body aching, he glanced over to where Anna sat. Tears were streaming down her face.

"What's wrong?"

Instead of answering, she rushed toward him, then jerked to a stop within inches of reaching him. "Wait. Are you hurt anywhere? Anything broken or bleeding?"

"I'm fine."

With that reassurance, Anna threw herself into his arms and held on. He didn't know which one of them was shaking the most. He only knew he wanted to hold her forever. When she'd almost fallen into the river... A giant ball of lead settled in his gut. He never wanted to go through something like that again. It reminded him way too much of what he'd lost years ago.

Anna pulled away slightly so she could look Aidan over. She was beginning to get her breath back, and her heart rate had slowed some. "Are you sure you're okay? You probably slammed hard against that mountain side."

He grimaced a smile. "I think the mud softened the impact." He sat back farther and started running his hands over her arms and legs. "What about you? Sorry I had to throw you like that, but I didn't see a choice. You're sure you didn't break anything?"

"Bruised and scratched. Nothing broken." She gave him her brightest smile. When this was all over, she'd allow herself a giant sobfest, but for right now they needed to celebrate a major victory. "We survived."

"Yeah. We damn well did." He went to his feet, wincing a little.

"Where do you hurt?"

"It'd be easier to say where I don't hurt." He waved away her concern. "Just bruises and scratches, like you. Do you need to take more time to rest?"

She pulled herself to her feet, a little slower than Aidan had. "No. We need to get going."

He grabbed her arm. "You are hurt. Dammit, don't give me that cheerful, stoic look. Tell me."

"I'm not hurt. I just bruised my side a bit when I landed."

"Show me."

Flushing a little but knowing that if she didn't show him, he wouldn't hesitate to roam his hands all over her until he found what he was looking for. Anna ignored the enticing thought of him doing just that. This was so not the time to think about things like that. She lifted her shirt on her right side.

"Holy hell, Anna," Aidan breathed. His hand gently ran down her side, from beneath her armpit to her waistband. "Pull down your pants. I want to see your hip."

"It's fine, Aidan. I—"

The uncompromising look he gave her said she was wasting time and breath by protesting.

"Fine." She unzipped her pants and lowered them, along with her panties, to show him her hip.

His fingers probed gently, looking for broken bones.

"Take a deep breath and let it out."

She did as he asked.

"Any sharp pains?"

"No. If I were hurt, I promise I would tell you, Aidan. Nothing's broken, fractured, or even bleeding. Just some bruising."

His fingers stayed on her skin for several more seconds. She wondered if he even knew his touch had gone from probing to caressing. The expression on his face had changed from concern to something dark and sensual. Anna couldn't prevent the shudder of desire that went through her. After everything they'd gone through today, the need to lose herself for a few minutes in his arms was almost overwhelming, but they had no time to spare.

As if he abruptly realized that, too, Aidan stepped back. "I agree. Bruising but nothing broken."

His cool tone told her he was back in control. She watched him go over to the tree where she'd tied the rope. He stooped down to release the knot and sent her an astonished look. "That's a perfect bowline knot. Where'd you learn how to do that?"

Feeling a little deflated at the return of his coolness, Anna wanted to lie and tell him she'd dated a really hot Eagle Scout who used to tie her up and do wicked things to her. Since that sounded as convincing as telling him she was an Olympic knot-tying champ, she told him the glum truth. "YouTube."

Though his mouth twitched slightly, as though he wanted to smile, he simply nodded and untied the knot. He walked over, put the rope in her backpack, and said, "Let's go."

CHAPTER FIFTEEN

It was almost pitch dark by the time they made it to the compound. Aidan knew they needed to rest. Anna had stumbled several times in the last hour, and it was all he could do not to give in and let her take a few minutes break. It was too dangerous. He couldn't risk using a flashlight in case there were lookouts guarding the perimeter. And knowing what he did about Garcia, he wouldn't put it past him to have set up booby-traps. The entire family was paranoid, for good reason, but living in a fortress on his own mountain, the youngest Garcia had taken it a step further.

Besides, walking in the jungle at night was just asking for disaster.

If he had suggested a rest, he already knew what Anna's answer would have been. In both the military and LCR, he'd worked alongside some of the toughest, gutsiest women he'd ever met. Anna was right up there with them. And she didn't have the training or the experience others had gone through. Much of her toughness came from sheer bravado and a good heart.

Aidan knew he was getting into seriously dangerous territory with her. Once this was over, and everyone was safe and home, he'd have to back away completely from Anna. Putting her at risk any more than he already had wasn't something he could continue to do.

"Let's stop here." Aidan spoke in low, quiet tones. They were maybe seventy-five yards from the fence that surrounded the compound. Julio hadn't gone for aesthetics. The fence was a twelve-foot chain-link monster with barbwire at the top. Was it to keep people out or to prevent them from leaving?

"I don't see anyone," Anna said softly. "Do you?"

Using his night vision binoculars, Aidan scanned the area once more. "Not a soul. Place looks deserted."

Dropping his backpack on the ground, Aidan stooped down and pulled out a device he had never had cause to purchase before. Standing, he handed it to Anna. "You know what this is?"

She took it from him without hesitation. "Sure. It's a bra holster. I have a similar one at home."

He refused to even let his imagination wander down that path. He nodded his approval and bent down to pull a secondary weapon from his ankle holster. As he handed it to her, his eyes carefully assessed her facial expression. He'd given it to her to hold in Cali, but the situation had been much less volatile. There was a real possibility that she'd have to use it this time. If she cringed or acted the least bit uncertain, he wouldn't give her the weapon.

Instead of appearing frightened, her face lightened. "Thank you. I was feeling decidedly naked."

Nope. He wasn't going there either.

"They'll expect me to be armed. They might suspect you are, too, but I'll deal with that when the time comes."

He wasn't surprised when she flushed slightly and turned away. He busied himself with checking his own weapons. When she turned, there was no indication that she had a weapon anywhere on her body.

Pulling his phone from his pocket, Aidan viewed the satellite map of the compound that McCall had texted him. He pointed to the northwest corner. "This is where we are." His finger moved up the screen an inch. "From talking with Carrie, I think she's here."

"Are we going to—"

Before she could finish the question, Anna's cellphone buzzed. She checked the screen and handed the phone to Aidan. "It's Carrie."

Aidan held the phone to his ear. "Are you all right?"

Sounding considerably wearier than she had a few hours ago, she said, "It's bad, Aidan. I've lost two more men. Two others won't make it till morning. Two additional men are sick."

"What about you? How are you feeling?"

"Asymptomatic so far. As you suggested, I've consumed only bottled water and prepackaged food."

Confirming his earlier suspicions. More and more, Aidan was considering this to be a poisoning. Question was, was it intentional?

"Where's Garcia?"

"In his bedroom. I checked him about an hour ago. He was conscious but in pretty bad shape."

Making a decision that he hoped like hell wouldn't come back to bite him in the ass, he said, "Can you get the phone to him?"

"Yes. You want to talk to him?"

"Yeah."

"Okay. I'll call you back as soon as I get to him."

The line went dead, and Aidan glanced over at Anna, who was looking both confused and worried. "Are you going to tell him we're here?"

"Yes."

"Are you sure that's a good idea?"

"No, I'm not."

**

Carrie slid the cellphone back into her pocket and headed out the door.

Diego stepped in front of her, blocking the door. "Where are you going?"

"I need to see Señor Garcia."

"Why?"

Telling him that she had a call he needed to take was a surefire way to get the cellphone confiscated. The man she'd stolen it from no longer needed it, as he'd died a few hours ago. That wouldn't matter to Diego. Now that his boss was ill, he was feeling his oats and issuing orders as if he were in charge.

"I need to check his temperature."

Diego jerked his head toward the door. Pretending he didn't scare her was useless. Out of all the men here, this one had the eyes of a cold-blooded killer. Wasn't it interesting that he was one of the few showing no signs of being sick?

They passed by the sliding doors that led to the pool. Though it was dark outside, the entire area was well lit. She didn't see Julio's wife.

"After I see to Señor Garcia, perhaps I should check on Señora Garcia. Make sure she isn't ill also."

"She's fine," Diego growled. "Move on."

Arguing with him was pointless. She would mention her concern to Julio. She also needed to figure out a way to get Diego out of the room when she called Aidan back. The last time she'd checked on Garcia, he'd been ill and holding his own. However, if the illness progressed the way it had for the other patients, Julio would soon be unconscious and unable to communicate. She had a bad feeling that Diego was waiting for that to happen.

Diego gave a brief knock and opened the bedroom door. Julio was sitting in a chair, but he was slumped so far down he was practically falling out of it.

Carrie rushed forward. "Señor Garcia?"

He raised his eyes to hers, and Carrie gasped at the change in just a few hours.

Turning back to Diego, she said, "I need you to get the medical kit."

"Why didn't you bring it with you, stupid gringa?"

"I didn't expect him to be this ill."

Despite the warmth of the room, Diego's glare chilled Carrie to the bone. No doubt about it, this man was trouble.

As soon as he'd closed the door, Carrie turned back to the sick man. "Señor Garcia, we don't have much time. There's someone you need to talk to. Someone who can help."

"What do you mean?"

Taking a chance that he wouldn't take it away from her, Carrie pulled the cellphone from her pocket and hit redial for Anna's number. She held the phone out. "Just talk to him."

Showing her just how ill he was, Julio did nothing but put the phone to his ear and say, "Si?"

Aidan answered in perfect Spanish. "Hello, Señor Garcia. My name is Thorne. I was hired by a friend of the doctor's to help you."

"Help? How?"

"The woman who hired me is an aid worker. She can assist Dr. Easterly."

"Where are you?"

"Right outside your compound."

"Why would you want to help?"

"Because your people are in need."

"You're not here for the doctor?"

"Yes, I am, but I won't take her away. Not until things are better. Your people need assistance."

Anna watched Aidan's grim expression as he made the offer. This could very well turn into a disaster if Julio Garcia decided he didn't want the help. The man could send someone for them and kill them on the spot. Even though Garcia's voice sounded weak and much older than a twenty-six-year-old's, it didn't mean that he was any kinder. He had kidnapped and terrorized Carrie. That wasn't something Anna could forget.

It seemed like they waited a lifetime before he said, "I will have a man come for you and bring you to me. You will surrender any weapons or phones."

"No. That's not the way this works," Aidan replied. "We're here to help, nothing more. I am willing to aid you in whatever you need, but I won't be put at a disadvantage."

There was a long silence, and then Carrie said, "He's very ill." Her voice went lower. "I don't know how long he has left."

Aidan cursed softly. "All right, Carrie. Tell him we're coming. We'll deal with whatever assholes come our way."

Anna touched the gun in her bra holster as reassurance. She'd become proficient with several handguns, so the small-caliber pistol had felt comfortable in her hand, as well as the holster in her bra. She knew what to do with it. She hadn't, however, ever pointed a gun at another person, much less shot at one. She took a deep breath and nodded to herself. Having learned that there was no point in having a gun if you weren't prepared to use it, Anna knew she would not hesitate to defend herself or someone she cared about.

Aidan pulled wire clippers from his backpack and started snipping at the fence to create an opening for them. Kneeling beside him, she pulled at each portion he clipped. Within a minute, they had an opening large enough to go through.

He put the wire clippers away, drew his gun from his side holster, and double-checked the clip. "We'll try to stay hidden until we get to the main house. They're expecting us, so that may not be possible. You stick to me like glue, okay?"

She nodded and followed Aidan as he went through the opening in the fence. Even though her heart was thudding and her adrenaline pumping, she noted that her feeling of purpose and direction gave her confidence she might not ordinarily have. A lot of it had to do with having a well-trained and confident LCR operative by her side. Aidan Thorne saved lives almost every day. He'd saved hers only a few hours earlier.

Together, that's what they would do here. Save lives.

CHAPTER SIXTEEN

There was nothing attractive about the compound. Garcia had gone to a lot of trouble to make it impenetrable, but he'd done nothing to enhance its looks. All the buildings they passed were either white-washed brick or adobe style. They were built for sturdiness and functionality, nothing more.

He and Anna were in the middle of the small community before they saw the first person. From the information McCall had obtained, there should be over a dozen men here, most of whom should be guarding the area.

A man, probably a guard, was leaning against one of the buildings. Aidan couldn't see his face, but from the jerking of his body and the gagging sounds he was making, it was clear the man was one of the many who'd fallen ill.

Pulling Anna's arm, Aidan eased by him. Drawing the guard's attention would probably get them shot.

At the end of the paved road was a monstrous-looking house. This was where Garcia had spent his money. The two-story ranch house sprawled out in every direction, a cattle baron's dream. The Ponderosa on steroids.

"Aidan." Anna grabbed his arm. "Look."

A short, squat man with a bad comb-over and an arrogant sneer sauntered toward them. He held an AR-15 rifle. On his left thigh was a holstered Smith & Wesson revolver, and at his waist hung a large knife. Aidan got the distinct impression that the man was overcompensating.

"Drop your gun," the man growled.

Aidan was about to argue the point when another man came up behind him, shoving a gun against his kidney. "Do what he says."

Aidan dropped his gun and stayed expressionless as he was frisked for more weapons. The man finished and took a step toward Anna.

"No," Aidan barked. "She's an aid worker. She is unarmed."

The man's greasy smile made Aidan's blood boil.

"Put one finger on her, and I'll split you in two, head to ass."

The man paused, his eyes skittering uncertainly to his companion. That was all the distraction Aidan needed. Whirling, he grabbed the strap of the gun hanging from the man's shoulder. Pulling him off-balance, Aidan slammed him into the other man, who was ineptly juggling his gun. He snatched the gun from the guy's fumbling hand and held it on the two men.

The astonishment on Anna's face had Aidan grinning. "I'll show you how to do that someday."

Returning his attention to the two men, he gave them his coldest glare. "Where's Señor Garcia?"

"In his bedroom. He sent us to bring you to him."

"Then let's go."

Watching Aidan at work put a whole new perspective on Anna's admiration and respect for him. She had known he was well trained, but seeing him in action made her realize that people like Jason Bourne actually did exist. She'd never seen anyone move that quick or efficiently in real life.

They walked down a long hallway, passing elegantly appointed rooms on the left and right. Whatever money Garcia had saved with the other buildings in his small community, he'd made up for in his own house. Every aspect of it screamed wealth and excess. The man apparently believed in living well.

The two men in front of them stopped at a closed double door. The shorter one sent a fuming look over his shoulder at Aidan. "Señor Garcia is in here."

"Open it," Aidan ordered.

Issuing what sounded like a curse, the man pushed open the door and stepped back.

"You first, amigo," Aidan drawled.

The man went through the door, along with his companion. Aidan, then Anna, followed them into the room.

At first, she saw only a gigantic suite. There were several sitting areas with sofas, chairs, and small tables throughout the room. A massive television covered one wall. Another wall had a large antique-looking bar. Anna felt a wince of sympathy for the poor guys who'd had to move the monstrosity anywhere, much less up an isolated mountain.

On another side, close to a large picture window, was a massive bed. Lying on that bed was a man in his mid-twenties. His eyes were closed, his skin a sickly yellow.

"Anna!"

Startled, she turned slightly and spotted Carrie standing at a door. She was holding a damp cloth and a plastic bucket. She looked tired and worried, but unharmed. Relief flowing over her, Anna rushed toward her, her arms outstretched, but halted when Carrie said, "You need to stay back from all of us. We still don't know if this thing is contagious."

"How's Julio doing?" Aidan asked.

"About the same. His temperature seems to have stabilized." She shot a glance at the unconscious man. "But he's still very ill."

"What about you? You still okay?"

"Yes. Just tired and feeling helpless, but no symptoms."

"Who else isn't showing symptoms?"

"Diego and Salvador." She indicated the two men who'd brought them here and now stood by the door. "And I'm told that Elena, Garcia's wife, isn't ill either. Although I've not been allowed to check on her."

Aidan jerked his head toward the bed. "Wake him up. I need to talk with him."

"I'll try. He lost consciousness right after he talked with you."

Carrie went over to the sick man and shook him gently. "Señor Garcia, wake up. It's important."

There was no movement of his eyelids, no change in his expression.

Carrie tried several more times without success.

Aidan stood to the side, still holding his weapon on the men who'd tried to take their guns earlier. Evidently deciding it was pointless to keep trying to wake the man, he said to Carrie, "These two are openly hostile. What about the other men here?"

"The ones who aren't sick have been extremely helpful. Diego and Salvador," she said as she glared at the two men, "are the only two who haven't been cooperative."

"We take orders from Señor Garcia only."

"Your boss is unconscious," Aidan said. He looked toward Anna. "Go with Carrie and do what you can to help. I'll find you when I'm finished."

Anna nodded. Even though she wanted to know exactly what he was planning to do, talking in front of Garcia's men wasn't wise.

Aidan motioned with his gun. "Let's go, you two."

***

Ten minutes later, Aidan walked into the small infirmary and got a glimpse of the hell Carrie Easterly had been handling by herself. The six beds in the room were occupied. The other patients were lying on air mattresses, sleeping bags, and blankets.

He found Anna in the middle of them. She was wearing a mask as she wiped the forehead and spoke softly in Spanish to one young man who looked like he should still be in high school. She raised helpless eyes to Aidan. "I don't know what to do for them."

"There's nothing more to do. I've contacted McCall, told him the situation. He just heard back from his contact at the CDC. They agree it doesn't appear to be airborne."

"Well, that's a relief." She pulled the white mask from her face. "This thing doesn't feel like it's doing much anyway." She looked over his shoulder. "Where are Diego and Salvador?"

"Locked them up in one of those brick buildings we passed."

"Bet that went over well."

"Took some convincing, but they eventually saw things my way." He didn't mention that both men would be waking up in separate rooms in a few minutes with massive headaches and their hands tied to posts.

"McCall's got a helicopter headed this way with a couple of doctors and some meds. It'll be a couple more hours before they arrive, so we'll do what we can for the patients." His eyes roamed the room. "Where's Carrie?"

"I convinced her, and the other two women, Evelyn and Constance, to lie down for a few minutes. They've not had a break in hours."

"How are you holding up?"

"I'm okay." The smile she gave him was sad. "Better than these guys are doing."

Her skin was so pale it was almost translucent. Half of her hair had come loose from her braid and hung limply around her face. Dark bruises were beginning to show on her arms and wrists where he'd gripped them to keep her from falling. Her pants were covered in mud, and her shirt was torn in several places. All in all, she looked a mess. And Aidan knew he'd never found her more appealing than he did now. Something wrenched inside him. Anna was exactly the kind of woman he—

Don't go there, Thorne. Just don't.

"Why don't we see if we can help any of these guys? When Carrie returns, we'll take our own break."

They worked side by side for over an hour. With limited medical supplies and no clear idea what had poisoned these men, there was little they could do but what Carrie had already been doing. Trying to keep their temperatures down and maintaining hydration was their best bet until aid arrived.

As they finished with the last man, Aidan remembered his internship where he'd gone almost two days without sleep. He didn't think he'd been nearly as tired then as he was now.

Hearing a sound behind him, Aidan stepped in front of Anna as he pulled his gun. Carrie jerked to a stop at the door. "Whoa. It's just me."

"Sorry. Can't be too careful."

"I understand. Every one of these men came in here armed to the teeth. When I told them I wouldn't treat them unless they took off their weapons, you would have thought I told them to chop off a body part."

"To some men, losing a body part might be easier." He grinned as he holstered his weapon. "I'm too fond of all my parts to make that claim."

Surprising him, Carrie sent Anna a small smile and said, "I see what you mean."

Before he could ask what she meant by that, Anna went into action, striding toward the door. "We're going to go find a bathroom and clean up. I mean, not together, but…" She shook her head, her color high. "We'll be back as soon as we can."

Sending her what looked like a grimace of apology, Carrie said, "Take all the time you need. If you want, you can use my room. It's on the second floor, third door on the right."

"Thanks, we will." When Anna looked toward Aidan, he was surprised at the vulnerability in her expression. Almost as if she was close to tears.

He followed her out the door and grabbed her hand before she could get away from him. "Hey, you okay?"

"Uh, um. Just tired."

He knew it was more than that but figured it would embarrass or upset her more if he pursued it. They headed down the hallway the way they'd come earlier. When they reached Carrie's bedroom, Aidan opened the door and searched it quickly.

"It's clear." He handed her two bottles of water he'd snagged from the infirmary. "Since we still don't know where this poison is coming from, I'd feel better if you used these to clean up with."

"You think it could be in the water tank?"

"It's possible. Until we know for sure, or we're out of here, don't drink anything but bottled water. If you're hungry, there are some bars and crackers in your backpack."

"Where are you going?"

"I'm going back to see if Carrie and I can talk to Garcia's wife. Carrie said she'd only seen the woman briefly, and she didn't seem to be showing any signs of sickness. She might be able to answer some questions about her husband."

He was about to close the door, but then looked back at Anna, who stood in the middle of the room, swaying with exhaustion. "Keep the door locked. Don't open it to anyone but me or Carrie. And keep your gun with you at all times."

She nodded, and he closed the door. The instant he heard the lock engage, Aidan walked away. He had wanted to stay. Wanted to hold her and reassure both of them that everything would be fine. Since he had long ago stopped making promises he couldn't keep, Aidan told himself to concentrate on what he could do. Finding out who was poisoning these people and then getting Anna and Carrie the hell out of here.

CHAPTER SEVENTEEN

Anna stood in the middle of the large bathroom. Every part of her body either ached, stung, or throbbed with pain. Even as much as she wanted to help Aidan and Carrie, she knew she'd be collapsing soon if she didn't rest a little. The last thing she wanted was to be a liability to either of them.

She eased her backpack from her shoulders and set it on the counter. Sitting on the chair at the vanity, she untied her boots and slid them off her feet, along with her socks. The cold tile against her hot, tired feet felt heavenly. That small amount of relief gave her enough energy to stand and start pulling her stiff, filthy clothes from her body. Removing the gun from her bra holster, she set it on the sink. Turning, she grimaced at the filthy pile of clothes on the floor. She was glad she'd brought a change of clothing, because there was no way those were going back on her body.

Grabbing a hand towel from a stack on the shelf, she wetted it and started cleaning. With each swipe, she discovered a new bruise or cut. Even though her injuries were uncomfortable, she was grateful they were superficial and she had no broken bones.

She used up one bottle of water. The stark-white hand towels she'd started with were now so muddy a bottle of bleach wouldn't save them. She, however, felt refreshed and almost clean. She chanced a glance in the mirror and made a face at the pale, exhausted woman staring back at her. She could do nothing about that, but she could at least put her hair back to rights. Untangling the messy braid, she combed her hair and then rebraided it. She pulled fresh khaki pants, a black tank top, and socks from her backpack and put them on. She put her boots back on, took the gun, and left the bathroom, feeling like a new person.

Even though she felt guilty for doing so, Anna made herself lie down on the bed. Collapsing from exhaustion would do nothing but cause problems. She inhaled and exhaled through a series of deep breaths, hoping a few minutes of meditation and rest would help. Ten minutes later, she sat up. This was doing no good. She couldn't stop thinking about what was going on outside those doors. While she was lying in bed like a ninny, any number of things might be happening to her friends. She couldn't just lie here. What if they needed her?

Grabbing the gun beside her, she went to the door and put her ear to it. Hearing nothing, she unlocked it and peered out. Still no sounds. Closing the door, she quickly returned the gun to her bra holster, opened the door again and headed back to the infirmary. She might have no medical training, but she could soothe brows and hold hands with the best of them.

She walked into the large room. Evelyn was there, mopping the face of one of the men.

"Hola, Evelyn. How can I help?"

Her smile tired, Evelyn said, "The two men over there could use some water."

Hurrying over to a large fridge, she took two bottles, turned around, and came to an abrupt stop. A beautiful young woman stood before her. Maybe a little taller than Anna, she had long, lustrous black hair, dark brown eyes, and dark golden skin. Wearing a scarlet halter top, skinny jeans, and bright red high-heeled sandals, she looked like she was ready for a night of clubbing. Finding her standing in the middle of an infirmary filled with sick and dying men was more than surprising. The dichotomy of the two was almost painful. This must be Elena Garcia, Julio's new bride.

Since Elena just stood there, staring, Anna gave her a pleasant smile and said, "Can I help you?"

"Who are you?"

"I'm Anna Bradford. I'm here to help these—"

"Where are Diego and Salvador?"

Aidan hadn't told her what he'd done with the men, but Anna knew he had most likely tied them up somewhere to reduce the threat. Telling that to this woman was probably not in Anna's best interest.

"I'm not sure. Is there something you need?" It occurred to her then that she might have come to ask for help for her husband. "Is it your husband? Is he worse?"

Confusion flickered across her face. "My husband? No. No." Then as if she'd just comprehended what Anna was asking, she said, "I just checked on him. He's sleeping, poor baby."

"And you?" Anna asked. "Are you feeling all right?"

"Of course." A slender, perfectly manicured hand waved away the question. "I never get sick."

"Then how can I help you?"

She held up a long black device that looked like a television remote control. "I need new batteries."

Before she could explain that finding batteries for the woman wasn't something she could help with, a gagging sound behind her caught Anna's attention. She hurried to a man a few feet away struggling to reach the bucket beside him. Holding it for him, she smoothed back his hair and spoke softly to him as he vomited into the bucket. When at last he finished, his head plopped back onto his pillow. Anna pushed the foul-smelling bucket away. Taking a cloth hanging from the railing of the headboard, she dampened it with water from a bottle and wiped his face and neck. The man closed his eyes and whispered, "Gracias."

Wishing she could do something other than wipe faces and hold buckets, Anna stood. She turned and was surprised to find Elena Garcia still in the room. She had assumed the girl would be disgusted by the stench or the gagging and leave.

The expression on Elena's face revealed no disgust. Anna tilted her head in wonder. If anything, there was a glint of something like satisfaction or glee in the beautiful woman's eyes.

Comprehension flashed like a beacon and before she could stop herself, she blurted, "It's you. You're responsible for the poisoning."

"What? How dare you accuse me of such a thing?"

Anna looked at the woman with a face of an angel. Years ago, she had trusted a young girl because she'd looked so beautiful, so innocent. That misplaced trust had resulted in Anna's abduction and torture. She had learned a hard lesson that day, one she would never forget. The most beautiful of faces could hide the evilest of hearts.

Elena must have realized her lies weren't being believed. A glimmer of what looked like amusement appeared in her eyes and she lifted a slender shoulder in an arrogant shrug. "So? What does it matter to you?"

"Why would you do something so callous? You poisoned not only your husband, but these men, too. Two of them have already died."

"You think I care about these men? These people?" Elena made a dramatic spitting sound. "They are filth beneath my feet. Not worthy to be in my presence."

"Then why did you marry Julio?"

"Our fathers arranged it."

In other countries, other cultures, arranged marriages happened all the time, often without the couple wanting to be married. However, few of those marriages ended in mass murder. "How did you think you could get away with it?"

Her chin tilted upward in a proud slant. "This was my father's revenge on the Garcia family."

"Your father is in on this? But why?"

"The Ruizes have been the most powerful family in this country for years. Juan Garcia thought he could take away our business. We do not mind competitors, but when they steal our business, we retaliate."

"This was over business issues?" Amazed and appalled, Anna's eyes swept over the ill and dying men in the room. Heaven only knew how many more there would be. "Why kill innocent men? Why would murder be the only answer?"

"You stupid puta," Elena spat, "with your holier-than-thou morality. Destroying the seed is the only way to kill the crop." She gave an arrogant jerk of her head. "It was my idea to marry the youngest son and destroy him. I made this sacrifice for my father, my family. It is an important warning to all. He who betrays a Ruiz will live to regret it."

Belatedly realizing that she was standing only a few feet from a murderer, Anna slowly began to back away. Hoping to distract Elena from noticing her retreat, she said, "You have to know that Juan Garcia will want revenge for the death of his son."

"You think we do not have a plan? We are prepared for war. Prepared to eradicate the entire Garcia family and all who get in our way. Once we are finished, the world will know our power."

"You don't care who gets hurt, do you?"

"You think I care about any of them? Putas. Whores. Sons and daughters of whores. They all deserve to die."

"And what about your child? You want him or her to grow up with this kind of life?"

She gave a trill of laughter, and Anna couldn't help but notice it sounded just as lovely as the woman herself looked. "I am not pregnant. I just told Julio that so he wouldn't touch me. Threatening to vomit on him every time he came near me was an excellent way to keep him away from me."

"You'll never get away with it."

"Oh, but I will." With admirable speed, Elena pulled a gun from a holster hung over a bed rail. Carrie had described the difficulty she'd had in getting the men to take off their gun belts to lie in bed. She had compromised by telling them their weapons would be right beside them if they were needed.

Elena held the gun with a chilling competence. She pointed it directly at Anna's head, her smile that of a cold-blooded killer. "Get on your knees, bitch."

Chapter Eighteen

Aidan was heading back to the infirmary with Carrie. Though Julio had given them permission to examine Elena Garcia, she hadn't been in her room when they arrived.

According to Carrie, the young woman hadn't been in to see her husband. Aidan wondered about their marriage. He didn't figure this had been a love match, but even so, wouldn't she have at least wanted to talk to Carrie about her husband's health and possible recovery?

He had hoped to learn more about her, but the only person they'd found in her suite was an older woman sitting in a rocker. Her name was Linda, and she'd been Elena Garcia's companion since Elena was a child. She said she was looking out for her charge and reassured them that Elena was showing no symptoms of an illness. She said Elena was in the shower, but she would relay the doctor's concerns. Aidan and Carrie could do nothing more than thank her and leave. This whole thing seemed messed up.

"Why don't you go get cleaned up? Maybe lie down for a while," Carrie said. "I'll head back to the infirmary and relieve Evelyn."

Aidan was about to agree to her suggestion when his cellphone buzzed. Grabbing it, he was relieved to see McCall's name on the screen. "McCall?"

"The helicopter with two doctors and various medical supplies will arrive there in about half an hour."

Relief swept through Aidan. At last some good news. "Excellent."

"How's everyone doing?"

"About as well as expected. No new deaths but still a lot of sick men. Garcia might not make it."

"The helicopter will take Anna and Carrie back. I'd like you to stay and keep an eye on the doctors."

Aidan refused to acknowledge the disappointment that he wouldn't be accompanying Anna. This thing with her needed to end before it could become a problem. Having the temptation removed was the best thing for both of them.

"Will do."

"Kelly and the rest of the team hitched a ride on the helicopter."

He had a feeling Diego and Salvador were going to be problems. Having backup from his team members would be welcome.

"Sounds good. I'll let you know as soon as things settle down." Pocketing his cell, he smiled at Carrie. "Help will be here soon. You and Anna can leave."

Carrie shook her head. "I'll stay until this is over. I think it would be good for Anna to leave, though."

He agreed with that but wondered what Anna might say. They'd face that when the time came. The urge to get Anna away from this place and to safety was becoming a strong need inside him.

Feeling a renewed energy, he said, "I'll go with you to the infirmary, see if there's anything I can do to help, and then head up to the bedroom to check on Anna."

Carrie's mysterious little smile made Aidan wonder what Anna might have told her about him. It was obvious she had recognized his name when they first spoke on the phone. Had Anna told her friend that he'd been part of her rescue years ago? Or did Carrie know more about their recent relationship, which consisted of him being a jerk to Anna every time she was around? He hoped it was the first one.

They were almost to the infirmary, and Aidan was about to ask that question when he heard the chilling words: "Get on your knees, bitch."

What the hell?

"Elena." Anna tried to keep the nervousness out of her voice. Using a no-nonsense tone she often used with recalcitrant parents, she continued, "Shooting me will not solve your problems. There are men here who are loyal to your husband. They won't let you get away with this."

"You think you're so smart. Don't you think we planned this carefully?"

"How do you think you'll escape from here? Do you fly helicopters?"

"I don't need to know how to fly. When the time comes to leave, I'll have all the help I'll need."

So she had men here who were loyal to her family. Anna thought she might know their names.

"Are you counting on Diego and Salvador? If so, they're locked up and can't help you."

"What do you mean they're locked up? Who would do such a thing?"

A harsh voice answered, "I did such a thing."

Keeping the gun pointed at Anna, Elena turned toward the door. Aidan stood there, his own gun pointing at Elena.

"Who are you?"

"That's not important. What is important is that you need to put that gun down and get away from Anna."

For the first time, Anna saw a flicker of doubt in Elena's eyes. Shooting one unarmed woman had probably seemed easy enough. But now she had two other people to consider, one of whom had a gun. The look in Aidan's eyes left no doubt that he would use his weapon in a heartbeat.

"We mean you no harm," Anna assured her. "You poisoned only the people who threatened your family. Correct?"

"Si. That was the plan."

"What items did you poison?"

"The cerveza and tequila in the cantina. And the coffee that's only for Julio's use."

If that was the truth, as long as everyone stayed away from the cantina and Julio's coffee, everyone else should be safe.

"What's in the poison?" Aidan asked.

Her brow furrowed in what look like real confusion. "I do not know. Why would I? It was doing its job."

Hoping to diffuse the situation, Anna said, "We came to rescue my friend, the doctor that Julio kidnapped. We have no wish to be involved in your family's feud with the Garcias. That's our only purpose here. Put the gun down and no one will be harmed. I promise."

"I promised my papa I would not fail," she whispered softly.

She saw then that Elena, while beautiful and vain, was just a young girl who wanted to please her father. She was a pawn in Pablo Ruiz's evil plan.

"Your papa wouldn't want you to be hurt, Elena."

"He will be disappointed in me if I don't finish this. He sent me here to destroy the Garcia family. I cannot fail."

What might've happened next if Anna had been able to continue to encourage Elena to give up, they would never know. A man screamed, "You whore!"

All eyes went to the door on the other side of the room. Julio Garcia leaned against the doorjamb. No one saw the gun until the shot blasted through the air. Anna thought she heard Aidan shout, "Anna, get down!"

Something wet splashed onto Anna's face and arms. She looked down to see Elena lying only a foot away, half of her face gone. Blood and brain matter was everywhere. In her numbed mind, Anna knew she was covered with Elena Garcia's remains.

Hard hands grabbed her, shook her. "Anna, look at me. Are you okay?"

In a daze, she looked up at Aidan and tried to speak. Nothing came out.

"Answer me. Are you hurt?" Even as Aidan asked, his hands were running up and down her body, looking for an injury. No wounds, thank God. He stood and, noting her eyes were glazed with shock, he cupped her face in his hands. "Focus on me, baby. You're fine. Everything is fine."

She shook her head and said in a thin voice, "Aidan? She's dead?"

He had to get her out of here. He glanced over at Julio, who had collapsed on the floor seconds after killing his wife. Carrie was tending to him.

He scooped Anna into his arms. On the way out of the room, he snagged three large water bottles from the stash on the table. Carrie and Evelyn could see to Julio. Anna was his priority right now.

She was still and stiff in his arms. Not caring that they were both now a bloody mess, Aidan shifted her closer to his chest and whispered a litany of comforting words as a whirlwind of emotions zoomed through him.

At Carrie's room, Aidan pushed the door open. Striding to the bathroom, he placed Anna on the closed toilet seat. He opened one of the waters, took a towel from the shelf, and dampened it. Kneeling in front of her, he said, "Close your eyes, baby."

Those eyes, deep pools of pain, looked at him so damn trustingly. He had promised to take care of her, and he'd damn well almost lost her. "Come on, sweetheart. Close your eyes for me."

Her lids closed, and Aidan began to clean her face. She was a mess. There was no way he could get all of the blood off without putting her in the shower. He wouldn't do that until they were off this mountain. It didn't matter that Elena Garcia said she'd poisoned only the alcohol and her husband's coffee grounds. Aidan was taking no chances. The woman had been bent on destroying the Garcias. Believing anything she said would be a mistake.

Anna sat quiet and obedient. Her shoulders were slouched with exhaustion, and Aidan didn't know if he'd ever seen her so dispirited.

"I need to change clothes."

It was the first time she'd spoken in a while and Aidan felt immeasurably better. Not only were her words clear and concise, they were calm. When she opened her eyes, Aidan could still see her horror, but he knew she was blocking it. Practical matters, like getting into clean clothing, were something she could hang on to and deal with. Later, he knew, she'd fall apart. He planned to be there when that happened.

"I have something you can wear." He stood. "Don't move. I'll be right back."

Anna waited until he'd left the room before she allowed the fierce shudder to go through her. At some point, she'd have to face the nightmare of what had happened, but for right now she had to stay strong. Aidan was doing everything he could to make sure she was okay. She needed to show him that she was.

He returned within a minute, holding a T-shirt, a pair of boxer briefs, and a belt.

His smile was a little crooked. "Not exactly haute couture, but I think we can make this work." He dropped the clothing on the side of the tub. "Come on, raise your arms."

She did as he asked, and he pulled her tank top over her head. She was glad to see there was no visible blood on her bra. Aidan went to his knees again and untied her boots, pulling them off.

She unzipped her pants and, wiggling slightly, managed to remove them without standing up.

Her panties and bra were made for sensibility and comfort, not sex appeal. They covered her better than most swimsuits, so while this wasn't what she'd dreamed of wearing if Aidan ever undressed her, she at least felt no sense of embarrassment.

She took a breath and, willing her legs to support her, stood. "I'm all right. I'll clean up and change. Carrie might need you."

"I'm not leaving you, Bradford."

Yes, he would. Eventually. But that wasn't what he meant, and that was a heartache for another day. This day had more than enough on its own. She wished she could give him a smile of reassurance, but it would have been fake. She sucked at fake smiles. Instead, she tried to convince him with words. "I'll be fine. I promise." Seeing he was about to object again, she added with a firmness she didn't feel, "I need to be alone, Aidan. Please."

"Fine." He backed out of the room. "I'll be out here if you need me."

Too tired to argue, she waited until he closed the door, and then her legs gave up their support. She dropped back onto the toilet seat, covered her face with her hands, breathed in and out several times. This was still not the time to fall apart, but she needed this moment, this small increment of time to center herself.

A few minutes later, her breathing had calmed, as had her heartbeat. Standing, she took a clean towel, wet it down, and wiped the rest of the blood from her face, neck, and arms. Aidan had gotten most of it, but she needed to do this herself. Scrubbing as hard as she could gave her a weird sense of accomplishment—she didn't know why.

She unbraided her hair and used the remaining water to pour over her head. When she saw the blood drip into the sink, she let out a little moan. *Stop it, Anna!* Straightening her spine, she worked through the strands as best she could, towel-dried her hair, and braided it. How odd that less than an hour ago, she was in here doing the very same thing and feeling if not happy at least optimistic. And now? Now she just felt empty.

Grabbing the clothes Aidan had given her, she put them on and looked in the mirror. Staring back at her was a pale, wide-eyed, scared little girl. She had left that little girl behind long ago, and dammit, here she was staring at her again. This wasn't what she wanted Aidan to see. She closed her eyes, took more deep breaths, and then opened them again. Better. Not good, but definitely better. She would make it through.

CHAPTER NINETEEN

Aidan paced the length of the bedroom suite. He wanted to go back in there and help her, but she was trying so hard to be brave. If he pushed, he didn't know how she'd react. She was holding up a helluva lot better than most people would have. How many people, trained for danger or not, could stay calm when they had a gun pointed in their face and remain that way seconds later when a head exploded all over them? He knew she'd never get the image out of her mind. He sure as hell never would.

Why hadn't he checked on her earlier? Why had he left her alone? Why had she left the room? Why the hell had he brought her here in the first place? This was no place for a woman like Anna. Yes, she was strong and smart, but that couldn't prepare her for dealing with drug lords or poisoned and dying men. And certainly not almost being killed.

The door opened, and when she walked out, he didn't bother to hide his smile. It felt damn good on his mouth. The olive green T-shirt was his color of choice when stomping around the Colombian jungle. It wasn't meant to be attractive, but Anna could make a paper sack look good. The shirt was about five sizes too big for her and should have swallowed her up, but she'd used his belt to create a sort of minidress. Combined with the hiking boots, the outfit that should have looked ridiculous was sexy as hell.

She had the gray boxer briefs in her hand and held them out to him with a small, quick grin. "I couldn't keep them from falling down."

He took the briefs and snagged her hand, too, pulling her to him. She came into his arms willingly, so trustingly. Aidan closed his eyes and just held her for a while. They both needed this. Maybe him more than her.

The sudden *whomp whomp* of a helicopter told him their time was up. He squeezed her tight one last time and let her go. "The doctors and supplies have arrived. Once they unload, they're going to take you to the airport. I'll have your stuff in Cali sent to you in Phoenix."

She was shaking her head before he could finish, about to disagree. Aidan leaned his forehead against hers. "Do this for me, Bradford. Please. I can't do the job if I'm worrying about you."

A breath shuddered out of her, and she sighed a soft, "Okay."

Knowing he might never have the chance again, Aidan pushed aside the knowledge that this was about the most inappropriate time to kiss her and did it anyway. Covering her mouth with his, he allowed everything he was feeling to show in his kiss. It was soft, sexy, hot, and needy. His mouth ate at hers, sucking and devouring. His tongue plunged deep, sweeping through her mouth, tangling and dueling with her tongue. She tasted sweet, warm, and so damn addictive he knew he could kiss her for a thousand years and never get enough.

He jerked away, his breathing heavy and erratic. Damn, he'd almost lost all sense of where he was and what he was here for. She could do that do him, and he couldn't afford it.

"Grab your backpack, and let's go."

His steps quick and decisive, he stalked to the door. He was about to open it when she softly said his name.

"Yeah?" Turning, he looked back at her and took in the beauty of Anna Bradford. Even though she was a physically attractive woman, it wasn't only her outward beauty that drew Aidan. Anna was what his Gram years ago referred to as *good people*. She had heart, courage, and goodness.

"Thanks for your help."

Even though it was ripping his insides to shreds to say goodbye, knowing they might never see each other again, Aidan did the only thing he could. Shrugging, he gave her his standard smile and said, "Hey, it's what I do."

It's what I do.

As Anna followed Aidan out the door to meet the helicopter, she told herself his words shouldn't bother her. It *was* what he did. And this was a job for him. He rescued kidnapped victims. How silly for her to believe this was anything else to him but a job.

Yes, he'd kissed her. Several times. Yes, he'd given her one spectacular orgasm. But he'd also made it clear on more than one occasion that there could be nothing between them. Even though it was obvious he was attracted to her, she knew he fought that with every breath. What could she do but help him fight it?

They stood a few yards away from the helipad until the helicopter blades stopped and people began to disembark. She decided the first two people, a man and a woman, were definitely doctors. The man was in his early sixties, had an Abraham Lincoln-like beard, and was about as tall and thin as the photos she'd seen of Honest Abe. The woman was in her mid-forties, wore wire-rimmed glasses, and had the serious expression Anna had often seen on other medical professionals.

The next person that jumped out of the helicopter, a petite, dark-haired woman, had Anna running forward with her arms outstretched.

Riley Ingram used to have a serious expression on her face twenty-four seven, but now that she and Justin had fallen in love, she was much less solemn looking. Even though her friend would never be what one would call bubbly, the quiet joy radiating from her was more than apparent. The instant Anna called her name, Riley gave one of her rare big smiles and ran to greet her.

They hugged each other and then stepped back. "I thought you and Justin were hiking up the mountain."

"We were, but when Noah told us that he was gathering a medical team, we figured we'd just hitch a ride. We probably got here faster this way." She gave Anna a once-over. "You okay? The uh…outfit…is interesting."

Like a falling rock, the smile dropped from Anna's face. "It's a long story."

Recognizing that that meant it wasn't a good time to explain things, Riley squeezed her arm in comfort. They turned back to the helicopter and watched as Elite operatives Justin Kelly, Angela Delvecchio, and Jake Mallory stepped out onto the helipad.

Aidan was greeting them, most likely explaining the events of the last hour. They turned once and looked at Anna. She raised her hand, and all three of them gave her what looked like nods of approval.

"The helicopter will take you to the airport," Riley said. "Noah's got a plane waiting for you and your doctor friend to take you back to the States."

As usual, Noah McCall had coordinated things with what seemed like magic. It would do no good to tell Riley that she didn't want to go back. There was nothing for her to do here other than get in the way. The biggest reason she wanted to stay was standing beside the helicopter with a look in his eyes that told her he wanted her to go. And soon.

As if she could read her mind, Riley squeezed Anna's arm again. "When I get back home, I'll call you, and we'll arrange a weekend to meet." She winked and added, "I'll bring the ice cream."

"Sounds wonderful. I—"

"Anna, can I talk to you a moment?"

She turned to see Carrie, who wore a worried frown on her face. She quickly made the introductions between Riley and Carrie and then allowed Carrie to pull her a few feet away. "What's wrong?"

"I'm not coming with you." Carrie looked back toward the house. "I just feel like I need to stay here and finish what I started."

That wasn't a surprise to Anna. Carrie's compassion and deep sense of commitment were among the many reasons she admired her so much.

"I understand. Take care of yourself. Okay?"

"I'm sorry I got you into this mess." She shook her head. "What happened in there. It shouldn't have happened, and you definitely shouldn't have witnessed it."

"I'm fine, Carrie. It wasn't anything we could have predicted. How's Julio doing?"

"Not well at all. I don't know if he'll survive this illness, and even if he does, I'm not sure he'll survive what he did to Elena."

"Or what Elena did to him," Anna added.

"Yes." She looked at the helicopter. "Looks like they've unloaded and are ready to take off again. When I get back to the States, we'll have a long sit-down and a good cry together."

Tears sprang to Anna's eyes even as she laughed and said, "I'll look forward to it."

She hugged the older woman. On the way to the helicopter, she gave Riley one last hug, waved at the other operatives, and then continued on to the chopper. Before she stepped up, she glanced back to find Aidan. He was several yards away with a cellphone glued to his ear and a scowl on his face. He gave her a brief, sweeping glance and then turned his back to her.

And she guessed that was that.

Her heart heavier than she could remember it being in years, she followed the safety directions of the pilot, who introduced himself as Howie. When he was sure she was buckled in safely, he turned back to the controls, and in seconds they were lifting from the ground.

Her eyes stayed on the man who was still talking on the phone, seemingly oblivious to her leaving. She willed him to look up at her, to reveal even one minuscule percentage of the pain she was feeling at having to leave him. She waited until he became a small, dark, unmoving blip on the landscape. When she could no longer see anything but trees, she sat back in her seat and allowed the hurt to wash through her. Silly, she knew. Why did it matter that he hadn't even acknowledged her leaving? It wasn't like he had promised her anything.

They were up in the air for maybe five minutes when something beeped on the instrument panel. She heard Howie mumble a few words and then say, "Roger that."

Suddenly, the helicopter made a wide turn in the sky, and she realized they were headed back to the compound. Had something else happened? Did she forget something?

They landed back on the helipad, and within a minute, Aidan opened the door and climbed inside. "I'm coming with you."

CHAPTER TWENTY

Aidan refused to reconsider the commitment he'd just made. McCall had phoned just as Anna was leaving. When his boss told him that Garcia and Ruiz were about to engage in an all-out war and that anyone who had been involved in the debacle at the compound could be a target, Aidan hadn't been able to make any other choice. Until this thing was over, he was sticking to Anna like glue.

She kept sending him little frowns, and he couldn't help but smile. She wanted to know what was going on, and he'd tell her soon. Right now he wanted to sit back and consider what he needed to do. Even though he and Anna were leaving Colombia, both Garcia and Ruiz had a reach far outside their own country. He needed a place that neither of them would ever know about or could find. And Anna needed a place where she would feel safe enough to let go and recover.

Her face was almost supernaturally pale. Dark shadows circled her eyes, and her mouth drooped with both fatigue and sorrow. In the last twenty-four hours, she'd had two near-death experiences, very little food, and almost no sleep. She might not know it, but she was staying upright on adrenaline and sheer will. Soon, everything would catch up with her. She would fall, and Aidan would be there to catch her.

When the location came to him, relief followed. But it was not without risk. Anna would be physically safe, but where he was taking her would put both of them in jeopardy of another kind. Being completely alone with this woman was something he'd fought against. It had been more than ten years since he'd had these feelings. He had believed they died when his wife was murdered.

Damned if he would allow anything to happen to Anna. He would guard her and keep her safe. And when it was time to say goodbye, he would make her understand that seeing him again was out of the question. After this was over, it would be over for good.

Anna kept her eyes focused out the window of the helicopter. If she hadn't been so tired, she was sure her stomach would be doing somersaults. Maybe her exhaustion was the reason she wasn't asking Aidan all sorts of questions. Like, why had he decided to come with her? Had something happened?

The helicopter hit an air pocket and lurched up and then down. It shook her enough out of her stupor to look at the pilot, then at Aidan. He gave her a reassuring wink and took her hand. He gave it a squeeze and held it between them on the seat.

It was then she realized why she wasn't demanding answers. She didn't care. Aidan was with her. Whether it was for the next hour or much longer wasn't something she was going to dwell on or question. When she'd gotten on the helicopter and he hadn't even acknowledged her leaving, she hadn't thought she would see him again. But he was here with her now. If there was one thing she'd learned from her experience of the past, it was to appreciate each moment for what it was. Worrying never solved one problem. So she would take this moment—and all the ones she could get—and enjoy them.

***

The LCR plane was ready and waiting when they landed at a small airport in Medellín. All Aidan and Anna had to do was get on board and inform the pilot of their destination.

After he ensured that Anna was buckled into her seat, Aidan went to the cockpit. He gave the destination to the pilot, requesting that an alternate flight plan be filed. This was an unusual request but not unheard of for LCR. The organization often took extra precautions such as these when undercover or hiding a rescued victim. Having their route made available to anyone other than those they trusted could mean disaster.

Satisfied that his request would be granted, he stopped in the galley and requested a light meal of sandwiches and fruit. After all she'd been through, he suspected that Anna's stomach would be a little unsettled. Something light until she'd had some rest and time to decompress would probably sit better.

When he returned to the main cabin, he wasn't surprised that Anna had reclined in her chair and was asleep. She wouldn't rest well there, but a light doze was better than nothing. As she slept, Aidan went to the back of the plane and settled into a seat. When they arrived at their destination, he wanted everything ready and in place.

He'd let McCall know where they were headed, but no one else. Not only was he hiding Anna from two drug lords, there was another man out there she wasn't aware of yet. This one was more dangerous than Garcia or Ruiz. This man's only focus would be to destroy her life. It was Aidan's responsibility to make sure the man never found out about her.

Retrieving his cell from his pocket, Aidan made his first call.

***

She didn't want to wake up, but Aidan wouldn't stop nudging her. Finally realizing that he wasn't going to stop, she opened her eyes enough to glare up at him. "What?" she snapped.

The man had the audacity to grin at her. "We're almost there."

Things moved in a blur after that. He allowed her a few minutes in the bathroom and then hustled her off the plane. They got into a black SUV and were whisked off the tarmac as if they were on an undercover mission. Aidan sat up front with the driver, and Anna was in too much of a daze to do more than look out the window. All she could see were giant trees and the occasional car as they zoomed down a narrow, well-paved road.

Half an hour later, they arrived at a small pier where a sleek black speedboat was waiting for them. Aidan got out, opened the back door for her, and then hurried her onto the boat as if he was hiding her from someone.

Aidan jumped onto the boat, started up the engine, and they were off.

Slightly more alert now and more than a little confused, Anna asked, "What's going on?"

Without looking at her, he gave an abrupt, "Not now."

He was distant and distracted. His eyes were alert and roaming, as if he expected a battalion of enemies to swoop down on them out of nowhere.

She might be bleary-eyed and feeling like she was living on her last ounce of energy, but she could recognize that this wasn't the time to try to get information. When the time was right, she would insist on answers. Bottom line was, she trusted Aidan. If he was worried for their safety, there was a reason.

So she stood beside him as he drove the speedboat through emerald waters, relishing the warm wind, the scent of the ocean, and the exhilaration of being with the man who had starred in her dreams for so long. She was exhausted and yes, even traumatized, but she wasn't one to look a gift horse in the mouth. Reality would rear its ugly head soon enough and allow everything to crash down on her. Until then, she'd ride the wave of this real-life fantasy for as long as possible.

As abrupt as a flash of lightning, a change came over Aidan. The stiff set of his shoulders relaxed, and his hands on the steering wheel loosened their death grip. He even slowed the speed of the boat so she no longer felt as if they were in a race. Apparently, he had decided that they weren't being pursued.

And now she wanted answers.

"Okay, Thorne. Spill it."

He kept his gaze straight ahead as he explained, "Garcia and Ruiz are in the midst of a war. Until this thing dies down, everyone who was at the compound is at risk. That includes you and me. We're going to hang out on a private beach for a little while until this thing blows over."

Her heartbeat thundered. "What about Carrie?"

"Angela and Jake have taken her to an undisclosed location. She'll be safe."

"But why would they blame us? We tried to help."

"Neither Ruiz nor Garcia are the type to listen before they start killing. If there's the slightest indication we had anything to do with his daughter's death, Ruiz would kill first and not have a bit of regret when he found out he was wrong. Garcia's only slightly less dangerous. Once they understand we hurt no one, they'll concentrate on each other. Until then, I don't want you or Carrie to be collateral damage."

She knew there were more questions she should ask, but reality was setting in quicker than she had anticipated. The small amount of energy she'd mustered was disintegrating at a rapid pace. If she didn't get some food and rest soon, she was certain she was going to do a face-plant.

"How far are we from our destination?"

"Ten minutes, tops." He grabbed a pair of binoculars from beneath the dash. "You can see it from here." He pointed to what looked like a tiny dot to her.

Putting her eyes to work when they could barely stay open kept her occupied. She could make out what looked like a little island, but she couldn't tell how large it actually was. The closer they came, the more she could see. It dawned on her then where they were.

"This is where Riley and Justin got back together, isn't it?"

"Yeah."

She remembered Riley telling her that it was like paradise. A beautiful white sandy beach, aqua blue water, a gorgeous house, and a large sparkling swimming pool. Riley had said the island was like heaven on earth.

Anna had wondered how much that feeling had had to do with being there with the man she loved. Lowering the binoculars, she looked over at the man driving the boat. She had a feeling she was about to find out.

Aidan didn't know if he'd ever seen anyone as tired as Anna still staying upright. In the Army he got used to pushing aside his fatigue. Didn't mean he wasn't exhausted now, just meant that he had a goal in front of him. Once he reached the goal, he could let go. Until then, he moved forward. Anna was apparently of the same mind.

Slowing the boat to a putter, he eased over to the pier. Once he had Anna settled in the house, he'd return and take care of the boat. The boathouse on the other side of the island was obscured from view and would hide that the island was occupied.

He could feel Anna swaying beside him, doing her best to stay on her feet. The boat settled gently against the dock, and Aidan grabbed the rope. "Stay here till we're secure."

He hopped up onto the dock, tied the rope, and jumped back into the boat. "Want me to carry you?"

She'd ordinarily shoot him a fiery look and snap out a sassy reply. In a telling sign of her exhaustion, a smile barely tweaked her mouth. "You get me horizontal, I won't be able to get vertical again for at least twenty-four hours."

"That's not a problem. There's nothing for you to do here but sleep, eat, and rest."

"I can't." She looked at him then, and he saw again her will-power. "Not yet. I have to shower. I have to—"

She didn't need to finish the sentence. Even though she had rinsed off at the compound and a little on the plane, some of Elena Garcia's blood was likely still on her.

"I understand," he said gently. Stepping back up on the dock, Aidan held out his hand. "I'll come back and get our stuff in a few minutes. Let's get inside."

Anna knew she was the biggest wimp, but the minute she stepped up on the pier, it was all she could do not to hold out her arms for Aidan to carry her up to the house. He had to be just as tired as she was, probably more so, because while she'd snoozed on the plane, Aidan had been on the phone. Unable to completely lose herself in a deep sleep, she had opened her eyes several times. Each time she had looked around for Aidan and found him at the other end of the plane speaking in low tones on his cellphone.

She made it off the pier and stopped to look up at their destination. The house was beautiful and quite large. Riley had described it as a plantation-like house with a colonial feel. After she'd slept for about a week or two, Anna looked forward to exploring.

A hard, muscular arm draped around her shoulders. "We can go as slow as you like."

She knew Aidan was just being his gallant, overprotective self, but being treated like an invalid didn't sit well with her. She straightened her tired shoulders, took a breath, and started up the hill. The sooner she got there, she sooner she could get a shower and then collapse. The steps didn't look all that steep, but halfway there, she had to stop.

"I can carry you the rest of the way."

"Nope. I can make it." She threw him a teasing look. "Just don't let go, because I have a feeling if I lost my footing, I'd tumble back onto the pier. If that happens, I'm sleeping there tonight."

His arm tightened around her shoulders. "I'm not letting you go."

Her exhausted brain refused to read anything into those words. Her heart, which wasn't nearly as tired as the rest of her body, leaped on the words like a starving lion pursuing a gazelle.

She stepped up onto the porch with a giant, heartfelt sigh.

"I'll show you around tomorrow."

She watched as he opened a small, hidden compartment beside the door and tapped in numbers. Seconds later, she heard a lock disengage. Aidan opened the door, and she stepped inside.

Anna was instantly washed in a welcome, beautiful coolness and, for the first time in days, felt at peace.

"Come on. There's a bedroom at the back of the house. While you shower, I'll fix us something to eat."

She wished she could tell him that she was too tired to eat. While that might be technically true, she also knew if she didn't get something substantial in her stomach, she'd wake in a few hours with a migraine. Not eating always did that to her.

"Sounds wonderful."

Aidan led her to a bedroom, and if she hadn't been so focused on getting into the shower, she was sure she'd be oohing and awwing over its beauty.

"Bathroom's through that door there. Should be plenty of towels, soap, shampoo. If you need anything else, let me know."

When she didn't move, he nudged her gently, and she headed in the right direction. Stopping at the door, she said, "Aidan?"

About to leave the room, he turned. "Yeah?"

"Thank you for taking such good care of me."

"I'll always be there if you need me."

As he walked out the door, she couldn't help but wish he'd said just one word: *Always.*

CHAPTER
TWENTY-ONE

Aidan calculated he had maybe forty-five minutes to an hour of upright time left in him before his body refused to obey his commands. He had a lot to do during this time frame. He moved the boat to the boathouse, and once he was sure there were no traces of their arrival, he carried their backpacks to the house.

When he went to the bedroom to drop off their gear, he heard the shower running full force. At last Anna was getting the shower she so desperately wanted.

In the kitchen, he opened the fridge and was relieved to see the food had been delivered and was to his specifications. Since he hadn't wanted any deliveries after their arrival, he'd had to move fast to get everything in place. Fortunately, Riley had taken a few minutes from the cleanup at Garcia's compound to give him an idea of Anna's favorite foods. He opened the freezer and was pleased to see three cartons of the ice cream Riley insisted would thrill and delight her friend. The thought of thrilling and delighting Anna sounded damn good to him.

Having lived on his own for more than half his life, he was at ease in the kitchen. He wasn't a gourmand by any stretch of the imagination, but he could put together a decent meal. As tired as he was right now, a cheese omelet and toast was the best he could do. It'd give both of them the protein they needed and would be easy on the stomach.

He put all the ingredients on the counter. As soon as he heard the shower cut off, he'd start the omelet. For now, he had a call to make.

McCall answered on the first ring. "Everything okay?"

"Yeah. We finally got here. How're things going?"

"Ingram and Kelly are still sorting through the mess. The sickest of the men have been transported to the hospital. Sinclair and Gates should be arriving there shortly to help out."

Aidan knew that Elite operative Brennan Sinclair and his new partner, Olivia Gates, had been on assignment in Puerto Rico.

"They're back already? How'd it go?"

"Better than we could have hoped," McCall said. "Three children rescued and already reunited with their families. Their abductors behind bars. No deaths."

"Can't ask for better than that."

"You got that right."

"Any word on what's going on with Garcia or Ruiz?"

"I've been on the phone with both of them. Garcia is being more reasonable. Probably because he's been able to talk to his son. Once he comprehends everything that's happened, I'm certain all his hatred will be targeted at the Ruiz family."

"What about Pablo Ruiz?"

"He's not going to be as reasonable or cooperative."

Grief had a tendency to make even the most sensible person blind. Pablo Ruiz had a reputation for being a coldhearted bastard with a strong sadistic streak. Considering the fact that he'd made his young daughter marry into a rival family with the intent of murdering as many as she could bore that reputation out. How reasonable was he going to be now that his daughter was dead and his evil plan had been uncovered?

"The men I told you about, Diego and Salvador, were two of the handful who didn't get sick. What's their story?"

"From what we've been able to piece together, both were on Ruiz's payroll."

"They knew Carrie Easterly wasn't a medical doctor when they abducted her, didn't they?"

"Yes. If they had brought a medical doctor to the compound, they feared their ruse would be up before Julio could die. Bringing Dr. Easterly to him and claiming they thought she was a medical professional bought them some time."

And to hell with abducting an innocent woman. Diego and Salvador's punishment would never be harsh enough, in Aidan's opinion.

"Mallory and Delvecchio get Carrie settled into a safe place?"

"Yes. She wasn't too happy about it, but when we explained that if she didn't hide, she could be putting her family in the US in danger, she changed her mind."

"Has the poison been identified?"

"Not yet. We've learned that Ruiz has his very own chemist who mixed up the poison. Good news is there were no more fatalities. The doctors stabilized everyone."

"So Julio is going to make it?"

"Yes. Juan Garcia sends his thanks for your help."

Helping to save Julio Garcia's life was definitely a mixed blessing. The man and his family weren't good people, but being on the good side of a drug lord was safer than being on his bad side.

"Carrie and Anna did all the work. I'll be sure to let her know he's grateful."

"Get some rest," McCall said. "I'll be in touch when things change."

Aidan put aside the phone. Since he could still hear the shower running in the master bedroom, he went upstairs and took a quick shower in one of the guest rooms. Feeling almost human, Aidan threw on a pair of shorts he had left behind last time he was here. He then went to the bedroom down the hallway and snagged something for Anna to wear.

Figuring Anna would be finished with her shower by now, he headed downstairs. He frowned when he entered the master bedroom. The shower was still running. He was about to knock on the door when he heard a distinct, heart-wrenching sound. She was crying.

Pushing the door open, Aidan's heart almost cracked in two. Through the frosted glass door, he could see that she was sitting on the floor of the shower, sobbing into her hands.

Opening the shower door, he said, "Anna?"

She raised tear-swollen eyes to his. "I still had her blood on me, Aidan. It was in my hair. And bits and pieces of…of…" She shuddered. "How could I not know that?"

"It's gone now, sweetheart." He held out his hand. "Come on. Let's get you dried off and some food into you."

She took his hand and allowed him to pull her to her feet. Ignoring a beautiful, naked woman shouldn't be that big of a challenge. He was so tired that his libido should be way below zero.

The fact that this beautiful, naked woman was Anna Bradford made all the difference. Grinding his teeth till his jaw ached, Aidan pulled her from the shower and grabbed a bath towel from the nearby shelf. Even though every inch of his body ached to carry her to bed and devour her sweetness, he dried her from head to foot with quick efficiency.

Besides, Anna didn't need him mauling her. She needed comfort, warmth, and security. He intended for her to get all three.

Satisfied she was dry enough, he took another towel and wrapped it around her body, hiding her loveliness and allowing his breath to return to almost normal.

Her dark eyes like large bruises in her bleached-white face. The trust in their depths gave him the strength he needed to say, "Hang on. Be right back."

Anna figured at some point she would be embarrassed by what just happened. Having a man see her naked was unusual on its own. Having that man be Aidan Thorne was too close to a fantasy come to life. Of course, that fantasy also included him being wild with desire for her. It definitely didn't include him pulling her off the shower floor, drying her body as if she were a child, and then covering her back up.

He appeared again, this time with a lavender sleep shirt in his hand. Feminine without being frilly, the shirt was something Anna would have picked out to wear. Who did it belong to? One would think she would be too exhausted or emotionally overwrought to feel even an inkling of jealousy. One would be wrong.

She didn't know if the jealousy was clear on her face, but for whatever reason, he gave her one of his gorgeous smiles and said, "My sister's."

With a boldness that surprised her, she dropped the towel and raised her arms. As if he'd done this a hundred times for her before, he put the shirt over her head and helped her slip her arms into the sleeves.

When he stepped back, she dared a quick look at his face, and her entire body flushed with heat. He might've been treating her like she was a child or an invalid, but the burning heat in his eyes said something else.

Showing off his self-control once again, he went to the door. "Come eat when you're ready. The kitchen is on the right side of the house, near the front. Second door on the left."

Losing all breath, Anna leaned back, grateful the shower door was behind her. There was only one man who could make her both weak in the knees and feel as though she could soar over treetops.

She turned to the mirror and was reminded once again of all that had happened. She had thought she was handling things rather well. By pushing aside the images and focusing on the present, she had been able to drive the horror to the back of her mind. But when she'd stood under the hot gush of the water and had looked down at her feet, blood had swirled around her, splattering on the shower floor. Elena Garcia's blood.

Memories had slammed into her, and she had lost it. Elena Ruiz Garcia had committed an incredible act of cruelty, and people had died. However, what had happened to her was horrific. The image of Elena's head exploding and the feel of blood splashing on Anna's skin wasn't something she would ever forget. Elena had been a young, impressionable girl who had followed her father's orders. Anna didn't know if that made her evil or just another victim.

Pulling herself away from the images, Anna quickly braided her damp hair and left the bathroom. As she passed the bed, she resisted the urge to fall onto it and let slumber take over. First, a meal, she promised herself, and then at least twelve solid hours of sleep.

She entered the gigantic kitchen and almost swooned to see a barefoot, bare-chested Aidan at the stove. This image had never been in one of her fantasies, but it was definitely something she would remember forever.

"Anything I can do to help?"

Sliding an omelet onto a plate with the expertise of a short-order cook, he said, "There's juice and milk in the fridge. Glasses are in the cabinet beside the fridge. If you'll pour me a glass of orange juice and get whatever you want, we'll be set."

She followed his instructions and a minute later was sitting at the kitchen table biting into a mouthwatering omelet. She told herself to eat slowly and savor, but she was too hungry. Besides, her eyelids were almost at half-mast. If she didn't eat fast, she feared she'd end up with her face in her plate.

"I talked to McCall. Angela and Jake arrived safely with Carrie. They'll stay with her until this is over."

"How soon do you think that'll be?"

"Hard to say. McCall said that Garcia is now looking only to the Ruiz family for revenge. Ruiz is looking for vengeance any way he can get it. We helped foil his plan, plus his daughter is dead."

"And he's responsible for both."

"The desire for vengeance isn't always rational. Blaming others for your own failings is as old as mankind."

"That's true." She blinked at her empty plate, noting that it was decidedly blurry.

"Time to get some shut-eye."

"Sounds heavenly."

Surprising her, he stood and held out his hand. When she placed her hand in his, he pulled her to her feet and scooped her into his arms. "What are you doing?"

He walked toward the door. "You're about a minute from passing out." He went back to the bedroom she'd been in earlier. As large as the room was, Anna assumed it was the master bedroom. He set her on the bed, went around to the other side, and pulled the bed covers back. "Hop in."

It took amazing effort for her to swing her legs onto the bed. The instant she did, she almost cried at the comfort. She was so tired, she figured she could be lying on a bed of nails and not really notice. But this was no bed of nails. She sank into the mattress with a grateful sigh and looked up at Aidan. "Where are you sleeping?"

"With you."

He pulled the covers back on his side of the bed, lay down, and pulled her into his arms. Feeling more safe and secure than she could ever remember, Anna snuggled against his chest and one second later was asleep.

***

Bogota, Colombia

"What do you mean they disappeared?"

"That's what my men have reported. Thorne and the girl left her hotel in Cali. We tailed them to a small takeout restaurant. They pulled over into a parking lot and ate. About fifteen minutes later, they got back on the road and—" Patrick hesitated.

"What?"

"My man saw him exit the parking lot, but then said it was like Thorne knew he was being followed. He said he just disappeared."

The news both disgusted and infuriated him. The incompetence of people no longer surprised him, but it didn't make him any less angry either. "Dispose of this imbecile in Cali. If he can't keep track of one man and woman, he doesn't belong in my employ."

"Certainly, sir."

"What else do you have for me?"

"We've done the background check on Anna Bradford. She was an easy subject to research."

Cook settled into his chair, readying himself to hear a long, boring story. Most people's lives were day-to-day drudgery, and though it was often necessary to know the most minute detail, it could often be as dry as hell.

"She grew up in Halo, Arizona. An only child. Parents are divorced. Has a bachelor's degree in both criminal justice and child psychology. A master's in child psychology, specializing in trauma. She's pursuing her doctorate."

Okay, he could see a small light at the end of this boring and staid tunnel. And he could see that Thorne would be attracted to someone in that kind of profession.

"There's one anomaly. In her second year of college, she was abducted."

He sat up in his chair. Now that was different.

"By whom?"

"A cult leader named Alden Pike."

"Tranquility."

Patrick looked up from his notes, surprise on his face. "You know about it?"

"Yes. I believe you were in prison at the time, so you probably missed the news. This cult leader had been abducting young women for a decade or so."

"For what purpose?"

"Mates for his followers."

What passed as a smile twitched at Patrick's lips. "A matchmaker."

He barked out a dry laugh. "Indeed."

"So what happened?"

"Authorities swarmed the compound, killed the cult leader, and rescued the women."

Patrick looked down at his notes again. "Bradford went back to school a few months later. Nothing on the radar since then. She works for the Timothy Foundation in Phoenix, Arizona, a children's advocacy organization. She's well-thought-of and, for her age, has an impressive résumé. Has even met with Congress and lawmakers in DC.

"Her main job seems to be traveling around the world treating traumatized children."

"Which explains why she was in Cali, but still doesn't explain how Thorne knows her."

"No, it doesn't."

"But you say he seemed to know her well?"

"Yes, sir. My sources say he carried her out of a bar, and they disappeared briefly into a market. Came out about half an hour later and took off on a motorcycle to the hotel she was staying in. They were there for a little more than an hour. My sources say he seemed extremely protective of her."

"Thank you, Patrick. That will be all."

As soon as his man walked out, a small smile cracked the hard surface of Cook's face. He had been waiting for this day for a long time. After the last incident, Thorne had virtually disappeared. He did, on occasion, see his parents, usually on holidays.

Cook had a man watching Eric and Susan Thorne, but for observational purposes only. They were in no danger from him. Even though he knew he could do irreparable damage to Thorne by hurting his parents, that wasn't the kind of justice he sought. While seeing Aidan Thorne broken, bleeding, and destroyed was his ultimate goal, there was only one avenue of vengeance he would allow himself. An eye for an eye, one might say.

He had been close to giving up. Time was running out, and he had been prepared to modify his plan. But now, if he wasn't mistaken, Miss Anna Bradford of Phoenix, Arizona, was going to give him the opportunity he had been waiting so very long to carry out.

But first he had to find her.

CHAPTER TWENTY-TWO

The Caribbean

Always a light sleeper, Aidan heard a low moan beside him and was awake in an instant. He turned to see Anna gripped in some sort of nightmare. He said her name softly, hoping to wake her without startling her. Her skin was still milky white, and the shadows beneath her eyes only slightly less prominent. They'd been asleep for only a few hours.

She moaned again and began thrashing around, her entire body jerking as if she were in restraints, trying to escape.

"Anna," Aidan said in a firm voice, "wake up."

When that didn't wake her, he shook her gently and said again, this time in the hard, commanding voice he'd perfected in the Army, "Anna Bradford. Wake. Up."

She woke screaming his name. Her eyes were wild and unfocused, the terror in them real.

Softening his voice, Aidan said, "You had a nightmare, sweetheart. You're fine."

Breath shuddered through her, and with a soft gasp, she threw herself into Aidan's arms.

Closing his eyes, he held her, savoring the feel of her soft, warm body, her special scent that reminded him of peaches and cinnamon.

In a muffled voice, she spoke against his chest. "I was so scared."

"Want to talk about it?"

"I haven't had a nightmare like that in a long time."

"After what you've endured the last three days, it's no wonder."

"It wasn't just about that. I was back in Tranquility. Alden Pike was torturing me. I kept begging him, pleading with him to let me go. Then all of a sudden, Elena Garcia was there. Pike was holding a gun to her head and telling me she would die unless I gave in to him. Before I could answer…" She stopped and shuddered again.

"He shot her?"

"Yes. No." She burrowed into his chest as if to get as close as possible. "Suddenly, it was you he was holding a gun on. I screamed yes, that I would do whatever he said. But he didn't listen." Her voice thick with emotion, she added, "He shot you, Aidan. Right in front of me."

Cradling her in his arms, he shushed and soothed her the way he had his nieces and nephews when they were babies. He said some of the same nonsensical things, reassuring her that all was well, that she was safe.

A final shudder went through her body, and then she relaxed in his arms. He felt her warm lips kiss his chest, and it was all he could do not to roll her onto her back and ease the unrelenting ache he had for this woman.

Forcing himself to do the right thing had never been so difficult. "You think you can sleep some more? You only got about four hours."

"Yes. I need visit the restroom first."

"While you do that, I'll just do a quick perimeter check. Make sure all is well."

She raised her head and gave him a sunny smile. He could become addicted to them.

"Meet you back here in ten?"

"Deal."

She bounded off the bed as if she had energy to spare. Aidan was glad to see that. One of the things he liked best about Anna Bradford was her incredible ability to rebound.

He headed toward the third floor. Unless one was looking carefully, you couldn't see that the house had an additional floor. The house had been built as a hideaway for Stuart Ritter, one of the most wanted criminals of the twentieth century. The third floor was a small room surrounded by windows that gave a three-sixty-degree view of the island. A giant high-powered telescope sat in the center of the room. With one sweep, any threat within a two-mile radius could be detected.

Aidan adjusted the lens and took in a slow comprehensive view of the entire area. He didn't expect problems. He had covered their tracks. And other than McCall, no one knew they were here.

Satisfied that all was well, Aidan headed back downstairs. He made his own visit to the bathroom, and after snagging a couple of bottles of water from the fridge, he returned to the bedroom. Anna was sitting up in bed, waiting for him. She'd released her hair from its braid and had brushed it to a dark, silken sheen. It flowed over her shoulders like a dark, shiny waterfall. Her eyes were slumberous, her smile sweetly sensual.

Swallowing hard, he gave her what he hoped looked like an impersonal smile and not the predatory look of a hungry wolf. Twisting off the cap of one of the bottles, he handed it to her. "Thought you might be thirsty."

"Thanks." She took the bottle, swallowed half of it down. "Cool, clean water is something I'll never take for granted."

During her captivity in Tranquility, she had been denied both food and water in an effort to break her. Thank God it hadn't worked.

Aidan downed his own bottle and tossed it into the wastebasket. She sipped hers a little more and then placed it on the bedside table. Then, as if they'd been together for years, she scooted over on the bed and patted the mattress in invitation.

Instantly hard, Aidan scrambled onto the bed, knowing the shorts he wore couldn't hide his reaction. He had brought her here to protect her, not to entertain himself. She would leave soon, and the last thing he wanted was to lead her on and hurt her.

Settling beside her, he gave her another impersonal smile and closed his eyes. "Sleep tight."

She didn't move for several seconds. He knew she was looking at him, and as tempted as he was to open his eyes and find out what she was thinking, he wouldn't. If he did, he'd give in to temptation.

Finally, she slid down beside him and snuggled against him. Unable to stop himself, his arms went around her, and he held her as he had before. If this was all he could ever have, then he would take it.

He was just drifting off when her heard her whisper, "Aidan?"

"Hmm?"

"Would you make love to me?"

Aidan's eyes shot open. Rolling on his side to face her, he found himself speechless for the first time in his life.

Anna swallowed nervously. The gorgeous man beside her was staring at her as if she'd just recited the Gettysburg Address backward and in Chinese. She didn't think she'd ever seen Aidan so astonished. Or more panicked. He had saved her from a raging river, almost fallen down a mountainside, and had disarmed two heavily armed thugs as if he were Jason Bourne, and not once had he appeared the least bit alarmed.

But this, evidently, was a different matter.

Asking him to make love to her was a giant step for her. She might be assertive and outspoken in other areas of her life, but when it came to intimacy, she was quite timid. A lot of that had to do with trust. It took a tremendous amount of faith in another person to allow yourself to be vulnerable. Would Aidan be surprised to know that she trusted him implicitly?

"I know I'm not like the other women you've been with."

"What other women?"

Feeling completely out of her depth, she gave a vague gesture with her hand. "I know there are other women."

"But how do you know you're not like them? Have you seen me with another woman?"

"Well…no." She swallowed past the giant lump of nervousness that had grown even larger in the last minute and a half. This wasn't going nearly as well as she had hoped. Aidan Thorne had a reputation for being a ladies' man. She had many friends at LCR, and more than a few had told her the rumors of all the women Aidan had dated.

"Then how do you know there are other women?"

"Come on, Aidan. You're no angel. I know you date."

"Rumors aren't always true, Anna. You should know that."

Now she felt like the town busybody who had nothing better to do than gossip about the local hunk.

Anna settled back against her pillow. "Never mind."

Yes, she knew she sounded like a sulky teenager who hadn't gotten her way, but she couldn't hide her disappointment. She had thought he wanted her. She might not be super experienced, but she recognized arousal when she saw it. When Aidan had gotten into bed, his erection had been impossible to miss.

She rolled over on her side, away from his searching eyes. So what if he didn't want her? She had known for years that there was something about her that irritated Aidan. Whenever she was around, he went out of his way to either be rude to her or avoid her. Just because she was crazy about him meant nothing.

"Anna."

"What?" She winced. She hated sounding like a snotty bitch.

"Turn around. We need to talk."

Okay, here it comes, she thought. *The talk*. The one where he told her she was a nice girl and he liked her as a friend, but there could be nothing between them. She'd never had that talk with anyone before, but she'd heard about it.

Willing herself to act like a mature woman who could take rejection without turning into a shrew, Anna rolled onto her back.

"You are without a doubt the most infuriating, irritating, maddening woman I've ever met."

"Hey!" She had expected a gentle letdown, not insults. "You know, you're no Prince Charming yourself, Aidan Thorne."

"Let me finish. You're opinionated. Bossy. Reckless, without a care for your own safety. And you're a cover hog."

Infuriated, she sat up in bed. "All you have to do is say 'no, thanks,' Aidan. You don't have to be so hateful."

"I'm not finished."

"Yeah, well, I am." She swung her legs over the side and was about to push herself out of bed, away from him. A hand grasped her arm, preventing her.

"Let me go."

"No. I said I'm not finished. You're also the most adorable, sexiest, sweetest, most unselfish, spirited, and beautiful woman I've ever known. In a word, you're perfect."

It was her turn to stare. "Huh?"

"Come here."

Her entire body suddenly the consistency of an overcooked noodle, she didn't bother to resist as Aidan pulled her into his arms.

Burying his face in her neck, he breathed in her special scent. "Anna. Anna. Anna. What am I going to do with you?"

She didn't answer, and Aidan couldn't blame her. He had been prepared to give her a simple no and an explanation of how he couldn't take advantage of her vulnerability. When she'd started spouting the ridiculous notion that she wasn't like his other women, as if she were flawed in some way, he hadn't been able to stop himself.

"For the record, there are no other women. I do date on rare occasions, but no one on a regular basis." For Aidan, dating involved getting to know a person and enjoying their company. With the past always on his ass, he couldn't take that risk.

"The LCR rumors are a crock of shit. Being known as the playboy of the organization keeps well-meaning matchmakers at bay."

"You mean like Noah?"

"Ha. McCall swears that's an urban legend."

She pulled away to look up at him. "Why do you always act like you don't want to be around me?"

"Camouflage, pure and simple. You, more than any woman I've met in years, make me realize what I'm missing. What I can't have."

"You've been hurt."

"That's part of it. I can't risk it again. I won't risk it. This probably sounds egotistical." He shook his head. "No, it will sound egotistical, but I can't think of any other way to put it. I can't take the risk of you falling in love with me, because there's no future for us. We cannot be together. Ever."

"What if I told you I'm willing to risk it?"

"Risk what?"

She pulled away from him, and Aidan reluctantly let her go. Leaning her back against the headboard, she bravely faced him. Another one of her traits that awed him.

"I haven't been involved with anyone since before I was abducted. I tried and…" She grimaced and tried again. "Every guy I meet isn't—"

Anna broke off abruptly. What she had been about to say was that every guy she met wasn't Aidan. Confessing that secret was a surefire way to push him away for good. He didn't want a relationship, and while she wasn't going to lie, neither would she admit that no man had ever made her feel the things he did.

"Every guy you meet isn't what?"

"My type. I know you're not looking for anything permanent. But you're the only man in years that I've been attracted to."

The concern in his eyes didn't diminish. She had done a lousy job of trying to convince him, but she could think of nothing else to say. She couldn't lie and tell him she didn't want a relationship or a commitment from him. Even if he didn't feel the same way, her feelings for him were authentic and permanent. But they were absolutely not what he would want to hear.

"And when this is over? When you go back to your life, and I go back to mine? What then?"

"We have memories, Aidan. Beautiful memories."

"And that will be enough?"

"It'll have to be."

"You deserve more, Anna. With a man who will love you the way you should be loved."

She took his hand then. It was now or never. "I want you, Aidan. I know you want me. Don't say no again."

His eyes locked with hers for the longest time. She saw desire, heat, need, and something else. Something more.

Leaning forward, his gaze still on hers, his mouth tenderly touched hers. Anna moaned at the first delicious contact. As if the sound of her approval spurred his momentum, Aidan kept his lips on hers as he started to pull her down onto the bed, but then he stopped.

"Wait."

Her pounding heart jumped to her throat.

His hands went to the bottom edge of her nightshirt, and with a wicked, little smile, he began to push up the fabric. Slowly, as if uncovering a cherished gift, he kissed each body part as it was revealed. First her knees, each thigh, then her stomach. By the time he uncovered her breasts, Anna was panting, her arousal so keen that every spot Aidan kissed felt as if she'd been stamped with fire. He paused at her breasts and just looked at her. Anna could feel her nipples peaking and goose bumps rising all over her body.

He groaned a heartfelt, "Beautiful," and instead of the scorching, soft kisses like before, Aidan licked a nipple until it was tightly drawn. Pulling away slightly, he smiled at the result.

Anna wanted more. She wanted his mouth covering her, suckling, taking, devouring. Instead, he moved on to her other breast, which received the same treatment. By the time he pulled away, her head had collapsed against the headboard, and she was moaning his name.

"Sit up, baby. Raise your arms."

Eager for more of whatever he had planned, Anna sat up and raised her arms. With a surprising speed, considering how slow he'd been before, Aidan jerked the nightshirt over her head and threw it on the floor. He then moved back and just looked at her. "Like I said. Perfect in every way."

Realistically, Anna knew she was far from perfect, but hearing those words from Aidan did something to her. Gave her a confidence and assertiveness she'd rarely felt during intimate moments.

Her own smile was quite wicked as she reached for him. When her hands touched his naked chest, she released a moaning sigh. He was hard and smooth, taut muscles covered in rough satin.

Everywhere she touched was a tactile delight. Broad shoulders tapered down to muscular biceps and corded forearms. His hands were twice as large as hers, callused and roughened by dangerous and difficult missions. She moved her hands back up his arms. If Aidan's face was a work of art, his chest was a beautiful sculpture, with two copper-colored nipples in a vast landscape of muscle and sinew. He had just the right amount of furring, which extended down to his hard-as-rock abs.

"Anna."

Her name was a tortured sound. She had been so immersed in the wonder of his body that she'd missed how very turned on he was. His eyes were golden-brown pools of heat, their depths gleaming with more need and desire than she'd ever thought possible.

"Touch me, baby."

Her gaze dropped down again, below his stomach. Though he still wore his shorts, she imagined they were extremely uncomfortable. His erection strained the fabric to breaking point.

Wonder and need dissolved any shyness she might have ordinarily felt. She reached for him, unbuttoning the waistband and unzipping the shorts. The hiss he released told her he was on edge just as much as she was. When she held him in both her hands and caressed his hard length, he said something in a harsh, guttural language she didn't even recognize. She leaned forward, eager to have her first taste.

Hands landed on her shoulders stopping her. "Oh no you don't. You've teased me long enough."

Before she could complain or resist, Aidan twisted around and pushed off the bed. He dropped his shorts on the floor, and with one smooth move of his hand, he jerked the comforter and sheets from the bed.

Grabbing Anna's ankles, Aidan slid her body down until she was in the middle of the mattress. Her eyes were wide with surprise and maybe a little trepidation. She had touched and teased him until he was as close to explosion as he'd ever been. And now he was going to return the favor. He had dreamed about holding Anna Bradford's soft, silken body, fantasized about having her long legs wrapped around him while he gave her pleasure untold. For every dream, every fantasy…for every time he'd had to turn away from her and grind his teeth to keep from touching her, he was going to make up for it all tenfold.

So aroused he could barely breathe, Aidan shut down every warning signal in his brain. He ignored the insistent little voice that told him that this was a bad idea. He had wanted this woman for so long, and despite how bad of an idea this was, he was going to take what he wanted.

His hands shook as they glided over her body. She was slender but curvy, firm and soft. From the top of her beautiful head to the bottoms of her long, slender feet, she was all woman. And for as long as they were here, together on this island, she was his woman.

He started at her feet, his lips paying homage as he moved up her body, stopping at shadows, crevices, and curves for a kiss, nibble, or lick. She had a multitude of bruises and tiny nicks from their experience in Colombia. Aidan pressed a soft kiss to each injury.

Since he knew he wouldn't want to leave for a long time once he got there, he bypassed the mound of soft, springy curls at the juncture of her thighs. He would return there soon and feast, but for right now, he wanted to continue his exploration. His tongue glided over her belly, and she arched, releasing a hissing sigh.

He spoke against her stomach. "You sensitive here, baby?"

"Yes. No." She spoke haltingly, as if confused. "Everywhere you touch…it feels like an electrical current is zipping through me."

"Good. By the time I'm finished, you'll be properly turned on."

Her husky laugh held a note of desperation. "By the time you're finished, I'll be unconscious with pleasure."

He smiled. "That's a worthy goal."

His mouth moving upward, Aidan continued his exploration. When he came to her breasts, he knew he wouldn't be able to just settle for a small kiss. Anna's breasts were perfectly rounded, lightly pink in color with plum-colored nipples that just begged to be nibbled on and enjoyed. He cupped both of the silken mounds and pressed them together.

"Aidan? What are you—" She broke off on a cry as Aidan covered both of her nipples with his mouth and suckled deep.

Throbbing increased in her core to a zenith. She had never orgasmed this way. Had never thought her breasts were particularly sensitive. Now she knew that it wasn't lack of sensitivity, but she had been with the wrong man. This amazing man with his strength, kindness, honor, and integrity was the right one. Now and forever.

"Aidan. Aidan." It was a litany, a plea for mercy, and a plea for him to continue.

Apparently realizing what was happening, that she was close to her peak, Aidan moved a hand to her sex and, using one finger only, pressed hard on the knot of nerves and then slid his finger inside her. Anna's entire body arched upward as she screamed out in her release.

Giving her no time to catch her breath or recover, Aidan moved down to where she was throbbing so deliciously. Settling between her sprawled thighs and cupping his hands beneath her knees, he lifted her legs, spread them wide, and lowered his head. The first swipe of his tongue set her on fire again, and when he suckled hard, Anna zoomed straight toward another climax. This time, he allowed her recovery as, with slow, steady thrusts of his tongue, he brought her down to earth gently, tenderly.

Her breaths shuddering through her, she barely noted that he opened a drawer beside the bed. She heard a crinkle and knew he was putting on a condom.

"Anna, look at me."

Opening her eyes, she gazed up at the gorgeous, golden-haired man who had come to mean so much to her. This was a dream come true for her, and if this was the only time she'd ever have with him, she wanted it to be one they would remember for the rest of their lives.

"Tell me you want this."

Holding her arms open wide, she said softly, "More than I've ever wanted anything."

Lowering his body over hers, Aidan carefully gauged Anna's expression. She was an open book, every expression revealing her thoughts and feelings. He pressed against her opening and briefly closed his eyes at the exquisite heat as he glided into her body. At the slight widening of her eyes, Aidan stopped and allowed her to adjust to his size. She'd told him she hadn't been with anyone in years, which meant he needed to go easy this first time. When he felt her muscles loosen, her body accepting him, he slid deeper. Gritting his teeth, his body screaming for him to bury himself as deep as he could go, Aidan forced self-control.

When at last he was as far as he could go, he paused. "You okay?"

Her smile both sexy and adorable, she whispered, "Never better."

Groaning at the sheer sweetness of this woman, Aidan kissed her softly, slowly, savoring, cherishing. And then he could no longer stop himself. Retreating, plunging, surging, and thrusting, his body and tongue in perfect rhythm, he rode them both to volcanic, explosive climaxes.

CHAPTER TWENTY-THREE

The next time Anna woke, the setting sun was casting a long, gray shadow over the room. She raised her head, taking in her surroundings. The bedclothes were back on the bed, covering her. She was alone. If not for the delicious ache between her legs and the flush of red on her chest from Aidan's beard stubble, she might have believed it had all been a dream. Just like all the others she'd had about him. Only it hadn't been a dream. She and Aidan had made love. Calling it anything other than that would be an insult to the experience. She had felt cherished, desired, and—

With a sigh, her head plopped back onto the pillows. No, she could go no further with her thoughts. Before he'd touched her, he had made her understand that no future together existed for them. She had agreed. Assigning a more romantic name to what had happened between them would be a betrayal of that promise. It didn't keep her from wishing things could be different, but what he had given her was more than she believed she'd ever have.

"Hey, sleepyhead." The gruff, sexy voice sent a rush of heat into her bloodstream.

Sitting up, she backed against the headboard, and unaccountably shy, she grabbed the sheet and covered herself.

Aidan stood at the doorway. He must have showered again, because his hair was damp, turning it a dark gold. He wore faded jeans, a T-shirt almost the exact shade of his eyes, and a satisfied smile. Anna couldn't help but smile back.

"Hungry?"

"Starving."

"Good. I made a feast. It'll be ready in about twenty minutes. Why don't you shower and ease some of your soreness?"

Heat infused her body again, but this time she could attribute the feeling to one hundred percent embarrassment. Her muscles were definitely sore from their ordeal in Colombia, but the most recent tenderness was all Aidan's doing.

As if he knew exactly what she was thinking, he winked and said, "Don't want you too sore for what I have planned next."

"Next?" Was that squeaky, breathless voice really hers?

"Exploring the island, of course. What else did you think I meant?"

Anna grabbed a pillow beside her and threw it in his direction. Her aim and arm strength were pitifully inadequate.

He sauntered over to her, snagging the pillow that had landed in the middle of the floor on the way to his destination. Stopping beside the bed, he leaned over and whispered in the softest, sexiest voice she could imagine, "You're outrageously sexy when you're embarrassed." Then he kissed her.

Her fingers tangling in his hair, Anna sank back against the pillows and savored the bone-melting, heart-stopping, achingly sweet kiss. His lips were soft and tender, his tongue gliding gently into her mouth in a leisurely, easy thrust. Sensual without being sexual, the kiss was both unique and powerful. Anna's heart, which she told herself hadn't yet tumbled over into love, made that final plunge. Aidan Thorne held it in his hands, whether he wanted it or not.

When he finally lifted his head, they were both smiling. His was one of a conqueror who'd just captured his prize. She figured hers looked exactly how she felt, goofy and smitten.

"See you in the kitchen." With that, he straightened and walked out the door.

Anna lay there basking for another couple of minutes until her stomach made a noise that sounded like an angry hyena. She bounded out of bed and headed to the bathroom. On the way to the shower, she caught a glimpse of her face. Yep, her smile was most definitely goofy and smitten.

Aidan lost his smile the minute he walked out of the bedroom. He had thought that castigating himself for his poor choices was a thing of the past, but apparently not. He had taken what he wanted and damned the consequences. And oh holy hell, were there going to be consequences.

Shoving the garlic bread into the oven, he slammed the door shut. He needed to get his anger under control before Anna came in and caught him. She was more sensitive to his mood swings than anyone he'd ever met. Having her know he regretted what had happened between them was the last thing he wanted. Because in his gut, where it really counted, he rebelled against that regret with every fiber of his being. It was, hands down, one of the best experiences of his life. That didn't mean that it should have happened. Where the hell had his discipline and self-control gone?

He stirred the tomato sauce, checked the boiling pasta for doneness, and uncorked the wine. Turning around, he took in the table and cursed himself again. Because instead of pulling back and trying to return to something approaching a platonic friendship, he had set the table for seduction. Candles, muted lighting, glistening crystal, fine china, and soft, romantic music. He didn't want platonic. He didn't want an easygoing friendship. For two long years, he had denied himself the delight of Anna Bradford. And now that he had experienced that pleasure, damned if he could go back to the way it was before.

"Smells amazing."

He turned, and his anger was demolished like a sandcastle beneath a rushing wave. She had evidently gone upstairs and found the clothing stash his sister had left. Jennifer and Anna were about the same size, though his sister was a little taller and thinner.

She waved at her clothing. "Hope you don't mind, but I snooped around and found this in one of the closets."

"I'm glad you did. It suits you."

The white sundress molded lovingly to her body, revealing a generous amount of skin without being immodest. Landing a couple of inches above her knees, the dress also showed off her golden, toned legs. He smiled when he noticed her bare feet.

"Couldn't find any shoes to fit?"

"No. They were a little large."

"My sister has Thorne feet. I remember my mother saying once that her children's feet size was the one feature she wished we hadn't gotten from my dad. My dad laughingly reminded her that her six-foot-three son would look quite strange with a shoe size of five."

"Wow, your mom must be tiny."

"Tiny but mighty. Barely five feet tall and rules the family like a miniature general."

"I'd love to meet them."

Aidan turned away before she could see his face. There would be no parental meetings. No family get-togethers, holidays, or otherwise. No *let me introduce you to the girl I'm crazy about* introductions.

A hand touched his arm and squeezed gently. He looked down at a lovely face filled with compassion and understanding. "I didn't mean anything by that. I promise. I remember our agreement, and I'm not expecting anything more. Okay?"

"You deserve more, Anna. You deserve everything good."

She leaned up and kissed his cheek. "I'll settle for the here and now and that delicious-smelling pasta."

Her humor and forgiveness broke the tension. Grateful for the reprieve, Aidan went back to work, determined to make as many memories as possible before this time was up.

While Aidan mixed the pasta and sauce together, Anna tossed the salad. She wanted them to get back to their easiness of before. Blurting out that she'd love to meet his family had been an impulsive response—one that she would make to any friend who talked about their family with such love. For a brief blip of time, she had forgotten that this new and close relationship was only temporary. Once the danger from Ruiz and Garcia had passed, she and Aidan would return to their lives.

Since it hurt to think of that, she set about thinking of other things. Like the amazing meal in front of her.

"Can all LCR guys cook like this? Riley told me that Justin is an amazing cook."

"Yes. McCall sends us to cooking school."

He made the statement with such a straight face, she believed him for half a second. His slow grin told her he knew he'd gotten her.

She took a bite of the pasta and forgot all teasing. "Oh my gosh. You should teach classes."

"You're easy to please."

For whatever reason, she took those words in a sexual context and found herself blushing to the roots of her hair. Aidan had pleased her over and over again. Dropping her gaze to her plate, she concentrated on her meal.

"When we've finished dinner, I'll let you explore anyplace you want."

She raised her head and faced a grinning Aidan. "You're doing that on purpose."

"What?"

"Embarrassing me."

"Like I said, you're easy, Bradford."

Refusing to let him bait her anymore, she asked, "How long have you and your family owned the island?"

"About six years."

"When you first told me about it—when we were talking about getting Riley and Justin together—you said no one hardly uses it anymore. Why's that? I would think this would be a perfect getaway."

He gave a one-shouldered shrug. "Too busy, I guess." He nodded toward her empty plate. "You want more?"

There were many things that Aidan Thorne was good at. Changing the subject smoothly wasn't one of them. She was learning the parameters in what he would and wouldn't talk about. Anything to do with his family, with the exception of the most basic things, was off-limits.

"Anna? You want more pasta?"

"No, thanks. It was delicious, though."

Aidan stood and held out his hand. "Let's take a walk on the beach before it gets dark."

She allowed Aidan to pull her to her feet, and then, as if she did it every day of her life, she went into his arms.

Burying his face in her neck, he breathed in and released a shaky sigh. "Oh, Anna, what am I going to do with you?"

Though his words were soft, even tender, she heard the frustration in his voice. Even as she wished she could help him with whatever was troubling him, she knew this was something Aidan would have to deal with alone. She just hoped he'd share it with her at some point.

Knowing they needed a lighthearted moment, she leaned back in his embrace and gave him her best effort at a wicked grin. "Is that another sexual innuendo? Because if it is, I have a few suggestions."

He barked out a laugh. "I'll bet you do. Let's take a walk and talk about them."

CHAPTER TWENTY-FOUR

Aidan held Anna's hand as he showed her around the island. He had never brought a woman here before. And other than arranging the meeting between Justin and Riley a few months back, no one other than his family had stayed here since they'd owned the island. Only a select few knew that the property belonged to the Thorne family. It was hidden deep beneath a couple of shell corporations and various fake names. This place was one of two locations Aidan and his family used for get-togethers. It was their safe haven.

After walking the entire length of the beach, they stood for a while and watched the tide come in, washing away the tiny prints sanderlings had made seconds before. The hand he held, small and delicate, felt perfect in his own, and Aidan felt something he hadn't experienced in years. Peace.

Anna's heartfelt gusty sigh seemed permeated with satisfaction.

He smiled down at her. "Nice, isn't it?"

"It's beautiful."

The island wasn't especially large. The entire circumference covered just over three-quarters of a mile. But the sand was sugar white, the water a crystal-clear blue, and the trees and bushes surrounding the house were filled with exotic flowers and several species of wild birds.

Even though he'd been here many times before, Aidan couldn't remember a time when he'd been more relaxed. He was intelligent enough to realize that the beautiful woman beside him made all the difference. He was also smart enough to recognize the danger of that thought.

"The island was given to my father as a thank-you."

"Given? You mean someone actually gave this island to your dad as a gift? What on earth for?"

"My dad is a pediatric oncologist. He saved the life of a young boy, and his father wanted to do something special for him. It's not Dad's way to accept gifts, especially something so extravagant. Saving a child's life is gift enough for him, but it was offered to him at a difficult time in my family's life—my life. So he accepted it for us."

"You and your family come here often?"

"At first, it was just me. I needed to…" He struggled with the right wording. "I needed some thinking time. Then we started coming here for family gatherings. Lately, with everyone so busy, we don't come here as often. My dad is semiretired, but my mom's practice is thriving."

"Your mom's a doctor, too?"

"Cardiologist."

"So medicine runs in the family."

"Yeah. My sister is an orthopedist."

"Wow."

Aidan let her absorb that, knowing questions would inevitably follow. He needed to explain things to her. She deserved to know everything. He had made love to this woman. Despite the fact that he'd warned her that no relationship was possible, she, more than anyone else, deserved to know the reason why.

Anna being Anna surprised him once again. "Do you have any ice cream?"

Smiling, he pulled her to him for a hard hug. "I think I have a few gallons of your favorites on hand. Let's go."

Her mind was once again buzzing with a thousand questions, but Anna wasn't going to ask them. The grim set of Aidan's mouth had told her he expected them. She'd learned in her profession and in her life that asking difficult questions involved more than just a curious mind. It also involved sensitivity and timing. She wanted to know Aidan's story because she cared about him. And because she cared, she wasn't going to pry. When and if he was ready, then so was she. Until then, she wanted to see something in his eyes besides the darkness he carried with him.

While Aidan cleaned up the remains of their meal, Anna scooped out generous bowls full of ice cream. Caramel vanilla for her. Fudge ripple for him. By the time she was finished, Aidan was through with the cleanup.

"Let's eat this outside by the pool."

Anna couldn't believe she'd yet to see the pool. For that matter, she hadn't seen the entire house either. As much as she wanted to do just that, she feared she'd have to wait till tomorrow for more exploring. Lethargy was already pulling at her muscles. After her ice cream, she was headed back to bed. Would Aidan join her again? She might be too tired for anything other than sleep, but the thought of him staying in another room after what they'd shared seemed preposterous. They might never have a future together, but they had the present. And she wanted to spend every moment possible in his arms.

Aidan led her through sliding glass doors onto a balcony surrounded by thick green foliage and blooming bougainvillea. Three steps down from the balcony was a lagoon-like pool with a small waterfall.

"Amazing. Riley tried to describe it to me, but now I know why she had such difficulty. This defies description."

"My nieces and nephews would spend every day here if they could."

"How many nieces and nephews do you have?"

"Two of each. Emily is the oldest at six. Cameron is four. The two youngest are two-year-old twins, Samuel and Serena."

She settled into a cushioned two-seat glider and patted the cushion beside her. The instant he sat down, she dug into her melting ice cream and closed her eyes as the creamy ice-cold confection hit her tongue. *Heaven!*

For a few moments, the only sounds were the clanging of spoons against their bowls and the occasional appreciative sounds Anna couldn't keep from escaping from her mouth.

"How did you know about my ice cream addiction?"

"Riley."

"Best friends are the best." She glanced over at him. "Who's your best friend?"

If she had stabbed him in the chest with a butcher knife, she didn't think he could have looked more pained.

She put her hand on his arm. "Aidan, I'm sorry." She wasn't sure what she was apologizing for. She only knew she wanted to get that tortured expression off his face.

"You have nothing to apologize for, Anna. I just…" He faced the pool, his eyes blank and distant.

And then, without the least amount of effort, Aidan found himself telling her everything. "I was what some people call a child prodigy." He glanced over at her, his smile crooked. "Yeah. Hard to believe, I know.

"I graduated high school when I was fifteen. Went to college, which was where I met Simon Cook. He and I were the same age, so we naturally gravitated to each other. After graduation, we started at the same med school in Michigan. That's where we met Melody. She was a year younger."

"So you were like a little group of Doogie Howsers."

"Something like that. We were book smart but not people smart. Didn't have any real-world experience. My family is well-off. Simon's was even more so. Melody had nothing. Her parents were dead, killed in a car crash when she was twelve. She was there on scholarships and grants. She had no extra spending money. Simon and I had more than enough, but we were all kind of in the same boat, maturity-wise. Made sense that we all became best friends.

"And I guess it was inevitable that I would fall in love with Melody. She was a bright, shining star. So full of energy and life.

"I got lucky and Mellie fell for me, too. We tried not to leave Simon out. He knew how we felt about each other and seemed to accept it as the natural way of things. Didn't act like he resented it. I never saw a hint of jealousy. Simon didn't date much, but we were so busy, none of us had a lot of free time.

"We graduated from med school and started our residency. Mellie was going into pediatric oncology. Both Simon and I were going to be surgeons.

"Mellie and I wanted to get married. My parents loved her, but thought we were both too young. They were right, but telling that to a headstrong twenty-one-year-old and a determined twenty-year-old did no good. We had the wedding, an abbreviated honeymoon, and that was that.

"We moved into a two-bedroom apartment close to the hospital where both Mellie and I worked." He took a breath. "And then we made the first big mistake."

"Don't tell me. Simon moved in with you."

"Yeah. Stupid, I know. But we talked about it, and leaving Simon out, especially since we'd been through so much together, just felt wrong. So we moved in together. Stupid...so very stupid.

"Carving out time for just the two of us was hard. When we weren't working, we were sleeping. Some days we'd go without more than a peck on the cheek as one of us was headed out the door and the other to bed.

"We didn't get into Simon's business a lot. He started spending more and more time away from the apartment. Mellie thought he had a girlfriend. I wasn't so sure."

He paused for a second. "Did I mention that Simon worked in a different hospital?"

She shook her head.

"He did, so neither Mellie nor I knew what was going on with him. Turns out that though Simon was a brilliant man, building personal relationships was difficult for him. Having to deal with patients, listen to their complaints, wasn't his thing. He got reprimanded a couple of times. I didn't know that until later. He was spiraling out of control, and I was so damned caught up in my own life, I completely missed the signs.

"Everything came to a head one day. I was taking a shower when I heard Simon and Mellie shouting at each other. I walked into the living room. It was a dumb argument over who took the last yogurt from the fridge. Turns out Mellie had lost a patient that day. She had worked a twenty-four-hour shift and was bone-tired, too. She complained about Simon taking the yogurt, he snapped at her, and it escalated.

"I broke it up. Simon shut himself up in his room, and Mellie and I had our first major fight. She wanted Simon gone. Said she wanted the privacy to walk around the house naked if she wanted. I was stupid and stalked out. I didn't really disagree with her thinking. Guess everything had gone so smoothly for so long, I was resistant to making any changes. I went for a run and gave her words a lot of thought. By the time I came back home, I knew what I had to do. Simon needed to move out.

"Mellie was already asleep, so I went to Simon's room, told him he needed to find his own place. He agreed. Didn't even seem upset. Said he'd been thinking about it, too. I thought everything was fixed. Still amazes me how damn naïve I was.

"I showered and went to work. Called Mellie during a break but got her voice mail. I told her Simon was moving out.

"I got busy at work. It wasn't until late that afternoon that I thought to check on Mellie again. Got her voice mail again.

Figured she was still sleeping. She'd been exhausted and was due back at the hospital at midnight.

"It was a little after nine when I got home. I'd stopped on the way and got Mellie some flowers."

Some things were frozen forever in his memory. He saw himself standing on the front stoop of that apartment with a bouquet of half-wilted flowers in his hand, and the thought had come to him that it was the first time he'd ever given Mellie flowers. He thought about how wrong that was. Mellie deserved flowers every day of her life. He had made a silent vow that he'd make sure that happened.

In his mind's eye, he saw the look on his face right before he put a hand on the doorknob, not knowing his entire world was about to be turned upside down. He'd been young in both years and wisdom. Book smart but so damn naïve about life. A cocky, wet-behind-the-ears doctor without any real knowledge of the gut-wrenching agony that can happen in the blink of an eye.

"I walked into the apartment. It was eerily quiet. Noticed immediately that Simon had moved out. His lamp on the desk in the living room was gone. Also, some weird painting that both he and Mellie had liked and put over the mantel had disappeared. I was kind of sad but glad, too. Mellie and I didn't have to worry about our privacy anymore.

"Since it was so quiet, I thought she might still be sleeping. The apartment smelled like disinfectant and bleach, so I figured she'd woken up, done some cleaning to tire herself out, and then had gone back to bed. She did that sometimes when she was too wired to sleep.

"I remember opening the fridge and taking out a beer. Drank half of it down, almost decided to watch some television. Then I thought I'd order some Chinese, and Mellie and I could spend some time together before she had to go into work. I was off the next day and was thinking about what I could do to make everything up to her."

He shook his head. "We always think about those things when it's too late.

"I went to the bedroom. Mellie was in bed, on her side, facing away from me. Some kind of chill zipped up my spine—like a warning. I'd never felt that before. Anyway, I leaned over to kiss her on her cheek. Noticed that her hand was drawn up in a clawlike position.

"I said her name and turned her over. She had this look of horror frozen on her face. Her eyes were open and fixed."

Aidan swallowed hard. The look on Mellie's face still haunted him. Late at night, when he was drifting off to sleep, he'd picture the awfulness of what her last moments of life must have been like. In the middle of the night when a nightmare jerked him awake, he imagined he'd heard her screaming his name. When he was planning an LCR mission, he'd think about how he hadn't been there to save her. About the only time he didn't get hit with those images was when he was on a mission. One of the reasons he stayed busy. Idleness brought the pain to the forefront.

His eyes dropped to his lap where Anna's delicate hand covered his own. He'd been so lost in the memories, he didn't know when she'd done that. A small frozen part of him warmed at her touch.

"She was…gone?"

"Yeah. Had been dead for hours. I don't know how long I sat with her. A rational part of my mind told me I needed to call 911, but I could do nothing but stare at her.

"Finally, I don't know if it was five minutes later or an hour, I called the police. The thought came to me then that I'd never get to hold her again, touch her. I wasn't thinking rationally. Fortunately, I wasn't stupid enough to pick her up, but I did lie beside her, touch her hair, talk to her."

For the first time in forever, tears stung his eyes. Those last few moments with Mellie were the hardest and the sweetest in his memory. He'd said all the things he should have said, all the things he'd always meant to say. All the things he'd never get to say again.

Aidan felt a soft squeeze on his hand and looked down. Anna's hand again, giving him comfort, support…strength to continue.

Drawing in a ragged breath, he said, "Cops found me like that. They dragged me out of the room to examine her, talk to me. Just as I was going to the door, I looked back at her one last time. They were pulling the sheet off her body. She was naked… covered in bruises and bites. Everywhere. It was obvious she'd been raped."

"Oh, Aidan…no."

"I went a little crazy then. Dove toward her. Took three men to pull me out of the room.

"They ended up handcuffing me to keep me from going back to her. They asked questions, I answered them. I was in shock. Wasn't thinking straight. It wasn't until they took me to the station for questioning that I realized they thought I might've done it.

"I agreed to DNA testing. Though I heard one of the detectives mutter that it was probably useless because the bastard had used bleach to clean her up. That was where the disinfectant smell had come from.

"They asked me to take my shirt off. I realized later they wanted to see if I had scratches on me. It was obvious that Mellie had fought hard against her attacker. No way the bastard wasn't bleeding. Once they saw I had no injuries, they loosened up a little, but they still had no other suspects.

"Insane, I know, but it never occurred to me to suspect Simon. When I was able to think straight again, I had the thought that I should call him. Let him know. I thought he'd be almost as devastated as I was.

"My parents were in Europe on vacation. My sister, Jenn, was only eighteen at the time but smart as a whip. And, thankfully, she was thinking rationally. Much more so than me. She called the family attorney. He got in touch with a top criminal defense attorney, who came to my rescue. The police let me go.

"I learned later that the police tried to find Simon, but he was nowhere to be found. They called his dad, who swore he hadn't heard from him.

"That was my first realization that it could have been Simon. I was assuming a break-in. Never once considered it could be someone I knew. A friend. Other than Mellie, my best friend.

"No evidence was left behind. Nothing that could tie anyone to the murder. But with Simon's disappearance, it became obvious to the police who'd done it.

"Took me longer. After a few days of not being able to find him, though, I finally accepted it. By then he was in the wind.

His dad swore…swore till the day he died that he didn't know where his son was. Said Simon had enough money to disappear without his help. He tried to defend Simon. Said the sex was consensual, but it must've got out of hand. That his son would never do something like that.

"I never saw Simon or his father again. His dad tried to contact me from time to time. I always sent back a message that until his son came forward and faced what he did, I didn't want any contact with him. He died a few years back."

"Did you go to the funeral?"

"Yes. Just in case Simon showed up. He didn't."

"What about your residency? You left your medical career behind?"

"I was twenty-three years old and felt like my life was over. I moved back home, to my parents' house. Didn't do anything for months other than try to find Simon. We hired private investigators. Finding him was the only thing I lived for.

"My family was my rock. Don't know what I would have done without them. About six months after it happened, I realized Simon wasn't going to be found. His father swore he didn't know where his son was, but I didn't believe him. Problem was, Dr. Cook had enough money and connections to hide his son forever.

"I knew I needed to get on with my life, but going back to being a doctor had no appeal. I just didn't have any passion for it anymore. I talked to my parents. Even though they didn't want me to, I joined the Army.

"I got a lot tougher, but the anger was still there. When I left the Army, I thought about going back into medicine, but the fire never came back. I worked construction for a while. Working with my hands soothed something inside me. And I started dating again. Nothing serious. Jenn was insistent that I find someone. She wore me down, so I agreed to go out with Kristen, a friend of hers. We only dated a couple of times…just didn't click.

"Then I met Amy. She was the niece of one of my father's friends. She came to a cookout we held for my parents' anniversary. We hit it off. It wasn't crazy love or anything, but we had fun together. We had been dating about three months when I got a frantic call from her. She had been attacked, beaten, and drugged. When she woke, she was naked and had a message carved across her chest. 'Simon says hi.'"

Aidan shook his head. Even after all these years, he still had trouble accepting his naïveté and stupidity. "After that happened, my sister told me that Kristen had been raped a few months before. Jenn said she hadn't mentioned it to me because she thought it would bring back bad memories. The guy was never caught, but she never considered it could have been Simon. Kristen was knocked unconscious…she never saw her rapist."

"Then are you sure it was Simon? Did he leave a message like he did with Amy? Was there any DNA?"

"He used a condom. No DNA was found, but an S was carved into Kristen's chest. The attack happened in Denver. Kristen was visiting her brother at the time. My sister didn't know about the carving. Only about the rape."

"But Amy wasn't raped?"

"No. I don't know why. She was knocked unconscious, too. But she was also drugged. The police thought he might've been scared away before he could rape her. Who knows? Maybe he thought the carving was enough."

"And you blame yourself."

"Of course I blame myself. How can I not? Two women I dated were attacked and cut up. One was raped. All because of me."

"Because of Simon. Not you."

"It doesn't matter. I knew then I could never have another relationship. And that I needed to disappear. My family is always on guard. They have personal protection, twenty-four seven. I don't think Simon would hurt them. That's not the way he wants to hurt me. But I won't take any chances. Not until Simon's no longer a threat.

"I force myself to see them only when we can get away privately."

"What happened to Kristen and Amy?"

"They've both recovered…as best they can. Kristen is married, has a family. And Amy?" He shrugged. "Last I heard, she was married again. Her third marriage. She moves around a lot.

"I can't risk any kind of contact with them. Not that either of them would want to hear from me, I'm sure."

"You've been looking for him all this time. Have there been sightings or leads?"

"No sightings, but I focused most of my search in Colombia. Simon's mother's family is from there. They have money and influence. It makes sense that he would go to them. They've denied that he's contacted them, but I have no reason to believe they're telling the truth."

"That's why you were there, in Cali? You got a lead on him?" She stiffened and twisted toward him. "And I prevented you from—"

Aidan held up his hand. "It doesn't matter. I knew going in it was likely either a hoax or a trap."

"A trap? Aidan, why would you—"

"Because I have to find him, Anna. Don't you see? Until he pays for what he did, I can't let go. Who knows? He could be raping and killing other women, too." Aidan shook his head. "I know in my gut that he's still out there somewhere, just waiting. Hoping I'll have some kind of relationship that he can destroy. I can't take that risk. With anyone."

She didn't respond to that, but her hand squeezed his gently again. He thought it was the sweetest touch she'd ever given him. She didn't protest or deny his statement. She was giving him comfort and support.

"So how did you hook up with LCR?"

He huffed out a humorless laugh. "I was infuriated by what Simon had done to Kristen and Amy. So I did a dumbass thing. I held a news conference and addressed Simon directly. Called him every bleepable name in the book. A coward. A lunatic. A sick, twisted, perverted SOB. I challenged him to come after me."

"You played right into his hands. He got to see you hurting."

A real smile pulled on his mouth. "Exactly what McCall told me. He caught the news conference. Called me, introduced himself. Wanted to know if I'd like to come work for him.

"He'd already done his research, of course. Knew everything about me. I met with him, and that was that."

"And in your spare time, when you're not rescuing kidnapped victims and damsels in distress, you look for Simon."

"Yeah. I'll never stop looking for him."

"What will you do when you find him?"

That question pulled him up, made him think. "I've gone from wanting to tear him to pieces to taking him out to the desert, stripping him naked, and leaving him for the buzzards."

"And now?"

"I want to beat the shit out of him and then put him behind bars so he can never hurt anyone again."

"And then you'll have peace?"

"Yes." He turned to her then, needing her to understand this if she didn't understand anything else. "Remember what you told me before we started up the mountain to rescue Carrie? That you couldn't bear it if anything happened to me? That's the way I feel, Anna. I couldn't bear it if something happened to you. And that's why whatever is happening between us can't happen.

"You understand that, don't you?"

CHAPTER
TWENTY-FIVE

Anna woke the next morning with an ache in her heart she didn't see ever going away. After Aidan's heartbreaking confession, they'd gone back inside the house. While Anna showered, Aidan had gone off to "secure the house." He hadn't told her what that meant, but she figured he needed some time to himself. Dredging up such hideous memories had to have left him both raw and hurting.

Beneath the shower, she'd let her own tears fall. The hurt she felt for him was not only intense to the point of pain, it revealed something she hadn't allowed herself to totally accept. She loved him. The now and forever kind of love. She had been aware that her feelings for him were stronger than any she'd ever felt, but until that moment she hadn't accepted how fierce or powerful they were.

After her shower, she'd walked out of the steamy bathroom to find him standing in the middle of the room. His eyes had held a pain so stark she'd almost started crying again. For once, his expression was easy to read.

Anna sat down on the bed and held out her hand. She had seen the surprise in his eyes. He had been expecting her to turn him away. A small part of her heart that still had an ounce of self-preservation left reminded her how much he could hurt her. She squelched it. This man didn't know it yet, but he already owned her heart. If she could help him, make him hurt less, then she would. Damn the consequences.

He had pulled her to her feet, gathered her in his arms, and held her for several long seconds. Then, as if it was as natural as daybreak, they got into bed. She lay on her side, Aidan pulled her against his chest, molding her against him, spooning her body with his. She had been asleep in seconds.

Several times she had woken in the night, and Aidan had been right beside her, holding her. She wished this could last forever, but she was too much of a realist. Aidan believed he would be putting her in danger by having a relationship with her. Now she knew why he'd been so insistent about staying off the streets in Cali. The helmet and the gosh-awful hat had been to cover her hair. Keeping her head down had been to hide her face.

His biggest fear was having anyone else hurt by the monster who, for reasons only known to Simon Cook, hated Aidan with such intensity.

"Good morning."

Lost in thought, she hadn't seen him appear at the doorway. How long had he been standing there, watching her sift through her feelings? Hiding her thoughts was not her best talent.

She worked up what she hoped was a sunny smile. "Morning."

He came toward her, holding a cup of steaming coffee in his hand.

"If you're bringing me coffee in bed, I'm nominating you for Man of the Year."

He handed it to her. "One sugar, no cream."

She accepted the mug, breathed in the rich, steamy brew, and took an appreciative sip. "You're my hero."

His expression didn't change. He looked serious and still so sad.

"You are, you know. My hero, I mean. Even before you came to my rescue in Colombia, you were. I admire and respect you." And because she desperately wanted to put lightness back into his eyes, if only for a brief moment, she added, "And you're a much better cuddler than Jack."

"Jack?"

"My stuffed pig."

"You have a stuffed pig?"

"Well, a fake stuffed pig. Not a real one because, well, that would be gross."

He gave a rapid headshake as if he couldn't believe he was talking about stuffed pigs. It was silly, yes, but the shadows had disappeared briefly from his eyes, and that was worth a bit of silliness.

"Breakfast is ready. Come out to the balcony when you're ready."

The instant he walked out the door, her shoulders slumped. She had no solution for Aidan's problems. Telling him things would get better would be a lie. How could they? For Aidan, nothing would be resolved until Simon was either dead or in prison. He had moved on as far as he believed he could.

Anna stood, threw off her nightgown, and dressed in another one of Jennifer's dresses. She had been taught that for every problem there was a solution. There had to be something that could be done.

Aidan slid an omelet onto a plate already loaded with hash browns and toast. Taking it and another one, he walked out onto the balcony. Anna would be here soon, and he needed to be prepared for whatever she threw at him. One of the most refreshing things about Anna was her unpredictability. He never knew what she might say or how she would react to a given situation. For a man who'd mired himself in obligation and duty, Anna's somewhat zany statements and antics were a welcome relief.

And now that was about to end.

"Smells wonderful." She scooted into the chair he held out for her. "If you ever leave LCR, you could open your own restaurant."

She took a bite of her omelet and made a moaning sound. She hid a smile as she noted that Aidan looked away briefly and shifted in his chair. Sometimes torture could be fun.

"When we're finished with breakfast, I'm going to explore this house from top to bottom. I can't believe I've been here for two days and I still haven't seen it all."

"We need to talk about that."

"You don't want me exploring the house?"

"Yes. No." He shook his head. "Explore it to your heart's content. That's not what we need to talk about. I've heard from McCall. The danger has passed."

"What do you mean?"

"He talked with Ruiz again. The man's calmed down enough from his grief to acknowledge that you, Carrie, and I were there against our will and had no part in what happened to his daughter."

Anna gave a disgusted snort. "I find it hard to believe he's that upset about his daughter's death since he's the one who sent her to murder who knows how many people, including her husband. He's the one who put her in danger in the first place. What did he think would happen to her if she was discovered?"

"That's something you'd have to ask him." He raised his hand and added, "Not that I intend for you to get within a thousand miles of him."

"He knew exactly what he was sending her into and didn't give a damn," she said. "He's the one who got his daughter killed. No one else."

"I agree. I don't think he's of the same mind, but at least he's decided we didn't have anything to do with Elena's death. And, bottom line, you can go home."

"Home? Not back to Cali?"

"No." He leaned forward, hoping she would take his words the right way. "Just because Ruiz claims he holds no grudges against you and Carrie doesn't mean he doesn't. It would be best if you didn't return. At least until this thing with Garcia and Ruiz settle down."

"*Will* it settle down?"

"Not completely, but at some point it should be less volatile."

"What if I don't want to…go home, that is?"

"I don't want you back in Colombia. I can't protect you if—"

"That's not what I'm saying. What if I want to stay here… with you?"

"Anna." His brow furrowed, and regret filled his eyes. "Sweetheart, I meant what I said last night."

"I know, and I accept that. But that's after we leave here. I don't have to be back at work for another week. Can we take this time, just for us?"

She saw the struggle, guilt warring with want. "And after we leave?"

"No contact. Nothing."

"Why, Anna? Why would you do that?"

If she told him she loved him, he might still agree to let her stay, but his guilt would be magnified. She couldn't do that to him, but neither would she lie.

"Because what we have is too wonderful to end right now. I want to make as many memories as I can." She cocked her head. "Don't you?"

He stared at her for the longest time. It was difficult, but she maintained eye contact. She hadn't lied, and despite his insistence that they could never be together after they left the island, she knew he enjoyed being with her.

Scooting his chair back, he stood and held out his hand.

Anna allowed him to pull her up and into his arms. When she put her arms around his neck, he cupped her butt and lifted, giving her no choice but to wrap her legs around his waist.

"What are you doing?"

He strode toward the door. "Making memories."

Giddy with happiness, she looked over his shoulder. "What about breakfast?"

"I'll make you another. After."

CHAPTER TWENTY-SIX

Bogota, Colombia

Patrick stood before him, the notebook he held in his giant hand looking incongruous. The man was much more comfortable holding a gun or knife.

"A woman, a psychologist named Carrie Easterly, that Ms. Bradford was working with at the clinic, disappeared. We don't know many details. It's become very hush-hush, but rumor is that Thorne and Ms. Bradford set out to find her."

Cook let that information settle within him. Yes, this was definitely something.

"We still don't know where they went, but she hasn't returned to her apartment or gone back to work yet."

"And no sighting of Thorne?"

"No, but that's not unusual."

He waved away Patrick's assertion that Thorne was elusive. While it was true that Cook didn't keep tabs on Thorne's daily activities, it was only because he hadn't put any effort into the matter. Thorne lived in fear, avoided any kind of serious, romantic relationship. The knowledge that Aidan Thorne could never have a normal life had been enough to sustain him through the years.

But recent events had changed his thinking. Fate had stepped in to give him a deadline.

"I have men staked out at her office and her home," Patrick was saying. "We'll know the instant she returns."

Rubbing his jaw contemplatively, Cook considered what he knew of Aidan Thorne. Arrogant. Decisive. Determined. Was this a trap? After all this time of searching and digging to find his adversary, was Thorne trying to draw him out by using the woman as bait? It was a possibility, but it didn't track with Thorne's personality. The man was overprotective to the point of paranoia. Even had bodyguards for his parents, his sister, and her family. If Cook hadn't found it so amusing, he'd be insulted. This vendetta had nothing to do with them. This was between Thorne and Cook.

Or could it be that Thorne no longer believed that danger existed? Had he become complacent? Did he think that the passage of time had absolved his guilt or lessened Simon's pain? If so, Thorne had a monumental surprise headed his way.

"Sir?"

Cook looked up, almost surprised to see Patrick was still standing there, waiting for further instructions.

"The instant Ms. Bradford shows up, alert me. We'll hold back a few days. Monitor her. See what happens."

"Very good, sir."

Cook waited until Patrick had walked out of the room before he allowed himself a smile. Whether Anna Bradford was actually romantically involved with Aidan Thorne or not no longer mattered. He cared about the girl, and that was enough for him.

His final act of revenge against Aidan Thorne would be a spectacular event. One from which the man would never recover.

***

The Caribbean

Aidan dove beneath the rushing wave, relishing the adrenaline rush as the warm water pounded his body. Day six of what they'd taken to calling their island paradise, and he wasn't near ready to give it up. But to keep her safe, he would do that and more. Tomorrow, Anna would return home, and that would be that.

The last few days had been, hands down, the best of his life. He waited to see if that thought brought any guilt and realized it didn't. He had loved Mellie with a young man's passion and an endless optimism. They'd had so much in common, and a deep friendship had turned to love. He had admired her drive, and their shared goals had merged perfectly. There would always be an ache in his heart for her. Not only had she died a horrible, agonizing death at the hands of a man they'd both considered a friend, but she had been so damn young. What she could have accomplished, the lives she could have saved, the beautiful children they could have had together—all gone because of one man's evil.

Now there was Anna. Witty, sassy, a little screwball at times, and so full of life and joy that just to look at her brought a lightness to his heart he'd never experienced before. For the first time in years, he was happy to be alive.

And it would all end tomorrow. He could not and would not take the chance of Simon coming after her. If she stayed with him, could he keep her safe? Yes, but that would mean curtailing her activities. Anna was a free spirit whose love of life and independence made her the amazing woman she was. Would she be willing to give all of that up just to stay with him? Maybe, but he would never ask her to make that sacrifice.

Aidan dove into another giant wave, swam deep, and then burst to the surface. He spotted the small lone figure on the beach and waved. She'd been in the kitchen all morning, claiming he had shown off his culinary talents long enough and now it was her turn.

He swam toward the beach, needing to touch her as much as possible before she left him. That desire became more urgent the closer he came to the shoreline. The agonizing knowledge that in just a few hours he might never touch her again made him swim even faster. The instant he reached solid ground, he started running toward her. Aidan had to give her credit. Though her eyes widened in surprise at his apparent urgency, she stood her ground, waiting for him.

The instant he reached her, he halted suddenly and just took in the whole of her. The sun had lightened her long, brown hair to a dark honey. Her golden skin had the sheen of good health again, and the shadows beneath her eyes had disappeared. She wore a sarong-style dress of blue and white that molded to her curves and fluttered around her long, bare legs. She was a combination of beauty, grace, and incredible sweetness.

The smile she flashed him held a bit of wicked teasing. "In a hurry?"

He touched her then, just a fingertip caress to her silky cheek. "You have no idea."

"Ready to eat?"

He pulled her to him, molding her body against his. "Yes." And then he kissed her, letting her know what he was hungry for.

Disregarding his wet, salty body, Anna stood on her toes and wound her arms around Aidan's neck. She couldn't get enough of him, and Aidan had shown her over and over that he felt the same way. She wanted him wet, dry, clothed, unclothed. Any way she could get him. Always.

His mouth explored hers with both tenderness and greed, his tongue delving and sweeping with unrestrained purpose. They had made love so many times in the last several days that it should be physically impossible for her to want him again. But that was the magic of Aidan Thorne.

As his hands roamed over her body, she felt a loosening of her clothes. She pulled back slightly to suggest that they go inside. The moment she did, her dress dropped to the sand, and she was nude. The dress wasn't made for wearing a bra, and Aidan had shown her over the last few days how irrelevant panties were in his presence.

Aidan took his own step back and let his eyes roam over her, from head to foot. Anna stood before him, not exactly nervous but still a little uncomfortable to be out in the open with no clothes. The look on his face and his hoarse words, "You're beautiful," pushed all shyness from her mind.

His hands cupped both her breasts and lifted them, causing her to shiver beneath the scorching sun. She closed her eyes the moment his mouth clamped down on a nipple. "Aidan," she whispered.

"Want me?"

"Yes."

"Here?"

"Yes."

"Now?"

"Yes."

The firm beach disappeared beneath her feet. Anna opened her eyes to see the world tip over as Aidan scooped her off her feet and laid her on the warm, soft sand. The sun was in her eyes, so she had to squint as she watched him pull off his swim trunks.

He dropped to his knees before her, and Anna touched him, marveling as she always did at the silky, hard smoothness of his erection. "You're so hard."

"A common malady when I'm within a hundred yards of you."

Feeling deliciously free, she smiled and stroked him. "I have the cure for that."

"Yes, you most certainly do."

Taking the hand that held him, he kissed her palm and lay beside her. "Do you know how special you are?"

"In what way?"

"In every way. From your sassy, sexy mouth to your generous soul. From your tender heart to your courageous spirit."

"Anything else?"

"Yes. You have beautiful eyes, gorgeous hair, the most tempting mouth, and a lovely neck." His gaze dropped lower. "Your breasts make my mouth water. Your skin is like a soft, fragrant rose. Your legs make my fantasies go wild, imagining them wrapped around me. Your ass is—"

She pressed her fingers to his mouth. "Okay. Okay. You like my body."

"The word like is too lukewarm. And you didn't let me finish. Your ass is firm, round, and makes me want to bite it." His hand glided down her stomach and stopped at her mound. "And your—"

Blushing outrageously, she said quickly, "I have plenty of flaws, you know."

He gave her a mock look of astonishment. "Dare you to name one."

"I have a voracious appetite."

"Oh yeah?" His mouth hovered over hers. "For what?"

"Ice cream, of course."

He kissed her smiling mouth, and once again Anna became lost in the glory of Aidan Thorne's lovemaking.

He stopped abruptly and raised his head. "What about brunch?"

"Brunch smunch."

He sat up. "You've worked too hard to spoil it."

"Aidan Thorne, if you don't finish what you started, I—"

His eyes glittered with laughter. "You'll what?"

"I'll…I'll…" Her mind was blank.

"Well, when you put it like that." He leaned back over her and, still smiling, kissed her, and Anna was once again lost in the lush, sensual world that only Aidan could create. No one had ever made her feel so wanted, admired, and, yes, loved, as much as this man.

Her hands eagerly touching him wherever she could reach, she gasped and arched her body when his tongue trailed from her mouth, to her neck, and between her breasts. How could she be so hot and shivering at the same time?

He lifted his head. His eyes glittered with a hot, wild desperation she hadn't seen in them before. "Tell me you want me, Anna."

"I want you, Aidan." Unable to stop herself, she added, "Always."

He looked at her then, touching her with only his eyes. His gaze moved down her body. Heat suffused her as if he caressed her everywhere.

After what felt like an eternity, he finally touched her, his hand settling at the apex of her thighs.

"Open for me, baby."

Refusing never entered her mind. Her legs moved apart.

Anna's heart thundered against her chest as Aidan's hand moved gently over her, caressing. When one finger touched the top of her sex, she groaned, breathless. And when he penetrated her, she gasped and arched upward, seeking more of him. He obliged. One finger, then two, slid easily into her. Rubbing, teasing, arousing.

"Aidan...please."

"I want to watch you, Anna. Want to see your face. Will you let me?"

Unable to articulate any coherent words, Anna could only give him what he wanted. Spiraling out of control, throbbing... needing, wanting, reaching for completion, the desire to get there a living thing. She never wanted it to end—this wild, untamed insanity.

"Keep your eyes on me, sweetheart."

Not realizing she'd closed them, she fluttered them open again. His expression both fierce and hot, he locked his gaze with hers. And then he gave her the most amazing, beautiful smile. Suddenly, she was soaring, reaching heights she'd never dreamed possible.

Giving her no time for recovery, Aidan eased his big body between her sprawled legs, lifted her hips, and plunged to the hilt inside her. Still reeling from ecstasy, Anna wrapped her legs around his hips and gave him everything. This man, her hero, her love.

CHAPTER
TWENTY-SEVEN

The rest of the afternoon passed in delicious splendor. After taking a shower together where things got so heated the hot water ran out long before they exited the stall, they dried off, threw clothes on, and headed down to the kitchen. The quiche was cold but easily heated in the microwave. The dish wasn't nearly as good as many of Aidan's had been, but she was pleased that he ate three slices and drank two glasses of an orange juice cocktail she had concocted.

After their meal, they quickly cleaned up and then spent most of the afternoon swimming in the pool. It was early evening, when they were walking along the beach and watching the sun settle into the horizon, that things went south.

"I've been thinking," Anna said.

"About what?"

"Have you thought about setting up a sting to trap Simon? I'm sure Noah would help."

"Yeah, McCall has offered to help numerous times."

She stopped walking to frown up at him. "LCR people train to catch the most vile criminals in the world. Why wouldn't you enlist their help?"

"The only thing that motivates Simon is hurting me by hurting a woman I'm involved with. That means putting someone at risk. I'm not willing to put another woman in danger."

"You don't think a female LCR operative could handle it?"

"Of course she could. That's not the point. I can't—"

"But that's exactly the point. Either you don't have a lot of faith in female LCR operatives, which I know isn't true, or—"

"Or what?"

Though blunt honesty wasn't necessarily something she avoided, Anna heard a small, cautious voice telling her this might not be the best time to give her opinion. She ignored the voice and spoke her mind.

"Or you're not totally committed to capturing Simon."

"Like hell I'm not. I've spent over a decade looking for that son of a bitch."

"And yet you're no closer to finding him than you were the first day you started looking."

"You know nothing about this, Anna, other than what I've told you. Judging me based on—"

"I'm not judging you, Aidan. I'm just saying that—" She stopped, frustrated with the way this conversation was going. She had him on the defensive, and that wasn't what she wanted.

"What's the saying? The definition of insanity is doing the same thing over and over again and expecting a different result."

"And that's bullshit. A blanket statement, and it doesn't cover all the things I've done to find the bastard. I've done everything I can."

"Everything but the one thing that might work."

"Stop it, Anna."

"I know you don't want anyone else hurt. I understand that, but—"

"But nothing. You didn't see them. What he did to Mellie... The horror he put Kristen and Amy through. You didn't see what he did to them. You weren't the one that had to explain to them why they'd been attacked. You didn't have to see the censure and hatred on their parents' faces when they realized that their daughters were targeted by a madman because they'd had the bad judgment of going out with me.

"So don't you damn well tell me what I should and should not do."

His voice had risen to a near shout by the time he was through.

She had hurt them both by stating her opinion, but she wouldn't apologize. Going for broke, she said calmly, "No, I didn't see your wife's body. I didn't see what he did to Kristen or Amy. And I didn't have to explain anything to them or their families. But think about this, Aidan. Is your guilt allowing Simon to win?"

"What the hell's that supposed to mean?"

"That maybe because of everything that's happened...the guilt you feel, you don't believe you deserve happiness. And that's exactly what Simon wants."

His eyes went hard as steel. "You think I'm not doing everything I can to bring Simon in because I feel guilty? That makes no sense. If anything, my guilt motivates me. Stop trying to psychoanalyze me, Anna. I'm not a traumatized child."

No, he wasn't a child, but he had been traumatized. She had learned a long time ago that telling anyone what their problems were didn't help. Just because she saw the issue clearly didn't mean Aidan would. He would have to come to that realization on his own, but maybe she had planted a small seed in his mind.

"I think I'll head back to the house and pack."

It was a deliberate statement on her part. Even though she was slightly ashamed to learn that she wasn't above a little emotional manipulation, she hoped the reminder that she was leaving would penetrate his defenses.

When he just nodded and turned away to look out at the ocean, she knew she'd gotten her answer. It wasn't the one she'd hoped for.

Feeling like shit, Aidan watched a crestfallen Anna walk down the beach, away from him. He had hurt her feelings, but there was nothing he could do about that. Her words had been like a knife to a long-festering sore. Images of Mellie flashed in his head. He might've known her for only a short time but they'd made thousands of wonderful memories together. Yet it was that last brutal image of her that stayed with him and wouldn't let him go.

Combined with that were the faces of Kristen and Amy. Women who'd had no idea they snagged the attention of a sociopath simply by being seen with Aidan Thorne. Their lives had been almost destroyed, their sense of safety gone forever.

How the hell was he supposed to get past that?

His cellphone buzzed in his pocket. He checked the screen and frowned. "Dad? Everything okay?"

"Everything's fine with us, son. What about you?"

"What do you mean?"

"I thought you might need to talk."

Coming from anyone else, that might've sounded strange, but Eric Thorne had a sixth sense when it came to his children. He always had. When either Aidan or his sister, Jenn, was hurting, they could almost always expect to hear from their father. His dad claimed it was just the deep love for his children that made him hyperaware, but Aidan wasn't so sure. Whatever it was, Aidan had been the beneficiary of that sensitivity all his life.

"It's been a difficult few days."

"Can you talk about it?"

Another reason he loved his parents was the unending trust they placed in their children.

"Can't say much about it. I—" For the first time since Mellie, Aidan found himself wanting to tell his dad about a woman. He wanted to tell him about how sweet, sassy, and funny Anna was. About how courageous she'd been and how she made him laugh.

"Son, you there?"

Though he trusted his dad implicitly, he had an ironclad rule about sharing anything related to LCR. Also, no one, not even his parents, could know about his feelings for Anna. The only way to keep her safe was to never talk about her. Ever. "Yeah, I'm here. Sorry, but no. Can't really talk about it."

"I understand."

"How're Mom, Jenn, Brent, and the kids doing?"

"Everyone's doing great." His father launched into several minutes of talking about how amazing his grandchildren were. It was expected. One of the many reasons his dad was such a great pediatrician was his deep love and affinity for children. He had the kind of personality that put children at ease.

"I hear your mother headed this way, so I'd better get off here. If I don't, she'll take the phone and insist on knowing what's going on. You'll tell us when you can, son. Right?"

"Yeah. I promise. Love you both. And thanks for the call."

"Love you, too, son."

Aidan slid the phone back into his pocket and continued to stare at the ocean as if there were answers out there. Problem was, he knew what the answers were, he just didn't like them. Not one damn bit.

Anna sat on the porch steps and waited until well after dark for Aidan to return to the house. She had stuck her foot in it and now couldn't figure out a way to make things right. He hadn't been ready to hear what she'd told him. Admittedly she sometimes opened her mouth without thinking, but she was usually very careful when it came to offering commentary or opinions unless she was invited to do so. And even then, she treaded carefully. People who were hurting often had triggers that even they didn't know about until they were set off.

Had she done that to Aidan?

Why couldn't she have kept her mouth shut? Mixing personal feelings with psychoanalysis was something she'd learned in her first psych class not to do. And this was more than just personal feelings. She had a vested interest in the outcome. How selfish she'd been.

When she at last spotted Aidan at a distance, headed toward the house, she breathed her first easy breath in hours. To know that he'd walked the beach, alone and hurting, because of her made her already aching heart feel as though it was bleeding.

As he drew closer, Anna struggled with what she wanted to say versus what she needed to say. She would wait, gauge his mood, and then speak. The instant she saw his blank expression, she knew whatever she said wouldn't fix things.

"I didn't know if you would be hungry. I made chicken salad. I can make you a sandwich, if you like."

"Thanks. Not hungry."

No longer able to hold it inside, she burst out, "Aidan, I'm sorry. I never should have said what I said."

"You're entitled to your opinion, Anna."

"It's not my opinion. I just—" She stopped. She was going back down the road she shouldn't have traveled in the first place.

"I know you're hurting, Anna, and I'm sorry. I never wanted to hurt you. That's why—"

"Wait. You think I said what I did because you hurt me? That's absolutely not true. I said it because you're hurting. I care about you and can't bear to see what your guilt is doing to you. I—"

"Drop it. Okay?"

More miserable now than she had been before, Anna nodded.

"I'm going to take a shower."

Only hours earlier, they'd showered together, laughing and loving each other until they were both breathless. The invitation for her to join him didn't come.

She allowed herself to absorb the hurt. What did she expect? He made it clear to her from the beginning that they had no future together. She knew she sometimes found herself on the unrealistic side of optimism, but even she should have seen the handwriting on the wall. Changing Aidan's mind after all these years was a fool's endeavor.

Anna didn't know how long she stayed there, staring into the dark, listening to the waves rush to the shore. Going inside where Aidan would likely ignore her again held no appeal.

When at last she could no longer see her hand in front of her face, she walked up the steps and into the house. There was only silence. The place already felt empty.

Hating that their last night together had turned into a monumental letdown, she went to the bedroom. Aidan had already told her a boat would be here to pick her up just past dawn. She doubted she'd sleep much, still she needed to at least try.

She halted at the door. Aidan stood in the middle of the bedroom. She couldn't tell if he'd been waiting for her or not. His expression was still just as blank as before, but she also saw the pain in his eyes.

"If you want, I'll sleep in the other bedroom tonight."

"No. Don't go," she whispered.

"Why? After I hurt you like that, why would you want me to stay?"

Oh, there were many answers to that question, and if she answered with what was in her heart, she would hurt him even more.

"Because you're hurting, too."

"It would be selfish of me."

"No, it wouldn't." She held out her hand to him. "Friends don't need a reason to give comfort, Aidan. They give it because they care."

"So you would sleep with a friend to make him feel better?"

She scrunched her nose. "It depends on which friend."

His conscience had no chance to win over something he wanted so much. Making what might have been the most selfish move of his life, Aidan took Anna's hand and led her to the bed. He wanted to take his time with her, savor every precious moment. That thought disappeared with the first button. The instant it came undone, he tugged hard until the others popped open, a few pinging against the hardwood floor.

She laughed softly. "Impatient?"

"You have no idea."

"Oh, I think I do." And with those words, her fingers went to his shirt, and she did the most agonizing thing of all. She unbuttoned each button with a slow deliberateness that had him groaning in frustration.

"Dammit, Anna. I want you."

"And you'll have me, Aidan. Soon. Very soon."

The smug, sexy smile teasing at her lips made him growl out a pain-filled laugh.

"You have a bit of sadism in you, sweet Anna?"

"No. I just know that good things come to those who wait."

"If that's a promise…" Willing his famous self-control to hold out, he gritted out the last few words. "Do your worst, then."

One more button came undone. "Oh no. You get only my best."

"You're killing me here, Bradford."

"Step out of your shoes."

He toed off his shoes, saying, "You do the same."

She stepped back. A beautiful siren. Hair slightly tousled, face flushed, teasing eyes gleaming with heat and excitement, pouty, smiling lips that looked like they'd already been kissed. Her blouse was ripped and hung haphazardly off one shoulder.

She slipped out of her shoes and reached for him again. He stepped out of her reach. Two could play this game.

"Slide your skirt off."

The smile grew wider as she apparently thought he was going to go along with her agonizingly slow seduction.

She slid the short skirt down her long legs and let it drop to the floor.

"Now, everything else."

"You, too."

Their eyes locked on each other as both shed their remaining clothes.

Still holding on to that smug, seductive smile, she said, "And now let's go even slower."

Grabbing her by the waist, he growled, "Like hell," and threw her onto the bed.

"Aidan!"

Coming over her, he slammed his mouth over hers and showed her exactly what she'd done to him. Devouring kisses gloried in her sweetness. His tongue thrusting deep over and over, Aidan took everything she offered and gave everything of himself in return.

Heat consumed her. Aidan's mouth was everywhere at once, licking, kissing, giving her unimaginable pleasure. They rolled around the bed, laughing, kissing, groaning, nibbling. Giving, taking, they made love like they had never made love before. Even in her sensual haze, Anna recognized the desperation in every movement, every groan. Even as a small silent part of her sobbed in denial, she refused to give in to the despair. She was in Aidan's arms, and she would relish every single second for as long as she could.

When at last the hot, male part of him slid deeply into her, she sobbed his name, in acceptance, in need, and in love. Heat spiraled out of control as she zoomed toward ecstasy and was flung among the stars. Seconds later, Aidan joined her, and they flew through the stars together.

He pulled away and dropped down beside her. Anna snuggled into his arms and held on tight.

Just as she was drifting off to sleep, Aidan said, "Anna?"

"Hmm?"

"Promise me you'll never give comfort like that to another friend."

And even though they both knew he had no right to ask for any such promise, she gave it easily. "I promise."

She fell asleep dreaming of things that might never be.

Aidan lay against the pillows. Though his eyes were closed, he had been awake for hours. He had heard Anna leave the bed. Had heard several broken sighs as she dressed and knew she was on the verge of tears. And he had felt her soft, sweet lips kiss his forehead and whisper goodbye. He hadn't planned on saying anything to her. No matter what he said, it would hurt her. He had planned to keep his big mouth shut and let her slip out of his life.

But at the last minute, just as he knew she was about to walk out the door, he opened his eyes, and said, "Anna?"

"Yes?" She halted at the door. She didn't turn around. He was glad for that because he greatly feared if he saw her face, he'd jump out of bed and never let her go.

"Thank you for spending this time here with me."

Her hand on the doorframe tightened noticeably at his words. "I would've spent the rest of my life with you, Aidan, if only you had asked."

The words slashed at him, more devastating than a machete.

She stood for maybe three seconds more, most likely waiting for a response. Since he couldn't give her one that wouldn't hurt her even more, he stayed silent.

She gave one last shaky sigh and walked out the door.

The instant the front door slammed shut, Aidan sprang out of bed and went to the front of the house. Standing at the window, he watched Anna walk down to the pier, where the boat waited. The instant Nico, the driver, spotted her, he jumped out of the boat and headed toward her. They exchanged a few words, and then he took her backpack from her hand and went back to the boat.

Anna turned and looked up at the house. Aidan knew she couldn't see him, but he still felt as if those soft brown eyes were penetrating right through to his soul.

I would've spent the rest of my life with you, Aidan, if only you had asked.

He shifted his gaze slightly, stared at the doorknob. All he needed to do was turn it, open the door, and call out her name. In his mind's eye, he pictured the scene. She would come running toward him with that breathtaking, sunny smile that lightened everything within him. He would hold out his arms, and she would throw herself into them with happy exuberance. He would tell her what was in his heart. That he wanted to spend the rest of his life with her, see her smile, hear her opinion on the variety of topics that interested her, and hold her in his arms every single night for the rest of his life.

His hand actually reached toward the door, and then Mellie's dull, lifeless image flashed in his mind, followed by Anna's face superimposed over his dead wife's. No. Oh hell no. He would not be so damn selfish.

Backing away, he didn't see how long she stood there. He couldn't watch her anymore. But what he could do was what he'd put off doing. He was damn well going to go after Simon Cook with everything that was in him. He would destroy the bastard once and for all. Then, and only then, he would go after what his heart, body, and soul longed for.

Aidan refused to give thought to the question of whether she would be waiting for him.

CHAPTER TWENTY-EIGHT

Phoenix, Arizona

Patrick sat in a small diner about half a block from Anna Bradford's apartment. He could easily see the complex from here. He knew she had arrived home in a taxi about an hour ago. He also knew she drove a seven-year-old white Jeep Wrangler, which would be easy enough to spot if she left the complex.

He tapped a speed-dial number for Simon Cook, then held the phone to his ear. There was no need to waste time on greetings. The instant his employer answered, Patrick said, "She's home."

"Excellent. Any sign of Thorne?"

"None."

"How did she arrive?"

"Taxi. My sources haven't determined how she traveled back to Phoenix. Nor do we know where she's been. No commercial airline or train itinerary lists her as a passenger. It's like she disappeared and then reappeared out of thin air."

"Thorne's doing, no doubt," Cook said.

Not sure he agreed but having no evidence to the contrary, Patrick grunted. "Could be."

"They've been together this whole time. I feel it in my bones."

The man's obsession with Aidan Thorne was understandable. Grief could have taken over Cook's soul, but he'd channeled it into vengeance, which in Patrick's estimation was much more productive.

"Keep her in your sights at all times, day and night. Let's see how Thorne plays this. See if he's finally willing to premiere his little psychologist to the world as his woman. Or if this was just a little light flirtation."

"And if it's nothing serious?"

"Doesn't matter. But knowing as much as we can will determine how we play the game. Either way, I'm looking forward to becoming acquainted with Ms. Bradford very soon."

Bogota, Colombia

After the call ended, Cook took a moment to consider his next steps. Truth was, he was tired in his heart and in his soul. Hanging on to hatred for so long was wearying.

Aidan Thorne had not had the life he'd envisioned. He had suffered. His family had suffered. That wasn't the revenge he wanted, but that, along with Thorne's eventual death, was what he had been willing to accept as his final vengeance.

But now a lovely young lady had caught Thorne's fancy. Once again, Cook couldn't help but believe that fate was giving him this final chance. It wouldn't fix what couldn't be fixed, but it was as close as he was going to get. It would be enough.

Taking a key from his pocket, he unlocked a door and stepped into a secret room. Only a few were allowed inside this peaceful sanctum. The temperature was necessarily cool. He stopped a second and pulled on the sweater hanging from a peg. He crossed his arms around himself, waiting for the sweater to do its job. Each time he came in here, the temperature seemed cooler than the day before. He knew that wasn't the case. The temperature was set by him. No one else had access to the controls.

He nodded at the woman in the corner. She sat in a rocker, and as he had insisted, there were no magazines, books, or television to distract her from her duties. Soft, soothing music was piped into the room to create an atmosphere of tranquil peace.

"You wish for me to leave?" Her voice was brusque and businesslike. Hildegard VanHousen was as no-nonsense as her name implied.

"No. I won't be here long."

The only acknowledgment was a slight blink of her eyes. She wasn't a talker—another point in her favor.

The woman he'd hired before this one had had a tendency to prattle on about inconsequential subjects. He'd no interest in her personal life or her opinion on anything. But she had been competent, and he'd snapped at her enough that she had eventually learned her ramblings were not welcomed. When he had caught her sneaking a book in to read, he'd fired her on the spot.

Feeling unaccountably sad, Cook didn't stay long. He stopped at the door and shrugged off the sweater. The cool air hitting him once again, he shivered. Just as he turned the knob to leave, he looked back into the room, whispered, "Soon," and then walked out the door.

***

Phoenix, Arizona

Returning to the real world was a harsh, unwelcome clash to Anna's senses. Having lived in paradise, how did one return to the mundane without some kind of culture shock?

As a psychologist, she knew it was normal to have a few adjustment glitches. What she had gone through in Colombia—facing death more than once, seeing a woman killed before her eyes—was enough to cause anyone to suffer a brief period of melancholy.

As a woman who had given her heart to a man who saw no future for them, it was a little more difficult than a textbook case of brief disorientation. Anna was grieving and hadn't come to terms with how to deal with it.

The instant she'd walked into her apartment, sadness had swamped her. Nothing pleased her. Telling herself that she needed to jump back into the swing of things hadn't helped either. She had gone to the grocery store and bought all of her favorite foods, hoping that comfort food would ease her discomfort. When she'd eaten only a half bowl of her favorite ice cream before throwing it down the sink, she'd known she would have to do something more drastic.

If moving on meant recovery, then she was going to do it in a big way. First, she would tackle the basics. Her apartment didn't please her. She walked from room to room, judging, assessing. After the charm and beauty of the island house, her apartment had all the appeal and imagination of a chain-hotel room. She had never really given it much thought. Traveling as much as she did, she hadn't felt that she was missing out on anything. But now she wanted something more, something different.

She was rational enough to recognize she was compensating for what she couldn't have, but for right now, that was all right with her. She would concentrate on finding another place, maybe even a small house. She would decorate it, pour all her energy into it, and that way, when she came home from a trip, she would actually be coming *home*.

Early evening came, and even though she'd bought plenty of food at the grocery store, she had no desire to cook for just one. She called out for a pizza.

After that, she had nothing to do but wait on the pizza delivery and make the calls she had been putting off. Her mom was the first one.

"Anna, darling. Tell me everything about your trip. Did you eat well?"

"Yes, Mom."

"And you took all your vitamins?"

She scrunched her nose. "Not all of them, but some."

"You have to keep your immune system healthy, Anna."

"I know that, Mom, but I feel perfectly fine." With the exception of a broken heart, but that wasn't something she planned to get into with her mother.

"Have you talked with your father yet?"

"No, you're the first person I called."

"I think he's dating that bimbo again."

Even though she didn't want to have this same old tired conversation, it was better than having her mother ask questions about her love life. So Anna settled back, said a lot of "uh-huhs" and "reallys," which was usually all her mother required when she went on a rant about Anna's father.

What was Aidan doing now? Had he gone straight back to Virginia, or had he been called in for a mission? Even now, while she was sitting in her quiet, safe apartment, he could be anywhere in the world, heading into danger to rescue someone.

What if something happened to him? The thought that she wouldn't know until Riley or maybe Noah called and told her slashed at her, adding another pain to her already aching heart. She wasn't his wife, significant other, or even, as far as anyone knew, a friend. In the opinion of the entire world, she and Aidan Thorne barely knew each other. That was the way Aidan wanted it. He believed she was better off, safer, if no one knew of their brief association.

"But enough about your faithless father. Did you meet anyone on your trip?"

Anna jerked at the question. "What do you mean? I met a lot of people."

"You know what I mean, Annabelle Bradford. Did you perhaps meet a young, gorgeous doctor who swept you off your feet? Maybe one who'd be interested in giving me some grandchildren?"

Tears sprang to her eyes before she could stop them. How could she tell her mother that she had indeed met a young, gorgeous doctor who had swept her off her feet? She couldn't, because that would also involve explaining that he had no intention of having anything else to do with her, especially nothing that involved giving her mother grandchildren.

She swallowed past the tears and said, "No. No one like that." And then because she felt guilty for lying, she said, "How about I come down on Friday, and we can have a girls' weekend?"

"That sounds lovely, sweetie. I'll make us appointments at the spa."

"Sounds perfect, Mom. I'd better go. I need to call Daddy before it gets too late. You know how he likes to go to bed early on weeknights."

"All right, darling. I'll see you Friday."

Anna got her father's voice mail and knew it was already too late. Her father often went to bed by seven on weeknights so he could get up before dawn. It was one of the many things about him that had driven her mother crazy.

She was about to call Riley when her doorbell rang. Her pizza had arrived. Grabbing cash from her wallet, she opened the door and jerked to a stop. Riley Ingram stood before her, pizza box in one hand, a half gallon of Anna's favorite ice cream in the other.

"I hijacked the pizza guy."

The volatile emotions she'd been holding back all day crashed down around her. Without a word, Riley walked into the apartment, dropped the pizza and ice cream on the hall table, and held out her arms. With a sob, Anna went into them.

CHAPTER TWENTY-NINE

LCR Headquarters
Alexandria, Virginia

Aidan stood in front of McCall's desk, unable to sit down. He needed to get this done before he changed his mind.

"You're sure you want to do this?"

Hell no, he wasn't sure. If this thing went sideways, he was screwed, and whoever else was working with him would be, too. He had no problem putting his own life on the line, but he damn well wasn't comfortable putting anyone else in danger.

But as much as he didn't want to admit it, Anna had been right. One of the reasons he hadn't agreed to McCall's offer years ago was because of his guilt. Over Mellie, as well as Kristen and Amy. He would always see Mellie's death as his fault. He had brought Simon into her life. And he had inadvertently brought Simon into Kristen's and Amy's lives. But punishing himself would never bring Mellie back. Would never erase what Kristen and Amy had suffered. There was only one thing left to give all of them, and that was justice.

"I've used every other avenue to find him. This is my last option."

"We've discussed this several times before, and you've always turned down the offer." A glimmer entered McCall's eyes. "Any reason you've suddenly changed your mind?"

He and McCall had always been brutally honest with each other and, because of that, had butted heads on more than one occasion. Neither liked to prevaricate or play games.

"Mellie deserves justice. So do Kristen and Amy."

"Yes, they certainly do."

"You want me to admit it's because of Anna? Very well, yes. She's a big part of it."

"The only admission I'm hoping for is that you've finally accepted that you deserve to have a life. One that includes happiness. You've denied yourself too long."

"Not nearly as long as Mellie was denied it."

"That's the guilt talking, Thorne. Regret and guilt have motivated you to do some damn phenomenal things. You've saved a lot of lives. But if you let that guilt destroy you in the process, the evil wins. And Simon Cook wins."

Anna had said the same thing. His gut told him hers and McCall's words were right. Knowing it and living it were two separate issues, though.

Needing to move forward, Aidan said, "As much as I'd like to get this done quickly, that can't happen and look authentic. Simon's a sadistic bastard, but he's not a fool."

"Agreed." McCall tilted his head toward the chair Aidan was standing beside. "Take a seat, and let's start planning."

***

Phoenix, Arizona

"Feel better?" Riley asked.

They sat on the floor across from each other, an empty pizza box on the coffee table between them. A ten-minute crying jag had done wonders for Anna's appetite. Now if she could only find an easy cure for a broken heart.

"Much. Thank you." Anna picked up a piece of leftover pizza crust from her plate and crumbled it. "How'd you know I needed you?"

"How do you think?"

"Aidan." She'd known the moment she'd seen her friend at the door that once again Aidan was trying to take care of her. He knew she would need comfort.

"He called me right after you left the island."

"What did he say?"

"Just that you might need a friend."

Her mouth twisted. Aidan knew how much she was hurting. Since he couldn't comfort her, he had sent Riley in his stead. How weird to be both angry and grateful that he had thought to do this.

"Thank you for coming. He was right. You weren't on a job, were you?"

"No. After we returned from Colombia, we took a couple days off."

"I know Carrie's back home, no one else died, and Julio Garcia is on the mend. Did anything else happen?"

"Not that I know of. I understand Ruiz and Garcia are still at war with each other."

Anna shivered. "It's hard to know who to root for."

"Neither, from what I can tell. Both families are responsible for multiple murders. Not to mention the death and destruction they've caused by trafficking drugs."

And their homebase was the area that Aidan went to frequently in hopes of finding the elusive Simon Cook. As an LCR operative, he was in constant danger when he was on the job, but Aidan put himself at additional risk by searching for his wife's killer.

"So you want to talk about it? Aidan wouldn't tell anyone where he took you. I'm assuming he stayed with you, wherever it was."

"He took me to the island. And yes, he did stay."

"It's beautiful, isn't it?"

"Paradise. Just like you described."

Riley gave her a sympathetic smile. "And you fell more in love with him than you already were."

No use trying to deny her feelings. Riley had seen through her protestations long ago and had been kind enough not to call Anna out on them. Besides, denying her feelings for Aidan went against everything within her.

"More than I thought possible."

"I won't ask you why you say that with such sadness. It's obvious something went wrong. Just know I'm here for you."

Anna reached across the table and squeezed her friend's hand. "Thank you. Actually, nothing went wrong. Not really. Aidan was upfront with me from the very beginning that once we left the island, it was over."

Temper flared in Riley's eyes. "What an arrogant asshole."

"No, no. It wasn't like that. I was the one who initiated things."

She blushed as she thought about that statement. While it was true that she had asked him to make love to her, days before that he'd shown her more than once how attracted he was to her. If not for that, she never would have had the courage to ask him.

"Did he tell you why you couldn't have a relationship?"

Aidan hadn't asked her not to talk about what had happened to him, but she didn't feel comfortable sharing the information even with her best friend. It was Aidan's story to tell.

"Yes. I won't say more, other than he feels he'd be putting me in danger if we see each other in the real world."

Riley's eyes narrowed with concern. "What kind of danger?"

"Someone hates him enough to go after any woman he cares about."

"He knows who this person is?"

"Yes, but he can't find him."

"Is LCR working on helping find him? He's got to know that Noah would bend over backward to help any of his employees any way he could."

Riley would know this better than anyone. Not only had Noah rescued her years ago and helped her create a new life for herself, he and LCR had finally been able to find and destroy the people who'd almost destroyed her.

"He knows that. He just…" Anna had no explanation, really, for why Aidan wouldn't let LCR do more. He had explained his reasons, but she knew in her gut it was more than his worry of allowing another person to be put at risk. The guilt he still felt over his wife's death, along with the other women Simon had attacked, wouldn't let him find peace.

"He just what?"

"I can't say more without giving you details I'm not sure he'd feel comfortable with me telling." She drew in a breath and said, "Enough about me. What about you? Have you and Justin found a house yet?"

A pink flush colored Riley's creamy complexion, but all she said was, "We've narrowed it down to three houses. We both want a house with some history—one that housed a happy family."

"Just like you guys will have someday."

Riley's blush deepened to a dark, pink rose.

"Oh my gosh. Are you pregnant?"

"What? Good heavens, no!"

"Then what's all the blushing for?"

Riley covered her cheeks with her hands. "It's just super warm in here, don't you think?"

"No, I don't think." She took her friend's hand again. "Spill it, Ingram."

Surprising her, Riley pulled her hand away and reached inside her blouse. She came out with a chain holding a gorgeous diamond engagement ring.

Anna squealed with glee. "Oh my gosh! It's beautiful, Riley! But why aren't you wearing it? And why didn't you tell me immediately?"

"I just—"

"No, no, no. Don't tell me you didn't because of Aidan. Don't do that. Sharing your happiness makes me happy." She jumped up and ran around the table to hug her friend hard. "I am ecstatic for you both. No one deserves happiness more."

Riley's blue eyes gleamed like sapphires. "I didn't even know he was going to ask. I mean…we'd talked about it, but in a one-of-these-days kind of conversations."

Anna pulled Riley to the sofa and sat beside her. "Tell me everything. Was it totally romantic? Did he get on one knee? Was there music? Flowers? Angels singing?"

Riley snorted out a laugh, and then her face went beet red. "Not exactly."

"Well, then, what?"

"We were, uh…you know. And he…well. And then I…I…"

Anna burst out laughing. "That's the most inarticulate sentence I've ever heard you say. Let me see if I've got this right. You and Justin were making wild passionate love when in the midst of that all-consuming passion, he popped the question. And you, Riley Ingram, besieged with ecstasy, overcome with desire, screamed out yes."

"Umm…something like that."

Anna nodded her approval. "Down-on-his-knees, hearts-and-flowers proposals are vastly overrated."

"To be fair, he was on his knees at the time. And I—"

Anna held out her hand. "Okay, too much information. Let's save the TMI for when we're on our second glass of wine or something."

"The flowers and music came the next night, with the ring. And the next night, we went to see his parents, who flew into town just to meet me."

"Wow, you have been busy. How did it go? Did they love you?"

"They were wonderful. It's easy to see why Justin is so kind and good. His mom and dad are so down-to-earth. They both hugged me and cried."

"I am so happy for you, Riley. Have you guys discussed a date?"

"We're thinking about November, as close as we can get to Thanksgiving without interfering with anyone's plans. Neither of us want anything elaborate or large. His family will be there and, of course, my LCR family. And you.

"Speaking of that..." Riley's expression went uncertain, almost shy. "Will you be my maid of honor?"

Happiness misted Anna's eyes. "It would be my honor."

CHAPTER THIRTY

Lake George, New York

Aidan maneuvered around a tree branch that had fallen across half of the road. He remembered a weather report from a couple of weeks ago had mentioned a severe thunderstorm had moved through the area. He was glad he'd come a day early. That would give him time to cut down some dead limbs and clear away the debris.

When he'd called his parents and suggested a get-together for this weekend, they had known something major was up. For the past couple of years, this place was where he and his family came for holidays and the occasional family meeting. Aidan had missed the last few and had never once initiated a meeting.

He'd heard the excitement in their voices. He hadn't given them any details because he didn't want to quell their hopefulness. He had no real clue if this plan would work. Either way, he wouldn't go forward without their knowledge and cooperation.

Aidan pulled up in front of the large two-story structure. Built more than thirty years ago, the house had gone through a half-dozen renovations before his parents had purchased it eight years ago. The place had been in sad shape, but his mother and sister, along with a team of architects and decorators, had practically rebuilt it. This house, more so than the beach house, had held the happiest memories for him. But now that wasn't the case. Hands down, his time with Anna at the beach house was the best time he'd ever had.

Anna had given him light he hadn't anticipated or asked for, but he found himself wanting it with every fiber and cell within him. The few days he'd been able to bask in that light had given him a happiness he hadn't felt in more than a decade. Maybe had never felt before. He wanted more. He wanted her for all time.

Until this was over, he had ensured Anna's safety. The Faulkner Agency, the private investigation agency he'd hired a couple of years back to watch over his family, would see to that. He'd made the call to them while Anna was still at the beach house. He had no reason to believe that Simon knew anything about Anna, but neither would he take the chance. When he implemented his plans, the danger would be heightened for everyone he loved. And that included Anna.

He wished he could call and check on her but refused to give in to temptation. He had no guarantee this would work. Letting her know about it would be selfish. If this plan to capture Simon was successful, Aidan would go to her, free for the first time in more than a decade. He didn't even mind the world-class groveling he would have to do. After the way he had behaved, Anna deserved her pound of flesh.

Riley wouldn't tell him anything about Anna, other than to say that she was holding her own. Even though she had refused to reveal what they discussed, Riley hadn't acted angry, which made him believe that, though Anna was hurting, she hadn't talked badly about him to her friend. Anna had every right to tell her best friend how badly Aidan had behaved. That she obviously hadn't, reinforced his opinion that Anna Bradford was one of the kindest and rarest people on earth.

More than anything, Aidan wanted this over with so he could go to her and tell her what was in his heart. But first he had a damn big task in front of him.

***

Phoenix, Arizona

She told herself that returning to work would be her life-saver. Staying busy had always been her way to cope with hurt in her own life. Besides, working with traumatized children had a tendency to put things in perspective. Her psychologist's mind told her this was avoidance, not healing. Her bruised heart said that was okay for now. By concentrating on others, she would heal. And then the day would come when she wouldn't hurt quite so much. If she continued to tell herself that, she was sure that one day she would believe it.

Though she wasn't due back to work for a couple of days, Anna called into her office and advised them she was returning sooner than expected. She had no consultations or meetings scheduled, but she was sure she could find something to keep her occupied.

As a freelance psychologist, Anna didn't have regular office hours or specific patients. She consulted on various cases, made presentations to medical organizations, and more than once had met with congressional leaders on the state of mental health for the nation's children.

Her job was higher profile than she'd ever anticipated. The monetary aspect had never entered her mind when she'd changed her major to psychology. She'd given little thought to how she would support herself. Silly and idealistic? Yes. If she'd never been kidnapped and tortured, her life and goals would have been radically different. But it had happened, and because of that, her life was changed. She would never wish her experience on anyone, but she was a big believer in things happening for a reason. She'd had two choices—learn from what she had endured and do something with that knowledge, or try to pretend it never happened. Sticking her head in the sand was not her style.

"Well, look what the cat dragged in."

Juggling a cup of steaming coffee and her purse in one hand and her briefcase in the other, Anna winced. Of all the people to encounter on her first day back to work, why did it have to be the one woman who hated her?

"Hello, Lucretia." Yes, that was actually her name. "You're looking lovely as ever."

Anna had learned early that complimenting the woman upfront softened her hackles to a manageable level. On top of that, Lucretia really was a physically beautiful woman. Anna had often wondered if she had a hideously ugly portrait hanging in her house in the way of Dorian Gray. An uncharitable thought, but Anna wasn't above such things, especially when it came to Lucretia Diamond.

"I went to Bora Bora for a week. To a fabulous spa that's to die for." She threw a critical look toward Anna. "Your vacation wasn't nearly as kind."

There was no point in correcting Lucretia. Telling her that she had volunteered to work with a free clinic in Colombia was of no interest to the woman.

"You really need to do something about those freckles on your nose."

A pang of both heartache and remembered joy hit Anna. The first day on the beach she'd forgotten sunscreen, and her face, especially her nose, had gotten sunburned. The result was a small explosion of freckles. Aidan had remarked on how cute they were and promised to kiss each one later that night. He had kept that promise.

"Is that a blush? Did you meet a madly handsome man on your little vacay, Anna? Do tell."

Telling Lucretia anything about her time in Colombia or with Aidan was out of the question.

"No. Must be the sunburn." She lifted her arms slightly to show how overburdened she was. "Guess I'd better get these things to my office."

"Better not get too comfortable. I overheard Glenda on the phone. There's a new bill coming up for a vote in Congress. Meetings are being set. There's no doubt who she'll send now that you're back."

The last part was said in a whine, which Anna ignored. Lucretia's jealousy was so well known that she didn't even bother to hide it anymore. The woman had more insecurities than many of the patients they counseled. Despite those and her never-ending cattiness, Lucretia's job was secure. She might have her issues, but she had an amazing rapport with the families she counseled. The first time Anna had seen her in action, Lucretia had soothed a sobbing mother, calmed an angry father, and comforted a suicidal teenager all at the same time. It hadn't made Anna like Lucretia any better, but she definitely admired her skill.

"I'll just head to my office, then."

Anna made a fast exit and rushed into the elevator. The instant the doors closed, she collapsed back against the wall with a whooshing sigh. Maybe Lucretia was wrong and Glenda wasn't planning to send her to Washington, DC, again. It wasn't that she necessarily hated going. The last time she'd been to DC, she'd actually felt she'd made a small difference. What disturbed her was the proximity to Alexandria, Virginia, and Aidan. Being that close without being able to see him would be like a recovering chocoholic visiting Hershey, Pennsylvania. The temptation to see him would be excruciatingly difficult to resist. In just a few short days, Aidan had become an addiction. One she had been forced to give up, cold turkey. Putting herself within reach of that addiction was not a good idea.

An hour later, her fears realized, Anna marched out of her office and headed home to pack. Her cellphone at her ear, she left a voice mail for her mother, canceling their weekend together. She had no idea how long she'd be away.

With her mind on the various tasks ahead of her, she never noticed the man in the black SUV that pulled out behind her.

Anna might not have been aware that she was being watched, but the man in the beige cargo van definitely took note. His employer was going to be very interested in this information.

***

"What do you mean someone is following her?" Cook said.

"I noticed him this morning but paid little attention until he parked outside her office complex. He was stationary until she came back out about an hour later. He took off right after she left the office. Followed her home."

"What do you know about him?"

"Had a friend run the plates. The vehicle belongs to a shell corporation. I've got people working on this, but it's obvious he wants to stay hidden."

"Is he taking photos?"

"No."

"Excellent! Thorne has hired someone to protect her, watch over her."

The joy in his employer's voice was only a surprise in that he could count on one hand the number of times he'd heard anything similar. Deathbed grim was the man's usual tone.

"Then she does mean something to him."

"Just as I told you, Patrick. You need to have more faith in my observations."

"You're right, Dr. Cook. How do you want me to proceed?"

"Wait and watch for a while longer. When the time comes, I trust you to know what should be done to her protector."

"Yes, sir." Patrick said the words calmly. His employer wasn't a fan of emotions so he couldn't let on how much the idea excited him. He usually handed down orders for a kill, per Cook's instructions. It had been much too long since he'd enjoyed one himself.

"What's going on now? Why did she leave work so soon after arriving?"

"She's on her way to DC to make a presentation to Congress."

"Oh my. How industrious, if not pointless. How do you know this?"

"Yesterday when she went for a run, I broke into her apartment and attached listening devices to some personal items."

"How very clever."

"She's taking a private jet provided by her employer. I've already made plans to fly commercial."

"Excellent. But there's been no contact from Thorne?"

"No, sir. Not as of yet."

"No matter. The fact that he's got someone looking out for her is all the confirmation I needed."

Patrick didn't bother to correct his employer. The news that Anna Bradford was under Thorne's protection wasn't something the man had really needed. Cook had made it clear that, no matter what Anna Bradford was to Thorne, he had plans for her.

Patrick had long ago lost any ounce of conscience. Years ago Simon Cook had pulled him out of the gutter and saved him from addiction and death. Because of that, he had pledged his loyalty until death. Still, he was human enough to shudder with revulsion at what he knew would be Anna Bradford's ultimate fate. She was a lovely young woman, full of life. Soon she would cease to exist.

Patrick gave a philosophical mental shrug. Damn shame, but he had a job to do.

"Unless something happens," Patrick said, "I'll contact you at the same time tomorrow."

"I'll look forward to your call. And as soon as Ms. Bradford returns home from her business trip, I want you to set up our meeting."

That was a surprise. He had thought Cook would wait a few more days to see if Thorne showed up. Not that it mattered. He was here to carry out his employer's bidding, nothing more.

"Very good, sir. I'll begin the arrangements."

CHAPTER THIRTY-ONE

Lake George, New York

"So you're finally going to do it."

Aidan looked over his shoulder as his sister, Jenn, stepped out on the deck. After a delicious, if somewhat raucous, dinner—his nieces and nephews had been in high spirits tonight—the kids had been sent up to the playroom to entertain themselves. Then Aidan presented his plan. As usual, each family member had their own reaction. His mother's was joyful, his father's relieved. His sister's was the expected "It's about damn time" affirmation. Her husband, Brent, seconded his wife's statement with a "Hear, hear."

While he believed Simon had no interest in hurting his family, Aidan still felt the need to warn them. Not once had they experienced a threat from Simon, but that didn't mean the bastard wouldn't change his course if it suited his needs. His family deserved to know that things might change.

Even though he wanted to tell them about the amazing woman he'd fallen in love with, he didn't tell his family anything about her. He and Anna hadn't parted on a good note. Just because he was prepared to bare his soul and grovel for forgiveness didn't mean Anna would accept his apology. Also, he had no guarantee this plan would work.

"Are you sure Simon is even alive?" Jenn asked. "It's been years."

Aidan stared into the dense forest. With the exception of a few hardy fireflies, there was nothing but deep, dark blankness, as if the entire area was empty. But that was all an illusion. Step into the midst of the forest, and one would see and hear all the life teeming within it.

"He's still out there. With his father's death, his wealth has only increased. He could stay hidden forever. He's waiting and watching. Sometime, somewhere, he'll strike. I have to be the one to control that strike."

"So tell me about her."

"What do you mean?"

She shot him a *you've got to be kidding me* look. "You might be able to fool Mom and Dad, but not me. I haven't seen that light in your eyes in years. You've finally found someone who makes you want to live again."

Should've known he wouldn't be able to hide the biggest reason for his monumental change in attitude. Jenn had been able to see through him all her life.

"She's got to be something special for you to take this chance."

"She is." He gave her a brief nod to acknowledge her correct assumption. "I can't tell you about her...not yet."

The less they knew about her, the safer everyone would be.

"All right, but you can at least describe her."

He smiled as he pictured Anna. "She's mouthy, sassy, won't let me get away with anything, and drives me out of my mind.

She has the softest, most compassionate brown eyes, a smile that lights up the world, the kindest heart, and I—"

"And you're in love with her."

"Yes." Such a simple, mild word for the immensity of his feelings for Anna.

A slow smile spread across Jenn's face. "It's about damn time."

"That's becoming one of your favorite sayings."

"That's because it fits so many occasions when it comes to my big brother."

"You think I should've been more proactive in finding Simon, don't you?"

"You've done more than most anyone would have or could have, Aidan. But with Simon Cook's connections and money, he's proven that he can stay hidden for as long as he wants."

"Unless I draw him out."

"Will you tell me how you're going to do that?"

"No."

"Succinct and to the point, as usual."

"The less you know, the better. I just wanted to warn you, all of you, to be on guard even more than usual."

"You could've said that on the phone or in an email."

Aidan shook his head, looked out at the darkness again. "I've missed the last three get-togethers." Regret hit him as he murmured, "Both Mom and Dad look older."

"Dad had mild cold a couple of weeks ago. Other than that, they're in good shape."

Aidan knew that his sister kept a sharp eye on the health of her entire family. But when telling Anna about his family, he had realized how much he'd missed. It was like he'd been frozen for years, and Anna, with her forthrightness and fearlessness, had melted the icy wall he'd erected around himself.

"My stars, she really must be something."

"What do you mean?"

"You're seeing and feeling things you haven't allowed yourself to experience since Mellie's death. It's like you've come alive again."

"She said something that made a dent in my stubbornness. That my guilt wouldn't let me be happy, even if I could."

"I cannot wait to meet her."

For the first time in years, Aidan felt a bubble of optimism, and he grinned. "You're going to love her."

***

Washington, DC

Anna stared at the cellphone in her hand. She had always considered herself a woman of self-control. Yes, she had her weaknesses, but they usually involved things that weren't good for her, like ice cream and purse sales. She refused to put Aidan in that category. Even if she never saw him again, she knew he had been good for her. But the temptation to call him just to hear his voice was so strong her entire body felt as if it might break apart.

He had given her his private number, in case she ever needed him in an emergency. But no matter how much she wanted to call him, aching to hear his voice didn't qualify as an emergency.

She told herself she was just bored. She'd flown to DC to meet with some policymakers and political leaders. Her master's thesis—At-Risk Children in War-Torn Countries and the Resulting Effects of Global Disharmony—had garnered more attention than she had anticipated. This would be her fifth meeting in DC just this year. While she was glad she had opened some people's eyes and created awareness, she would like to think that all the meetings had produced positive results. She couldn't say that about today's meeting. James Timothy, founder and head of The Timothy Foundation believed by speaking to lawmakers as often as possible, she was planting seeds for future progress. She loved her employer but thought perhaps his optimism sometimes got the better of him.

Anna glared at her phone again. She either needed to make the call or forget about it. Staring at the thing and agonizing over her indecision was getting her nowhere. Grinding her teeth to give her courage, she tapped in the number Aidan had made her memorize. At the first ring, she started to panic. What was she going to say? This was crazy!

Just as she was about to end the call, his voice mail answered. She almost sobbed, because the voice that answered wasn't even Aidan's. Just some androgynous voice that told her to leave a message. Either too desperate or too embarrassed not to say something—she'd ask herself later which one it was—Anna couldn't prevent the words from tumbling out of her mouth.

"Hey, it's me. I know I'm only supposed to call if it's an emergency, and it's not. I...I just wanted to hear your voice. And how stupid is it that not only didn't you answer, some robotic voice did it for you? And here I am just babbling like it's you and you're actually interested.

"You know what? Just ignore this call. I'm ice cream deprived, that's all." She cleared her voice and added, "Um, well. Hope you're well. Uh...take care."

She ended the call, threw herself onto the bed, and covered her head with pillows. Now, not only would he know how desperately she missed him, she'd sounded like a nitwit to boot.

Being in love sucked.

CHAPTER THIRTY-TWO

Phoenix, Arizona

Anna returned home from DC and decided she was even more dispirited than when she'd left the island. Aidan hadn't called her back. Not that she should have expected to hear from him. Especially since her voice mail message had sounded so pathetic. She winced every time she thought about how needy she probably appeared.

It helped a little when Riley returned her call and informed her that Aidan was out of town. Of course, she was still embarrassed by having made the call in the first place, but at least she could tell herself that he was most likely on a mission and too busy saving lives to take the time to return a personal phone call. That sounded so much better to her bruised feelings than thinking he just didn't want to talk to her.

Later that night, just as she was drifting off to sleep, reliving the last time she was in Aidan's arms, her cellphone rang. Lost in the memories, it took a few seconds for her brain to comprehend and recognize the noise. Grabbing it, she held the phone to her ear and said groggily, "This is Anna."

"Hey, it's me."

She sprang up in bed like a fire had been lit beneath her. Fumbling for the switch of her bedside lamp, she knocked several things to the floor.

"Are you okay? What was that noise?"

"I'm fine. Just dropped something on the floor."

"I got your message."

Of course he had. Anna was about to give an apology and then stopped herself. She wasn't going to say she was sorry for calling. Okay, yes, she could have sounded a little less desperate, but considering the circumstances of their relationship, he should cut her a little slack.

"I wanted to hear your voice." She didn't tell him she'd been in DC. Even though he had never told her to avoid personal details on the phone, Anna refused to put Aidan in further danger by giving specifics.

"I…"

Just that one hesitant word told her so much. How silly to think anything would be different. Aidan wasn't going to suddenly change his mind about seeing her. He believed that any kind of relationship would put her in danger. Telling him that she would be willing to take that risk would be ludicrous. No way in hell would he agree.

"It's okay," Anna assured him. "I'm fine."

He was silent for so long, she thought they'd lost their connection. "You there?"

"Yeah. I—" More silence and then a muffled, "I gotta go."

Blowing out a shaky sigh, Anna dropped the phone on her lap. Call her crazy, but she felt a million times more optimistic than she had before the call. The few words Aidan had said, combined with his awkwardness, was the most telling conversation she'd ever had with him about his feelings for her. She'd known he cared about her and had been sure that if circumstances were different, he would have pursued a relationship. But Aidan was always direct, blunt to the point of hurting her feelings on more than one occasion. Even when it hurt, she had been glad to know where she stood with him. The phone call tonight revealed something she hadn't anticipated. He was hurting. And not in the *I wish we could see each other naked* kind of hurting.

For the first time since leaving him, Anna felt optimism where Aidan was concerned. No, it didn't negate that he wouldn't allow himself to have a relationship with her, but now that she knew for sure how much he cared, she believed it could work itself out.

Refusing to listen to the little voice inside her that told her this kind of optimism was delusional to the point of insanity, Anna settled back into bed and fell asleep with a small smile on her face.

***

Lake George, New York

"Of all the stupid-assed, idiotic, asinine things to do, that had to be the dumbest thing you've ever done, Thorne."

At any other time, Aidan might have found the situation amusing. Not only had he just made a fool of himself with Anna, he was sitting in his bedroom muttering obscenities and insults at himself.

When he'd taken the time to check his messages and had heard the loneliness in her voice, he hadn't wasted a moment in calling her back. Not because he was concerned for her safety, which should be his number one priority. No, he had done it because she'd sounded exactly the way he felt—lonely and aching for the one person he couldn't have.

Impulsiveness was not in his DNA. Nor was hesitancy in speaking his mind. So the only explanation he had was the fact that, dammit, he just needed to hear her voice.

Reaching up to kick his own ass wasn't enough punishment for the sheer selfishness of his actions. Calling her likely gave her some kind of hope. He didn't want her to have hope that they would ever be together. Hope led to disappointment. He'd disappointed Anna enough already.

If he succeeded in this plan he and McCall had worked up, and Simon Cook was put behind bars where he could no longer hurt the innocent, then and only then would he contact Anna again. Calling her just to hear the sound of her voice had been nothing more than a selfish indulgence on his part. He would not do that again.

He was saved from trying to figure out the proper punishment for himself when his cellphone sounded with a familiar tone.

"What's up, McCall?"

"Can you get back here tonight? We've got a situation and need as many team members as possible."

"I can be there in a few hours."

"See you then."

Pushing his personal issues to the back of his mind, Aidan headed out the door to tell his family goodbye.

***

Phoenix, Arizona

After finalizing her notes for her last patient of the day, Anna logged off her computer for the night. Even though she didn't have a private practice, she took on the occasional client when asked. Truthfully, it was her favorite part of her job. So much so that she had already decided that when she earned her doctorate, she would open a private practice.

She had learned an enormous amount by working for The Timothy Foundation, but developing relationships with individual clients was where she felt she could do the most good. She hadn't yet decided when or where she wanted to open her practice, but she still had a few months to decide.

She grabbed her purse hanging on a peg behind her door and headed out of her office. As she wound her way around a small maze of sofas, chairs, and desks, she abruptly noticed the silence. The office was empty. Most everyone else who worked here had families or significant others at home.

Refusing to give in to the self-pity that hovered right above the optimistic glow still gleaming from last night's phone call from Aidan, Anna shoved the pitiful thought as far down as she could and trudged down the hallway toward the elevator. Most of the lights had been turned off, but the office was well lit enough for her. Still, for the first time that she could remember, she felt uneasy as she walked through the empty building.

Anna unsnapped the clasp on her handbag and touched the pepper spray inside. Knowing the weapon was there and would be in her hand in a half second gave her extra courage. She no longer worried that she was paranoid or being silly. She had ignored those feelings once before and had been abducted. Being prepared saved lives. She'd rather decide later she was being silly than wake up dead, regretting it. Stupid thought, but there it was.

Her heart racing for no accountable reason that she could figure out, Anna stepped onto the elevator and pressed the button for the first floor. Just as it was about to close, a large hand appeared, grasping the edge of the door to keep it from closing. Gasping her surprise, Anna jumped back a couple of feet and grabbed hold of the pepper spray.

A man she'd never seen before walked onto the elevator. "Evening, ma'am."

Sixtyish, with thick white hair, a deep tan, and hazel eyes, he had a smile that was both impersonal and polite. "Didn't realize it was so late. Looks like everybody else had the right idea and went home earlier."

Anna gave a vague smile, acknowledging his statement. There was nothing about the man that was the least threatening or weird. He looked like someone's kindly grandfather. But listening to her instincts would always be her best defense. If this nice-enough-looking guy was actually a psycho, being trapped in an eight-by-eight box with him was not a good idea.

Just as the door was closing shut again, she muttered, "Oops, forgot something in my office," and ran through the open door.

She turned back to see an expression of concern on the man's face. Okay, so maybe she had overreacted. Better safe than sorry.

She waited a couple of minutes, giving the elevator time to land on the first floor and the man to walk out into the parking lot. She stood at the window and watched as he came out of the building, looked at his watch, and turned to go down the sidewalk.

Shaking her head at how spooked she'd been, Anna pushed the button for the elevator again. The instant it arrived, she jumped on and pressed the first-floor button. Just to be on the safe side, she hit the close button to prevent any other late-leaving employees from boarding.

The door closed without incident, and Anna breathed out a relieved sigh. She returned the pepper spray to her purse but kept her hand on it just in case. The car traveled to the first floor without stopping. Her earlier concern gone, she thought again about the phone call from Aidan last night. When she woke this morning, she'd actually double-checked her cellphone log just to make sure he had indeed called her and that it hadn't been a dream. Sure enough, his number was on the list.

She walked out of the building with a smile on her face. Maybe she was a fool for being optimistic, but since she'd had almost no hope before he'd called her, how could she not feel upbeat?

Okay, admittedly, one awkward phone call wasn't exactly a declaration of love, but it was definitely a sign that he was thinking of her. And maybe if he missed her enough, he'd go after Simon Cook once and for all.

At that thought, her smile slipped. What if something happened, went wrong? No, she wouldn't let herself think that way. Aidan was in danger almost daily with LCR. She had witnessed firsthand how he reacted to danger. He could handle himself.

Later, she would wonder if she hadn't been so lost in her thoughts of Aidan and had been more aware of her surroundings, could she have prevented what happened next.

A giant hand grasped Anna's upper arm and spun her around. The pepper spray gripped firmly in her hand, she faced her assailant. She caught a glimpse of a large man with empty eyes an instant before she pressed the spray button. The liquid hit his face, and he let out a loud yowl, releasing her arm. Anna took a running start to her car. She slammed face first into another man. Swinging her arm up, ready to spray this guy, too, she was stunned into immobility by the immense pressure on her wrist.

"Drop it, bitch."

Anna let loose a scream that she was sure could be heard in the next city. Adrenaline pumped like a geyser through her bloodstream, and she vaguely noted a dull pain in her wrist as she was forced to drop the canister. She answered the assault with a right hook to her attacker's jaw and followed with a targeted kick to his kneecap.

The guy let go of her wrist, but more hands grabbed her. Brutal fingers dug painfully into her shoulders. She fought against the man holding her, her frantic brain wondering just how many assailants she was going to have to battle. A fist slammed into her face and then into her stomach. Retching and gagging, she struggled in the man's arms, but he had too firm of a grip for her to move more than a few inches. She raised her eyes to face the man in front of her and could do nothing but wince as his fist headed toward her face again.

"Stop!" a man shouted.

It was too late. The fist connected with her face but her pain-dimmed mind acknowledged that he must've pulled back at the last second, because the impact wasn't as stunning as the first hit.

Anna turned her head slightly and saw the man from the elevator. A rush of gratitude flooded her that he was still around and was going to help her.

"Dammit, I told you I didn't want her hurt," the man said.

He wasn't going to be her savior.

"She hurt me. I paid her back. Fair's fair."

Knowing she was losing the battle to stay conscious, Anna focused on the white-haired man, who appeared to be the ringleader.

"Who are you?"

His expression still just as kind as it had been before, he gave her a small apologetic smile. "Sorry, Anna." His gaze shifted to the man holding her. "Keep her still."

She saw the hypodermic needle in his hand and jerked frantically, trying to get away. "No, no, no!"

"Don't worry," the man said, that scary smile going even wider, "it'll make you forget the pain."

She was hurting so much, she barely felt the pinprick in her neck. Within seconds, her vision blurred even more, and events began to unfold in slow motion. All fight within her disappeared, and powerful arms lifted her. She was floating, and then something solid but soft appeared beneath her body.

She heard a male voice she thought probably belonged to the older man say, "Dr. Cook will be upset that you were hurt, but he's going to be extremely pleased with you."

Dr. Cook! As she drifted into unconsciousness, her mind screamed a silent, *I'm so sorry, Aidan.*

CHAPTER THIRTY-THREE

Bogota, Colombia

Except for the hideous bruises on her face, she looked exactly as he had envisioned her. Wanting their first meeting to be as spontaneous as possible, Cook had deliberately not asked for photos of Anna. Beneath her injuries, he could clearly see the loveliness. And he could easily understand Thorne's affections.

His ire still up from the injuries she never should have sustained, he said softly, "If the men weren't already dead, I would have had you bring them here. I'm in need of new lab rats. They got off lucky."

"I made them suffer a bit. It was unfortunate that we didn't have time to find more-competent men."

Cook grimaced, gave a small shrug. He would reveal the truth to his loyal employee soon enough. "I found myself unable to wait any longer to make her acquaintance. The things I've read about her since learning her identity spurred my imagination."

His gaze returned to the unconscious woman on the bed. "You talked with her in the elevator?"

"Yes. Only briefly. She has excellent instincts. I've been told my face could rival Santa Claus's for kindness. She wasn't taking any chances, though."

"Doesn't surprise me. Thorne wouldn't fall for just any woman. She would need to be a match for him in every way."

"Considering what she'd been through, the self-defense training wasn't a surprise. However, the fact that she nearly incapacitated two men twice her size was a bit alarming."

"A woman of beauty, intellect, and strength. I cannot wait until she wakes up so we can get acquainted."

"She started to come around about an hour before the plane landed. I gave her the second injection, per your instruction."

"She'll be out for at least another six hours. When she wakes, she'll have a few unpleasant hours ahead of her. Plenty of time to put the rest of my plan into action."

"Are you sure you want to proceed as we've discussed? It's not too late to change direction."

Cook's shoulders stiffened. "This plan has been in the making for a long time. Just because I'm ramping up the timetable doesn't mean I'm any less committed."

As if realizing he'd overstepped his boundaries, Patrick gave a silent nod and took a step back.

Cook relented slightly. Patrick had been his loyal servant and companion for so long, it only made sense that the man would show concern. While Cook had only ever felt affection for one other person in his life, he could recognize the emotion in others.

"You will be taken care of, Patrick. Your retirement is secure. All that I have will go to you."

"I appreciate your generosity, sir."

"Nonsense. Who else would I leave it to? Everyone I care about is gone, or will be very soon. I'm taking matters into my own hands, as I always have. Going out on my own terms and in this manner is all I have left."

"Yes, sir."

"Now, leave me alone with her. We'll be contacting Thorne soon." Cook turned back to the unconscious woman. "In the meantime, I'm going to have a private talk with dear Anna. Even though she can't respond, it's my hope that she can still comprehend at this stage in her unconsciousness. I want to prepare her for our forthcoming adventure."

"Should I restrain her? Despite her small size, she could still fight back. When she wakes, she could do damage."

"No need." His mouth lifted slightly. "On waking, Ms. Bradford will not have the energy of a newborn lamb. The second injection you gave her was one of my favorite creations. For several agonizing hours, she will find it almost impossible to catch her breath between writhing in pain and vomiting her guts up."

Patrick wrinkled his nose in disgust. "Sounds quite unpleasant."

"It will be for both of us. However, I think it will be the most effective way to control her. She's already proven she's strong and tenacious. But when your gut is roiling, it's amazing how amenable one can be."

His expression showing a hint of fear as well as respect, Patrick nodded and backed away farther. "I'll be close by if you need me."

Cook turned back to the woman on the bed. "I have everything I need to, um…what's the phrase? Get this party started."

***

With a slight grimace of pain, Aidan adjusted his big body on the cushioned airplane seat. Flying first class had its perks, but even with the extra comfort, his side still ached like a sore tooth. Getting kicked in the ribs by a size-thirteen boot would do that every damn time. After the excitement had passed, one of the medics had wrapped his ribs up tight, but he'd be hurting for a few more days. Frustrating, but he'd endured worse.

The op had been bigger and more successful than anyone had anticipated. Not only were several young women being returned to their lives and their families, a group of sleazy human traffickers were behind bars. The icing on the cake had been the apprehension of one of the most-wanted criminals in the world. Darius Ronan had his fingers in various illegal pies, and they had lucked out when he had appeared during one of their ops.

LCR had a very specific reason for wanting to bring Ronan down. He was responsible for the kidnapping and torture of both Declan Steele, Sabrina's husband, and Sabrina herself. His elusiveness had reminded Aidan of his search for Simon. But now Ronan was behind bars. Aidan hoped this was a portent of good things to come in his own frustrating search.

Sabrina and Declan were now headed for a well-deserved vacation. He hadn't told his partner about Simon Cook or the new op he was about to embark upon. He'd never told Sabrina about his past. He trusted her in every way possible, but talking about what happened without any hope of resolution had been too damn painful. Now that there was hope, he would tell her when she returned from her time off. Telling her before she left would have meant one thing—she would have delayed her vacation to help him out. He couldn't do that to her or Declan. After all they'd been through, they deserved this time together.

McCall had suggested, and Aidan had agreed, that Elite operative Olivia Gates would be the one to help him implement his plan. Gates was Brennan Sinclair's new partner. Tall and blond, she was similar in looks and coloring to Mellie, as well as Amy and Kristen. Maybe it was too easy, but the hope was that Simon would think that Aidan was attracted only to a certain type. The more convincing they could be that this was a real relationship, the better the chances that Simon would fall for the ruse. Having Olivia look like his type couldn't hurt.

Olivia had been an LCR operative for a while but had recently moved over to the Elite team. When McCall had suggested her, Aidan hadn't been sure. Other than knowing she had some resemblance to Mellie, he knew almost nothing about the woman. After he'd seen her in action the last couple of days, his opinion had changed and his doubts had disappeared. Olivia could handle anything that came her way.

He pushed aside the knowledge that he had worked with many female operatives who would have gladly partnered with him to trap Simon Cook. He still didn't feel right about putting any operative at risk, but McCall had drilled holes in his tightly held beliefs. Simon was not going to just appear out of nowhere. He was going to have to be trapped. If Aidan intended to ever have a life with Anna, this was his only option.

So he would go home, work on logistics, and when Olivia arrived back home, they would put their plan into action.

He could have waited and flown back to the States on the LCR jet, but that would've delayed him a couple more days. McCall hadn't been able leave yet, and the other operatives on the team had gone their own ways.

His cellphone buzzed in his pocket. He checked the readout and felt a familiar thudding of his heart. It only made sense that she was calling him, especially after that ridiculously awkward call he'd made to her.

He answered with a smile in his voice. "Hello, Anna."

"Sorry, Dr. Thorne. Anna is otherwise occupied right now."

Aidan jerked up in his seat. "Who is this? Where's Anna?"

"A friend of a friend, you might say."

"Where's Anna? If you've hurt her—"

"Relax. Other than feeling a little under the weather, Ms. Bradford is perfectly fine. How long she stays that way is entirely up to you."

"Where's Simon?"

"Dr. Cook is getting acquainted with Ms. Bradford. He asked me to call you."

"I swear, if he hurts her, I—"

"You'll what?" the man asked mockingly.

"I'll personally gut you," Aidan snarled.

"I'll look forward to the challenge, Dr. Thorne. But since we only have a limited time to talk, let's move on, shall we? I have specific instructions from Dr. Cook."

"I'm listening," Aidan ground out.

"You'll be landing in about two minutes. Get off the plane and go straight to baggage claim. You'll be met by two gentlemen.

No need to look for them. They'll recognize you. These men will give you instructions for the next part of your journey."

"I want to talk to Anna. How do I know you even have her?"

"You don't. However, you know that I have her cellphone. You're welcome to contact the bodyguard you assigned to her. He is unfortunately no longer able to talk, but you can do your best. Dr. Cook told me you were once a gifted doctor, so who knows what miracles you can perform?"

"How do I know she's alive? This could be a trick to trap me."

"Also true. You'll just have to wait for further proof. If it makes you feel any better, we're preparing a video for you."

"How can—"

"I'm not finished, Dr. Thorne. Please refrain from contacting anyone. We have spies everywhere. One could be on the plane. If we see you talking to anyone or using your phone, Ms. Bradford will suffer for your disobedience. Is that understood?"

"Yes."

"Excellent. We'll chat again soon."

The instant the call ended, Aidan studied his fellow passengers. A woman and a child sat across from him, two businessmen were in the right front, an elderly couple sat directly in front of him. None of them looked like spies for Simon Cook. Aidan couldn't take the risk. If Cook knew he was on a plane, headed back to DC, then he could damn well have placed spies here to watch him.

Having no other choice, Aidan slipped his cell back into his pocket. If anyone were watching, they'd see him comply with the instructions. What couldn't be seen was the finger he'd used to uncover a small, hidden compartment on the left side of his phone. Most people would think it was a cover for an earphone jack, which it was. But next to the jack was a tiny alert button. One press, and McCall received an immediate notice that one of his operatives was in trouble. GPS tracking would begin immediately.

Knowing he'd done all he could for now, Aidan stared into space, his heart racing as he envisioned all the horrible things Anna was going through. Dammit, how had Cook gotten to her? Aidan had been so damned careful.

None of that mattered now. He would save Anna. There was no doubt in his mind about that. It might be the last thing he accomplished on this earth, but he would be successful. The confrontation that had been ten years in the making would soon take place, and Aidan was sure of only two things—Anna would survive and Simon Cook would not.

CHAPTER THIRTY-FOUR

Darkness surrounded her, consumed her. Hands, thousands of them, grabbed at her, clawing, pinching. Giant teeth tore into her flesh. Anna fought, struggled to scream, to call out for help. She was bound, legs, hands, mouth. She couldn't move, couldn't speak, couldn't breath.

What was happening? Why was she being tortured? Sobs built to a crescendo but she couldn't make a sound. Who was doing this? Why? Her mind prayed, begged for help. Tears filled her eyes, rolled down her face. Whimpers rose in her throat as she realized she was going to die.

A golden haired man appeared before her. With beautiful brown eyes and a dazzling smile, the man filled her heart with hope. She wanted to call out to him, warn him. Why, she didn't know. She needed to tell him something. What? Who was he? Had he done this to her?

No, not him.

His smile dimmed, his eyes went dark with sorrow. Agony zoomed through her entire body. She swallowed her screams and let the darkness devour her once more.

Minutes or days later, she woke again. Darkness still surrounded her. She was still bound, still unable to scream but she was alive. She heard a noise. She blinked, assuring herself that her eyes were open. Was she about to be rescued? Had the golden haired man returned?

Light appeared. The face of evil hovered above her. No, no, no! Not him. Not him. He was dead! Alden Pike had been shot and killed. Her mind scrambled to explain the horror. A little voice in the back of her mind whispered the mantra, *Pike is dead, Pike is dead.* Yet he was here, beside her. Had everything been a dream? Was she still in Tranquility? Everything that had happened—her rescue, her degrees, her career—were they all in her imagination? How was that possible? How...?

Aidan! Aidan Thorne was not a figment of her imagination. He was the golden haired man, the man she loved. He was real.

Fighting back the hallucinations, the hideous memories, Anna kept Aidan's face locked in her mind. Alden Pike's evil countenance hovered on the periphery, but as long as she held onto Aidan's image, she could fight the beast that threatened to throw her back into hell.

Darkness washed over her once more, but this time it was softer, welcoming. Warmth wrapped her in a comforting embrace.

She woke again, this time to horrendous agony. Streaks of fire ripped through her stomach as if the devil himself were dancing inside her gut, shredding her insides with his vile, evil claws.

Pounding, piercing misery erupted in her brain, drilled into her skull. Anna screamed, her dazed mind recognizing that she had been released from her bonds. Freedom no longer mattered. She was dying...she was sure of it.

As much as she wanted to roll around in her misery, cry out in her suffering, she forced herself to lie still. Taking even, shallow breaths, she acknowledged and absorbed the pain. Her racing heart slowed, the panic within her calmed. The hideous pain was still there but by focusing her thoughts she could lessen it somewhat.

She zeroed in on her surroundings. The surface beneath her was soft, giving. She heard no sounds or noises. She knew she should open her eyes and face the knowledge of her circumstances, but something held her back. Not just the violent nausea and hideous headache. Something else stopped her. A shadow hovered at the edge of her consciousness. A dark, ominous feeling of dread that told her to put off facing reality for as long as she could.

Unable to bear not knowing, Anna forced her eyes open.

What she saw was nothing she'd anticipated. She was in a beautiful bedroom decorated in different shades of green. It was both feminine and practical. Nothing frilly or ostentatious. In fact, if she had chosen the décor herself, she couldn't have been more pleased. Problem was, this was not her bedroom.

She lay still as possible and tried to think. What was the last thing she remembered?

Her mind refused to give her the memories. Hoping for a clearer perspective, Anna gingerly sat up in bed. In an instant she knew she'd made a massive mistake. As if a monster had been let loose inside her, her belly roiled like a massive wave, and the pain turned into a fit of vomiting. Noting the bucket beside her bed, Anna reached for it just in time. She retched and gagged. Beneath the misery, a small voice inside her was telling her something else was wrong. Something even worse than the sickness. That worry would have to wait. Another bout of nausea hit her.

"Hello, my dear."

Anna raised her head and looked around. Saw no one.

"Don't bother looking for me. I'm in another room. I have to admit to having a weak stomach, one of the many reasons I never did well with patients. So please excuse my rudeness in not greeting you in person."

As if a movie played in her head, she saw herself fighting against two men. She had pepper-sprayed one of them, punched the other. Then another man, the kindly looking man in the elevator, had appeared. He had drugged her and abducted her. She didn't remember much else other than the name mentioned right before she'd lost consciousness.

"Hello, Simon."

"Excellent. I see Thorne has apprised you of the situation. That will save us some time."

"What the hell did you give me to make me so sick?"

"Just a little concoction I created. It's so rare that I have the opportunity to experiment on a healthy specimen. I hadn't anticipated the delightful addition of hallucinations. It's been enlightening to watch you these last few hours."

"You bastard! What was in that shot?"

"Now, now, don't get too upset. You'll just feel sicker. Let me reassure you that it won't kill you, my dear, if that's what worries you."

"It'll just make me wish I were dead."

"Exactly. I can already tell that we are going to get along quite well. You speak your mind, and that's a quality I've learned to appreciate in a woman."

"What do you plan to do?"

"That's nothing for you to worry your pretty head about. Now that you're awake, you've got several hours of unpleasantness ahead of you. Do be sure to keep your bucket close."

Nausea overtook her once more, and Anna did the only thing she could do. She rode the wave of agony and endured.

***

Reagan National Airport
Arlington, Virginia

The instant the door was opened, Aidan strode off the plane with an unleashed urgency. He didn't bother looking around at the other passengers as they disembarked. Whether Simon had someone on the flight no longer mattered. Whatever the man had planned, Aidan would go along with it. Getting to Anna was his only priority right now.

McCall would be tracking his phone. He would know where he was, and a team would be headed his way soon. Unfortunately, not soon enough.

As instructed, he went to baggage claim. He hadn't checked any bags, so he stood in the middle of the large area where dozens of exhausted and harried travelers waited. It didn't take long.

A hard hand landed on his shoulder, and a man growled into his ear, "Let's go."

Aidan didn't see the man or the one he sensed on his other side. He walked with them toward the glass doors. When one of them pushed the door open, he noted the scorpion tattoo on his hand. Looked like a gang symbol.

"This way," the tattooed man said.

They led him to a black Hummer. The back door opened, and Aidan was pushed inside. The two men got in with him, one on each side. He couldn't see who was driving. The vehicle took off.

"Your cellphone, please."

Knowing he had no choice, Aidan handed over his cellphone. The man pressed a button on the door, and the window slid down. Aidan's phone disappeared through the opening.

"What now?" Aidan asked.

"We wait for further instructions."

They drove out of the airport and toward the Beltway. Though the atmosphere inside the vehicle was one of grim silence, there was also an air of expectation. These guys were as much in the dark about what would happen next as Aidan was. He didn't find that the least reassuring.

A cellphone buzzed, and the guy on Aidan's left answered with, "Yes?" The man listened for several seconds, said, "I understand," and ended the call.

"Your wrists, please."

"Why?"

"You're to be restrained."

"Why now?"

The man on his right jabbed a gun in his side and snarled, "Do it!"

Having little choice, Aidan held out his hands and watched as his wrists were zip-tied. If these guys thought that they were safer this way, let them. Zip ties wouldn't slow him down for one second.

The man then pressed a button in the ceiling, and an overhead monitor lowered to eye level. The screen flickered briefly, and as eerie music surrounded them, a scene right out of a horror movie appeared. The setting was a graveyard. Fog and mist swirled and danced with slow, graceful abandon. Twisted and gnarled trees with Spanish moss hanging from the misshapen branches encircled ancient-looking tombstones. The camera panned the area, revealing monstrous crypts and crumbling encasements. The only thing missing were ghost and goblins.

The camera that had been moving slowly through the graveyard abruptly picked up speed and zoomed forward, then jerked to a stop before three tombstones. The one in the middle was large and elaborate, made of expensive-looking marble and stone. The ones on either side of it were much smaller and looked like they were made of concrete blocks.

The writing on the tombstones was out of focus. Aidan moved closer to the screen, trying to read the inscriptions. As if the cameraman wanted to make the most impact, the picture focused abruptly and the writing became clear.

Here lies Simon Cook, Jr. A brilliant doctor destroyed by evil. May his betrayers rot in hell.

The camera shifted to the right. The etching on the cement, jagged and messy, read:

Here lies a betrayer and liar: Aidan Thorne

Even though he didn't need to read what was on the other tombstone to know who it had been prepared for, Aidan shifted his gaze to it anyway.

Here lies the innocent Anna Bradford. She used her last dying breath to curse the man who killed her, Aidan Thorne.

Aidan pushed aside the knee-jerk reaction of fury. There were clues here, and he needed to find them before the images faded.

First clue: This wasn't the result of Simon's imagination. It was too tame. When it came to horror movies, the Simon he knew was all about the gore. This was too mild, almost stereotypical of an old-time horror movie.

Second clue: Simon was one of the most-foul-mouthed people he'd ever known. Twice in college he'd been almost kicked out for the vile language he used in public. So why was Aidan's epitaph so mild if Simon hated him that much?

Third clue, and the one that confused Aidan the most: Simon's epitaph. Problem was, Aidan couldn't put a finger on why the wording bothered him. And while it was obvious that the endgame was for all three of them to die, why would Simon want to end his life when he was finally getting exactly what he wanted?

Something didn't add up.

The screen faded to black, and a voice, reminiscent of Vincent Price, said, "The time has come for you to pay, Dr. Thorne. It's unfortunate that Ms. Bradford will have to die, too."

Aidan didn't know if there were cameras inside the Hummer. Not that it mattered. Showing any kind of emotion other than icy coldness during this ordeal wasn't something he could allow. Simon would feed off of any anger or pain Aidan revealed.

The man who'd taken the phone call earlier pressed a button on a side compartment. A door opened, revealing a small bottle of clear liquid. The man took the bottle and handed it to Aidan. "Drink it."

"No."

He smiled and said, "Good."

The man on the other side of him pressed something hard against his side, and a jolt of electricity zipped through Aidan's body. Jerking uncontrollably, Aidan shouted. In that instant, something foul-tasting splashed against his tongue. He spewed out as much of the liquid as he could, but within seconds, he knew enough of the drug had gotten into his system to impair him.

Slumping into his seat, Aidan watched a blur of the world pass by. The man to his right chuckled. "Enjoy your trip."

***

Bogota, Colombia

A weak and listless Anna Bradford lay on the bed. He hadn't yet met her in person. He'd spoken the truth when he'd told her that he had a weak stomach. The stench of bodily fluids was one of the many reasons he had changed course in his medical training. Whiny, complaining people were another.

He had to give Anna credit. She wasn't a whiner or complainer. For the past five hours, she had vomited and heaved as though she were dying. But not once had she called out to anyone. Not that it would have done her any good, but he had developed a certain measure of respect for her stoicism. Women who endured without complaint were his favorite kind.

The poison was now out of her system, but she would remain lethargic, unable to defend herself against the weakest of opponents.

One of the day nurses he'd employed several years ago stepped into the room. At just under six feet tall and as strong as an ox, Sybil Dempsey could arm-wrestle a steroid-using body builder and win. Anna would be no challenge.

"Get up. I'm here to clean you up," the woman said brusquely. Sybil wasn't known for her bedside manner.

Showing that the girl had more than a little gumption, she tried to sit up and made it almost halfway before she collapsed back onto the bed.

With a combination grunt and huffing noise, Sybil lifted Anna into her strong arms and carried her out of the room. The instant they disappeared, another nurse entered. This one was much smaller and more feminine. Secretly, she was his favorite of all his nurses, simply because she was pretty and rarely said a word. She did her job with a competent pleasantness that he found most appealing.

Though her nose wrinkled at what was probably a terrible stench, she set to work. After disposing of the offensive bucket, she put fresh linens on the bed and sprayed air freshener throughout the room. She then opened the windows and allowed the early morning breeze to blow away any remaining sickroom odors.

Half an hour later, a fresh-looking Anna returned. Though still carried in Sybil's arms, she wore a wide-awake and wary expression. She was now coherent enough for him to proceed with the next phase of his plan. She would soon learn her fate.

CHAPTER THIRTY-FIVE

LCR Headquarters
Alexandria, Virginia

Noah stood at the front of the conference room filled with Elite operatives. Everyone's expression was a reflection of his own concern. They knew three things: Thorne had signaled he was in trouble. His last known location was Reagan National Airport. And Anna was missing.

"Do we have any idea who took Anna?"

The question came from Ingram. Even though she and Anna were best friends, Noah had no worries that the operative couldn't do the job. Riley Ingram was one of the best he knew for being able to put her personal feelings aside to achieve her mission. Her friendship with Anna might spur her initiative, but it would never hinder her performance.

Sharing the background of any of his operatives with others, even with the people he trusted most in the world, wasn't something Noah took lightly. His commitment to each of his people was as strong as any oath ever taken. However, when it came to saving their lives, discretion had to take a backseat.

"Here are the basics. Thorne has an enemy named Simon Cook. The man murdered Thorne's wife years ago. Since then, Cook has made it his personal mission to destroy any romantic relationship Thorne has ever had. He's attacked two women, both of whom were involved with Thorne."

"Attacked them how?" Fox asked.

The instant he'd received Thorne's alert, he'd contacted Sabrina Fox, knowing she would want to be involved in the rescue. Noah detected no hint of anger or betrayal in her voice. She and Thorne had been partners for several years, but they led separate lives and respected each other's privacy.

"The first woman was knocked unconscious and sexually assaulted. The second was knocked out, not sexually assaulted, but was mutilated with a message across her chest. 'Simon says hi.'"

"Shit," Kelly said softly.

"Thorne has been looking for Cook for over a decade. He believes he's in Colombia, as that was Cook's mother's homeland."

"What's Simon Cook's background?" Mallory asked. "And what's his beef with Thorne?"

"From all accounts, Simon Cook is, or was, a brilliant doctor. A genius who got his medical degree at the ripe age of twenty. His beef with Thorne is harder to determine. Cook and Thorne were best friends up until the day Cook raped and murdered Thorne's wife."

"How'd Thorne know him?"

"They were in school together. College and medical school."

"So Cook has made it his life's goal to destroy Thorne's life." Sinclair summed up the situation in his succinct way.

"That's the gist of it, yes."

"What do we know so far?" Ingram asked. "Were there no witnesses to Anna's abduction?"

"None that we've been able to find. What we do know is that Thorne was met in the baggage claim area of Reagan National by two men."

Noah clicked a button on the remote in front of him. Video appeared on the screen showing a grim-looking Thorne talking briefly with two men. One of the men said something. Thorne gave an abrupt nod, and they walked out together. Another film clip showed Thorne getting into the backseat of a Hummer.

The feed froze on the screen, and Noah turned back to the group. "That's all we've got."

"Why abduct Anna?" Ingram asked. "He attacked the other two women but didn't kidnap them. Why'd he change his MO?"

"That, among many other things, is something we don't know." Pressing his hands down on the table, Noah leaned forward and took in everyone's gazes. "All we know is that both Anna and Thorne are in trouble, and we damn well better figure something out quick before it's too late for both of them."

***

Hours passed before Aidan regained use of his mind and his limbs. A few minutes after he'd imbibed the drug, they'd stopped at a small airstrip. With the help of his two captors, Aidan had stumbled onto a plane and collapsed onto a seat. One of the men had been concerned enough about his safety to buckle his seat belt, and then they'd left him alone for the duration of the long flight.

Existing in an altered state of awareness, he had been alert enough to comprehend what was going on around him. However, the drug he'd been forced to ingest had inhibited his ability to respond.

He didn't know if the drug was designed to incapacitate more than it had, or if by spitting some of the liquid out, he'd prevented the full effects. Whatever the reason, he was now alert and strong enough to take on these assholes. The instant they landed, he would be ready. One advantage to the drug was the lack of pain in his damaged ribs.

Since letting his captors know that he had recovered was not in his best interest, Aidan continued to keep his body sprawled out on the seat, his head lolling to one side. He kept his eyes half open to alert him if anyone approached, and he listened. And he learned one important thing—these men didn't know dick about what was happening. They were being paid to do a job and take him to a location. Meaning they followed the money and had little loyalty to their employer.

The men spoke Spanish with a Colombian dialect. It gave Aidan no sense of satisfaction to know that he'd at least been right that Simon was in Colombia.

The talking stopped as the plane began to descend and the men settled back, readying themselves for landing.

Aidan forced himself not to think about what Anna was going through. Simon wouldn't kill her yet. The monster would want him to watch, unable to save her.

He told himself that just because Mellie and Kristen had been raped, that didn't mean Simon had done the same to Anna. Nor did it mean Anna would be mutilated as Amy and Kristen had been. He told himself that Simon would refrain from hurting her until Aidan arrived. Problem was, he didn't know if he told himself these things because he believed them, or if they were lies to make himself feel better.

Knowing it was useless to torture himself, he returned his mind to the horror-movie vignette Simon had created and its message. Why would Simon include his own tombstone?

Aidan remembered a late-night conversation with Simon close to the end of their med school days. Sleep-deprived and running on fumes, they had turned their discussion to death and dying. Simon had given a surprisingly vulnerable statement about his fear of death and how he would hang on with all his might when his time came. Had he changed so much that death no longer scared him? Something wasn't adding up. Aidan's mind scrambled for an answer. What was he missing?

The plane made a smooth touchdown and taxied down the runway. Aidan drew in an even breath, preparing himself for what lay ahead. He would play his role of incapacitated captive until the last minute. The more impaired he appeared, the better his chances of taking them by surprise.

"I'm glad my part of the job is over," one of the men muttered.

"I still don't think we were paid enough," another man griped.

So someone would be meeting the plane, and these men would be gone. As much as he'd like to kick their asses, he wouldn't waste his energy on them.

One of the men lifted the handle and opened the door to the outside. The other two men helped Aidan to his feet. Still acting drugged, he slumped forward and shuffle-walked down the steps. Aidan felt mild amusement as one of the men cursed at him for being so weak and helpless. These guys didn't know it, but they were going to get off easy.

When they reached the tarmac, Aidan lifted his head, looked around. Another Hummer sped toward them and jerked to a stop a few feet from where they waited. Two men stepped out.

Aidan let his head drop slightly, as if it weighed too much. That gave him the opportunity to inventory the weapons the new men were carrying. Basic, nothing elaborate. Each had a Glock sidearm and a KA-BAR knife strapped at the thigh. They likely had a secondary weapon at one ankle. The clothing was camo, the stance military. These guys were trained killers. Probably mercenaries.

Satisfied that he knew what he was up against, Aidan gave a convincing drug-induced sway. The men ignored him as if he didn't exist. And they talked.

"Where are you taking him?"

"That's not your concern. Dr. Cook has paid you for your services. Your job is over."

The man who had complained about his payment earlier—Aidan decided he was the dumbest of the three—sneered, "What if we want to renegotiate our contract?"

Aidan knew what was going to happen the instant the idiot asked the question. Even though the deed was done in less than two seconds, Aidan noted each movement as if it were in slow motion. He saw a slight shift to the mercenary's body, heard the glide of the Glock as the man lifted it from his holster, and the almost imperceptible click of his finger as it pressed the trigger. A grunt and then the thud of the body.

"Anyone else want to renegotiate their contract?"

The other two men backed away, making hurried assurances that they were quite happy with what they'd been paid. Seconds later, they could be heard running back up the steps to the plane.

A giant paw grabbed Aidan's arm. "Let's go."

Aidan stumbled forward. The fact that they'd left the body lying on the tarmac was telling. They weren't bothering to hide their activities. Which made him more certain than ever that this was the endgame for Simon. Whatever he had planned, he wasn't planning on surviving, which made Aidan's job a little more complicated.

***

Bogota, Colombia

Though weak as a newborn kitten, Anna couldn't help but feel grateful that the nausea was gone. Whatever had been in the syringe she'd been stabbed with was pure evil. As was the man who had created it. Simon had bragged about his concoction as if it were some kind of miracle drug. Though she had yet to meet him, she had already decided he was the personification of the evil, mad scientist.

A nurse with an expression fierce enough to intimidate a four-star general had bathed her. The woman's demeanor had been cold and heartless, but Anna hadn't cared. Getting the stench of illness off her body had been of utmost importance.

After her bath, she'd been allowed to rinse her mouth with a minty mouthwash. Then she'd been dressed in a long, flowing white nightgown. Even as ill as she still felt, Anna recognized the artistry and talent that had gone into creating the garment. Why would Simon go to such extravagant expense? Her wild imagination came up with several answers, and they all creeped her out.

She was now seated in an overstuffed armchair with her legs propped on a matching ottoman. It was obvious no one saw her as a threat. With good reason. The effort to lift her legs onto the ottoman had used up all her strength. Fighting her way out of this place would have to wait until she could at least stand on her own.

At that thought, a hard lump settled in her throat, and her heart gave a frantic jump. She already knew why she had been brought here. She would be used as a pawn against Aidan. The other two women Simon had attacked and brutalized had been left at the location of their assaults. But this time, instead of attacking her as a taunt to Aidan, she had been abducted. Simon had changed his game.

Anna knew exactly what the man she loved would do. He would come after her. Simon would be waiting for him. What the fiend had planned once Aidan arrived was anyone's guess.

She had to be ready. She had to be strong enough to help him.

A door opened, and the man she'd first seen in the elevator in Phoenix walked into the room. In his hands was a tray holding a steaming bowl and two bottles of water.

"Hello, my dear. You must be famished."

Was she hungry? Surprisingly, yes. Other than the debilitating weakness left by the poison, she felt fine. And she was ravenous. Problem was, eating anything this guy put in front of her wasn't going to happen. He'd been the one to shoot her up with poison.

He placed the tray on her lap. If she'd had an ounce of strength in her body, she would have lifted the tray and slammed the thing into his face. Since she doubted she'd even be able to lift the spoon sitting beside the bowl of broth, she did the only thing she could and gave him the coldest, meanest stare she could conjure.

"Ah, my dear. I thought perhaps you wouldn't trust me after what happened at our first meeting. Therefore, if you don't mind eating after I do, let me show you that the broth is completely harmless."

He picked up the spoon, dipped it into the broth, and carried it to his mouth. He swallowed, then said, "A little saltier than I prefer, but still tasty for all that."

Anna knew that if she wanted to get strong enough to assist Aidan in escaping, she was going to have to eat.

"Take three more bites."

He smiled his appreciation of her tactics and obliged. He left the spoon in the bowl and said, "It's cooling rapidly. Best eat it while it's still warm."

She wasn't finished yet. "Take a drink from both bottles of water."

"They've not been opened, my dear."

"Do it anyway."

"Very well." He unscrewed one bottle, took a swallow, and did the same with the other one.

Satisfied that they didn't plan to drug or poison her again, at least not yet, Anna attacked the food with genteel greed. Her hollow stomach gave a grateful grumble as it welcomed the nourishment. When the bowl was empty, she drank an entire bottle of water, then started on the second one, drinking it a little slower.

The man sat at her side, watching her eat but not speaking. When she looked up at him, questions in her eyes, he shook his head. "I'm sorry, my dear. I have nothing to tell you. Dr. Cook is your host. He'll be the one to talk with you about your stay here."

"You act as if I'm here of my own accord. You kidnapped me and poisoned me."

"If I'd thought you would come willingly, I would have been a little less aggressive."

She ignored the obvious lie and said, "When will I meet Simon?"

"When he deems it the appropriate time." He stood and lifted the tray. "Best thing for you to do is rest and recuperate. I'll be back in a few hours with another meal." He grinned as he added, "Baked chicken and rice is on the menu. I'll look forward to taste-testing for you."

"Simon's plans for me are obviously not good. Why bother to feed me, make me feel better?"

The kind smile was still in place, making his next words seem all the more ominous. "Dr. Cook wants you well enough to appreciate the full experience."

The instant he was out the door, Anna shifted in her chair, thinking to get up and explore the room. The effort to move even a little changed her plans. If she tried to get up, she would fall. And if she fell, she doubted she'd have the energy to even crawl to the bed. The only thing she could do now was comply with what the man had told her to do. She would rest, recuperate, and when Aidan arrived, she would fight alongside him to win.

Leaning back in the chair, Anna closed her eyes, and as tears rolled down her cheeks, she began to pray.

She and Aidan would win…they had to. There was no other choice.

CHAPTER THIRTY-SIX

Aidan and his new captors flew to their destination on a helicopter. He had considered throwing one of the men out of the chopper and forcing the other one to fly to their destination. The thought had been brief. He'd seen these types before. They'd crash the helicopter into the mountain, killing them all, before they'd fail at a mission.

When they'd gotten onto the chopper, the zip-tie around his wrists had been traded for handcuffs that secured him to the armrest. His ankles were chained to a steel rod beneath his seat. Figuring they'd been told to drug him if he appeared to be alert, Aidan made sure they believed he was still high as a kite. He'd need all his faculties once they arrived.

Since he wasn't expected to do anything other than look drugged, Aidan leaned his forehead against the window. Once they were in the air, he couldn't hear anything over the whirl of the rotor blades, so he concentrated on the mountains below them. The terrain was mountainous, but nothing he and Anna hadn't faced before. Hard to believe that was only a few weeks ago.

Even though regretting what had happened was pointless, Aidan couldn't prevent damning himself for his failure. Simon had to have spies in Cali. And Aidan had stupidly thought he had hidden his feelings for her so well. It would have taken little effort for Anna's identity to be discovered.

The protection Aidan had provided her had been inadequate. The one man assigned to watch her was dead. Instead of worrying that he would infringe upon her freedom, he should have hired a half-dozen people to ensure her safety.

The chopper made a sudden sharp left, and Aidan spotted the fortress that he had been trying to find for almost a decade. He felt no vindication that the large structure was almost invisible, blending into the jungle as if it were as much a part of the wildness as the giant trees that shielded it. The anger that had been simmering, waiting to erupt, reached its zenith. The two men in front had ignored him the entire flight. They still didn't see him as a threat. He would play that advantage out until the very last moment.

The chopper circled the estate a couple of times—Aidan figured this was to alert the occupants that they had arrived—then headed to a clearing about a quarter mile away.

Timing would be everything. Since he was still handcuffed and chained to the seat, he could do nothing but wait until he was released. After all this time, he doubted that the men would believe he was still too incapacitated to fight. He also didn't believe that Simon would want him unable to comprehend what was going on, which meant the men wouldn't force more shit down his throat. Brute force would be their method to make him cooperate.

The instant the chopper touched down, the man in the front passenger seat went to his feet and came for him. He unlocked the chain at Aidan's feet first and then, as he reached for the handcuffs, growled, "One wrong move, and you get a bullet."

Having no problem with that, Aidan nodded. Making any kind of move in these close quarters would be suicide.

The man uncuffed him from the armrest and said, "Turn around."

Aidan presented his back to the guy and allowed his hands to be cuffed behind him. Once Aidan was secured, the guy stepped out of the chopper, pulling Aidan with him.

The minute his feet were on the ground, Aidan said, "I gotta take a leak."

"So go."

Giving the other man a smarmy smile, he said, "You gonna unzip me?"

With a growling curse, the guy pulled him a few steps away from the chopper and dug into his pants pocket for the key. He unlocked Aidan's cuffs and stepped back. "You got a gun pointed at your kidney. You do anything other than take a piss, you're a dead man."

As Aidan unzipped his pants, he assessed. Situated only a few feet away from a glass building, he had a perfect view of what was going on behind him. The surly guy did indeed have a gun pointed at his kidney. Behind him was the other man. His back was to them as he rummaged around in a duffle bag.

Finishing, Aidan zipped up and, in the guise of adjusting himself, made a move backward. With a subtle, quick turn, Aidan grabbed the man's gun and pulled him around with it. The guy looking through his bag turned, a gun in his hand. Aidan fired two shots, both hitting their mark. Just as the man dropped, the guy Aidan was holding kicked out toward Aidan's legs. Pivoting, Aidan swung the man around again and slammed his booted foot into the man's chest. The man fell backward, releasing the gun.

Aidan stood over him, gun pointed at a non-life-threatening part of his body, and said, "What are your orders?"

The mercenary glared up at him and remained silent.

With no time for subtle questioning, Aidan fired a round into the man's leg, shattering his tibia. As he rolled around on the ground, screaming, Aidan snapped, "Tell me, or you'll have a matching pair."

"We're just supposed to take you to the house and leave you at the front door." He swallowed and added, "That's all. I promise."

Aidan smiled. "Now, was that so hard?"

"You'll never get away with this, asshole."

"Maybe. Maybe not."

The man rolled over, grabbing at his leg. When he rolled back, he was holding a gun. Aidan fired a second shot, this time into the man's forehead.

Knowing that Simon would be expecting his men to show up with him any minute, Aidan had only a limited amount of time to prepare. He searched the duffle bags belonging to the two men, found a few nice surprises, along with a cellphone and a bottle of water.

He sheathed both knives, one in each boot, took three guns and all the ammo. Taking off at a run, he drank down the water as he dialed McCall's number. When nothing happened, he checked the readout and cursed. No signal.

Hoping for a better signal when he got closer to the house, he kicked into high gear. Every second counted.

Though there was a small access road running from the helicopter landing area to the mansion, Aidan opted for the cover of trees and shrubbery. He anticipated there would be cameras alerting Simon to his presence, but he wanted to avoid any advance warning if possible. Taking Simon and his men by surprise was the best chance of survival for both him and Anna.

When he got to the edge of the estate, he halted behind a tree. There were no fences, no gates. Simon apparently trusted that his location was hidden enough that he didn't need additional security. Aidan checked the signal on the cellphone. Still nothing. Even though he'd rather have a half-dozen LCR operatives going inside with him, there was no way he could delay any longer.

Holding one of the Glocks in his hand, Aidan headed to the front door.

***

Anna stiffened at a noise outside the bedroom. She'd been dozing on and off since dinner. About an hour ago, she had eaten a delicious, if bland, meal of chicken and rice. The man, who'd finally introduced himself as Patrick, kept his word, taking a large bite of everything on her plate and consuming several sips of her water.

She was still so weak that her hand shook when she lifted her fork to her mouth. Simon's poison had done a number on her. She felt foolish for consuming a meal like she was a guest when she had no idea where Aidan was or what was going on outside the bedroom door, but until she regained her strength, she would be no use to him or herself.

The door opened abruptly, and Anna sat up in the chair, trying to ready herself for whatever these men had planned. Patrick entered first, and then a man she'd never seen walked in behind him.

"Who are you?" She looked behind them. "Where's Simon?"

Neither man answered her, but the new man sent Patrick a smiling look. "You're so right. Perfect choice."

They both came toward her, and the intent expressions on their faces gave her warning that things were about to get ugly again. Refusing to just sit still and take whatever they had planned, Anna forced herself to rise. Her legs felt like jelly, and her entire body was shaking. She made it around the chair and then had to lean against the back of it to keep herself upright.

"Stay away from me."

The stranger gave her an oddly gentle smile. "I'm sorry, but that's just not possible. You're here to fulfill a promise. Now be a good girl, and we'll try to make this painless."

Patrick stood on her left, and the other man was on her right. They were both older than she was, but they were at full strength. Since they wouldn't be fighting for their lives, as she would be, she told herself she had the advantage.

Anna pushed away from the chair and ran toward the door. Halfway there, two pairs of hands grabbed her arms. Using every bit of strength she had left, Anna jerked and fought them off, scratching and kicking. Her feet were bare, and she felt the jarring impact all the way through her body when she made contact with various body parts. She heard curses and more than a few grunts.

She took another step, and then thick, strong arms wrapped around her torso, trapping her arms. She realized Patrick was holding her when the other man came to her side. In his hand was another syringe.

"No. Dammit! No!" Anna jerked and screamed, kicking violently. The last injection had almost killed her. She couldn't take another one.

Correctly interpreting her fear, the man said, "Don't worry, my dear. This will just relax you." The needle slid into her arm.

The world whirled around her. "Why?" Anna whispered.

She was vaguely aware that she was lifted and placed on something soft but firm. Her mind acknowledged she was back on the bed.

"Please, stop." She managed to get the words past her rapidly numbing lips. "Please don't hurt Aidan."

A wild, hideous kind of laughter surrounded her, and Anna screamed in silence for the man she loved and might never see again.

CHAPTER THIRTY-SEVEN

Aidan opened the front door and walked into the mansion as easily as he would at his own home. The interior wasn't what he'd expected. The outside looked almost homey, but the inside was both cavernous and austere. The floor was a cold, gray marble, and the walls a slightly dull shade of beige. Since he probably didn't have a lot of visitors on top of the mountain, Simon had skimped on the décor.

"Hello, Dr. Thorne."

A man stood at the top of the stairs. White hair, sixtyish, with a kind-looking face. His hazel eyes were empty and emotionless.

"Where's Anna?"

"All in good time."

Aidan aimed his weapon at the man's crotch. "I'm not going to ask again."

"Very well," the man said. "Ms. Bradford is sleeping. She's perfectly fine, and you'll see her soon."

"I want to see her now."

"Really, Dr. Thorne. Your rudeness would be amusing if it weren't so gauche."

Aidan fired a warning shot at the man's left foot. He jumped back and stumbled on the stairway. Grabbing hold of the railing, he snarled, "That was uncalled for."

"It was very called for. Tell me where Anna is, or you'll be missing a few toes."

"All right. You've made your point. Please place your weapon on the floor, and I'll take—"

"I don't think you're understanding me. I keep my gun. You take me to Anna. End of story."

"End of story? I don't think so."

The steel of a gun was pressed into his back. "Do as the man says. Drop your gun."

Aidan leaned down and placed the Glock on the floor.

The man behind him growled, "Search him."

Two more men appeared, and Aidan stood still as they removed weapon after weapon, along with the cellphone.

The man on the stairs began to walk toward him. "Well, you certainly came prepared. I guess I don't need to ask what happened to the men who brought you here?"

When Aidan didn't answer, the man smiled. "Dr. Cook is eager to see you again after all these years. Follow me."

With no choice but to comply, Aidan followed behind the older man. The three guys behind him were all armed, and while they might not shoot to kill, they'd likely enjoy shooting some non-vital areas just for the fun of it.

The white-haired man led Aidan down a long hallway and stopped at a door. He knocked, and when a voice said, "Enter," he put his hand on the doorknob.

Aidan heard the familiar voice, and his mind was trying to come up with an explanation when the door was pushed open. Comprehension slammed into his brain.

Now he knew why the words on Simon's tombstone in the homemade horror movie had bothered him. Simon had detested being referred to as Junior. There was no way he would have willingly put that on his tombstone.

His mind whirling with new questions, Aidan stepped inside and faced a ghost.

Smugness might not be a virtue, but in this instance, Simon believed he was entitled to a small amount of it. The shock in Aidan Thorne's eyes eased, if only slightly, the rage Simon Cook, Sr. had held on to for more than a decade.

"Shall I quote Mark Twain? The report of my death was grossly exaggerated."

Recovering quicker than Simon had anticipated, Thorne snarled, "Where's Anna?"

"Tsk-tsk, Dr. Thorne. The women in your life have always caused you trouble of some sort."

"I don't know what sort of sick, twisted game you and your son are playing, but leave Anna out of it. She's got nothing to do with this."

"But of course she does. She's the final masterpiece in a decade-long endeavor."

"If you want me dead, then damn well do it and get it over with. There's no reason Anna has to be involved."

"Such an altruistic man. I'm surprised you left the medical profession. You could have done such wonderful things. Saved so many lives."

"What do you want, Dr. Cook?"

"Call me Simon."

"That's what I call your murdering bastard of a son."

Rage erupted like a volcanic explosion, and Simon lunged toward the man who'd ruined his and his son's lives. He got only halfway there before a voice shouted behind him, "Dr. Cook. Stop!"

Simon halted, infuriated that Thorne had caused him to lose his temper so soon. Anticipating that his emotions might get the best of him, he'd asked Patrick to stay close in case he overreacted. There was so much more to accomplish. Ending things now would ruin everything.

Stepping back, Simon grimaced a smile. "Have a seat, Aidan. Let's catch up."

"Not until I see Anna."

"You really have a thing for her, don't you? And why shouldn't you? She's a lovely young woman."

Simon jerked his head slightly. "Patrick, if you please."

The wall behind him slid open to expose the large observation window that looked into the bedroom he'd had especially prepared for this momentous occasion. In the middle of the room was a king-size bed. And on the bed lay the lovely Anna.

For as dramatic a showing as possible, the lights inside the room brightened in slow increments, much the way daybreak began. Then, with a burst of brilliance, the entire room flooded with light. And that was when Simon heard the most beautiful sound of all. A pain-filled gasp from Aidan Thorne.

Fury unleashed, Aidan had his hands wrapped around Cook's neck before he realized he'd moved. "What did you do to her, you son of a bitch?"

Clawing at the fingers around his neck, Cook rasped the words, "She's sleeping."

She didn't look like she was asleep. Her cheeks were bleached of all color, bruises covered one side of her swollen face, and she was as still as death.

"Dr. Cook?" The white-haired man appeared on the other side of the glass partition, beside the bed where Anna lay.

"If you want her to stay unharmed you need to let me go, Thorne," Cook wheezed. "Patrick is quite capable of breaking her arm with his bare hands."

Aidan eased his grip on Cook's neck, but only slightly. "He touches her, you die."

"But, my dear young doctor, you've definitely lost your touch. I'm already dead."

"What are you talking about?"

"Let's have a seat, and I'll tell you a story."

"I want to see Anna first, face-to-face. I need to make sure she's okay."

"Very well, but under certain restrictions."

"Restrictions?"

"You'll be restrained."

Aidan held out his hands. "Fine. Whatever."

Beaming as if he'd earned a major concession, Cook zip-tied his wrists. "Come with me."

Cook led him out the door and into the other room where Anna lay. He didn't wait for the old man to keep up as he strode to the bed and checked her pulse. It was steady and even. Her breathing was good, and her temperature felt normal.

"What did you give her?"

"Just a little sleeping potion. Something I created myself. She's perfectly fine."

"What happened to her face?"

Cook made a clucking sound. "An inadvertent injury, I'm afraid. Your Anna put up more of a fight than was anticipated. The hoodlums we hired weren't as careful as they had been instructed. If it makes you feel any better, they're both dead now. And though she's bruised, nothing's broken."

Wanting nothing more than to haul Anna into his arms and take off with her, Aidan forced restraint. He wouldn't get one step outside before he was shot. No way in hell would he put Anna at more risk. He had to figure out a way to get her out safely. If talking to Cook Sr. and his crazy-assed son was what was required, that's what he'd do. Aidan knew it wasn't going to be that simple, but he'd cross that bridge when it appeared in front of him.

"All right. Let's talk."

"Excellent."

He followed Cook back out to the other room. Why the bastard was allowing him to keep an eye on Anna while they talked was suspicious, but Aidan wasn't going to question the reason. If he had to, he told himself, he could be at Anna's side in seconds.

"Have a seat. Would you like something to drink? Coffee? Tea?"

"Get to the point."

As the elder Cook settled into his chair, Aidan ran down the things he remembered about the man. Widower. Gifted chemist. Father of one son, whom he doted on to the point of obsession. Ten years ago the man had been slightly stocky, with thick hair, bushy eyebrows, and a ruddy complexion. This man, with his thinning hair, pale face, and slender body, held little resemblance to the Cook Sr. that Aidan had once known.

After Simon disappeared, Cook Sr. had become a hermit, still claiming his son was innocent and swearing he had no idea where he'd gone. No one had believed him, but neither could they prove otherwise. So was Simon here? Had father and son been holed up in this place like two evil moles?

"Why'd you fake your death?"

"Because it was the only way to get rid of the constant surveillance. No one believed I didn't know where Simon was hiding. I couldn't go anywhere, do anything without being followed and harassed."

His smile one of triumph, he added, "I do wish I'd thought of it years before. Amazing what you can accomplish when people don't know you exist."

"Like abducting a young woman?"

"There is that, but I promise, this was a one-time venture. So much work is involved."

"What do you want, Dr. Cook?"

"I want what any father of a wrongly accused child would want. Vindication."

"Simon was not wrongly accused. And do you think kidnapping and drugging Anna makes him look less guilty?"

"I've given up on the idea of Simon looking less guilty to the world. It's you who needs to absolve him of a crime he didn't commit. A crime you were responsible for."

Aidan's fingers dug into the arms of his chair. If he went after the bastard and strangled him as he wanted, he'd be killed, and Anna would likely die, too. He wouldn't jeopardize her life for the satisfaction of ending Cook's life. "You want to tell me how the hell I'm responsible for your son raping and murdering my wife?"

"You kicked him out of the apartment. You were his friend, his best friend, long before that whore came into your life."

"You may think you're safe from me because of your armed men, but hear me now. You insult Melody one more time, I will rip your tongue from your mouth and stuff it down your throat."

As if realizing he'd gone too far, Cook gave a shaky, ill-at-ease smile. "Of course, Simon could be difficult to live with sometimes."

"Why don't we bring Simon in here and let him be part of the conversation?"

Cook's expression flickered with an odd kind of sadness.

"Simon's the one who died, isn't he? Was it his body that was buried at what was supposed to be your funeral?"

"You think you have it all figured out, don't you, Thorne? You know nothing. The body in that coffin belonged to a John Doe homeless man. Instead of disposing of his body as if he had no family, I gave him quite a lavish send-off."

"If Simon is still alive, where is he?"

"We'll get to that in a moment. I won't let you deter me from my plans. Do you know how long I've waited for this?"

The more Cook talked, the more Aidan realized that the man was right. He had no clue what was going on and apparently hadn't for years. Despite his denial years ago, Simon's father not only knew where his son was, the bastard was deeply embroiled in his son's sick, twisted games.

"Then get on with it, Cook."

"Very well." He leaned forward, the glint of madness in his eyes a chilling reminder of what Aidan had at stake. "Let me tell you how you murdered my son."

CHAPTER THIRTY-EIGHT

Anna was quietly going insane. She couldn't move. Everything was frozen, numb. There was no feeling anywhere in her body. Limbs she told to move stayed unresponsive. She couldn't even open her mouth to scream or her eyelids to see. Her brain was working perfectly. In fact, this was the most alert she'd felt since she'd been here. The rest of her body was useless.

What had that bastard given her?

When she'd heard Aidan's voice, she had wanted to scream at him, warn him how crazy the man was. Instead, she could only lie here, helpless and terrified. Then she'd felt his hands on her, checking her pulse, her temperature. Why couldn't he see that she wasn't sleeping as Cook had claimed? She could hear everything. She just couldn't move. Couldn't he see that?

Aidan's hands had felt wonderful. Every particle of her wanted to lean into his touch, savor the feel of him. She silently screamed, willing her body to respond. There were tears in her eyes, she was almost certain they were there, but she couldn't release them. How had Cook done this? He had created a living corpse. Able to hear, breathe, and think, but unable to move even an eyelash.

How was she going to be able to help Aidan escape when she couldn't even open her eyes?

She heard footsteps as they walked away from her. She assumed they'd left the room, but then she heard their voices again. Aidan's and that of the man she now knew was Simon Cook, Sr., Simon's father.

The voices were so loud and clear that Anna knew they were coming from the speaker that Cook had used before. The man knew that she was awake, knew she could hear everything. And for some reason, he wanted her to hear his discussion with Aidan.

Whatever the reason didn't matter. She clung to every word Aidan said. The anger and bitterness were apparent, but so was the determination. That gave her hope. Aidan hadn't come here to give up and surrender. He had come here to rescue her. And he would.

***

Above the Caribbean Ocean

Infuriated by the lack of progress, Noah continued to stare at the screen displaying the map of Colombia. He had almost nothing to go on. Thorne had spent years trying to find this man. Without some kind of divine intervention, there was no way they were going to locate Cook in time to save Anna and Thorne.

Even though it was risky, he and the Elite team were headed to Colombia. Noah had no choice. Thorne had strongly believed that Cook was hiding out on one of the vast mountains of that country. Since that was all they had to go on, Noah was taking a calculated risk. Problem was, where to go when they arrived? He had no freaking clue. He had contacted every man and woman he knew who had information or ties to the country, in hopes of gleaning some kind of intel. So far he'd come up with zilch.

The cellphone lying on the conference table in front of him buzzed. A reminder that he had more than one LCR mission going. He glared at the thing, an unusual pessimism hitting him. These days, for every successful rescue they achieved, five more horrific events took place. LCR was larger than Noah had ever dreamed possible, but dammit, it still wasn't enough.

Grabbing the phone, he frowned at the unknown caller on the display. Wondering what new disaster had hit, he growled, "McCall."

"Señor McCall? Juan Garcia here."

"Hello, Señor Garcia. Is there something I can help you with?"

"No. But I believe I can help you."

Noah's heart picked up a cautious, optimistic beat. "How's that?"

"I am calling to offer my assistance in locating your friends Señor Thorne and Señorita Bradford. Those young people went out of their way to help my son. I would like to return the favor."

Noah couldn't suppress the smile that spread across his face. Just when the darkness looked as though it would eat up all light, a glimmer of hope appeared. Stupid, but he hadn't even considered calling Garcia. The man wasn't known for his kindness or generosity.

"You know where they are?"

"Si. I have people who know people. They claim the two were taken to a large mountain estate just outside Bogota."

"Do you know who owns this estate?"

"I have a name, but beneath it is another name. I believe this is a sham."

"Can you send me the location?"

"Si. I'm sending it to you via email. I have men who will be glad to assist you."

Helluva note that one of the most notorious drug lords, known to be ruthlessly cruel to his enemies, was providing him with the information he needed to save two lives.

"Thank you, Señor Garcia. I have the personnel. I just needed a location. Your assistance has been invaluable."

"Your man Thorne helped to save my son's life. Señorita Bradford worked to save his men's lives. I could do no less."

The call ended. Noah glanced at his laptop screen and noted he had a new email with attachments.

His optimism now sky-high, he went to the conference room door and took in the tense faces of his operatives. Some were on their cellphones, others on their laptops. Each of them working different angles, digging for any kind of information available on Simon Cook.

"We've got something."

They rose quickly and followed Noah. Sitting at the conference table, he clicked the link on the email and began to read.

***

Bogota, Colombia

Aidan and Simon Cook, Sr. sat across from each other as if they were having some kind of friendly social visit. As if Aidan didn't want to strangle every ounce of breath from his body.

His only solace right now was that the light was still on in the other room where Anna lay. He could see that she hadn't moved. He hoped she was simply sleeping, as Cook had stated. He hoped she had no idea what was happening. Just being able to see her, know where she was, gave Aidan the ability to focus. Figuring out how to get her out of here was his next goal.

"You know," Cook said in an odd, conversational tone, "you broke Simon's heart when you demanded he leave."

"Look, Cook. We've been through this. I—"

"Yes. Yes. I know. You believe you were in the right. But actions have consequences."

"And the consequences were Melody's rape and murder? The rape and mutilation of Kristen? The attack and mutilation of Amy? And now Anna's abduction? All because your insane and fragile baby boy was asked to find his own apartment?"

"Neither your sarcasm nor your insults are appreciated, Thorne. What looked like a simple request to you broke my son's heart. He came to me and told me what happened. He tried to be brave, but I could tell he was devastated. Simon was intellectually brilliant but still such a child when it came to his emotions. He loved you and Melody so much. Trusted you to always be there for him.

"Being forced to leave the apartment you shared made him feel as though his life was over."

Aidan chose not to respond. The longer the delay, the longer it would take to help Anna. Besides, the lunacy of Cook's defense of his son was beyond Aidan's ability to comprehend.

"I tried to explain to him that he would find more friends, better friends. But he was inconsolable."

Aidan reflected back on the moment he'd asked Simon to get his own place. He'd seen nothing but understanding and acceptance in his demeanor. Had he been so focused on his own life that he hadn't seen what was happening to his friend? If he had been more sensitive, could all of this been prevented?

Aidan glared at the older man. It didn't damn well matter if he had been an insensitive asshole. "People get their feelings bruised every damn minute of every damn day. How many of them rape and murder because their feelings are hurt? Or attack two women? Or stalk a man for ten years? Tell your son's lame-ass sob story to someone else, Cook."

"The past ten years have been your punishment for what you did. You're the cause of it all."

"You're as crazy as your son ever was."

"Say what you want. Defend yourself if you can. However, I know the truth. You took my son away from me. My beautiful, precious son."

"I did nothing to your son, you lunatic freak," Aidan ground out. "He. Murdered. My. Wife."

"It was an accident."

"Rape isn't an accident. Strangling a person with your bare hands till they stop breathing doesn't happen by accident. Biting and punching her until she's bruised and bleeding was not an accident." Aidan spoke through clenched teeth. "Your son murdered Melody."

The evil gleaming in Cook's faded-blue eyes should have warned him, but nothing could have prepared Aidan for the man's next words.

"No, he didn't. I did."

CHAPTER
THIRTY-NINE

His mind reeling, Aidan managed only a hoarse, "What?"

"I went to see you and Melody, to ask you both to reconsider." Cook's tone held a mild tone of confusion, almost as if he was still trying to figure out the events of that day. "Simon didn't know I was going. He was out looking for an apartment. I knew he wouldn't do well living on his own. The boy needed companionship. He looked at you and Melody as his family. I thought I could make her see reason. I needed to fix this for him. Make both of you see that what you were doing to Simon was wrong.

"You were working, but Melody was there. I thought I could talk to her…if she relented, then she could make you change your mind, too. But she wouldn't. She said she loved Simon like a brother but felt it was time for him to be on his own. She told me that I coddled him too much. That I should let my son work out things on his own."

Cook's eyes went wide with offense. "The very idea that this woman…this little bitch…would lecture me on how to raise my son… Needless to say, it infuriated me. So I slapped her. Just to knock some sense into her, you understand. And she had the audacity to hit me back.

"No woman had ever done something so disrespectful, so outrageous to me. I admit I lost control. In a small moment of weakness, of indiscretion, I hit her again. And then I did it again and again. When I finally came to myself, she was alive but barely conscious. I had no choice but to end her life. She would have told Simon what I'd done. I couldn't allow that."

"So you raped her, then killed her." Aidan couldn't believe how calm he sounded, because on the inside, a monumental eruption was about to take hold of him.

A small, almost self-conscious smile flickered on Cook's face. "I admit that was an indulgence on my part. The violence left me aroused. And since I was going to kill her anyway, I took the time to enjoy myself."

As if it made a damn bit of difference, Cook hurriedly added, "I want you to know, I had never done anything like that before. A part of me was horrified…" He gave another slight smile. "And, I'm almost ashamed to admit, another part found it incredibly satisfying."

The asshole had actually said the last part as if admitting a silly little indiscretion, something harmless and inconsequential. The question of whether the man in front of him would live or die today had already been answered in Aidan's mind, but he forced himself to stay still. He needed to hear it all.

"Once it was over…and I'd done the deed, I knew I had to cover it up. I cleaned up my mess, erased all evidence of my presence in the apartment and on her person. Then I left." He sighed. "I had no idea they'd blame Simon for my blunder."

"Blunder?"

"You know what I mean. Anyway, I went home, thinking they'd blame the incident on an intruder. Or perhaps her husband."

Cook blinked up at him, and the madness Aidan had glimpsed earlier was now in full force.

"You deserved no less, you know. You're the one who started it all, Thorne."

"Does Simon know what you did?"

"Unfortunately, yes." For the first time since this whole insane conversation had started, Cook's expression revealed remorse and sorrow. "When he heard the news of Melody's death, he was devastated. He was going to go to you, to comfort you, but I stopped him. By then it had come to me that he could be considered a suspect. I couldn't let him be seen. He would have been arrested...questioned. He couldn't be punished for something he didn't do. And I, of course, couldn't allow myself to be arrested."

Cook shrugged his thin shoulders as if everything he was saying made perfect sense. "I had to hide him, which meant I had to tell him the truth."

At some point, Aidan would face the reality that he'd hated his friend for all these years for something he hadn't done. But that would be later, much later. Right now, he wanted the truth and Simon Cook Sr.'s death. And then he and Anna were leaving. Aidan didn't care if he had to kill every person on this hellacious mountain.

"My son, as you might expect, was extremely upset. He was going to go to the police. Actually expected me to go with him and turn myself in. As if I were some kind of common criminal. I couldn't do that, and I couldn't allow him to go to the police."

Already seeing what was coming, Aidan said, "What did you do to him?"

"Well…I had to stop him, of course. You do understand that, don't you, Thorne? I couldn't go to prison."

"So you killed him?"

"No. Well…not really. I just…" He swallowed and looked around the room as if surprised by his surroundings. "You know of my work. My brilliance in chemistry is unrivaled. Even faking my death hasn't stopped people from wanting my creations. People, even governments, from all over the world place orders for a variety of potions they'd never find anywhere else."

Cook paused as if waiting for a response. Was the freak waiting for a compliment?

When Aidan said nothing, the man huffed out a small breath and continued, "At the time of my quarrel with Simon, I had been experimenting with a behavior-modification drug. I had yet to use it on a human, but we'd had great success with a couple of chimpanzees and a pig. I was designing it to change brain patterns to eliminate bad behavior. You know, to stop bad habits such as smoking or overeating.

"I thought if I could use it on Simon and make him understand why I did what I did, he would wake up and understand he couldn't turn me in. I was going to hide him away, give him an opportunity to work with me. With his brilliance, along with mine, we could have accomplished so much together."

"It didn't work."

Tears of both anguish and fury glinted in his eyes. "No. He stopped breathing. I was able to bring him back, but he…" He swallowed hard. "His brain was dead. His heart was beating, but that was all that was left of him."

"How long ago did this happen?"

"Three days after your wife died, so did my son."

"And the two women who were attacked. You did that? You raped another woman? Knocked them out, carved into their skin?"

"Of course not. I'm not a common criminal, you know." His voice went ice cold. "However, I did, and still do, hold you responsible. You ruined my life, my son's life. It was only fair that yours should be ruined, too. Simon never got a chance at happiness. Neither should you."

"You hired a man to rape Kristen? To mutilate both her and Amy?"

"Yes. If it helps, the two men I hired to do the deeds are dead." He shrugged. "I couldn't have anything lead back to me, could I?"

"You did all of this just to get back at me?"

"It prevented you from having any kind of long-term relationship, didn't it? It was more than Simon was able to have.

"Oh, I know you've had your dalliances. I had no problem with that…a man has his needs, after all. As long as you made no serious commitment to a woman, I was satisfied with your punishment."

"Why take Anna? You obviously believe there's something between us. Why didn't you hire someone to attack her like you did the other two women? Why bring her here?"

"Circumstances have changed, and my timetable has been moved up. My final act of revenge had to be expedited."

"And what is that final act, Cook? You plan on killing both Anna and me?"

"No." His eyes went cold. "Oh, I admit, I had planned for you to die as well. But now I realize your demise would be the easy way out for you. Instead, I want you to live a long, long life. You'll be haunted with the knowledge of what you've destroyed with your selfishness. And it's one last gift I can give my son."

"One last gift?"

"Patrick?" Cook said.

The lights behind them went dark. Aidan could no longer see Anna. Breaking the flimsy zip-tie with one quick snap, Aidan zoomed to his feet.

"Sit down, Thorne. I said I don't want you to die, but that doesn't mean I won't have you shot or maimed. Ms. Bradford is not being harmed in any way."

"Then what the hell is going on?"

"We're ready, Dr. Cook," a voice announced from the darkened room.

"Then please turn the lights up, Patrick."

The lights went on again. Aidan's eyes went straight to Anna. She looked the same as before. Everything looked the same as before, with one glaring, heartbreaking exception.

"Holy hell," Aidan breathed. "You kept him alive?"

Thin and pale, his features almost painfully peaceful, Simon lay beside Anna on the bed.

"Of course. I had the money. Why shouldn't I?"

"Because you'd already killed him, you bastard."

"He may be dead to the rest of the world, but he's not dead to me. At least not yet."

"I'm getting damn tired of asking you what you mean, Cook."

"Very well. Here's everything you need to know. I'm dying. I have a month to live, perhaps less. I want to go out on my own terms. My son and I, along with the lovely Ms. Bradford, will soon be engulfed in an explosion that will destroy this house."

Shit. Shit. Shit. The bastard was crazier than he'd guessed.

"And you expect me to just walk away and let that happen?"

"Oh, I'm sure you'll try some heroics. But it will do you no good. I will not be deterred. Everyone in this house has been paid handsomely to ensure that my final wishes are carried out. You will not stop me."

"Like hell I won't." In two strides, he was at the door. He opened it and faced the same three men as before, guns at the ready.

Aidan whirled and faced the devil. "You will not do this, Cook. Kill me if you have to. Isn't that what you want? To see me suffer? Then just do it. But leave Anna out of it. She's an acquaintance, nothing more. You left the women I had flings with alone. That's what she was to me. A fling. You won't be hurting me like you want. She's nothing more than someone I had sex with."

"It no longer matters. My mind is already made up. I took the only woman my son loved away from him. Anna might be a poor substitute, but it's the best I can do for him."

Cook nodded toward his men. "Please escort Dr. Thorne out of the house and secure him safely away from here. I wouldn't want a stray spark to singe one hair on his head."

One of the men grabbed him. Aidan shook him off. "You're a lunatic, Cook! You cannot do this!"

"Of course I can. Goodbye, Thorne."

"No!" Aidan shouted and lunged for the door. Searing agony exploded in his head, and the last thing he saw was Anna's pale, too-still face. And he knew he had failed her after all.

Chapter Forty

The LCR plane landed at a small airstrip on the north side of Bogota, and the team of operatives traveled to the base of the mountain together. Unfortunately, Garcia's coordinates hadn't been exact, so they had no choice but to split up.

"Kelly and Ingram, take the eastern side," Noah said. "Delvecchio and Mallory, take the west. Gates and Sinclair, you'll take the north. Fox and I will take the south. We stay in constant contact. We know nothing about Simon Cook or his plans. He could've planted booby traps in anticipation of Thorne finding his hideout. Be safe and be aware."

He nodded at the group. "Let's go."

They parted in grim silence. His people were always motivated to rescue and save lives, but when it was personal, there was always an added sense of urgency. Having no idea what Cook had planned for Thorne or Anna brought an unknown element to the mix. No one knew what to expect.

He and Sabrina hiked a couple of miles up the mountain before Noah finally said, "Sorry you had to cancel your vacation plans."

"I wouldn't have it any other way, and neither would Declan. Aidan isn't just my partner, he's my friend. And Anna…" She shook her head. "If she doesn't make it out of this, Aidan will never forgive himself."

Since Noah couldn't argue with the truth, he said instead, "They're both smart and resilient."

She looked away but not before he saw a flash of emotion on her face.

"You upset with Thorne for not telling you about Cook?"

"Yes, but not in the way you might think." Her brow furrowed as she explained, "When Aidan and I became partners, we both agreed that our pasts weren't up for discussion. I certainly didn't want to talk about mine, but looking back on that, I wish I had confided in him about Declan. About what I'd gone through.

"I'm not angry that he didn't tell me. I'm angry with myself for not asking. He's been hurting all this time, and I should have been there for him."

"You have been there for him, Fox. You're exactly the kind of friend and partner he needed."

"How so?"

"You helped him focus on the present. Thorne's been mired in guilt for ten years. Having a partner who didn't want to relive her own past made both of you better operatives."

"You put us together for that reason?"

"That, and because you have great chemistry."

"He's the brother I wish I had instead of the one I got." Her voice went grimmer. "I just hope we can find them before it's too late."

"We will. Getting that information from Garcia was exactly what we needed."

"It'd be nice if we got breaks like that more often."

"Yeah. Damn nice." Noah gave his operative a sideways glance. Fox wasn't always easy to read, but there was something else going on with her.

"Something else on your mind?"

She sent him an admiring look. "You're one of the few people who can read me."

"It's a gift that comes in handy, especially with LCR operatives, as well as my children."

"I'll bet." She was silent for a moment, as if searching for the right words. "Declan and I have been talking."

"Always a good thing in a marriage."

"He wants to make some changes."

"And you don't approve?"

"Yes…I mean, no, I totally approve. I just don't know what I'm going to do about them."

"You want to leave LCR?"

"Oh no. Never that. This is where I need to be. Where I belong. But Declan is considering leaving EDJE. He says the agency isn't what it once was. He doesn't feel that he's making the difference he wants to make."

"That's understandable. He's one of the most focused individuals I've ever known. Not accomplishing what he wants has got to be frustrating."

"Exactly. So he's thinking about branching out on his own."

"Doing the same thing?"

"Yes and no." For the first time in Noah's memory, Sabrina looked uncomfortable with him. "He wants to do something similar to LCR, but with some variations."

"Variations?"

"An organization that includes finding missing people, rescuing, and recovery, like LCR. But also cybersecurity, protection services. Things like that."

"The world's becoming a much more dangerous place. The more people willing to rescue, the better. And Declan's one of the best I've ever seen." He shot her a questioning smile. "Did you think I'd look at him as competition?"

"Declan said you wouldn't, but since I work for LCR, I worried it might cause problems."

"I can't think of anyone more qualified to run such an organization. And I admit to having an ego about a lot of things, but when it comes to saving people's lives, I don't give a damn who does the rescuing as long as it gets done."

Her smile was one of relief and gratitude. "Good. I agree. I hope that we can work—" She halted as a rumble like distant thunder echoed through the trees.

Noah was about to comment on the coming thunderstorm when the ground beneath their feet shook with the violence of an earthquake. He looked up to the top of the mountain and felt his heart stop. Even from this distance, he could see fire and debris shooting into the air. Someone had set off a massive explosion. And he knew without a doubt that Anna and Thorne were right in the midst of it.

***

Aidan was halfway to the helipad when he regained consciousness. Two men, half dragging, half carrying him, were moving at a rapid pace. He was thankful they were so rough, or he might not have woken so quickly.

With his head dropped to his chest, he was able to see they both still held their guns. Another man was in front of them, leading the way. Waiting for an opportune time to attack wasn't possible. He had to act now. The farther they moved from the house, the less his chances of getting to Anna. If Cook was telling the truth, the mansion could explode any second.

He slumped farther to the ground, pulling at the two men. One of them used his other hand to help catch him. Aidan snatched the gun and fired one shot into the head of the other man holding him. With a quick turn, he fired off two shots each into the other two men. There was only one life he could save today, and that would be Anna's.

His heart racing, his blood flooded with adrenaline, Aidan ran full out down the dirt road. Every step he took felt like too many. If she died... No, no, no. She wouldn't.

Sneaking back inside would be pointless. He wouldn't stop until he got Anna out of there. Whoever got in his way wouldn't survive.

He took the last few steps in a flying leap, landing on the porch. Shoving the door open, he ran toward the back of the house to the room where he'd last seen Anna. This would be Cook's location, too. As obsessed as he was, he'd want to go out with his son.

"Stop!" Patrick shouted.

Without slowing down, Aidan half turned and fired several shots toward the man. Aidan heard a grunt, knew the bullets had made contact. A gun blasted behind him. Aidan felt a slight punch on the back of his left shoulder, followed by a burn on his side. He ignored both.

"You'll never make it in time!" Patrick yelled.

"Yes, I will."

He burst through the door of the room. The stomach-churning image of an unconscious Anna lying between an almost-dead Simon and his deranged father wasn't something he'd get out of his head, ever.

Cook lifted his head and glared at him. "How did you get back in here? You're going to spoil everything. Patrick!"

Aidan strode to the bed and fired two shots, one into Cook's chest, the other into his groin. Leaning over Cook's body, Aidan scooped Anna up into his arms. Her eyes were open, but she was unnaturally still. Had the bastard given her more drugs?

He gave her what he hoped was a reassuring smile. "I'm here, baby. Hold on." Lifting Anna's limp body up, he placed her over his shoulder in a fireman's carry and took off. Instinct told him he had only seconds, if that, to get the hell out of there.

He sped through the house, an oppressive feeling of imminent doom nipping at his ass. Thankfully no one was around to try to stop him. He was on the porch when he heard the first rumble. Aidan tightened his grip on Anna and sprang from the porch. He landed on his knees, made it back to his feet, and tore off down the road. He felt the heat of the blast a second before a resounding roar bellowed around them. The massive expulsion of air slammed against his body, throwing him off his feet again.

Aidan managed a midair turn and landed on his side, protecting Anna from being smashed into the ground.

Holding her in his arms, he spared a second to watch the mansion burn. Within that mass of blazing wood and shattered glass was justice for Melody, for Amy and Kristen. And for Anna. The crazed bastard was dead.

But there was also the heart-wrenching knowledge that the man he'd blamed all of these years, and hated with such bitter passion, had been a victim himself. His friend had not betrayed him.

"Aidan?"

He glanced down at the woman in his arms. Though her eyes were glazed, her pupils dilated, she was awake, and she was alive. For now, that was all he needed.

CHAPTER
FORTY-ONE

Disoriented and so groggy she had to keep pinching herself to stay awake, Anna nevertheless refused to allow Aidan to carry her any longer. She had tried to get him to let her see to his injuries, but stubborn man that he was, he'd said not yet.

A minute after Aidan had been forced out of the house, Cook had come into the room and administered another shot. He'd kissed her on the forehead, saying he wanted her to be aware of everything. And then he'd lain down beside her.

The shot had an immediate effect, and she had at last been able to open her eyes. Unfortunately, she'd still been too weak to move, to do anything other than lie there and wait for whatever was going to happen. Even as she was praying that Aidan would come and save her, she was also praying that he would stay away and be safe.

And then, because he was who he was, Aidan had been there and spirited her away, saving her life once again.

His hand holding hers, Aidan pulled her down the dirt road, away from the burning building. "When we get somewhere safe, we'll check each other out."

She gazed around. She might not be as alert as she wanted, but she could at least keep an eye out. They'd already veered around three dead men on the road. She knew Aidan was the one who'd taken them out.

"You don't think all his people are dead?"

"I hope they are, but I can't take that chance. Once we get up in the air, I'll feel safer."

"Air?"

"I was brought here in a helicopter. You probably were, too. We'll take it and…" He jerked to a stop. "Shit."

"What's wrong?"

"Someone already took it."

They walked to the middle of a flattened area. Anna could see the imprint of where the helicopter had once been. She shifted her gaze and spotted the bodies of two large men a few feet away.

"Your doing?" she asked.

"They're the ones who brought me here."

She looked up in the air but saw only the setting sun and dimming skies. It would be dark soon.

"So we walk down the mountain. We've done it before."

His face was grimy and etched with pain, but the brightness from his smile warmed her heart. "You're one in a million, Anna Bradford. You know that?"

She returned the smile with a cheeky one of her own. "Tell me something I don't know. Not too many women could sleep through all the ruckus you made."

"I have a lot to tell you." He nodded toward the single story glass building to the left. "For right now, let's check here for supplies and then get out of here. Even though it's a roof over our heads, I'd just as soon not stay here."

She couldn't argue with that. The farther away she got from the monsters, even though they were dead, the better. Glancing down at her body, she grimaced. "Think we can find me something other than a nightgown to wear?"

"We'll find you something. I promise you."

In the end, they found more than they'd expected. The building housed a small gym as well as a changing room with individual lockers. Apparently, Cook's employees spent time in the building. Which, considering who their employer was, made sense. Getting some privacy, away from the lunatic they worked for, would have been important to save their own sanity.

Ten minutes later, they walked out of the building, both dressed in clothing they'd found in lockers. While Aidan had grabbed a small duffle and filled it with some medical supplies he found in a cabinet, as well as an antibiotic he'd discovered in one of the lockers, Anna had collected water bottles and snacks from a vending machine that Aidan, with the aid of an ax, had busted open for her.

Feeling a little more secure and a lot more awake, Anna followed Aidan's lead. An hour later it was pitch dark, and they had no choice but to stop or take the chance of falling and hurting themselves more. She had seen blood on Aidan's shoulder and his side, as well as the back of his head.

The instant they found a small, enclosed area that shielded them from sight, Anna instructed Aidan to sit down and let her look at his injuries. She moaned at what she found.

"It's not that bad."

"Aidan, you have bullet holes in your shoulder, a bloody slice on your side, and a lump the size of an apricot on your head."

"That's good news."

"Why?"

"It feels like a watermelon."

Tears sprang to her eyes. "Stop trying to make me laugh. That's not even funny."

"Come on, sweetheart. Get me patched up, and then I want to check you, too. Whatever that asshole gave you put you out for hours."

She didn't mention what had happened beforehand. Telling him she still felt as weak as water from the hours of vomiting and the torturous nightmares she had endured wouldn't help.

Following his instructions to the letter, Anna cleansed the blood from Aidan's shoulder and side with antiseptic wipes and applied bandages. There were two holes in his shoulder, front and back, so at least the bullet was no longer still there. She was grateful for that because she wasn't sure either of them could have survived her extracting the bullet. The cut on his side, several inches long, was from a bullet that had sliced into his skin at least an inch deep. The cut needed stitches, and while Aidan could probably have talked her through that, they had nothing to sew it up with.

She touched the wrapping around his torso. "Why are your ribs wrapped?"

"Some SOB kicked me during an op. Just cracked a couple."

"Oh, is that all?"

Letting her know her sarcasm wasn't lost on him, he gave her a quick grin.

Muttering to herself, she cleaned the blood from the giant lump on his head. It looked even more massive once she'd washed the blood away.

"You must have the mother of all headaches."

He shrugged. "I dry-swallowed some aspirin back at the building. It's not too bad."

Not too bad for Aidan was probably *agony* for anyone else, but since she could do nothing about it, she simply nodded.

"Okay now," he growled softly, "let's take a look at you."

Despite the circumstances and in spite of what she'd overheard him say to Cook, Anna felt a wave of longing so immense she had to grip her hands together to keep from reaching for him. Not only was this not the time or place, he was injured. Besides, she was still so weak, even one small kiss would probably knock her sideways.

He checked her pulse first, which was probably skyrocketing, but he just gave her a narrow-eyed look and said, "Let me see your eyes."

He used the flashlight to test her pupil reaction. She had a slight headache, and the light made it worse, but she wouldn't complain. Aidan's head had to be pounding.

"Any dizziness?" he asked.

"No."

"Blurred or double vision?"

"No."

"Nausea?"

She shook her head. "No."

"When we get to back to the States, I want you to go to the hospital for a full checkup and an entire panel of blood work. The drugs the son of a bitch gave you were his own inventions."

Revulsion swirled within her at the knowledge that unknown chemicals had been injected into her body. Cook could have given her any number of illnesses or diseases.

"He really was crazy, wasn't he?"

"Way past it. You hungry?"

After what she'd been through, she was relieved to be able to say, "Starving."

"Let's eat, and then tell me what you remember."

He handed her a bottle of water, a bag of chips, and a small pack of cookies.

Feeling as though she hadn't had an ounce of moisture touch her mouth in weeks, Anna downed half the water in one long gulp. She then started on her chips, and Aidan did the same. They ate in companionable silence for a few moments.

Feeling moderately better, Anna sat back against the rock. "How did you find out I'd been taken?"

"I got a call from Patrick from your phone." He gave her a nod. "Tell me what you remember."

She told him about leaving late and the man in the elevator. "It was Patrick. Even though he was incredibly polite, and there wasn't anything threatening about him, he gave me the willies. I made an excuse and got off the elevator.

"I waited a minute or so and then left the building." She gave a wry grimace. "I thought I was home free. I was a few feet from my car when two men attacked me."

He tenderly touched the bruises on her face. "I could kill the bastard again for this alone."

"I got in a few punches, but then Patrick showed up and shoved a needle in my neck. I was out for hours. When I woke up, I think I must've been on a plane. I remember hearing a drone, but he must've seen me move. He stuck me with another needle. The next time I woke, I was in a bed at Cook's house."

"Did he do anything to you? Touch you?"

"No. Not at all. He was creepy but treated me very politely. When I realized what had happened…I was so scared. I knew you would come for me."

"Are you finished with your chips?"

"What?" She glanced down at the bag she'd crumpled in her hand. "Yes."

He took the bag from her and put it away, then held out his hand. "Come here."

She went into his arms as if she was coming home. As if she belonged there, forever.

Aidan allowed himself one second of closing his eyes to savor the feel of her, whole and healthy. In those long hours of not knowing where she was, what had happened to her, he had almost convinced himself he would never get the chance to hold her again.

His head pounded as if someone were slamming a hammer into it every second, his shoulder and side throbbed, and the ribs that hadn't had the chance to mend were probably cracked even more. None of that mattered. Anna was alive. That was all that mattered. It was the only outcome he would have been able to live with.

Her voice was muffled against his chest. "I think those few moments when they forced you to leave and I was lying beside Simon were the worst of it all. I didn't think I'd ever see you again."

He shifted a little to look down at her face. Daylight was almost gone now, but this close, he could see the gleam of tears in her eyes. "You could hear us?"

"Yes. The drug…whatever he gave me…made me unable to move. I was paralyzed, but I was aware of everything. Could hear everything."

Fury roared through him. The sick son of a bitch had wanted her awake, helpless to do anything but lie there, aware of what was coming.

"When you came into the room to check on me, I was screaming…but you couldn't hear me."

He buried his face in her hair. "I'm sorry, Anna. So very, very sorry."

"It's not your fault, Aidan. I should have been able to fight them off. Believe me, when I get home, I'm going back to my self-defense instructors for some major training."

Telling her she had been outnumbered and drugged would do no good. Besides, he wanted her better trained.

"So I think I heard everything correctly. Cook Sr., Simon's father, was the one who'd been doing this all along. And your friend Simon…"

"Was innocent." Aidan shook his head, still trying to get his mind wrapped around the idea of how wrong he'd been all these years.

"In a way that's got to be a comfort. The man you believed was your best friend really was your best friend. He didn't betray you."

"Yeah."

She went silent, and Aidan figured she was probably asleep. He shifted her onto the ground so he could lie beside her but still hold her. He didn't intend to sleep. Just because it looked as though everyone had either died in the explosion or had escaped beforehand didn't mean that was what happened. He wouldn't let down his guard. Not again. Not until they were out of the jungle, and he could be assured once and for all that no one was coming after her.

He kept himself awake, thinking about regret, allowing himself to come to grips with all that he had learned. All the preconceived ideas that had been all wrong. He thought about Melody. Now that he knew who had really killed her, how it had all happened, a fresh wave of pain washed over him. And he thought about Simon. Had he known that Aidan blamed him? Or had he trusted Aidan to know he would never have hurt Mellie?

There were people he needed talk to, arrangements he needed to make. For the first time in over a decade, he actually had a future. And the woman he held in his arms was the biggest part of it. That was, if she would still have him.

CHAPTER FORTY-TWO

Anna woke just after dawn feeling almost normal. The first night after their escape, she had slept like the dead and had woken to find Aidan's concerned face hovering over her. She vaguely remembered that he had tried waking her several more times, and she had refused. She had still been so weak, and he had insisted they stay in their little hideout for one more day. She hadn't had the strength to argue.

This morning, though still a little tired and disoriented, she could feel her energy and stamina returning. Most certainly she would be able to travel today.

She shifted slightly, and her exhausted mind worked to figure out why she was lying on the surface of the sun. A searing heat encompassed one side of her body. She struggled to get away from the heat source and finally managed to sit up. The instant she was upright, she knew where she was and what was happening. Aidan was the heat source. He was lying beside her, burning with fever.

Going to her knees, she touched his forehead and gasped. His temperature had to be well over a hundred. His eyes were closed, and though she hated to wake him, she needed to know if he was in pain.

"Aidan?" she whispered.

Bloodshot eyes popped open immediately. "How are you feeling?"

"I'm fine. Much better than you are. You've got a fever."

"Yeah. Came on a few hours ago. I took that Amoxicillin we found. That'll help some. I'll pop a couple more aspirin and we'll be good to go."

"You're not going anywhere until we get your temperature down."

He grinned up at her. "You're cute when you're bossy."

Despite her worry, she couldn't help but laugh. "And you're a flirt even when you're sick."

She pulled the nightgown from the duffle bag. Even if the thought of it gave her shivers, she was glad she'd brought the thing with her to use as bandages. She ripped off one of the sleeves. Dampening the material with bottled water, she placed the damp cloth on his forehead.

"Hold this here. I need to take a look at your shoulder and side."

"I replaced the bandages about a couple of hours ago."

"How bad?"

"Shoulder might be getting a little infected. Side looks like it's thinking about doing the same thing. Nothing a few more doses of antibiotics can't cure."

And unfortunately the bottle they'd found only had a few pills left in it. "What about your head? How does it feel?"

"Still hard as a rock."

Her raised brow told him she wasn't moving until she got what she wanted.

A smile tugging at his mouth, he turned slightly so she could examine the lump on his head. The size had decreased, but more blood had crusted around it.

She dampened another cloth and cleaned the wound, relieved to not see fresh blood.

"Does your head still hurt?"

"Not as much as my ass. I've been sitting on this hard ground too long. Let's get up and stretch our legs."

Pleased that he felt well enough to stand, considering how he looked, Anna scrambled to her feet and assessed the surrounding area. She'd been so out of it yesterday, she could have been lying in a pit of vipers and she wasn't sure she would have noticed.

She could understand why he had insisted they stay here one more night. The place Aidan had chosen for them was actually like a little garden. Wild, vibrant flowers of various colors surrounded the area, while giant leafed bushes gave exceptional coverage. The flat area where they'd slept was covered in low, lush grass. Massive trees shaded them from the worst of the sun, and a large boulder jutted out from the ground to shield them from the inevitable rain. It reminded her of the place where they'd sought shelter a few weeks ago. With everything that had happened, it was hard to believe it hadn't been that long ago.

She turned to make that remark to Aidan and stopped. He'd just gotten to his feet and had the oddest look on his face.

"Aidan?"

He whispered, "Oh shit," and fell forward at her feet.

Anna didn't know how long she had been working to get Aidan's fever down. After he'd collapsed, she had rolled him over. First, she had checked to make sure he was breathing and hadn't injured himself further, then she had taken a look at his shoulder and side. His shoulder wound was red and inflamed. The bullet crease on his side looked angry, too. There was no doubt that the two injuries were the sources of the fever rampaging through his body.

Getting his temperature down was her first priority. She worked for over an hour, wiping his body with a wet cloth. He regained consciousness within a few minutes of passing out, assuring her that he was fine and just needed an hour or so of rest. A few minutes later, he was unconscious again.

On the inside, Anna was a mass of volatile emotions, fear being the biggest one of all. This beautiful, heroic man could not die. He had endured so much, lost so much. Had saved her life, as well as so many others. And now that he could actually allow himself to have a normal life, to have it snuffed out like this was injustice in the extreme. She could not allow that to happen.

Yes, she loved him with all her heart. Yes, she wanted to be with him more than anything. Her wants and needs didn't matter right now. She put all of those things aside to focus on one thing. This was one of the most selfless, noble men she'd ever known. The world needed more men like Aidan Thorne.

So she worked endlessly for hours to bring his fever down. Whenever he had moments of consciousness, she fed him little sips of water and talked about nonsensical and ridiculous things. Whether she did that to make sure he knew he wasn't alone or to keep herself from panic, she wasn't sure. She only knew that she had to keep up this one-sided dialogue.

It was late afternoon, she had gone through four bottles of water, and her voice was almost gone from talking so much, when Aidan's fever finally broke. During the longest hours of her life, in between her diatribe on everything from politics to reciting her master's thesis, Aidan had done his own share of rambling. Most of it was incoherent, but he mumbled Melody's name several times.

She could not imagine the pain he had endured, losing Melody in the way he had. And not only had Aidan heard the bastard who'd murdered her describe in detail what had happened, he'd learned that everything he had believed was a lie. It only made sense that this was at the forefront of his mind and would haunt him in his delirium.

But she couldn't deny that, as understandable as his pain was, her own hurt clawed at her like a wildcat, ripping her heart to shreds. She had heard every word he'd said to Cook about her and about Melody. He had said that Anna was just like the other women he'd had sex with. She was nothing special. They'd had a fling, nothing more.

The rational part of her mind told her he'd said those things in the hope that Cook would release her. That if the fiend didn't think she was important to Aidan, he would reconsider killing her. The other part, though, one made up of all the gut-churning emotions she felt for this man, told her what he'd said was true. Aidan had never given her any indication that he felt anything for her other than desire and perhaps friendship. He had even refused to consider her suggestion of using LCR to trap Cook. That, more than anything, spoke of a man who was still mired in the past and didn't want to move forward. Didn't want to have a new life with another woman.

She didn't begrudge his feelings. If Melody had been the love of his life, how could she resent his deep love for his wife?

Wasn't it just too bad that Aidan was the love of her life?

***

"You look tired, baby."

She had been sitting beside him, seemingly lost in thought. The instant he spoke, a smile of pure radiance brightened her face to an almost ethereal glow. Though she did look weary and worn out, happiness washed away the exhaustion.

"You're awake and speaking coherently."

"Apparently two things that haven't happened in a while. How long have I been out?"

"On and off for about a day and a half."

Aidan cursed himself. Almost two days of leaving her alone and unprotected.

"Are you okay?"

"I am now." She leaned over and kissed his forehead and then his cheek. She did it so automatically, he had a feeling she had done that many times over the last two days.

"Sorry I left you to fend for yourself. You must be exhausted."

She turned away and started rummaging in the duffle bag, but not before he saw her face crumple with emotion.

"Anna?"

Turning to face him again, a bottle of water in her hand, she whispered, "I've felt helpless before, but never like that. I thought I was going to lose you, Aidan."

He took the bottle she held out to him and then grabbed her wrist, pulling her forward. She went into his arms, and once again Aidan savored the contentment of having her so close. He was far from well, and they were not remotely out of danger, but they both needed this time.

"Why's your voice so hoarse? You been yelling at me and I missed the fun?"

"Only a few times. We've mostly just chatted about mundane stuff. Well, I chatted." He felt her smile against his chest. "You're a great listener, by the way."

"Thanks. One of my few talents when I'm unconscious." He squeezed her gently, noting how fragile she felt in his arms. "I haven't taken very good care of you."

She huffed out an exasperated breath. "No, you've just saved my life a half-dozen times, but who's counting?"

"We're even, then. If you hadn't kept me hydrated and cooled down, I wouldn't have made it."

"We're not even by a long shot. I'm just so glad you're better."

At some point, he needed to get up and try his legs out. For now, he wanted Anna to rest. He knew she'd stayed awake to keep him safe. She would downplay her heroism, but that didn't mean he would. He knew what it must have cost her. She was still recovering from all the shit Cook had pumped into her. And yet she had kept watch over him, protecting him. He couldn't think of anyone he'd rather have at his side for the rest of his life.

CHAPTER FORTY-THREE

Anna slept for several hours. Now that she was sure Aidan would make it, she allowed herself to relax. Still, she kept the small pistol he'd given her right beside her, and she woke several times to ensure everything was okay. Several times when she woke, Aidan was awake, too.

She'd asked him why he wasn't sleeping, and with his classic sexy smile, he'd said, "Because watching you sleep is a helluva lot more fun."

It was late afternoon when she woke again, feeling about as rested as she figured she was going to be until they were on level ground and far away from here.

"I need to get up and walk around."

Anna scrambled to her feet and held out her hand. "Let me help you."

His look was both disgruntled and sheepish. "I'd be insulted if it wasn't for the fact that I'll probably need your help."

She rolled her eyes. "Because I'm a woman?"

"No. Because I outweigh you by about a hundred and twenty-five pounds."

She doubted the number was one twenty-five but was vain enough to like that he thought so.

"I won't tell anyone if you don't."

He took her hands, and between the two of them, they got him on his feet. He swayed for a few seconds, and she knew it was all he could do to stay upright. She also knew he would persevere.

"Okay. I'm going just beyond those trees over there. You hear or see anything out of place, give me a yell. And don't hesitate to use your gun, if need be."

"You think any of Cook's men are still around?"

"I doubt it, but I don't want to take any chances."

She watched him make his way slowly through the bushes. He stumbled a couple of times but did better than she'd expected. Once he'd disappeared, she was vigilant, her gun at the ready, alert for any unusual sounds. Wild birds cawed, and small four-legged creatures scampered beneath the foliage. Other than those normal sounds, she heard nothing.

Less than ten minutes later, Aidan returned. His face was once again flushed, and his eyes were dull with pain. The short walk had cost him.

He must've noticed her worried frown, because he was quick to reassure her. "We'll stay here one more night, and then we'll get out of here. Promise."

She nodded. Either way, they were going to have to leave tomorrow. Their water supply could be replenished with rain, and they still had some candy bars and crackers, but Aidan desperately needed professional medical care.

They split a candy bar and a pack of crackers and settled back beneath the overhang of the rock. The rains came, and even though they both got a little damp, Anna was at peace. Tomorrow, things would be better. They would continue their journey down the mountain and would be safe soon. She fell asleep dreaming of a hot shower, clean sheets, and Aidan's strong arms surrounding her.

She woke with a gun to her head.

Aidan soundlessly eased around the clearing, cursing his carelessness with every breath. He should have woken Anna before he left, but she'd looked so peaceful, and he was gone only a few minutes. And now Patrick, Cook's main minion, had found her.

The only thing Aidan had going for him was that he had managed to circle around without getting caught. Patrick's back was to him. Aidan just needed to figure out how to get him away from Anna. The bastard had a gun to her temple. If Aidan took the shot now, Anna was dead.

"Where is he?" Patrick growled.

"I don't know. We got separated."

"You're telling me that the knight in shining armor who fought like hell to save you just lost sight of you?"

"He fell down a hill. I've been trying to find him, but I injured my back. I can't move very well."

Good for you, sweetheart, Aidan thought. Let the asshole think she was injured. He'd be less on guard.

"Well, now, isn't this a pretty pickle."

"Look, Mr. Patrick, I don't know what all of this is about. I've done nothing to you. I just want to go home."

"I'm sure you do, but it's too late for that now. Getting mixed up with Aidan Thorne was a bad decision."

"But I barely know the guy. Why would—"

"Tell it to someone who gives a shit. You're no use to me. I sure as hell can't carry you down this mountain. Might as well shoot you and put you out of your misery."

"But I—

"Get away from her, asshole."

With one smooth move, Patrick pulled Anna to her feet and whirled her around until she was in front of him, shielding him. The gun was still at her head.

"Well, looks like he's found you, love."

"Let her go. This is between you and me."

"I'm afraid it isn't. You ruined the plan. Dr. Cook intended that the girl die, too. There's no reason that still can't happen."

"Except if she dies, so do you."

"Not if I kill you first. Dr. Cook was the one who wanted you to live with your grief. I'd just as soon you die, too. Less complications for me. Plus, I owe you for the bullets lodged in my arm and leg."

"Then you better kill me, because if you harm one hair on her head, you are a dead man."

The gun turned away from Anna and pointed toward Aidan. "I've got no problem with you going first."

It wasn't planned, but Aidan knew Anna's ingenuity, he knew she was smart. And he was right. The instant the gun moved away from her, Anna eased a knife from her belt and plunged it to the hilt into Patrick's thigh. The man released a loud squeal and loosened his hold on her just enough for her to twist away. Aidan didn't waste any time. He fired a shot into Patrick's chest and followed it with a headshot.

The man was still falling to the ground when Aidan reached Anna and jerked her away. "Are you okay? Did he hurt you?"

"No. I'm fine." She glanced down at the now dead Patrick. "There you go saving my life again."

"This time I think we can call it a draw."

He gave her a quick, short kiss, mostly just to reassure himself that she was really fine.

"Why don't you go take a quick walk, loosen up your legs?"

"What are we going to do about him?"

"Leave him here. When we get to civilization, I'll tell the authorities where to find him. I doubt that they'll care."

Aidan waited until she'd walked away before he went to Patrick's body. In the last few weeks, Anna had been around more dead bodies than most people saw in a lifetime. He rifled through the man's pockets and confirmed what he thought had probably happened. Patrick was supposed to have gotten away, probably on the helicopter, and because Aidan had delayed him, he hadn't been able to escape. Cook's remaining men had gone off and left him. The man was unprepared, having almost nothing on him. But the one thing he did have was the exact thing they needed.

Anna came back to the clearing. "Why are you looking so happy?"

Aidan held up the treasure he'd found in Patrick's pocket. "Want to make a phone call?"

Delight in her eyes, she rushed forward. "Yes!"

A little surprised at the old-school device, Aidan flipped the phone open and clicked on the phone icon. He punched in McCall's number, and when nothing happened, he growled out a curse. "Dammit. What is it with this mountain?"

"No signal?"

"Not a single bar. Let's grab our gear and get started. The closer we get to civilization, the better our chances of getting a signal."

Aidan reached for the duffle bag. The snap of a twig had him turning, simultaneously going for his gun as he pulled Anna behind him. Hell, what now?

A familiar face appeared between the bushes. "You guys interested in a ride out of here?" Justin Kelly asked.

CHAPTER
FORTY-FOUR

Alexandria, Virginia

Aidan stood beside the empty hospital bed and reviewed Anna's chart. She was out of the room, having more tests done. So far, the test results were negative for any kind of damage Cook's drugs might have done to her organs. Every time he thought about the shit that had been forced upon her, he grew infuriated again.

They had been back almost three days. Once Justin and Riley arrived, things had moved fast. It figured that McCall and his Elite teammates were already on the mountain looking for them. When Aidan had learned who'd informed McCall of their whereabouts in Bogota, he had been surprised at the irony. Sometimes you never knew where the hell help was going to come from. You're just damn glad you got it.

Thankfully, Kelly had had a radio that worked. He had called for a rescue helicopter and then notified the other operatives.

Within an hour, McCall and the other team members had arrived. Not long after that, a helicopter had appeared, and he and Anna had been airlifted out of the jungle. They'd landed at an airport where the LCR plane was waiting. A few hours later, they'd been back in the States.

Aidan had been out of commission for a day or so. The infection that had been raging through his body had needed strong antibiotics. The bullet wound in his shoulder had caused no muscle or bone damage. Though it still throbbed, the pain was bearable. A little rehab, and he'd be good to go. The crease on his side had required a dozen stitches and had already started itching, telling him he was healing. He'd had a slight concussion, and the ribs he'd cracked last week had indeed been cracked further. All in all, he'd gotten out damn lucky.

His biggest concern was still Anna's health and well-being.

"Hey."

Aidan turned as a nurse rolled Anna into the room in a wheelchair. She was still too pale for his liking. There was a worrisome dullness to her eyes, and her appetite, which he'd always admired, was still off.

"Hey, yourself." He nodded at her wheels. "Enjoying your ride?"

"No, but I've been told it's hospital policy." She stood and came toward him. The weight she'd lost in the last few days hammered at his conscience. It was time he started taking better care of her.

"Why didn't you tell me that the drugs Cook first gave you caused hallucinations and made you violently sick?"

"How did you know?"

"I read your charts."

"Hmm." She didn't smile, but amusement glimmered in her eyes. "Isn't that some sort of violation?"

"When it comes to your welfare, I'm willing to take the risk."

Her hand caressed his arm. "I know," she said softly. "I'm alive because of you."

"So why didn't you tell me? After we got away...when you told me about your abduction, you didn't say anything about the hours of vomiting and migraine. The hallucinations about being back in Tranquility."

"Because there wasn't anything you could do about it. After I got the poison out of my system, I was fine."

That wasn't quite true, but he wasn't going to argue the point. The test results had indicated she'd received a concoction that had included some kind of bacteria that commonly caused food poisoning. Cook had combined that with a strong sedative. The bastard had been an evil genius, able to create a variety of illnesses.

Since their return, McCall's best researchers had discovered something so chilling, so gut-wrenchingly horrifying, that Aidan had still not come to terms with the reality. Dr. Simon Cook Sr. had crafted the poison that had killed some of Julio Garcia's men. If he had given that particular concoction to Anna, she would probably be dead.

"It's over now, Aidan."

Anna's gentle voice pulled him from his grim thoughts. She knew exactly what was on his mind.

"McCall told you...about the connection between Cook and Ruiz?"

"Yes." She gave him that smile that caused his heart to jolt every time he saw it. "I'm very lucky."

And that was it for Anna. She had survived the ordeal. So far, they had discovered no lasting side effects or consequences from what she'd been given. She was ready to move on.

He would do that, too…or at least try. The fact that she never would have been exposed to Cook if it hadn't been for Aidan was something he would have to live with. Going forward was the only option.

Taking the hand that was still caressing his forearm, he led her to the sofa. He sat down and pulled her to sit beside him. He wanted to hold her but couldn't afford the distraction right now. His time was limited. He had a plane to catch.

"I'm leaving in a few hours."

She frowned up at him, her worry and disapproval evident. "You're going back to work? Isn't that too soon? You haven't healed yet. Your shoulder and side, not to mention your concussion, are still causing you pain."

"I'm not going back to work. Not yet. I need to see Kristen and Amy. They need to know who was responsible for their attacks. And they deserve the closure in knowing the bastard is dead."

Anna swallowed past the growing lump in her throat. Aidan was right. These women had every right to know the truth. Telling them on the phone would be cold and cruel. Not telling them the truth would be worse.

But she couldn't help but want to cling to him. When they'd been out in the jungle, just the two of them, she had felt so close to him. Connected in a way she had never been with another person. Since their return, they'd been separated for large blocks of time. Necessary because of all the tests she'd had to endure, but the connection they'd had was lessening. No, that was too mild. It felt as though it was disintegrating at an alarming speed. And she had no idea how to stop its progress.

"When will you be back?"

"Hard to say. Kristen is still in Connecticut, but Amy moved to Vermont a few years back. While I'm in Connecticut, I need to see my family. They've been through hell with me. They deserve the truth, too."

And so his answer was *I don't know.* She wasn't shy when it came to most things. It was her experience that you didn't get far in life by being a shrinking violet. When it came to her heart, though, and the immense emotions she felt for this man, she couldn't be the straightforward, tell-it-like-it-is person she was in other things. He just meant too much to her. Because if she told him what was in her heart and he said no, that there was no future for them, she wasn't sure she could handle the pain. Even if he indicated they could date and see each other in public, she wouldn't react well.

Dating wouldn't be enough for her. Not without commitment. There was nothing shallow, casual, or fleeting about her feelings for Aidan. She was in love with him, totally and forever. There could be no halfway for her. For Anna, it was all or nothing.

"Hey." His voice jerked her from her thoughts.

She gave him her best understanding smile. "You're right. Everyone deserves to hear the truth in person."

"When I get back, we need to talk."

"Okay." What else could she say?

Cupping her face, he leaned down and captured her mouth in a tender, mesmerizing, exquisite kiss.

Anna's heart, soul, her very being ached for more, but she responded with the same degree of tenderness and caring. If this was their last kiss, she wanted them both to remember the moment as beautiful and magical.

When he pulled away, she didn't even try for a smile. There was no way she could fake one. Instead, she said what was expected of her, what would ease his mind. "I'll see you when you get back."

A few minutes later, Aidan walked out the door. Not taking any chances that he would come back and catch her, Anna sped to the bathroom and locked the door before she broke down into a sobbing mess of tears.

***

Ann Arbor, Michigan

Standing in the quiet of the small park, Aidan let the isolation soothe him. The last few days had left him raw. He had been face-to-face with both Kristen and Amy. The two women were alike in a lot of ways, but how they took his news was the polar opposite. Kristen had sat beside her husband, holding his hand when Aidan had delivered the name of the man responsible for instigating the rape. When he had explained the details and that Cook Sr. claimed that her rapist had been killed, she had wept in her husband's arms.

Aidan had apologized profusely once again. He had wanted to do more, but whatever he could offer would never make up for what she'd been put through simply because he had dated her. But after her tears, she had given him a gentle smile of understanding and told him she was glad to know the truth, but she had been able to move on. She told him she hoped he could move on, too.

Aidan had left her home, still sad but slightly buoyed by her gracious forgiveness. Perhaps that was why his meeting with Amy had been so intensely painful.

Amy had not been able to move on as Kristen had, though it was obvious she had tried. She had lived in five different cities since her attack, married twice, divorced twice, and had been employed at no less than a dozen places.

Some would say that the violation she'd suffered was less traumatic than what Kristen had endured. Aidan wouldn't go that far. Not only did Amy still bear the physical scars from her attack, the way each person dealt with trauma was their own. Her pain was genuine and so raw, it was like the assault had happened only a few days ago instead of years ago. Aidan had left her apartment feeling as though he'd been flayed open. The suggestion that she seek more counseling and his offer to pay for whatever she needed had been met with bitter contempt.

His parents, as he had expected, received the news that the threat was over with both joy and relief. Aidan had left soon after with the promise that he would return soon. He hoped that Anna would be with him. He still hadn't told them about her. Since he was about as unsure of her as he'd been about anything in his life, he'd simply told them he hoped to be sharing more good news with them soon. From the quick, delighted looks they'd given each other, he knew his sister had already spilled the beans.

And now here he was, his final stop before he went home. This place of solitude and comfort held so many memories, both happy and painful. It only made sense that this was the place he would visit last.

He had proposed to Melody here, right under this giant oak tree. They'd been grilling each other for a final. She had asked him a question, he had answered. When it had been his turn to ask a question, Aidan had asked her to marry him. She'd simply smiled, given him a yes, and then went on to ask him another quiz question. That had been Melody, unflappable and serious, even in the midst of a marriage proposal.

Beneath this giant oak was also the place he had come that cold December day to spread her ashes. And he had sobbed… Oh, how he had sobbed. Lying on the ground, uncaring of the snow and wetness, he had poured his heart and soul out to her.

Today, he had come for another reason. He wanted to talk with her about what he had learned. And then he had something else very important to discuss with her.

Sitting beneath the tree where they'd sat so long ago, Aidan began. "Hey, Mellie. Sorry it's been so long since we've talked. Guess you know what's happened—that I finally found out the truth. Something you've known all along.

"I can't even begin to imagine what you felt that day, Mellie. It still rips at my guts to even think about it. I'm sorry, sweetheart. I'm sorry that happened to you. I'm sorry I wasn't there for you. To protect you.

"You probably got pissed that I blamed Simon. I feel bad about that, Mellie. Hating him for all these years for something he didn't do. And to think I'd had conversations with his father… and all the while he—"

Swallowing with difficulty, Aidan continued, "But now the truth is out. Both Simon and his father are dead. I'll mourn my friend Simon the right way this time."

Ragged breaths gushed from his lungs. "Aw, hell, Mellie, how did things get so messed up and confused? But it's done… over with. Guess you know what else I've come for. I've come to say goodbye again. I've met someone…guess you know that, too.

"You would love her, Mellie. She's smart, sassy, so full of goodness and light. I'm crazy about her. I'll always love you, you know that. But I got lucky. I fell in love again. Never thought it could happen. She's different from you in a lot of ways, but in the ways that matter—the things that would make you friends—she's a lot like you, too.

"I'll bring her here someday to meet you. She won't think I'm crazy for talking to you like you're actually here. That's one of her greatest gifts—she understands me. Gets me.

"So, here we are. Saying goodbye once again. I hope you'll look down on me from time to time and remember the good times we had. The love we shared. And if Simon's up there with you, will you tell him I'm sorry for being such a boneheaded nitwit?"

Aidan got to his feet, wiped the tears from his face. "Thank you for loving me, Melody Thorne. I was so damn lucky to have you in my life. And thank you for understanding that I have to let you go. Anna is my future."

Turning, he walked away from the past, both beautiful and sad. A few feet in front of him, a redbird swooped down and perched on a branch. Its trilling, melodic song followed him as he walked away. And he knew a peace he hadn't felt in more than a decade. His Mellie had just wished him well.

CHAPTER FORTY-FIVE

Phoenix, Arizona

Anna stared at her image in the mirror. This was a face only a mother could love, and she had a feeling her mother might even have her doubts. Green goo was so not an attractive look for her.

She'd returned home a couple of days ago. The final test results had shown there was no residual damage to her body. Other than dehydration and exhaustion, she was in excellent health. There had been no reason for her to stay.

She hadn't heard from Aidan since he'd walked away more than a week ago. She told herself it was fine. What he was going through would be agonizing. Talking it out with her would only make him relive the pain. He'd said they would talk when he returned. She would hold on to that.

Her employer had given her a few more days to recuperate, and while part of her appreciated his generosity, another part just wanted to jump back into work and bury herself in other people's problems. But that would be wrong. Her job required her full attention. She would not use other people's pain to help her forget her own.

This morning, she'd looked in the mirror and had been disgusted with herself. She had let herself get mired in worry, and as her mother had told her many times before, worry wasn't good for the complexion. There were still shadows of bruises on her cheek, but those could be covered with make-up. It was the lack of vitality in her overall appearance that bothered her. So she had set out to do something about it.

Last Christmas, her mother had given her an expensive spa therapy kit—everything a woman would need to have her very own at-home spa experience. Since she had no plans for the day, she had decided to indulge.

She had washed and conditioned her hair with the honey-suckle-scented shampoo and conditioner. And because she loved the big waves they gave her, she had rolled her damp hair in giant curlers. She had soaked in a tub of hot water with aromatic beads filled with some kind of gel that was supposed to make your body feel like sunshine. She'd gotten out feeling cleaner but not especially sunshiny.

After her bath, she'd spread forest green goop on her face that made her look like a bad Hollywood version of an alien. While that set, she had buffed her nails, both fingers and toes, and painted them an Exquisite Dawn, which just looked orange-red to her.

Now here she sat in her recliner with a glass of red wine, cheese, crackers, and fruit, with some kind of guitar music playing on her iPhone. Since her face was getting kind of tight, she'd get up in a few minutes and clean off the green goo.

All in all, not a bad way to spend a Saturday afternoon. Who needed an expensive spa when she could do all of this alone, in the privacy of her own home? She closed her eyes, took a deep, cleansing breath, and allowed peace to wash through her.

And then the doorbell rang.

Aidan had been stunned when he'd arrived at the hospital and learned that Anna had gone home. Stupid not to have considered that once the final results of the tests were in, she would be discharged. He had talked to her doctors several times since he'd left, finding reassurance that so far, no damage to her organs had been found. After one last discussion with her primary physician, relieved beyond measure that Anna was indeed healthy, he'd gone back to the airport and caught the next plane to Phoenix.

He hadn't called her while he was gone. That was likely a mistake. One of his many where Anna was concerned, but he had been so damn torn up inside, he had figured she'd come away from their conversation worried for his sanity.

Today, if she let him, he would rectify all his screw-ups where she was concerned. That was if she would answer the door. He pressed the door buzzer and knocked again.

He knew she hadn't returned to work. Riley had said she had a few more days off. Could she have gone to see her mother or father? Again, the knowledge that he'd been stupid not to call her was kicking him in the ass.

Turning from the door, he pulled his cellphone from his pocket and pressed her speed-dial number. Wherever she was, he'd go to her. As it rang, he heard an echoing ring. He put his ear to the door. Her phone was in the apartment. No way in hell would she leave her phone behind.

Aidan pounded on the door. "Anna, I know you're in there. What's wrong? Why won't you let me in?"

"Nothing…um. Why didn't you call before you came?"

"Sorry. I—" He jiggled the doorknob. "Dammit, I don't want to talk to you through a door. Open it up."

"It's not really a good time right now, Aidan. Maybe later."

Confusion gave way to alarm. Her voice sounded both nervous and upset. There was someone in there with her. He had checked and rechecked, assuring himself that there would be no more threats from Cook, but he must have overlooked one. And now Anna was once again in danger.

He answered with as much nonchalance as he could fake. "No problem. Just call me when you want to talk."

"Oh. Okay."

Aidan charged down the hallway and down the stairway to the first floor. A sensible man would go to the main office, explain the problem, and get a key to Anna's apartment. When it came to Anna's safety, sensible was not in his vocabulary.

He had to get into that apartment right now.

Anna stood at the door and heard Aidan practically run away. There was no way she could have opened the door. Having him see her like this would have humiliated her beyond bearing. She hadn't, however, expected him to take her refusal so well. He hadn't even argued with her.

Dejected, she padded on her heels, toes in the air, to the bathroom. She would get this goop off her face, remove the curlers, and take out the cotton she'd put between her toes to keep her wet nails from smearing. Then she would call and ask him to come back.

She was halfway to the bathroom when she heard the sound of breaking glass coming from her living room. Her heart thudding, Anna forgot all about her toenails as she dashed into the bedroom and grabbed her gun from the nightstand. She tiptoed back to the hallway, pressed her back against the wall and, with silent footsteps, eased sideways toward the living room. She peeked around the corner and gasped. Aidan stood in the middle of the room surround by glass from her broken patio door. Gun in hand, he was wearing the fierce expression she'd seen more than once. He was ready to destroy whatever threat was in his way.

Without giving it a second thought, Anna stepped out from her hiding place. "What on earth are you doing?"

"Anna? Are you okay?"

"I'm fine."

"Well, then why didn't you let me inside? I thought someone was in here holding you hostage."

"Of course not. I just—" The realization of what he was seeing suddenly hit her. Wanting nothing more than to sink through the floor in total humiliation, she muttered, "The visit was a nice surprise, but I just wasn't in the best position to receive company."

A grin stretching from one side of his face to the other, Aidan holstered his gun and came toward her. "I've noticed you're at your most polite when you feel at a disadvantage."

She frowned, and when she realized she couldn't frown because the mask had hardened and her features were frozen, she glared instead. "I'm always polite, even to men who break into my apartment. Even the ones who don't call me and let me know how they're doing."

He stopped in front of her, and though she was sure he was having trouble not laughing, she saw no amusement in his eyes, only tenderness. He took the gun from her slack hand and placed it on an end table. "I missed you at the hospital. I didn't know you'd been discharged."

"That's what happens when they decide you're perfectly healthy."

"Yeah, I talked to your doctor."

"Someday we need to have a discussion about privacy laws."

"Just one of the many discussions we need to have." He touched her cheek where the mask had dried to the point that she was having trouble even moving her mouth. "This is an interesting new look for you."

"It's a mm…sk."

"A what?"

She rolled her eyes. "Sp…pa."

His mouth twitched, but again she had to give him credit for not laughing. "You look like you're having some difficulty speaking. Is it time to take off the mask?"

She nodded, not only greatly fearing that the mask wouldn't let her talk anymore, but that she'd start crying. Fat tears streaking down her green face would be even worse.

He took her arm. "Let's get this off of you so you can tell me what an insensitive, hardheaded idiot I've been."

She wasn't necessarily going to do that, but getting the mask off her face was fast becoming a necessity. She headed to the bathroom, and since he didn't seem inclined to leave, she grabbed two washcloths, dampened both of them, and handed him one. He worked on one side of her face while she worked on the other. He didn't speak, but from time to time his beautiful, sensual mouth would turn up, and she knew he was doing his best not to laugh out loud.

"There. My side is all done." He gently touched the lingering bruise on her cheek. "Does it still hurt?"

"Not at all."

"Good." He quickly kissed the bruise and then asked, "Want me to finish your side?"

"Not. I've got it." Relieved to finally be able to form words, Anna made short work of the remainder of the mask. She tried to tell herself that her soft, dewy-looking skin was worth the embarrassment she'd just suffered, but she couldn't make herself believe the lie.

"So what do we work on next? The curlers in your hair or your fuzzy toes?"

In for a penny, in for a pound. Nothing could happen that was going to embarrass her any more than she'd already suffered. She sat on her vanity stool and held out one foot. "You can start on this. I'll take the curlers from my hair."

That beautiful smile now in full force, Aidan took the foot she offered and removed the cotton between her toes. When he finished, he pressed a soft kiss to the top of her foot and said, "Now the other one."

So mesmerized by his Prince Charming looks and actions, Anna gave him her other foot and completely forgot about her curlers.

Once again, Aidan removed the cotton, even blowing on her toes to get rid of the final wisps. Once again, he pressed a soft kiss to the top of that foot before lowering it to the floor.

"Want me to do your hair, too?"

Torn between an immense desire to throw herself at him and ravage him on the bathroom floor and the equal need to sob her heart out in his arms because she'd missed him so much, she quickly shook her head. "I'll do it. Why don't you pour yourself a glass of wine? It's on the kitchen table. I'll be there in just a minute."

Showing her he had the sensitivity to go along with his gorgeous face, he gave her another look, one of heated longing and then walked out of the room.

A shaky sigh gushed from her as soon as he disappeared. The things that man made her feel were probably illegal in most states.

She jumped to her feet and quickly went to work on the curlers. Within minutes, her hair was a gleaming mass of thick dark waves. She applied a light moisturizing cream to her face, a little concealer on the bruises, lengthened her already long lashes a bit, and then added color to her lips with a light coral lip gloss.

Taking a step back, she viewed the results and decided that, despite her embarrassment at getting caught looking like the green-faced glob from another world, she was happy with the results.

She rushed into her bedroom and grabbed her favorite dress from the closet. Even though the style was a bit dressy for wearing around the house, with its short, flared skirt and lacy sleeves, the shimmering aqua-blue was the exact color of the water on the island. Those few days there with Aidan had been the happiest of her life and Anna couldn't resist the reminder.

The tender looks Aidan had given her had made her so optimistic, her heart was pounding in anticipation. But if she was wrong and he was here to break her heart? Well, then, she wanted to look nice for that, too. A girl needed a confidence boost when her heart got shattered.

Determined to act like a mature, reasonable adult either way, Anna walked out of the room. She found Aidan in the kitchen where he had rummaged around until he had found what looked like the ingredients for some kind of pasta dish.

Anna didn't say anything. She couldn't. All she could do was lean against the doorframe and watch the man she loved with all her heart and wonder exactly why he was here.

Aidan stopped abruptly when Anna appeared at the door. He had never seen her lovelier. Nor had he ever seen her so uncertain. He planned to address that in just a second. But first he had to taste her.

Standing in front of her, he lifted a long brown strand of hair that lay in a soft curl on her creamy shoulder. "You are one of the loveliest women I've ever known."

"Green goop can do wonders."

"Your beauty has nothing to do with green goop, hair curlers, or nail polish. It's all you, Anna. Your courage, your strength, your perseverance. You have a smile that lights up a room, a beautiful, compassionate heart." He lowered his head. "And the softest...sweetest mouth."

She tasted even sweeter than he remembered. He wanted more...he wanted all of her. He allowed himself only a small taste. They had things to talk about, and there was a lot he needed to say.

Lifting his mouth from her luscious lips, he kissed the tip of her nose, her forehead, and stepped back, away from temptation. For the first time, he noticed what she was wearing.

"You dressed up. Would you rather go out to dinner?"

"I didn't dress up to go out. I dressed up for you."

Would this woman ever stop making his heart turn over? He knew she wouldn't.

Unable to keep himself from another taste, he bent forward for another kiss. Before he could make contact, she stepped out of his reach and said, "What can I do to help?"

Her move was what he needed to get back on course. First, he wanted to know what was going on in that quick, intelligent mind of hers. Then he had some confessions of his own to make.

"If you'll put together a salad, I'll finish up the pasta, and we'll be set."

They worked together in silence, but not the companionable one they had shared on the island. The atmosphere was tense. He figured part of it was anticipation, but he also detected something else. Anna had a sadness about her that disturbed him.

When they sat down to eat, the conversation covered current events and weather-related news. He wanted to keep the conversation light for one very important reason—she needed to eat. By his calculation, Anna had lost at least five to seven pounds with this last ordeal. Aidan had never been hung up on size, but he sure as hell was hung up on keeping Anna healthy.

When at last both their plates were clean, he stood, held out his hand, and led her into the living room. "I'll take care of the dishes later."

As she settled on the sofa, Anna tried to pull her hand away. Aidan wasn't having it. He sat beside her, and as if that didn't quite satisfy him, he abruptly lifted her in his arms and settled her on his lap. "There. Much better."

The move was exactly what Anna had needed to settle herself down. Since they'd returned from Colombia, she'd felt awkward with him, disconnected. Wanting to get back to their earlier closeness, she lay her head on his shoulder and said, "How bad was it?"

His arms around her squeezed in appreciation for her understanding. "It was painful for both of them. Kristen has done a great job of moving on with her life. She said that what I told her just gave her more closure. I hope that's the case. Amy didn't feel the same way. She's still struggling and is understandably bitter toward me. I've offered to help her in any way I can, but—"

"Don't beat yourself up, Aidan. People process their grief in their own way, in their own timeframe. Sometimes it takes years for a person to come to grips with trauma. Sometimes they never do."

"I just hope to hell I didn't make things worse."

She hugged him to comfort him. Sometimes there were no answers, only more questions.

"My parents, on the other hand, are thrilled."

"I imagine they are. Having to be on guard all the time must have been stifling. Now they don't have to worry."

"That's not the biggest reason. They are of course glad that the nightmare of Simon Cook is over."

"Then what's got them so thrilled?"

"You."

She raised her head from his chest so she could see his face. "Me?"

"Yeah, you. They cannot wait to meet you."

Speechlessness wasn't something Anna often suffered, but this bit of news completely numbed her mouth and her mind.

Aidan grinned. Yeah, he loved seeing that shocked look on her face. He planned to put it there as often as he could.

"So I was thinking maybe this weekend, we could go see your mom and dad," he said. "I know they live a few hours from each other, but we should be able to see them both in a weekend, don't you think? Then next weekend, we'll go see my family."

Before he could stop her, Anna shot up out of his arms. "Now wait just a minute. This is putting the cart before the horse, counting chickens before they hatch, and several other farm animal analogies I can't think of right now.

"Don't you think it would be a good idea to actually talk about you and me before we become an 'us' to other people?"

"Have I ever told you I admire the way you talk?"

"No. It seems there are lots of things you haven't told me."

"Have I told you that I love you?"

Tears sprang to her eyes. "No," she whispered, "you haven't."

"I do, Anna. I love you so much it scares me. Seeing you in danger…" He shook his head. "Not being able to get to you, help you. Hell…I aged a decade in seconds when I realized Cook had you."

She sat down beside him again. Her heart was soaring, and there was nothing more she wanted than to throw herself into his arms, but she had to know the truth. "What about Melody?"

Aidan frowned his confusion. "What about Melody?"

"I heard you, Aidan. Remember how I told you the drug Cook gave me made me unable to move, but I was wide awake? The room I was in had a speaker connected to where you were with Cook. I heard every word you said."

"What did I say?"

"That I was just someone you'd slept with—like so many other women. A fling and nothing more."

"Anna. Sweetheart. I would have told that bastard anything to get him to release you. I thought if he believed you meant nothing to me, he might consider letting you go. If lying to the devil would have gotten you out of there alive, there's nothing I wouldn't have said."

"That's what I told myself, but I—"

Aidan pressed a finger to her lips. "But nothing. You're too smart to let your insecurities get in the way of what you know to be true. Yes, I loved Melody, with all my heart. I was devastated when I lost her, but you were right about a lot of things that you said to me on the island. I was using Simon as an excuse to not move on. I felt such guilt for bringing him into her life. For what happened to Amy and Kristen. Something I didn't realize I was doing was allowing my grief to hold me back from loving again. You made me see that, Anna. You made me want more.

"I didn't tell you, mostly because we haven't really had a chance to talk about it, but McCall and I were implementing a plan to capture Simon. We hadn't yet had a chance to put anything in place, but it was in the works."

"Why?"

"Because I fell in love with an outspoken, opinionated, compassionate, tenderhearted little rebel who had the audacity to challenge me, make me see things I'd refused to acknowledge for years."

He brought her hand to his mouth for a soft kiss. "Thank you for that, Anna. For not letting me get away with my old standby lines and excuses."

Aidan drew in a shaky breath. He'd been talking forever, and Anna had yet to speak. Had he been reading her wrong? Was he in this by himself? What if she didn't love him?

"Okay, baby, I've spilled my guts till I'm raw inside. Talk to me. Tell me what you're—"

She threw herself into his arms, kissing his cheek, his chin, his mouth. "I love you, Aidan. With everything that's within me…I love you."

Aidan swooped down and took her mouth. It was a claiming, a declaration, and a promise. He devoured her lips like he'd never get enough of her, and Anna gave him her all. Her heart, her mind, her very being were his for the taking.

The kiss was everything, and then it wasn't enough. Aidan pulled away. He wanted to explore every inch of her, but they still had things they needed to talk about. Once he got her naked, he didn't plan on speaking with any coherence for several hours.

He held her shoulders and locked his eyes with hers, wanting to make sure he could read her correctly.

"We don't have to decide everything today, but I don't want to go another night without you. I have a couple weeks' leave from LCR, but when I return, I have to live in the DC area."

"That shouldn't be a problem. Several psychologists for the Timothy Foundation live in other cities. Even a couple in other countries. As long as I'm with them, I can work remotely."

"You're thinking of leaving?"

"Once I get my doctorate, I'd like to open my own practice." Her smile grew brighter. "I'm sure I can find lovely office space in the DC area."

She went to move back into his arms, and while he wanted that more than anything, he needed to make sure of one thing.

"You're not just saying that, are you? I'm old-fashioned in some ways, but when it comes to this, I want to make sure you're doing what you want, not what you think I want."

She gave him that cheeky grin he so loved. "When have I ever held back my opinion with you, Thorne?"

"Have I told you that you're the most amazing woman and that I adore every single thing about you?"

"Even the things that drive you crazy?"

"Especially the things that drive me crazy."

Her expression confidently sexy, she lay back on the couch and held out her arms. "Show me."

With a growl of intent, Aidan followed her down, his mouth devouring as his hands roamed everywhere at once, pulling and tugging. Seconds later, she was completely bare, and Aidan hadn't yet shed one item of clothing.

"Hey!" She reached for his shirt. "Not fair."

"We'll work on me for the next round." He started at her feet, kissing, nipping, caressing. Everywhere he touched, she melted. By the time he worked his way up her body to look into her eyes, Anna was a mass of heated desire like she'd never felt before. Need rippled through her in waves, and the instant he slid inside her, she zoomed to climax.

When she returned to earth, she opened her eyes to see Aidan hovering over her with an expression of such sweet tenderness she wanted to cry.

"Thank you, Anna."

"For what?"

"For being who you are. For not giving up on me. For putting up with me. For bringing me back to life." He lowered his head, gently touched his mouth to hers. "I love you, Annabelle Bradford."

Her heart so full she thought it might burst, Anna whispered, "And I love you so much, Aidan. You're everything I've ever dreamed of. Everything that I could ever want."

"Say you'll be mine forever."

"For now. Forever. For always."

"Always."

And as his lips met hers, Aidan once again swept Anna away to a world of beauty she'd only ever imagined in her dreams.

Epilogue

Alexandria, Virginia

Classical music soared through the rafters of the gorgeous old church, setting just the right ambience for the ceremony. Flowers of every variety and color graced the windowsills. The pews were decorated in colorful ribbons, and candles, interspersed throughout the auditorium, gave off a soft golden glow of both intimacy and reverence.

Standing at the altar, holding a lovely bouquet of white roses and delicate peach orchids, Anna willed herself not to cry. Everything was so perfect. This was an LCR collaboration unlike any other operation that had ever been planned. Who knew that hard-boiled operatives could create such beauty?

The woman walking down the aisle toward the man she adored was one of the biggest reasons everyone had worked so hard. Riley Ingram had overcome so much, and today she would join her life with Justin Kelly, her friend, her partner, the love of her life. How could it get any better?

The wedding dress was almost as lovely as the bride herself. Silk, satin, and ivory lace—elegant but far from elaborate. The simple design was perfect for Riley's petite frame and looked wonderful with her dark hair and creamy complexion.

The man at her side, walking her down the aisle, made everything better. Stoic as always, the gleam in his dark eyes told the tale. Noah McCall, LCR leader and one of the toughest men Anna had ever known, was showing his softer side. The slight curve to his mouth revealed how special this day was for him, too.

Anna's gaze shifted slightly to get a glimpse of Justin's reaction as his bride-to-be came toward him. The naked emotion on his face squeezed Anna's heart. These two were so much in love.

Her eyes moved to the man standing just behind the groom. Her heart flooded with love. Dressed in a black tuxedo, his thick blond hair slightly ruffled from the wind, Aidan Thorne was the epitome of gorgeous, sexy male perfection. And he was all hers.

Completing her perusal of the best man, she returned her attention to his face and swallowed a laugh. While she'd been ogling him like the eye candy he was, he was doing the same with her. The smoldering heat in his eyes left little to her imagination. Anna shivered with anticipation. Later tonight she would make sure the invitation he was issuing with that sexy look was thoroughly and deliciously satisfied. He gave her a conspiratorial wink as if he knew exactly what she was thinking.

Feeling more than a little flushed, Anna turned her attention back to the bride. Her throat clogged when she spotted a glistening of tears in her friend's eyes. Riley wasn't one to cry, but today of all days it was understandable.

When Riley and Noah reached the altar, the music ended, and the minister asked the question, "Who gives this woman to be married to this man?"

Noah answered in his deep, strong voice, "Her family and I do."

Pressing a kiss to Riley's forehead, Noah was about to back away when Riley caught his arm. She whispered something only Noah could hear. Noah grabbed her, hugged her hard, and then let her go.

Riley turned to face the man she was going to join her life with. Her smile both beautiful and brilliant, she held out her hand. "Okay, Kelly. Let's do this."

With a shout of laughter, Justin pulled Riley into his arms and gave her a brief, hard kiss. "I love you, Ingram."

The wedding reception was winding down, and he had yet to dance with the maid of honor. Aidan had seen his beautiful Anna from time to time and had exchanged numerous heated looks with her. That wasn't nearly enough. He wanted to hold her, dance with her, kiss her luscious peach-frosted lips.

It was still hard to let her out of his sight. He had come so close to losing her. Still woke up in the middle of the night and reached over to touch her just to make sure she was there and safe. He knew that Simon Cook and his minions were all dead. Aidan, along with LCR researchers, had dug deep and uncovered everything about the evil bastard's empire. Cook's wild ramblings about governments purchasing his creations had been accurate. Cook's clients had included Mafia kings, drug lords, one well-known actor, a couple of politicians, and yes, several government officials from various countries.

The Colombian government was having a field day with all the information uncovered, but Aidan's primary concern had been to ensure that Cook had not set up a contingency plan. He hadn't. Simon Cook and his insane, twisted evil was in hell where he belonged.

Standing in the middle of the room, Aidan's eyes roamed the crowd. He had lost sight of Anna. He told himself he wasn't worried. With the exception of Justin's family, he knew every person here. It wasn't every day that two operatives married each other. LCR people from all over the world had flown in for this very special event. But he still didn't see the one person he most wanted.

Her light touch on his shoulder made him smile. He turned to the woman who had changed his life and held out his hand. "Dance with me."

Wrapped in Aidan's arms, her head against his chest, Anna swayed to the music. The wedding had been perfect. The bride and groom had left a while ago, their faces bright with happiness.

Her duties as maid of honor had ended, and now Anna wanted to concentrate on the man holding her in his arms as if he'd never let her go. It had been almost a month since Aidan had told her he loved her, but she still had to pinch herself sometimes to make sure all of this was real.

His parents had been as wonderful as Aidan had claimed, welcoming Anna into their home as if she were already family. And Jennifer, Aidan's sister, was exactly as he had described her. Anna already knew they were going to be great friends.

Her own parents had been a little less effusive. Not because they didn't like Aidan. They were both thrilled, and for the first time in years, she'd seen her parents actually smile at each other. What didn't thrill them was the fact that she had moved away from Arizona. Even though she promised frequent visits, it had taken half an hour to get her mom to stop crying. And in an odd but encouraging moment, her mother had thrown herself into Anna's father's arms, and he had comforted her.

Not a reconciliation, by any means, but for Anna, who had witnessed more acrimony than happiness between her parents, the moment had been a nice one.

"Happy?" Aidan whispered in her ear.

"More than I ever thought possible."

Aidan pulled away slightly so he could see her face. She did look happy. There were no shadows from the past, no doubts about his love for her. Not for a second did he want her to think that he didn't adore her with every breath.

She looked especially beautiful tonight. The color of her gown—what she'd told him was a light ginger-peach—gave her creamy skin a luminous radiance. Her hair was a dark, silky waterfall flowing over her soft, bare shoulders. She glowed with good health and contentment. And Aidan was so much in love with her he couldn't see straight.

Today had been a special one for both of them, watching their best friends get married. Tonight was going to be even more so. The moment they walked into their apartment, she would know what was about to happen. Rose petals would lead a path to their bedroom, where champagne was chilling. He'd brought the ring with him to the wedding and hadn't asked himself why. And suddenly he knew the reason.

Aidan had wanted everything to be perfect for her. She deserved nothing less. But as he looked around the room and at Anna again, he realized this was the perfect place. There were flowers, romantic music, and wine. Best of all, almost everyone in this room was LCR personnel. He had hidden his true feelings for Anna for much too long. He would wait no longer.

She had her eyes closed again and wore a sweet, slightly goofy smile on her face.

"Anna?"

"Hmm?"

"Get ready to be embarrassed."

Her eyes flew open. "What?"

Aidan withdrew the small ring box that had been burning a hole in his pocket and went to one knee. Removing the three-carat, round-cut diamond engagement ring, he held it up to her. The music was now a soft romantic ballad, perfect for the occasion. Everyone around them, realizing what was about to happen, had stopped dancing, shamelessly staring.

"Aidan!" she squeaked in a whisper. "What are you doing?"

"I'm showing the world that I love and adore you. Annabelle Bradford, will you marry me?"

Forgetting all about embarrassment, she squealed, "Yes!"

Aidan surged to his feet, and surrounded by thunderous applause, wrapped his arms around Anna, staking his claim for all the world to see.

Dear Reader: Thank you for reading Running Wild! I hope you enjoyed Aidan and Anna's story. If you would consider leaving a review to help other readers find this book, it would be greatly appreciated.

If you'd like to be notified when I have a new release, sign up for my newsletter. http://authornewsletters.com/christyreece/

To learn about my other books and what I'm currently writing, please visit my website. http://www.christyreece.com

Follow me on Facebook. https://www.facebook.com/AuthorChristyReece/ and on Twitter. https://twitter.com/ChristyReece

OTHER BOOKS BY CHRISTY REECE

LCR Elite Series

Running On Empty, An LCR Elite Novel
Chance Encounter, An LCR Elite Novel
Running Scared, An LCR Elite Novel

Last Chance Rescue Series

Rescue Me, A Last Chance Rescue Novel
Return To Me, A Last Chance Rescue Novel
Run To Me, A Last Chance Rescue Novel
No Chance, A Last Chance Rescue Novel
Second Chance, A Last Chance Rescue Novel
Last Chance, A Last Chance Rescue Novel
Sweet Justice, A Last Chance Rescue Novel
Sweet Revenge, A Last Chance Rescue Novel
Sweet Reward, A Last Chance Rescue Novel
Chances Are, A Last Chance Rescue Novel

Grey Justice Series

Nothing To Lose, A Grey Justice Novel
Whatever It Takes, A Grey Justice Novel

Wildefire Series writing as Ella Grace

Midnight Secrets, A Wildefire Novel
Midnight Lies, A Wildefire Novel
Midnight Shadows, A Wildefire Novel

Acknowledgements

Special thanks to the following people for helping make this book possible:

My husband, for your love, support, numerous moments of comic relief, and almost always respecting my chocolate stash.

My mom for patiently listening to my ramblings about stubborn characters and frustrating plotlines.

My Aunt Billie for the loan of your home on the river to help me get to know Anna and Aidan better. And for always calling me the day you finish one of my books to tell me how much you enjoyed it.

Joyce Lamb, for your awesome copyediting skills and fabulous advice.

Marie Force's eBook Formatting Fairies, who always answers my endless questions with endless patience.

Tricia Schmitt (Pickyme) for your wonderful cover art.

The Reece's Readers street team, for all your support and encouragement.

Anne Woodall, my first reader, who always goes above and beyond, and then goes the extra mile, too. You're awesome!

My beta readers, Crystal, Hope, Julie, Kris, and Alison for reading so quickly and your great suggestions.

Linda Clarkson, proofreader extraordinaire, who, as always, did an amazing job. So appreciate your eagle eye, Linda!

And to all my readers, thank you for your patience and your emails requesting Aidan's story. Without you, this book and all the others, past and future, would not be possible.

ABOUT THE AUTHOR

Christy Reece is the award winning and New York Times Best-selling author of nineteen romantic suspense novels. She lives in Alabama with her husband and numerous fur-kids.

Christy loves hearing from readers and can be contacted at Christy@ChristyReece.com.

Have you met Grey Justice?

There's more than one path to justice.

Turn the page to read excerpts from the first two books in the Grey Justice series, Nothing To Lose and Whatever It Takes.

NOTHING TO LOSE
A GREY JUSTICE
NOVEL

Choices Are Easy When You Have Nothing Left To Lose

Kennedy O'Connell had all the happiness she'd ever dreamed—until someone stole it away. Now on the run for her life, she has a choice to make—disappear forever or make those responsible pay. Her choice is easy.

Two men want to help her, each with their own agenda.

Detective Nick Gallagher is accustomed to pursuing killers within the law. Targeted for death, his life turned inside out, Nick vows to bring down those responsible, no matter the cost. But the beautiful and innocent Kennedy O'Connell brings out every protective instinct. Putting aside his own need for vengeance, he'll do whatever is necessary to keep her safe and help her achieve her goals.

Billionaire philanthropist Grey Justice has a mission, too. Dubbed the 'White Knight' of those in need of a champion, few people are aware of his dark side. Having seen and experienced injustice—Grey knows its bitter taste. Gaining justice for those who have been wronged is a small price to pay for a man's humanity.

With the help of a surprising accomplice, the three embark on a dangerous game of cat and mouse. The stage is set, the players are ready…the game is on. But someone is playing with another set of rules and survivors are not an option.

***

Nick opened his apartment door and headed straight to his bedroom to change into a pair of shorts and an old sweatshirt. About the only way he had to battle the hopelessness inside him was to beat the hell out of his boxing bag and work himself into exhaustion. He was halfway to the kitchen for a bottle of water when he realized he wasn't alone. The dark figure of a man sitting in a chair in the corner caught his eye.

Cursing his inattentiveness, he grabbed the closest weapon—a bust of Sherlock Holmes—and turned toward the intruder.

"Before you allow Mr. Holmes to bash my head in, wouldn't you like to know why I'm here?"

The crisp British voice sounded familiar, but he couldn't place it. Nick replied coolly, "I'm more of an attack-first-and-ask-questions-later kind of guy."

"Pity. You don't seem the type to go off half-cocked."

"Depends on the situation. Having some asshole break into my house is the type of thing that pisses me off."

"Understandable, but you can often learn more things if you wait awhile."

"Or you can get yourself killed. Now, tell me who the hell you are and why you're here."

"Let's talk first. Then we'll decide if we want to exchange personal information."

If the man was going to shoot him, he would've done so by now. Nick lowered the statue to his side but held on to it just in case. He reached for the light switch on the wall.

"No lights."

"So I'm not allowed to know your name or what you look like?"

"Not yet. Have a seat."

Despite the aggravation of having a stranger break into his house and the man's numerous rules, Nick was intrigued. He pulled his hand back from the light switch. "I'll stand. Now tell me what the hell you want."

"I want what you want—to bring Mathias Slater and his goons to justice."

If he hadn't captured Nick's attention before, he sure as hell had it now. "What do you know about Slater?"

"That he's into more shit than anyone could ever imagine."

"And why do you care?"

"Let's just say that seeing bad guys get what's coming to them is a hobby of mine."

"And how can you assist me in seeing that Slater gets what's coming to him?"

"By giving you access to information you can't get through your channels."

"You mean illegal channels."

"Semantics. What you see as illegal, I see as creative license."

Still wary but more interested than ever, Nick returned the statue to the end table and dropped down onto the sofa. "Okay, you have my undivided attention."

"Excellent. However, we need to come to an agreement before we go further."

"Such as?"

"If you decline my proposal, this discussion never happened."

"Agreed."

"Excellent."

"You're just going to take my word for it?"

"I wouldn't be here if I didn't already know you can be trusted, Mr. Gallagher."

Where and how he'd gotten information on Nick could wait till another time.

"Okay, I'm listening."

"Mathias Slater and his antics hit my radar several years ago. I've tried penetrating his tight-knit circle. Unfortunately, I've gotten only so far before someone ratted out my informant."

"And how can I help? If you know that much about me, then you already know that I've run into a road block in every avenue I've taken against Slater."

"That's true. However, you have an avenue you don't even know you can take."

"And what's that?"

"There's a folder on the table in front of you. Take a look inside."

Nick didn't move…considered what could be inside.

"I'm glad to see that my informants were correct. You have a short fuse, but it's tempered with a deliberative cautiousness."

"I'm assuming that I'll be allowed to turn on the lights to look at the folder."

"That's correct. Another reason why your deliberation is important. You turn on those lights, you will have information that could destroy not only me, but negatively impact the lives of thousands."

Nick reached up and flipped on the lamp beside him. Light illuminated the man sitting in the corner and he knew why the voice had sounded so familiar. This was a man known to millions. And he was right—if anyone discovered the truth, thousands of lives would be affected.

Deciding to mull over the man's identity later, Nick grabbed the folder and opened it. The instant he saw the first photograph, everything within him froze. He looked up at the man who sat so calmly across from him and whispered hoarsely, "What do I need to do?"

Whatever it Takes
A Grey Justice
Novel

To Save His Family, She May Be His Only Hope

Working for the shadowy division of the Grey Justice Group is the perfect job for Kathleen Callahan. Compartmentalizing and staying detached is her specialty. Get in, do the job, get out, her motto. Wealthy businessman Eli Slater is the only man to penetrate her implacable defenses and she fights to resist him at every turn.

Eli Slater has worked hard to overcome his family's past and repair the damage they caused. A new light comes into his life in the form of security specialist Kathleen Callahan. Even though she rejects him and everything he makes her feel, Eli is relentless in his pursuit, determined to make her his own.

Darkness has a way of finding and destroying light and Eli learns his family's troubles are far from over. Dealing with threats and attempts on his own life is one thing but when those he loves are threatened, it's a whole new game. And he'll stop at nothing to win.

But evil has a familiar face, along with an unimaginable goal of destruction, putting both Eli and Kathleen in the crosshairs and threatening the happiness they never believed they'd find.

***

Kathleen willed her legs to move, one step and then another. Up the stairs to her apartment. She'd shut off her emotions over the last few days. Had barely slept or eaten. Holding on by a thread, just waiting until she could finally let go. The second she entered her apartment, she was planning a meltdown of epic proportions.

The key slid into the door of her apartment, she twisted the knob, and felt the emotions swell.

"Miss Callahan?"

She jerked around. Exhaustion and emotional devastation had slowed her instincts. A man stood in the shadows. He was dressed in black, and she could see nothing of his features other than he was tall, with a muscular physique. If he was here to attack her, he would win. She was way too tired to give a damn. And if he was here to rob her, he was in for a major letdown. She had nothing worth stealing…nothing left, not anymore.

Her fuzzy brain registered that he'd called her Miss Callahan. People weren't generally that polite right before they attacked.

"Yes?"

"I'd like to talk to you about your sister."

Another damn reporter. The burn of hatred was strong and true, singeing and cauterizing the bleed of grief. "Haven't you bottom-feeding reporters had enough fun? Haven't you tortured me enough? What more do you want?"

"I'm not a reporter, Miss Callahan. I'm here to help you."

"Help me how?" Her voice went thick as she added, "I just buried my sister. If you'd wanted to help, you've got piss-poor timing."

"I know. I'm very sorry. I—" He broke off when voices came from the stairwell. Her neighbors were coming home. "Look. May I come in?"

"No, you may not. I have no idea who you are or what you want."

He moved closer, stood in the light. Her breath hitched as she immediately recognized his famous face. This man was on the news more times in one week than Kathleen had been in a lifetime. But what was he doing here?

"My name is Grey Justice, and I'd like to help you find the person who framed your sister."

Made in the USA
Middletown, DE
25 March 2018